The BALLAD of PERILOUS GRAVES

The BALLAD of PERILOUS GRAVES

ALEX JENNINGS

REDHOOK

Redhook Books/Orbit
Hachette Book Group
1290 Avenue of the Americas
New York, NY 10104
hachettebookgroup.com

First Edition: June 2022
Simultaneously published in Great Britain by Orbit

Redhook is an imprint of Orbit, a division of Hachette Book Group.
The Redhook name and logo are trademarks of Hachette Book Group, Inc.

The publisher is not responsible for websites (or their content) that are not owned by the publisher.

The Hachette Speakers Bureau provides a wide range of authors for speaking events. To find out more, go to www.hachettespeakersbureau.com or call (866) 376-6591.

Library of Congress Cataloging-in-Publication Data
Names: Jennings, Alex, 1979- author.
Title: The ballad of perilous graves / Alex Jennings.
Description: First edition. | New York, NY : Redhook, 2022.
Identifiers: LCCN 2021046057 | ISBN 9780759557192 (hardcover) |
ISBN 9780759557215 (ebook) | ISBN 9780759557185
Subjects: LCSH: New Orleans (La.)—Fiction. | LCGFT: Fantasy fiction. | Novels.
Classification: LCC PS3610.E5574 B35 2022 | DDC 813/.6—dc23
LC record available at https://lccn.loc.gov/2021046057

ISBNs: 9780759557192 (hardcover), 9780759557215 (ebook)

Printed in the United States of America

LSC-C

Printing 1, 2022

For Hartford Terry Jennings Sr., who is twelve feet tall.

Map by Stephanie A. Hess

I

I

HERE I'M IS!

Perry Graves tried not to think about summer's arrival—the heat devils hovering, breathless, over the blacktop as if waiting for something to happen—or even about the city streets. Tomorrow was the last day of school, and he'd be free to roam the neighborhood soon enough...But it *wouldn't* be soon enough. Perry and his little sister, Brendy, sat cross-legged on the living room floor watching Morgus the Magnificent on the TV. The unkempt, hollow-eyed scientist was trying to convince a gray-haired opera singer to stick his head into a machine that would allow Morgus to amputate the singer's voice with a flip of the switch. From here, Perry could hear his parents and their friends gabbing on the front porch as they sipped sweet tea and played dominoes.

"Why you ain't laughing?" Brendy said.

"Don't talk like that," Perry said. "Daddy hears you, he'll get you good." Then, "I don't always have to laugh just because something's funny."

"Oh, I know, Perry-berry-derry-larry." Brendy stuck her tongue out at him. "You in a *mood* 'cause you ain't seen Peaches in a week. You don't want me talkin' like her because it remind you of the paaaaaain in yo heaaaaaaaaaart!"

Perry scowled. "Shut up."

"I'm sorry," Brendy said. "I'm sorry you luuuuuuuvs Peaches like she yo wiiiiiiiiife!"

"Little bit, you be sorry you don't shut your mouth," Perry threatened. He had no idea what he could do to silence her without getting into trouble.

"*Nyeeeeowm! Zzzzzrack!*" For a moment, Brendy absently imitated the sound effects from Morgus. "You just want her to say 'Oh! Perilous! I luuuuuvs yew tew! Keeeeeeess me, Perry! Like zey do een—'" Perry was ready to grab his baby sister, clap his hand over her mouth at least, but before he could, a clamor rose up outside. "Looka there!" some grown-up shouted from the porch, his voice marbling through a hubbub of startled adult exclamations.

Whatever was going on out there had nothing to do with Perry, so he ignored it. He was sure that someone had just walked through some graffiti, or that a parade of paintbodies was making its way down Jackson Avenue. He grabbed Brendy's wrist, all set to give her a good tickle, but when the first piano chord sounded on the night air, Perry's body took notice.

Perry let go of his sister, and his legs unfolded him to standing. By the time the second bar began, his knees had begun to flex. He danced in place for a moment before he realized what was happening, then turned and made for the front door. Brendy bounced along right beside him, her single Afro pouf bobbing atop her little round head.

Oooooooh—ooh-wee!
Oooooooh—ooh-wee!
Ooo-ooh baby, oooooooh—ooh-wee!

Outside, Perry's parents and their friends had already descended to the street. Perry's grandfather, Daddy Deke, stood at the base of the porch steps, pumping his knees and elbows in time with the music. "Something ain't right!" he shouted. "He don't never show up this far uptown—not even at Mardi Gras!"

Perry bounced on his toes in the blast of the electric fan sitting at the far end of the porch. The night beyond the stream of air was hot and close—like dog breath, but without the smell. As soon as Perry left the breeze, dancing to the edge of the porch steps, little beads of sweat sprang out on his forehead and started running down.

From here, as he wobbled his legs and rolled his shoulders, Perry saw a shadow forming under the streetlight. It was the silhouette of a man sitting at a piano, and the music came from him. The spirit's piano resolved into view. It was a glittery-gold baby grand festooned with stickers and beads, its keys moving on their own. Shortly thereafter, Doctor Professor himself appeared, hunched over, playing hard as he threw his head back in song. He wore a fuzzy purple fur hat, great big sunglasses with star-shaped lenses, and a purple-sequined tuxedo jacket and bow tie. Big clunky rings stood out on his knuckles as his hands blurred across the keyboard, striking notes and chords. Perry smelled licorice, but couldn't tell whether the smell came from Doctor Professor or from somewhere else. The scent was so powerful, it was almost unpleasant.

All Perry's senses seemed sharper now, and he tried to drink in every impression. He danced in place to the piano and the bass, but as he did, guitars and horns played right along, their sound pouring right out of Fess's mouth.

Ooh-wee, baby, ooooooh—wee
What did you done to meeeee . . . !

By now, everyone for blocks around had come out of their houses and onto the blacktop. A line of cars waited patiently at Carondelet Street, their doors open, their drivers dancing on the hoods and on the roofs. It was just what you did when Doctor Professor appeared, whatever time of day or night. They danced along to the music, and those who knew the lyrics even sang along.

You told me I'm yo man
You won't have nobody else
Now I'm sittin' home at night
With nobody but myself—!

Perry gave himself up to the sound and the rhythm of the music. The saxophone solo had begun, and it spun Perry around, carried him down the steps and across the yard. His feet swiveled on the sidewalk, turning in and out as he threw his arms up above his head.

Just as quickly as he'd come, Doctor Professor began to fade from sight. First, the man disappeared except for his hands, then his stool disappeared, and then the piano itself. He had become another disturbance in the air—a weird blot of not-really-anything smudged inside the cone cast by the streetlight, and just before he had gone entirely away, Perry heard another song starting up. The music released him, and the crowd stopped moving.

"Oh, have mercy!" Perry's mother crowed. "That's what I needed, baby!"

"That Doctor Professor sure can play."

"Baby, you know it. Take your bounce, take your zydeco—this a jazz city through and through!"

Wilting in the heat, Perry turned to head back inside and saw Daddy Deke still standing by the porch. The old man wore a black-and-crimson zoot suit, and now that he'd finished his dance, he took off his broad-brimmed hat and held it in his left hand. He looked down his beaky nose at Perry, staring like a bird. "Things like that don't happen for no reason," he said. "Something up."

"Something bad?" Perry asked.

"Couldn't tell ya, baby," he said. "Daddy Deke don't know much about magic or spirits. But I gotta wonder...why *that* streetlight in particular? That one right there in front of Peaches's house?"

Now Perry turned to look back at the space where Doctor Professor had appeared. Daddy Deke was right. It stood exactly in front of Peaches's big white birthday cake of a house.

"I didn't see her dancing," Perry said. "Did you?"

"If she'da been there, we'da known it," Daddy Deke said. "Can't miss that Peaches, now, can you?"

Perry and Brendy's parents resumed their seats on the porch, but Daddy Deke headed past them into the house. Perry and his sister followed. In the foyer, Daddy Deke paused to breathe in the cool of the AC and mop his brow with a handkerchief. "Ain't danced like that in a minute," he said.

The living room TV was still gabbling away. Brendy twirled and glided over to shut it off—and Perry wasn't surprised. After seeing Doctor Professor, the idea of staring at the TV screen seemed terminally boring—but so did porch-sitting.

"What you doing tonight anyhows, Daddy Deke?" Brendy asked.

"Caught a couple bass in the park this morning," the old man said. "Might as well fry some up and eat it."

"You went fishing without us?"

"Y'all had school," Daddy Deke said. "If you comin', come on."

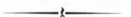

Daddy Deke's house sat around the corner on Brainard Street, a stubby little avenue that ran from St. Andrew to Philip, parallel with St. Charles. The low, ranch-style bungalow with the terra-cotta roof and stucco walls looked a little out-of-place for the Central City—it was the kind of place Perry would expect to see in Broadmoor, crouching back from the street like ThunderCats Lair.

As Perry and Brendy crossed the lawn, Daddy Deke broke away to head for his car, an old Ford Comet that seemed like a good match for the house in that it was also catlike. But instead of ThunderCats Lair, it reminded Perry of Panthor, Skeletor's evil-but-harmless familiar. Daddy Deke turned to look at his grandchildren over his narrow shoulder. "Gwan, y'all. I just gotta stash something real quick, me."

As always, the door to Daddy Deke's house was unlocked. Perry let himself and Brendy inside and took a deep breath. Daddy Deke's place had a smell he couldn't quite identify, but it was unmistakable. A mix of incense, frying oil, and Daddy Deke's own particular aroma—the one he wore beneath his cologne and his mouthwash, the scent that was only his.

At one time, the house had been a doubled shotgun. Daddy Deke had had the central dividing wall and a couple others knocked down, but the second front door remained. Perry and Brendy took off their shoes and stored them in the cubby underneath the coat rack. By then, Daddy Deke had followed them inside.

"Do the fish need scaling?" Perry asked. Daddy Deke had shown him how to descale, gut, and fillet a fish, but Perry was still refining his grasp on the process. There was something about it he enjoyed; figuring out how to get rid of all those fins, bones, and scales felt a little like alchemy—transmuting an animal into food. It made Perry think of the Bible story where Jesus fed thousands on a couple fish and two loaves.

"Naw," Daddy Deke said. "Did it my own self this time—wanted to get them heads in the freezer. Gonna make a stew later on."

Perry's mouth watered. Daddy Deke's fish-head stew was legendary—no matter what form it took. He could make it French-style, Cajun, or even Thai. On those nights when Daddy Deke made a pot for the family and carried it around the corner, the family would eat in near silence, punctuated with satisfied grunts and hums of approval.

"Why I can't never fix the fishes?" Brendy asked. "I wanna help make dinner!"

"You didn't want to learn," Perry said. "You said it was gross."

A flash of anger lit Brendy's face, but it blinked away as quickly as it had come.

"You promise to be careful with the knife," Daddy Deke said, "and we put you on salad duty, heard?"

"Yesss!" Brendy hissed. "Knife knife knife knife *knife!*"

"Lord," Perry said with a roll of his eyes.

In the kitchen, Daddy Deke turned on the countertop radio and stride piano poured forth to fill the room like water. "You know who that is?" Daddy Deke said.

Perry listened closely. He recognized the song—"Summertime"—but not the expert hands that played it. Hearing it made him feel a sharp pang of loss. He hadn't touched a keyboard in more than a year. He pushed that thought away—thinking about playing was a dark road that led nowhere good. "No," Perry said. "Who is it?"

"That's Willie 'The Lion' Smith," Daddy Deke said, "outta New Jersey. Used to work in a slaughterhouse with his daddy when he was a boy. He said it was horrible, hearing them animals done in, but there was something musical about it, too. That's the thing about music, about a symphony: destruction, war, peace, and beauty all mixed up, ya heard?"

Perry frowned and shut his eyes, listening more closely. He could hear it. At first the tone of the music reminded him of water, and it was still liquid, but now he imagined a bit of darkness and blood mixed in. He saw flowers unfurling to catch rain in a storm. Some of them were destroyed, pulverized by the water or swept away in the high wind.

"That's the thing about music," Daddy Deke said. "It can destroy as much as it creates. It's wild and powerful, dig?"

Perry opened his eyes. "Yes," he said, trying to keep the sadness from his voice. "I understand—a little bit, I think."

"Hey, now," Daddy Deke said.

Perry shook his head. His attention had been off in the ozone somewhere as he, Daddy Deke, and Brendy played rummy. Perry liked rummy okay—he liked the shape of the rules, the feel of the game itself—the cards against his palms, raising and lowering them to the table, keeping track of points—but tonight, he'd been going through the motions. "I'm sorry," he said. "What's going on?"

"What's going on is you won and you don't even care!" Brendy huffed.

"Y'all, I'm sorry," Perry said. "I just—I still feel the music on me. I'm thinking about what it means and what Doctor Professor wants with Peaches."

Brendy rolled her eyes. " 'And where she at? What she doing? She thinking bout me?' Blah blah blippity."

Daddy Deke laid down his cards and shook his head. "Don't tease ya brother for caring—and besides, Perry ain't the only one miss Peaches when she gone. Is he?"

Brendy pulled a face where she flexed her neck muscles and drew her mouth into a flat, toadish line. Then she let the expression go and sucked in a huge mouthful of air to pooch out her checks. She let that go, too. "Okay, no he ain't," she said. "We all be missing Peaches. I get left alone, too, but I don't make a big deal. Just like when—"

Perry knew his expression must have darkened because Brendy cast aside whatever she'd meant to say next. "En EE ways, Peaches *always* go away for a lil bit after a fight."

This was true. Thirteen days ago, Peaches had fought Maddy Bombz on the roof of One Shell Square after Perry and Peaches figured out how to predict the location of her next display. Each of her fusillades was part of a grander display—similar to the ones above the Missus Hipp on Juneteenth or on New Year's—and since she didn't care about the safety of her "audience," of course she intended to launch her grand finale atop the tallest building in Nola. Perry and Brendy watched from a Poydras Street sidewalk as one of the explosions tossed Peaches down to the street.

She hit hard and lay still for a moment, then sat up, shaking her head angrily. A glance into the parking lot to his right told Perry what she'd do next. Peaches pushed up imaginary sleeves and bounded over to a big green dumpster. She lifted the bulky metal thing over her head easy-as-you-please and jumped. *Hard.* Watching her reminded Perry of the moon landing videos. It was as if gravity simply worked differently for her when she wanted it to.

When she leaped back to the street, the dumpster she carried had been crimped closed like a pie crust. She set it down right there on the pavement.

"Five-oh on the way," she said. "I seen 'em from up above. Let's get to steppin'." And they had. Perry and Brendy had spent the night at Peaches's house, watching TV and eating huckabucks and Sixlets late into the night because there was no school the next day.

Perry and his sister awakened the next morning to find Peaches's pocket of pillows and blankets empty—and nobody had seen her since.

"I know she coming back," Perry said.

"I know you know," Daddy Deke said. "But I'll tell you sumn for free—there ain't nothing wrong with the feelings you having, but them feelings are yours. Ain't nobody else responsible for 'em, dig? You can't carry nothing for nobody else, and cain't nobody carry what's yours for you."

Perry frowned. In the past, Daddy Deke had never failed to offer him comfort when he was feeling low, but this advice seemed important. He turned Daddy Deke's words over in his mind for the rest of the night. *Cain't nobody carry what's yours for you.* What burdens did he carry, and why? Well, there was the dream he'd had...but some dark, quiet presence in the back of Perry's mind told him that it hadn't been a dream, it had been a warning, and he'd be a fool not to heed it.

Music might be the most powerful magic in Nola, but it couldn't help Perry—not really.

Dryades Academy was an old square-built art deco building that looked more like a courthouse than a place of learning. Its façade was a riot of ivy, full of ladybugs the size of baseballs, which marched up and down the outer walls, keeping them clean. Chickens roosted in the trees out front, and one of the substitute teachers, Mr. Ghiazi, had told Brendy that every evening, after hours, when the last students and teachers had gone home, the chickens would come inside and hold their own lessons, learning about corn and how to find the best worms and bugs. Something about the way he said it made Brendy think Mr. Ghiazi was probably joking—or at least that he thought he was.

Inside, the building boasted green marble floors, old-fashioned mosaics, and vintage furniture maintained by an invisible custodial staff. What Brendy loved most about the place, what she couldn't imagine ever parting with, was its smell. Crayons, glitter, oil soap, and cooking. It smelled best on cold winter days, but even on the last day of school, Dryades Academy smelled like home. How her brother could leave it made no sense to her.

This year, Perry and Brendy had attended separate schools. Last summer, Perry abruptly asked to transfer out of Dryades Academy and wound up at a new school over on Esplanade Avenue. Brendy didn't understand the choice, and she knew she should have asked Perry about it, but every time she tried to bring it up, Perry's face took on a lost, hunted look, and she backed down. Still, it made her sad and angry to be without him, and sometimes those feelings formed a little knot of tension in her throat—like she'd tried to swallow a pill and failed.

All year she had avoided thinking about it, but now, as she sat at her desk by the window in Mr. Evans's class, ignoring the movie playing on the classroom livescreen in favor of a Popeye the Sailor Man coloring book, she wondered whether Perry had decided to leave because he wasn't good at music.

Brendy bore down with her Fuzzy Wuzzy brown, filling in the outline of Popeye's left arm as he slung a string of chained-together oil barrels over his head. She'd taught herself a trick earlier this year: She liked to color in her figures hard, in layer after layer—careful, of course, to stay inside the lines—then go back with a plastic lunch knife and scrape away the wax. The process resulted in smoother, richer colors that had won her an award from the Chamber of

Commerce in its Carnival Coloring Competition. The grand prize had been a beautiful purple-and-white bicycle that Daddy Deke taught her to ride without training wheels.

Brendy frowned, listening hard, as she finished coloring Popeye's exposed skin and tried to decide what color Olive Oyl should be this time. The chickens in the tree outside had gone quiet. Brendy had earned the right to sit by the broad classroom window because Mr. Evans thought she did such a good job fighting the temptation to stare outside at the trees and the play yard, and the neighborhood beyond. This was only partly true. Brendy found it easy to keep from staring out the window because she tended to listen out it instead. Most of the time she spent at her desk found her listening to the swish of cars on the street, the noise of other classes bouncing balls and running riot on the play yard blacktop, the squabbles of the chickens and the neighborhood cats— who seemed, lately, to have resolved their differences by banding together against the raccoons and possums.

Hey, girl!

Was that Peaches? Brendy raised an eyebrow.

Hey, girl. Hey!

Brendy frowned and selected another crayon. "Peaches?" she whispered.

Yeah, girl. Come on. We gots to go!

Brendy considered briefly, then raised her hand.

It took a while, but Mr. Evans noticed. "Brendy?"

"Can I go use it?"

Mr. Evans nodded curtly. "Two minutes." But he'd never remember.

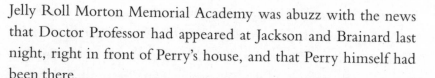

Jelly Roll Morton Memorial Academy was abuzz with the news that Doctor Professor had appeared at Jackson and Brainard last night, right in front of Perry's house, and that Perry himself had been there.

"What did you do?" kids asked.

"Oh, you know," Perry said, basking in his fame. "I do like you do. I danced."

"What song he played?"

"'Missed Yo Chance,'" Perry answered. "It happens to be a favorite of mine."

"Who else was there? The backup singers? Any P-bodies?"

"At this time of year?" Perry asked. "It ain't Mardi Gras, you know."

"My daddy says it couldna been him," Mickey Ledoux said with a shake of his head. It was just after nine that morning, and the fifth grade was putting the finishing touches on that year's Learning System. The project was designed to represent everything the fifth-grade class had learned—about the Huey Long Bridge, about the Chinese Revolution, about fractions, adding and subtracting time, and about Albert Einstein.

The fifth-grade students had been divided into teams of five, and each student was responsible for designing and creating a representational planetoid to affix to the System—a giant mobile where every planet was an idea. Perry and Mickey were on the math team, and Perry had made an abacus from Ping-Pong balls and PVC pipe, papered with cutouts from magazines and show flyers featuring musicians and clubs from around town. It had taken Perry weeks to come up with the design, and weeks more to execute it. Daddy Deke had brought him every magazine he could find that had even a mention of a Nola musician, but here it was, complete, staring him right in the face.

When Perry looked at Mickey's sculpture, he felt like he'd been duped. Mickey had made a sundial that looked like it had taken him maybe twenty minutes to put together—or no time at all if, as Perry suspected, Mickey's older brother had just done it for him.

Now, the entire fifth grade had taken over the cafeteria under the supervision of the art teacher, Miss Erica, and were completing the final assembly so that the project could be hoisted on wires and suspended from the cafeteria's high ceiling until next year's fifth-grade class completed its own. The usual lunch tables were absent—there'd be no lunch at school since today was a half day— and instead they stood at beige folding tables wearing their fathers' cast-off dress shirts backwards to avoid messing up their uniforms.

Mickey himself had already started puberty, and his long legs combined with his light musculature made him the fastest runner at Morton Academy. When Mickey kept his mouth shut, running or playing ball, Perry envied the way he impressed everyone— especially the girls. When Mickey talked, though, it was usually to parrot something some dumb grown-up had said.

"You think anyone in Nola could mistake anybody else for Doctor Professor?" Perry asked.

Mickey considered. "Not really," he said slowly. "But what if it was a trick? What if it was somebody else impressonating him?"

"'Impersonating,'" Perry corrected without meaning to. "Why would anybody who could play like that pretend to be anybody else?"

"I don't know," Mickey said with an irritated shake of his peanut-shaped head. "But it couldn't be him. It ain't Mardi Gras, and Jackson is too far uptown for Doctor Professor to just show up there."

Perry didn't answer right away. Biting his lip, he finished duct-taping a plastic coat hanger to the top of his abacus and picked it up by the hook, testing the hanger against the sculpture's weight. The hold seemed more than secure, and he sighed softly at the culmination of his efforts. Carefully, he laid the sculpture on the work table.

"Maybe he didn't just appear," he said, still staring at his work. "Maybe he wanted something. Or he was looking for somebody."

"Like who?"

Perry found it hard to keep the exasperation out of his voice. "Like Peaches, that's who! Important people come looking for her all the time."

"I heard Peaches don't live there no more anyhow," Mickey said. "I heard she left town."

Now Perry's face heated, and his fingers twitched. His hands wanted to curl into fists. "Oh yeah, Mickey?" he said, turning to face the other boy. "Who you heard that from? Cuz Peaches my best friend, and she wouldna left without telling me, ya heard?"

"Sure she is," Mickey said. "If she's such a good friend, when's the last time you seen her?"

Perry's heart sank. It had been a while. Two weeks, at least. What if Mickey was right? What if Peaches had run out on Perry? What if she'd run out on Nola?

"I see her every damn day, dummy," Perry said. "She lives two houses down from me. You don't never know what you're talking about. All you do is run fast and talk out your ass, and everybody knows it."

"Hey!" Mickey said, balling his own fists. "You take that back!"

"Sure I will," Perry said. "As soon as you admit you don't know nothing about nothing—and neither does your stupid daddy!"

Mickey actually drew back his fist to throw a punch, but Miss Erica had appeared behind him like magic. She caught Mickey's wrist and held it. "Boys!" she barked.

Miss Erica was a tallish white woman with dark hair and great big eyes. Today she wore a poet's blouse with frilly cuffs and a long crimson skirt that looked like a giant upside-down rose. "It's the last day of school. There will be no fussing and *no fighting*!"

"He called my daddy stupid!" Mickey said.

"Perry," Miss Erica said. "Is that true?"

"I didn't—I didn't start it," Perry said. "I called his daddy stupid, but it was because... I said it because..."

Perry couldn't find the words. He felt like the last boy on Earth.

"Apologize to Mickey."

Perry knew what Brendy or Peaches would say in his place: *Mickey Ledoux, I'm sorry you and yo daddy is so-o-o-o stoopid.* But he wasn't Brendy, and he certainly wasn't Peaches.

"I'm sorry," he said. "I'm just—I didn't mean it."

Deflated, Perry Graves went back to work.

II

Tha Ghost of Beanie Weenie

Time ground to a crawl as the shortened school day reached its middle hour. After the students finished their Learning System, Miss Erica and Miss Renee led them back into the fifth-grade Team Lair, which was a set of three different classrooms arranged around a central common area. The students sat crisscross in five rows to face a screen, and the teachers turned on the projector.

Perry loved *The Phantom Tollbooth*. Daddy Deke had read it to him and to Brendy years ago. The rise and fall of Daddy Deke's voice, the way he performed the characters rather than simply reporting what the book said, had fired Perry's imagination, made him dream of far-off places and people, of taking up a quest of his own—even if such things weren't possible in real life, certainly not for shy, bookish boys like Perry.

Perry still remembered what Daddy Deke had told them the day he finished reading the final chapter. "Let me tell y'all sumn for free: Nola is a pure wonder of a city. You are truly blessed to call it home—but there's other places out there. Make sure to get out and see 'em when you can. The city will always be here when ya get back."

At the time, Perry hadn't understood what his grandfather meant.

Of course there were other places, and of course they mattered. But why go traveling far and wide when Nola was enough?

In years past, he had looked forward to seeing the movie on the last day of school. He was lucky they showed it at both his old school and his new one. After all, that screening was the first real sign that summer had officially begun. Today, though, with the hours standing still, the minutes creeping by, and the seconds moving not at all, the film felt like a sentence to be endured. Besides, Perry very much preferred the book. He had gone through three copies since he got his first one for Christmas however long ago, and his newest copy was on its way out. The paperback was dog-eared in the extreme, some of its pages ready to fall right out. The spine had long since been broken, and every time Perry opened it, he felt the book sigh softly, as if it were getting tired.

Some nights, when he couldn't sleep, instead of reading comics or Billy 7 Adventures, Perry would get out his flashlight and his trusty *Phantom Tollbooth* and read under the covers in a fort made of pillows and blankets. Well, what he did couldn't quite be called reading. He would hold his flashlight like a telephone receiver between his chin and shoulder and thumb through the pages, running his fingers over the letters without sounding the words inside his head. He didn't need to. He knew them all better than if he'd written the book himself. He'd mouth a word or sentence—*Dodecahedron, Doldrums, killing time*—and realize dimly that he didn't actually need the flashlight to enact this rite. The words flowed into him through his fingertips—or no, they didn't, because they already lived deep inside him, inhabiting his core. Perry needed only to touch the print in order to create a sympathetic vibration in his chest, and the story would tell itself to him, and every last word was magic every single time.

Perry liked the movie version—liked it a lot. Most everything was more or less the way he imagined it when he first read the book—well, mostly less—but he didn't care to sit through it today. He wanted to jump from his seat on the floor by the column and disappear behind it, then, on tiptoes, skulk right out of Jelly Roll Morton Academy to freedom and the boiling Nola summer.

Instead Perry pulled his right leg up so he could rest his elbow on his knee as he stared at the screen almost without seeing. Milo had just discovered the giant red-and-white striped package in the foyer of his row house.

Hey. Perry.

Perry frowned. Milo had found the card whose envelope read FOR MILO, WHO HAS PLENTY OF TIME.

Perilous Antoine Graves!

Distracted from his sort-of watching, Perry looked around. At first he thought he'd heard Peaches trying to get his attention, but anyone who knew her knew that Peaches would never set foot inside a school. He couldn't find the source of the whispering anyway.

Don't look round, boy. Act like you ain't heard me.

Perry's heart lurched in his chest. That was *definitely* Peaches's voice! She must have broken her cardinal rule to sneak into Morton Academy and sit at Perry's side, unnoticed by the teachers or the students.

Teacher ain't looking. Get up and head straight outside. Now! Now!

Perry wavered, then slowly folded himself into a crouch. Creeping slowly, he edged around the column to keep it between him and everyone else. Then, carefully, soundlessly—holding his breath, even—he crept out into the hallway. He froze, staring at his red-and-white shoes contrasted against the beige linoleum tile. One, two, three, four, five beats passed as he stood with his back to the Team Lair, and no voice called him back.

"Castle in the air!" the tollbooth called out from the movie. "By way of Dictionopolis and alllll points west!"

Keep it movin', baby. Don't get caught. She sounded just as near to him as she had inside, her voice insistent and distinct, but coming from nowhere and everywhere at once.

"Peaches!" Perry whispered back. "Where you at?"

When she didn't answer, Perry resumed his creep, walking on

the sides of his feet so as to make no sound in the hall. When he reached the Academy's front doors without incident, he pressed the handle slowly, then waited a couple more beats before pushing the door open into the summer air.

Outside, sunlight fell like rain. It was so thick, so powerful that Perry expected it to ring as it bounced onto Esplanade Avenue. He held the door, careful to let it swing noiselessly shut, then visored his hand over his eyes to survey the scene before him.

The air smelled intensely of day and of outside. The avenue was silent. Not a single car, not a single zombie. Tall, fat oaks stood sentry along the opposite sidewalk, scattering the shadows of their leafy branches to break the light like mosaics upon the walk. A patch of graffiti rippled in the air several yards down toward City Park. Perry was a little surprised to see it. P-bodies never came to this part of town, because the graffiti got cleared away so quickly here. Perry stared at the stylized letters, trying to read the tag. After a moment or two, he was mostly confident that it said BOAT AKK.

But reading it solved nothing. If Peaches had called him, where was she?

"Peaches!" Perry said, almost at full volume. "Here I'm is!"

Now the whisper giggled at him.

"Stop playing," Perry said. "I get caught out here, I'll be grounded for a month!"

Doooooown dem steps!

Perry took one look behind him through the glass of the front door. The hallway stood empty. Nobody seemed to have detected his escape. Satisfied—more or less—Perry descended the steps to stand on the sidewalk outside the school. The rectangular shadow of the Jackson/Esplanade sky trolley slid slowly up the avenue, and Perry looked up to see the trolley's glass belly puttering along its route. It stopped a couple blocks up and descended gently to the street, purring hoarsely like an elderly cat. A couple passengers stepped off and ambled on their way.

Perry looked the other way down Esplanade toward City Park.

The graffiti made it hard to tell for sure, but he saw nobody lurking that way.

Crooooooss dat street!

Perry checked both ways, then did as he'd been told.

On the other side of the avenue stood a venerable old house with dark purple paint and red trim. It sat back from the street at the end of a twisty little walk, and low hedges lined its yard. What would Peaches be doing here? Perry knew her taste, and she would call this house "daaaaawg oogly!"

Perry shrugged and started toward the front door.

"Here I'm is!" a giant voice rang out, and Perry whirled so fast he lost his balance and spun right down on his butt.

Brendy was so thrilled with herself that she danced a little jig. "I got you!" she crowed, shaking her little fists. "You got *got!* Oh! Aw! *Ha!*"

Perry glowered at her. "What you even doing outside? We're gonna get in so much trouble!"

"You ain't in no trouble," Peaches said as she emerged from the hedge. There hadn't been room enough for her inside the branches, but she must have used some trick to make herself and Brendy fit.

Seeing Peaches in her worn red dress with its white collar and buttons caused a slight constriction in Perry's chest. Her knees and elbows were knobby and a little scuffed, and her hands and feet were both too big for her body. Her legs had lengthened out in the time Perry had known her, and he noticed now, to his embarrassment, that her chest was beginning to grow.

Perry's face heated, and he hoped the darkness of his complexion would hide his blush. "You came in the school?" was all he could think to say.

"Not me, baby," Peaches said. "I already got my brains."

"She throwed her voice," Brendy said with a nod.

"That far?" Perry asked.

"I'm pretty strong," Peaches said with a smirk. "I throw far as a mug! Now, let's get to steppin'."

Without the barest effort, Peaches lifted Perry to stand before her.

"What song Doctor Professor played last night?" she said, her brown eyes wide.

" 'Missed Yo Chance Blues.' "

"Ooooh. My favorite!"

Perry couldn't help but feel that would have been her response no matter his answer. "So where you been?" he asked.

"Here and there. Keepin' it cool. But later for all that," Peaches said. "Right now, we got bidness. Somebody took something from me, and we finna get it back."

Brendy clapped both hands on her cheeks and bugged out her eyes. "Somebody stole from you?"

"Baby, ain't nobody more surprised than me," Peaches said.

"Who would do that?" Perry asked. "I mean, Kill Grems is probably still pretty mad at you for beating his butt right in front of everybody in Audubon Park."

"It ain't him, though," Peaches said.

"What did they take?"

Peaches took a breath. "It's complicated," she said. "But it's sumn real special, heard? Something I need. I'm pretty sure I know who got it, and I know where he at."

Perry wanted to ask more questions, to plan the heist or what-ever this was, but being near Peaches again after so long made him giddy. He felt a tingling in his chest that made him—well, he wasn't sure what it wanted him to do. Going with Peaches to steal her property back would give him a chance to—to smell Peaches, to look at her and listen to the rhythm of her voice.

"Well, all right then," Perry said. "You know we ready to back you up." But he had to ask: "You didn't leave town, though, right?"

Peaches wrinkled her nose. "Leave town?" she said. "That's the dumbest thing I ever heard."

As the three of them headed for the sky trolley stop, Perry found himself thinking on the past. Previous events loomed large for him today, and now that Peaches was back, Perry thought about how they'd first met.

Just after the Storm, when Perry turned five, his parents threw a cookout in the Graves family yard. Brendy was still a toddler, so she wasn't up to much. Perry's mama stayed with her on the porch, bobbling the girl on her thick honey-colored knee as Perry, his twin cousins, and some of the neighborhood kids ran around the yard or frolicked in the bouncy castle. As the party wore on, the twins got tired of jumping, and Perry caught them trying to sneak away.

"Where you going?" he asked as Pink and Danni stood at the edge of the sidewalk just at the border of the lawn.

"We gone check out the ghost house," Pink said. Even then, she wore her hair combed straight up into a kinky tower.

"You stay here," Danni said. "We report back."

"I want to go," Perry said.

"Naw, you can't—" Danni said.

Pink cut her off. She called the shots between them. "Let him come," she said. "We won't let nothing happen. Besides, what if there really is a ghost? We'll need a big strong man to protect us."

Perry was a little scared, but he puffed out his chest anyway, and together they went.

"It looks like a big cake," Perry said as they stepped into the house's overgrown yard.

"Moldy cake, maybe," Danni said. "All creepy."

It *was* creepy, Perry had to admit. While the house itself reminded him of a wedding cake, the gnarly, leafless oaks, the sagging porch, and the falling-off shutters reminded him of *Scooby-Doo*.

Pink led them around the side of the house and to the screened-in porch in back. The rusted storm door stood open, fallen half off its hinges. Inside stood a splintery porch and what looked like a stack of newspapers made mush by the wet, but still bound together by a yellow plastic ribbon. The place smelled damp and old, the way Perry imagined a mummy's tomb would—or no! Dracula's coffin room!

"You scared?" Pink asked.

Perry couldn't tell whether she was asking him, her twin sister, or herself. "I ain't scared," he said, just to be safe. "But if *you* scared, we can go back."

"I ain't scared," Pink said. "Let's go."

WHAT Y'ALL WANT?

The voice boomed hollow. At the sound of it, without a word, Danni up and left. Perry saw her go out of the corner of his eye, and he could tell from the way Pink stood very, very straight that she would have gone, too, if terror hadn't rooted her in place. Perry's own limbs felt light and springy. He knew that if he turned and ran, his legs would carry him faster than they ever had before, but he stood his ground because this was something *new*, and such strangeness so close to his everyday world could not be ignored.

WHO YOU IS, LITTLE GURL? WHAT Y'ALL WANT WIF MY HOUSE?

Pink reached down and grabbed Perry's left arm. The motion had been painfully slow, but her grip was hard enough to hurt. "Let's go," she said.

"I ain't scared," Perry said, and this time, even as he said the words, he realized they were true. "What *you* want, haint?"

I WANTS YOUR TOY CARS AND A MONKEY ON A UNICYCLE, said the voice. AND BRING ME ONEA DEM SNO-BALLS FROM THE MACHINE WHILE YOU AT IT.

"Haints don't need toys," Perry said. "And haints can't eat sno-balls, noway. You the dumbest haint I ever met."

Pink yanked at Perry's arm, but she couldn't seem to get herself moving any other way. They just stood there while Perry challenged the disembodied voice that rang from the darkness of the haunted house.

WELL, THEN WHAT ABOUT MY MONKEY? AND ANYWAY, HAINTS CAN *TOO* EAT SNO-BALLS. I EATS 'EM ALL THE TIME. SNO-BALLS IS HAINT FOOD. ERRYBODY KNOW THAT.

Now Pink seemed to realize that while the voice was scary, its words were utterly ridiculous. "Wait a minute. Who that is?"

WHO *YOU* IS? I AXED YOU FIRST!

"I'm Pink Marie-Antoinette Duvally."

WELL, I'M THA GHOST OF BEANIE WEENIE!

Silence descended, and then, moments later, the air broke with the silliest laugh Perry had ever heard. It sounded almost like Goofy from the cartoons—but girlish and brimming with joy. Perry laughed himself, just to hear it.

"You ain't no haint!"

"Got me there, baby," she said, and out she stepped from the shadows inside the porch. Back then she was shorter, leaner, and her limbs weren't quite so knobby, but she had the same big red Afro puffs, the same wide brown eyes, and her skin was the exact color of Daddy Deke's morning coffee.

"Here I'm is," she said. "My name Peaches—Peaches Lavelle—and I done sailed the Seven Seas." She paused, seeming to consider. "I guess you can forget the monkey. Y'all do got sno-balls, though. I seen 'em from my window. What your name is?"

"Puh-Perry," Perry said.

"Well, happy birthday, Puh-Perry. How old you is?"

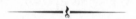

The trolley smelled of clean laundry. Peaches took up her own seat, sitting with her legs crossed and her arms spread out over the back of it. She bobbed her head gently, humming silently to herself, and every so often, she met Perry's gaze and wiggled her bubble-gum tongue at him.

Brendy sat next to Perry, leaning down with her head between her knees as her chubby legs dangled above the transparent floor. Her feet were bare—as they almost always were when she and Perry adventured with Peaches. Perry held his sister's patent-leather Mary Janes for her, thinking dimly and without much interest that he should complain about that one of these days.

The man sitting in front of Perry wore cheap headphones, and Perry could hear his music, tinny and faint.

Brendy had ridden the sky trolley more times than anyone could remember—they all had—but she always seemed transfixed by the view. Perry guessed it was Brendy's limited sense of propriety that kept her from lying spread-eagled on the floor, her entire body pressed against the bottom of the sky as she watched the city scrolling underneath her.

After meeting up, the three of them had caught the 91 up to Rampart Street, then walked up St. Claude to wait for the Elysian Fields trolley. The noonday sun was boiling hot, so they'd stopped at Gene's—a ridiculously pink house at the corner of St. Claude and Elysian Fields—for virgin daiquiris while they waited for their transfer.

As they stood at the corner, Perry looked down the avenue toward the lake and saw a crazy lady marching up the way. Tall and long-legged, she wore a bright red fortune-teller's turban and a long, flowing coat that looked made from several different sweaters all sewn together. Even though she wore a turban, the coat's hood was up, but it was so long and pointy that even from where he stood, Perry could see its length bouncing behind her in time with her steps. The woman seemed unaware of anyone else on the street; she just trudged on, wide-eyed and frowning.

"Look," Perry said. "Look at her go."

"Who?" Brendy said, looking round. Her gaze fell on the woman. "Oh!"

"She just a street crazy," Peaches said. "Don't matter if she dressed like a Mardi Gras. Crazy is crazy."

On the corner across St. Claude, a fortyish man with salt-and-pepper hair stood talking on his cell phone. He gestured wildly, obviously giving orders or yelling at someone. He stood right in the crazy lady's path.

Either she didn't see him or she didn't care. The woman didn't slow her gait. The man caught sight of her and tried to move aside as she reached him, but he was a little too slow. She brushed past, knocking him down.

Then, without looking for the light, the crazy lady stepped right into traffic. Cars honked and swerved, but she just kept going. Nothing seemed to touch her or draw her interest.

"We better get out the way," Peaches said.

The three of them stepped back into the parking lot of the Foot Locker behind them and watched the woman stride past. As she rushed by, Perry heard a quick snatch of music. It was just a couple quick piano chords, and he couldn't identify the song. He couldn't tell for sure, looking at her back, but he didn't think the woman had been wearing headphones. Still, if she was, that might account for her behavior, just a little. She was lost in the music, marching instead of dancing. But that didn't explain the flowing hooded coat or the turban—or why she didn't seem to see anyone or anything in her path.

"That was—I dunno what that was," Perry said.

"That was a street crazy, Perry," Peaches said. "You seen your share."

The Elysian Fields trolley had arrived. It purred to the ground and Peaches climbed on. Perry let Brendy on, then climbed in after. As he paid both their fares, he thought about what he'd seen. The lady was crazy, all right, but Perry couldn't help but feel there was more to her than that.

He watched the man with the headphones, considered asking him to turn his music down. Something in the idea made Perry feel small and craven. The music wasn't bothering him, after all, so why hassle anyone about it?

Goddamn jungle music.

The thought bubbled up from somewhere dark, in a voice not Perry's own. He knew it, though. It was the voice of—

Perry tensed. He'd almost fallen asleep. He had promised himself never to fall asleep on the sky trolley again.

Brendy sat back. She slouched a little, crossing her arms over her chest. "So," she said. "Where we going, anyway?"

Perry adjusted his own posture. Peaches sat on the forward-facing bench at right angles to him and Brendy, gazing thoughtfully at the grubby fingernails of her right hand. She was due for a wash—the bottoms of her bare feet were nearly black with grime—but as far as Perry knew, Peaches never bathed indoors. It had been almost a week since the last good rain, and wherever Peaches had been and whatever she'd been up to in that time, she hadn't taken her usual weekly swim in Big Lake at City Park. It was a wonder she didn't stink.

Perry looked down through the rose-colored glass as the trolley hummed along. The humming stopped abruptly, and the trolley glided silent for a few seconds as its motor rested.

"We going to a boneyard," Peaches said.

"Foy Street!" the pilot called over his shoulder.

Peaches reached up and pulled the bell. This was their stop.

If they were getting off at Foy, heading to a cemetery, Peaches must mean Mount Olivet—which happened to be where Doctor Professor was buried. Could this mission be connected to him somehow? Surely, he wouldn't have stolen from Peaches...

The trolley drifted down, and the three of them disembarked. Perry started to sweat immediately, but it was only a few blocks to their destination.

At one time or another, the three of them must have been to every other cemetery in town to visit family or on school field trips. Mount Olivet, though, was outside their usual stomping grounds. The walk down Gentilly and up Norman Mayer went quickly enough, and as they went, Brendy babbled happily about this and that. She always talked this way after a longish trolley ride, but her companions didn't have much to add. Peaches answered the occasional question in monosyllables, and Perry spent most of the time watching her. She'd seemed totally normal when they met up, but now she seemed extra quiet—not sullen, but...distracted.

Now they were in sight of the boneyard's front gate. Perry expected to see at least a zombie or two hanging round, but the street—the entire neighborhood, it seemed—was empty of them. He frowned and reached for Peaches's elbow. From her mood he expected her to shrug him off, but she didn't, and they walked like that for several paces, Perry's hand resting on her cool, dry skin. Perry realized now that he'd never seen Peaches sweat, and he wondered if she felt the heat the way normal folks did.

Perry pushed the thought away. It didn't matter. Peaches was Peaches.

He curled his fingers a little, slowed his walk. "Hey."

"Hey, what?"

"You okay?"

"You ain't gotta be worrying bout me all the time, Perry," she said with a roll of her eyes.

Perry just watched her, feeling caught without knowing why.

"You know what I mean," she said. "I'm fine. How *you* doing?"

"I'm okay," he said. He grinned and danced a few manic steps. "Summatime, baby!"

"Summa. Time," she agreed. "Here I'm is."

"Here I'm is!" Brendy crowed.

"Yeah," Perry said. "Here we is together." But a chilly unease had begun to gather in his belly.

MELT YO HEART

August 2018

The International Collaborative School of New Orleans was situated in the old Rabouin Technical College building on Carondelet Street. The building made Casey Ravel think of a sandcastle sculpted by an obsessive child—all shaved planes and soft angles. At the height of summer, before the fall semester began, the school building seemed to lie in an enchanted trance. The resigned hush of its empty halls seemed like a bated breath, and Casey imagined the school ached to live again.

When he accepted the job, he thought he'd simply be writing grants, but it turned out the school expected more from him. He attended every board meeting and leadership session, though he wasn't a teacher. Where he drew the line, though, was in policing the students' behavior and dress. Dr. Pullen had asked that all school leadership make sure that students' ties were tied and that their powder-blue uniform shirts were tucked in. Casey had smiled and agreed enthusiastically, knowing even as he did that he had no intention of following through. Listening to the circular conversations to decide whether to decide about this or that detail of whatever-the-fuck procedure was one thing, but being a dick to kids just to do it didn't sit right with him.

Casey's office was tucked away to the left of the lobby stairs. It had once been a supply closet, and a few items were still stored there—the threadbare Panther mascot costume, extra fire extinguishers, and some seasonal decorations—but the ceiling was high, and the room was small enough that the single window unit kept it comfortably cool even as wet heat smothered the city like a great fat belly. Now classes had begun and the building was alive again for the 2017–18 school year, and the place smelled of teenage funk and rubber cement.

Casey had submitted two grant proposals and a Letter of Interest that week, but there was nothing else to do while he waited for Ms. Mounir, the Arabic teacher, and Mr. Crawford, the Mandarin teacher, to turn in their program narratives for the Language Expansion Report due next week. The thought that he hated this work flashed dull in Casey's mind, and he shoved it gently away, squinting at his flat-screen computer monitor to check his calendar for what must have been the fiftieth time that day. He hated fundraising, all right, but he was damn good at it.

Casey's phone dinged and he flipped it onto its back to see who had messaged. Oh. Wrong phone. He was still getting used to being the kind of cat that carried multiple iPhones. The ding came again, and this time he realized it was coming from the top left desk drawer. He fished it out.

Nigga, tha FUKK???

Casey reached under his glasses to hold his eyes shut. Jayl was right to be indignant. Casey should have told his cousin he was moving back to town, but every time he'd tried to form the words, he had failed, and he wasn't sure why. He snatched up the phone and called.

"Excuse me, sir? Excuse me. Language, sir. Language."

"Uh, excuse you?" Jaylon said.

"No, I know," Casey said. "My fault."

"Mane, you done me downbad. I don't expect Uncle Trev to tell me shit with his absent-minded tomato-cobbler-eatin' ass, but you my nigga, nigga!"

"I know. First I didn't want to tell you because it didn't look like it was going to happen, and then when it did it happened so fast that—"

"That you just forgot my ass? I see I see."

"Never that. I figured I'd tell you in person, but your ass be jetting around everywhere all the time."

"Aw."

"Where you calling from right now?"

Jayl sucked his teeth. "Mane, that's—"

"*Where*, though?"

"See, I ain't even that far: Houston."

"Where were you Monday, though?"

"Okay, Montreal."

"*Well.*"

"Trev tell you what I'm workin' on?"

"No, he said it was big and hush-hush."

"'Big Hush Hush.' That sounds like him. Can you me at the Spot tomorrow night?"

"Already there, baby. Later on." Casey ended the call and considered the sensations playing across his skin. He was excited to see his cousin again—thrilled—but he had to admit there was a little fear there, too. In a flash, he remembered running as hard as he could, a stich in his side. Scrambling up a chain-link fence as Jaylon broke to the right behind him, unable to get over. There was no sin in it, Casey knew. Jayl had always been big, a little slow. He couldn't run like Casey. But leaving him felt... The regret gathered in the back of Casey's throat.

He swallowed it and went back to work.

———— ❧ ————

Casey's relationship with his parents was not ideal—but it was better than some. From Casey's youngest years, he remembered his father, Raymond, teaching Casey's brother H. T. the rules of manhood. First and foremost was We Take Care of Our Own. When Ravel men had children, they raised those children; when family asked for help, they gave it. Casey had listened intently to those lessons without knowing exactly why. When he decided to begin his transition, he was living with his girlfriend Ximena in Bowie, Maryland. He stayed away from his parents for the first few weeks, begging off the Sunday dinners they hosted at their house in Catonsville. At the end of Casey's second month on T, he and Ximena had gone to dinner.

The house was a five-bedroom brick-and-siding split-level with a broad stained deck Raymond Ravel had built himself. Casey arrived with Ximena in tow and was surprised to find that his Teedy Billie and her wife Laverne were there as well. Billie was his mother's older sister. She'd been married to her man, Wood, for almost forty years until he died of cancer—then she'd married her lifelong best friend.

By then, Billie's move was no scandal in the family—the tug-of-war over Casey's lesbianism had more or less ended because his parents had come to understand that it was more than a passing phase—and the next year, Casey had told his brother that the inner child he'd been wrestling with for years was a little boy.

The dinner itself went well. No snide comments came Casey's way. The family treated Ximena warmly, told her stories of Casey's girlhood—how he would peel off his dress and take to the suburban streets and bike trails, running until his brother caught up with him and led him home by the hand. Casey had been embarrassed by the anecdote, but he hoped his brother telling it meant that he understood, at least a little, that Casey had always hated the dresses and skirts his parents had given him to wear, that they'd never fit.

Over the course of the dinner, Ximena mentioned that Casey

had been down for the count for almost a week with a chest cold he found hard to shake. At the end of the night, as they were preparing to leave, Raymond had quietly asked Casey whether it had really been a cold or "whatever you been taking to grow a beard."

"No," Casey said. "It wasn't the hormones." But the comment withered him, ruined his night.

He hadn't known it at the time, but that was when Casey resolved to move back to New Orleans.

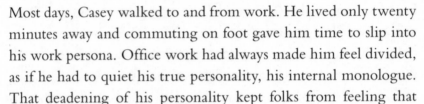

Most days, Casey walked to and from work. He lived only twenty minutes away and commuting on foot gave him time to slip into his work persona. Office work had always made him feel divided, as if he had to quiet his true personality, his internal monologue. That deadening of his personality kept folks from feeling that Casey watched them too intently—as if he was sizing them up for something. Of course, what he'd been sizing them up for, in his younger days, was sketches, but he hardly drew at all anymore.

Nowadays Casey felt like a stranger to the city, but by walking he felt he was getting to know it again. He half jogged down the school's front steps and turned right on Carondelet street, heading uptown toward the Lower Garden District.

Even now, twelve years after the storm, everywhere Casey looked he saw the scars left behind by the Failure of the Federal Levees: crosses spray-painted on boarded-up windows, whole high-rise towers standing empty in the Central Business District while luxury condo buildings popped up like toadstools after rain. When Casey referred to the Failure in conversation—which was not often—folks unfamiliar with the details of the destruction looked at him strangely, wondering why he termed it so formally. What they didn't understand was that the hurricane itself wasn't responsible for the damage. Instead, it was the levees designed and built by the Army Corps of Engineers—the fact that they'd never been as strong as New Orleanians had been led to believe. Katrina and Rita were manmade disasters, and while Casey felt like a traitor for abandoning the city in its darkest hour, at least he could remember that much, name it to himself.

To be fair, the city looked better than it had when he'd first returned after the storm. Yes, the scars were still evident, but miasma of injury had faded, or at least transformed into something quieter, a sort of background static. As Casey walked under the I-10 overpass, he saw a forest of tents and even a sofa or two sitting in the shadow of the highway. At least three churches stood close by the encampments, and Casey's religious upbringing sent twinges of anger through his chest—hot little slivers like the bits of shrapnel that threatened Tony Stark's heart. He hated the way New Orleans treated its poor, its less fortunate. He hated what his mother would have called the "do-lessness" of the clergy here and elsewhere.

Casey had first felt the same pale, dull anger when he'd come down from Maryland in February of 2007. Then, he and Jaylon had driven from Chalmette up to Bay Saint Louis and back, touring the area. Casey had looked out the passenger window at acres and acres of dead trees choked by floodwaters. Even Lake Pontchartrain had changed from a silver-blue expanse stretching to either side of the causeway bridge to a darker, muddier blue, as if it were considering another uprising. And everywhere, blue tarps lay draped over damaged roofs. In Chalmette, Casey saw a house that had drifted off its foundation and split horizontally in half. The upper section of the house had caught fire even in the flood and now lay across the street, broken and blackened. In Mississippi, Casey saw families camping on what had once been the foundations of their houses—with not even FEMA trailers to shelter them.

Casey snapped back to the present to find that he'd reached his building. His apartment was cheap by DMV standards, but here in New Orleans it was on the steeper side. The Georgian was an ivied brick building sitting on St. Charles Avenue.

When he was young, Casey had spent summers staying with his Mamaw Relma in her big old place down on France Street.

Gardenias perfumed the city, and the bizarre street names sounded like secret incantations. *Rocheblave, Tchoupitoulas, Henriette Delille*... Some nights, as he lay in the attic room twin bed, listening to Jaylon and H. T. mumble and snore, Casey would recite those names quietly to himself. If he went long enough without repeating one, the words would gradually transform in his mouth, ferment like the floral spirits his grandmother kept in the living room sideboard. If he went longer still, the air seemed to vibrate, and he would feel pressed against an invisible membrane, and if he learned the proper key, he could push through into... what...?

Usually, as Casey walked, he'd silently recite the name of every street he crossed. He must truly be distracted. He shook his head, irritated with himself. Of course he was distracted! He was bone-tired from the stress of the move and living in the unfurnished apartment made him feel as if he barely existed.

He stood in the kitchen sipping grape juice, scanning the bare living room: not so much as a TV in here. Well, New Orleans didn't lack for entertainment no matter how much had changed since the storm. He needed to eat something anyway, so he might as well head over to Frenchmen and see who was playing.

The same day he flew in, Casey found a beat-up '97 Lumina on Craigslist. Six hundred dollars later, he was on the move. It was the last of his savings, but his first check from the new job had been enough that he could get an apartment straightaway, even if he couldn't yet furnish it.

The city simmered in its bowl as Casey parked the Ole Girl by Washington Square. As he strolled through to Frenchmen Street, he remembered that this wasn't his first time here since leaving town. The other visits had been part of holiday excursions—Halloween, when the street was a river of drunken costumed revelers, and Carnival, when it was... well, an ocean, he supposed.

Today there were no costumes, no off-brand Transformers or

zombie clowns, just doughy tourists in cargo shorts and polo shirts and locals who understood how to handle the lingering heat as the daylight dimmed to evening. Best to move as little as possible and keep to the shade.

A hush stole over the street. Casey felt a strange sensation of openness, as if someone had lifted the lid off the sky. He felt watched. He thought he heard someone call his name in the silence, and the impression was so powerful that he wheeled for a moment, looking to see who had named him. As he did, the ambient noise of the city—the grumbling engines, the commotion of crows, and the skittering of squirrels—returned as if it had never gone. Cautiously, Casey resumed walking.

Two older men sat outside the Marigny Brasserie. One was thin and dark-skinned with a mane of salt-and-pepper hair and glasses with thick bubbly frames. He wore a diagonal-striped polo shirt and sandals with socks. As Casey stepped past him, the man stood, and the tone of his conversation elongated as if he was considering leaving but hadn't yet made up his mind.

Casey checked out the menu at Three Muses, and his eyes immediately fastened on the lamb sliders. This would be the place. Casey was a sucker for miniature foods. In Casey's eyes, this bar was a prime example of the sort of place opening up on Frenchmen Street in the past several years. The clientele was largely white, either transplants or tourists who knew enough to bypass Bourbon Street and the Famous Door in favor of real music. The walls were painted a cloudy blue, with crimson curtains in the window and vibrant portraits of jazz men Casey mostly didn't recognize hanging on the walls.

He ordered his sliders and some truffle fries at the bar and a Spaghetti Western for the wait, then slid into a seat near the small stage where a tech was setting up for the show. He didn't know who was playing tonight, but it didn't matter. It would be good to lose himself in music again. He made a mental note to buy a new needle the moment his turntable arrived.

Casey was scrolling through his Discogs wantlist on his phone when the band started up with a blazing riff that yanked him back to the present. Something about the sound reminded Casey of arcing a bright line of spray paint across a concrete wall.

The thin, bespectacled man Casey had seen down the street stepped up to grab the mic with his right hand as he held his trombone at his side.

I said, I will I will I will I will I will
Melt your heart like butter!
Under the goddamn cover of night
I will make you make you shudder!
Hey!

The singer drew his horn back to his lips and played along as the band launched back into the opening riff. They were playing a version of Dr. John's "I Walk on Guilded Splinters." Casey didn't know what he'd expected, but it wasn't this. The set made him hoot and stomp as the band veered between joyful but reverent jazz standards, original songs, and reinterpretations of cherished favorites from all over the map.

Casey shouted out loud when they launched into a rattling version of "Revival" by Deerhunter. In response, the singer jumped up on the bar to play his own version of the guitar solo while Casey and the rest of the crowd stood from their seats and threw their hands up. Afterwards, Casey was left with that ringing feeling behind his breastbone that he only felt at the tail end of a solid show or when he knew for certain he'd lost his pursuers after a chase.

"Thank y'all! Thank y'all, Three Muses!" the singer shouted at the end. "I have been Foxx King and *errybody free!*"

Casey settled up his tab and headed back to his car. On the way, he saw King standing outside the brasserie again.

"Hey, man," he said. "That was amazing!"

"Aw, thank ya, baby," King said lazily. Casey couldn't believe how chill this man could be after such a fiery set. "We here every Thursday."

Afterwards, as he reached the spot where he'd felt overshadowed by that strange silence and openness, Casey expected something strange to happen again—but there was nothing. His fingers twitched and, absently, he reached into his pocket for a pack of cigarettes that wasn't there. He caught himself, and the action made him frown. It embarrassed him, but a feeling of defiance swelled in him. He was a grown-ass man, and if he wanted to smoke, that's what the fuck he'd do...

For days, the Muses show stuck in Casey's mind. The opener, especially. The original track was one of Casey's favorites. He had heard it by chance when he was young, playing at some record shop in Baltimore's Inner Harbor that Casey's older brother had dragged him to looking for this or that cassingle. As H. T. ignored him in favor of the tapes he was thumbing through, Casey turned away in search of amusement. In those days, Casey wore rompers. They were meant as a compromise, since he and his mother had done battle over his unwillingness to wear dresses.

The music on the PA was just background noise until Casey heard the singer's voice, smooth and gravelly at the same time, mention the word "zombie." H. T. had shown Casey *Return of the Living Dead* last week, and the movie had terrified and thrilled him at the same time. Now he listened more closely to the song. It moved like a carousel, foreboding chords rolling across an enchanted mix of tom-toms and bongos.

When the singer promised to "melt your heart like butter," Casey frowned. Nothing about the song sounded heartwarming to him. It sounded foreboding, like a threat made in a midnight churchyard. Casey was as frightened by it as he'd been by the "Thriller" video when he saw it at four years old. This fear was colder, though, and there was something delicious in it.

The next time he heard the song, it was a different version. Flatter, paler—almost as if the singer had no idea what the lyrics meant. He couldn't remember which of the many many covers that had been. Paul Weller? Sonny and Cher?

It wasn't until Casey was a freshman at Smith that he listened to *Gris-Gris* from start to finish. All of the tracks amazed him, but "I Walk on Guilded Splinters" pierced him through the heart—made him feel as if he was way out on a collision course with something he had not yet begun to understand.

———————❧———————

The sun had begun to drop away behind Metairie as Casey hurried the old car north up I-10. He took the Chef Menteur exit, and for a moment he had the queer feeling that he'd been transported back in time. The only difference he noticed as he came off the freeway was that the apartment building to the left of the road had been tagged-up something fierce. FREYA, ARBUS, YANKY, but no JAYL—the car behind him at the light bleated to let Casey know the stop had turned, and he continued on, trying not to think *What if? What if? What if?*

Jaylon's spot was in the Franklin Manor complex.

The compound itself was a series of four six-story buildings connected by what Casey first took for walking bridges before he realized they were merely decorative awnings. The place reminded Casey of the dorms at UNO, but the facades were brighter, with crisp edges and broad balconies. Jaylon's place was a three-bedroom corner apartment. Art prints and originals hung on the walls, and each room had its own color scheme.

As his cousin showed him around, Casey realized why he was so surprised: The last time he'd been to one of Jaylon's apartments was five years ago, and the place on Leonidas had looked like what it was—a transitional space between adolescence and adulthood. Some of his posters and art prints had been framed, while others were tacked directly to the wall. The kitchen trash was tucked neatly under the sink, but out on the balcony sat a Big Shot bottle full of Kool butts. Now Jayl had brought his artist's eye to bear, and the place looked professionally decorated.

"You didn't tell me it was like *that*," Casey said, grinning, as they sat on opposite ends of the sectional. Jayl had taken the long side, where he could stretch out. He'd always been big—well, fat, really—but even that had changed in recent years. He was still barrel-chested with a belly, but it didn't protrude the way it used to.

"Thanks," Jaylon said. "And I'm grateful, no cap. But—and I honestly don't talk to anybody bout all this..." He paused, frowned as he parsed his words. "I mean, I'll talk about my work in interviews and shit, but it's not like, real talk. Then I'll talk to other artists and shit, and that's great...but I thought it would be different by now."

"Different?"

"Yeah, you know. Since all that Shepard Fairey Andre the Giant shit, I thought white folks was really feeling street art. They say so, but you know: There's a vibe. Like low-key 'you don't really belong here,' ya heard?"

Casey nodded. "Good."

Jaylon stopped short, surprised, then his understanding seemed to shift. "Yeah. *Yeah*," he said. "We an invasive species. We thrive where we don't belong."

"Like nutria and weeds, nigga."

"Goddamn, I'm glad you're here!"

"Me too, man. Me too," Casey said. "Listen. You, ah...I know I haven't been in touch like I should."

"Please," Jayl said. "You here now."

He was; following through on his decision to return had cost him more than he expected. The years since the storm had shaped Casey into someone new—and it wasn't just the transition. It was—

"Ximena left me," he said, finally.

Jaylon's expression darkened and he shook his head. He and

Ximena had gotten along famously. "Aw," he said. "Aw, man. I really thought y'all was gone make it."

"I know," Casey said. "I thought we were over the hump. I figured if we made it through transition, we could make it through anything."

"How long y'all was together?"

"Ten years, man."

"Goddamn," Jayl said. "Longest I made it is five years, and I started running out of shit to talk about. You ever look at bae and be like, 'Could you please get kidnapped or some shit?'"

Casey laughed. "Well. It was never boring. Maybe that was the problem."

Her image rose up in Casey's mind. Her almond eyes red from crying. *Case, I love you so much,* she'd said, *but I can't come with you where you're going.* His fingers twitched in his lap.

When Casey looked back to Jaylon, the other man was watching him with an unreadable expression.

"What?" Casey asked.

"I don't know," Jaylon said. "We just living in some wild-ass times, I guess. I'm just, uh, you know. I'm glad you're back. For real for real."

Like Casey, Jaylon was pushing forty, but for a moment he looked much older. What had Casey missed? What had Jaylon been through that he hadn't the words to tell?

"I'm just sorry it took me so long."

Jaylon shrugged off the apology. He wriggled his eyebrows. "You wan see something dope?"

"Indeed I do," Casey said in his Johnny Carson voice.

Jaylon rose, snatched his car keys up from the coffee table. "Then come on."

IV

AT THE BONEYARD

Yakumo dreamed of fire, flood, and shipwrecks. Of an enormous cotton gin grinding black bodies like peppercorns. He dreamed of starless nights crowded by storms. He didn't dream his wife or children. Even here, in his sleep, the cold clung to him in a wet, frigid webbing. He could feel his bones, the icy rage inside them, and a skittering aliveness beneath his skin, smaller bodies crowding his flesh. Vermin.

With some effort, he opened his eyes. He wasn't sure which body he wore now, but a quick glance at his legs told him: He had none. Though he could feel his feet pressed bare against the stone floor, he saw nothing below his knee, and he felt suspended from above, seething in the dark air.

Claws scrabbled desperate at the back of his throat. Yakumo curved his back into a question mark and fought to swallow the creature. The rat was tenacious, though, and clawed its way into his mouth. He tasted its hair and fright against his rotten tongue. Its terror, its hatred. But it was him, wasn't it? Some of him?

Yakumo spat the rat onto the dirty floor. It lay still for a moment, stunned. He stretched his cold darkness to wrap a black-on-black tentacle around the creature. It squealed as he thrust it back into its mouth and swallowed, savoring its struggle against the softness of his throat.

Gathering this piece of him back into himself ignited a small lightning storm in Yakumo's haunted skull. The electricity there was black, and the rain fell sideways, and once again, he felt himself borne up and down by the waves of a darkened sea. He—

He'd dozed again. He looked down at the paper crumpled in his left hand and grinned a yellow grin. Ah. The letter. There was no way of knowing whether the rat he'd just swallowed had been the same one that brought him this document, but it mattered not at all. What mattered was that he had his letter, and there was nothing its intended receiver could do about it. Yakumo unfolded the paper and inhaled its contents. More of the sea, but this time he tasted salt sunlight along with the ink. And what was this flavor? Care? It filled his sinuses with a bittersweet vapor, created an ache in the bones of his face.

His gorge rose. A swell of vermin wriggled in his belly, trying to force its way up. He swallowed again, careful not to let it get too far this time. The earwigs, the roaches, the rats, the blowflies and maggots settled back inside him and, content, he crawled back onto his slab to wait for... he couldn't remember what. Ah. Yes. The Old Man. Soon, he'd have a prisoner to interrogate, a means of rupturing this idiot eternity and finding his way out.

He gurgled a hateful laugh, then his mouth yawned like a grave. Koizumi Yakumo began to snore.

———— ♪ ————

They could hear the music from the street. At first Perry thought Doctor Professor must be playing somewhere inside, that this was where his spirit must reside when he wasn't playing around town. If that were true, though, wouldn't his music be strongest of all right here? Perry liked the sound of the piano, the horns, the guitar, and the hoarse singing, but his body remained his own. He didn't feel compelled to dance.

Besides, he realized as he listened more closely, it wasn't just one song they heard. There were at least two others going on at the same time—one with saxophone and stand-up bass, and another with just brass and drums. A funeral, maybe? More than one? The front gate stood closed and, as with most cemeteries here in town, a high concrete-and-iron fence stretched all the way around the property. Perry was a little surprised to find the place shut tight. He guessed the grounds were closed to tourists.

"So what now?" he asked.

Peaches scratched her chin. "Guess I'll throw y'all over."

"Throw us over?"

"Yeah. I throw you over the wall."

"You throw... *really* far, though," Perry said. "How we do this without getting hurt?"

"Well," Peaches said thoughtfully. "You be okay if I don't put too much spin or nothing on you. And if you drop out of the throw before you hit the ground."

"Drop...?"

"You know," she said. "Like when you fall from real high, but you don't wanna land too hard, so you fall into another fall lower down that's slower? I do it all the time."

"Why?" Perry said. "You can't get hurt."

"That ain't—" Peaches sighed, exasperated. "Falling down too hard ain't no fun, Perry. You know that."

"But what you're talking about... I don't think normal people can do that. I don't think Brendy and me can do that."

"Ever tried?"

Perry just watched her, his mouth open. He knew exactly how things would go now. Peaches would convince him and Brendy to do this ridiculous thing, as she'd convinced them to do so many others, and in spite of everything Perry knew about the world, it would work, more or less. Perry might be slightly banged up if he failed to follow directions to the letter, but Peaches would never let her friends come to harm.

"Okay," he said. "Throw me first."

"Aight," she said. "Now, to make sure you go where I want, I'm gonna have to spin you round, so you might feel kinda dizzy, okay? Just make sure you come outta that fall before you hit the ground, okay? Even if you come out too soon, that'll be better than staying in the whole time, ya heard me?"

Perry felt something dark inside him waiting for an opening to pounce. He couldn't tell whether it was the sort of doubt that should be swept aside or common-sense trepidation. Still, when Peaches was around, he felt like a better version of himself. "Right," he said. "Okay."

"Now gimme dem hands," she said.

Perry held out his hands, and Peaches took him by the wrists. Could she feel his heartbeat?

"Don't worry none," she said.

"I ain't worried," Perry said—and it was mostly true.

"Good. But don't hit nothing."

"Don't—? What?"

"Now, one...two...*three!*"

Perry thought she'd spin him the way he would have spun Brendy—with her legs hanging out behind her as she giggled through the air. Peaches's movements were so fast, though, that before Perry knew it—quick-cut—she had let go and flung him into the air. He spun from his center, turning so fast that the sky and the ground blurred together. Perry panicked, grasping internally for his sense of gravity, willing himself into a different trajectory even as he feared he'd fall the wrong way.

He landed on his side, a little too hard, and rolled onto his back, breathing in short, shallow sips. He sat up swiftly, as if waking from a nightmare, and just breathed, realizing as he did that he could have hit a headstone or a vault on the way down. He jumped to his feet.

"Here I'm is!" he shouted.

"All right!" Peaches called. "Brendy coming over!"

"*Waaaaaaaaaugh!*" Brendy bellowed as she spun into the air above the cemetery lawn.

"Drop out!" Perry shouted. "Drop!"

Brendy's arc wavered for a split second, and she seemed to stick against the baked-blue sky. Perry ran like a wide receiver, staring up at her, as she began to fall. He didn't see the headstone standing in his way.

Perry hit the stone and squawked as he somersaulted over it to land flat on his back. He couldn't see Brendy now. Had she fallen too fast? Was she—?

"Here I'm is." Brendy stepped into view, grinning down at him. "Look at your face!"

Perry shook himself and rose to his feet just as Peaches came over. She landed in a crouch, her fingers spread in the grass before her. The landing, and even the twenty- or thirty-foot jump she'd taken over the wall, seemed to have cost her no effort at all. Quickly, she straightened.

"Good," she said. "Only thing worried me is if onea y'all fell up insteada down. I can jump like a mug, but I can't fly, so catching you woulda been a *beast*."

Perry's scalp tightened. "...What!"

Peaches giggled and stuck out her tongue at him.

Perry blushed and looked away, but something at the edge of his hearing caught his attention. He cocked his head, listening. "Wait. What happened to the music?"

The cemetery grounds smelled of turned earth, cut grass, and flowers, but no bird chirped, no bee buzzed, and no music played near or distant.

"It's fine," Peaches said. "It's just we ain't supposed to be here. That music for the dead folks."

"They's haints here?" Brendy asked. "Zombies?"

"If you woke up dead, whyinhell would you wanna hang around your grave?" Peaches asked. "Cemeteries is the least haunted places in town. Now, come on. We don't wanna get caught."

"Caught?" Perry asked. "Who by?"

"Don't matter none," she said. "Long as we don't get caught."
She visored her left hand above her eyes, scanning the distance.
"All right, then...thataway!"

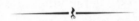

Most Nolan cemeteries are full of vaults and mausolea, with banks
of stacked drawers lining the walls. This one was less compact than
most. Headstones and vaults stood up on the well-kept lawn with
bouquets of flowers, votive candles, fetishes, and sometimes piles
of hell notes set before them. Perry had learned all about hell notes
in school. They were fake dollar bills—like Monopoly money, but
with crazy denominations, $50,000 or $75,500—that dead folks
used to conduct business. As they walked, Peaches stopped to grab
notes off the lawn, so long as they lay far enough from a grave.

"Ain't it bad luck to go picking those up?" Perry asked.

"Not if they don't belong to nobody," Peaches said.

"What you need them for?"

"Don't never know when you gotta go to the Dead Side of
Town."

"There's a dead side of town?" Perry said. "I mean, we got
enough haints and zombies hanging round anyway."

"Right," Peaches said as she bent to snatch another bill. "But
you ever go to East Nola?"

"Sure," Perry said. "Sometimes, with my folks or Daddy Deke."

"See?" Peaches said. "Y'all ain't from there, but you go there
anyhow."

"So, it's just a neighborhood?"

"A big one," Peaches said. "Bigger than Central City and Mid-
City together. I mean, think about it. There's more dead people in
town than live ones, right? They gotta live somewhere."

Perry had no response to that.

Their destination was a stained white tomb with a peaked roof and a statue of a pelican sitting on top, its head hidden under its wing. The legend on the vault didn't even seem like a proper name to Perry—not a Nolan one, anyway. The carving on the plaque read KOIZUMI YAKUMO. It looked older than the other graves, standing between two oaks that leaned together overhead, shading it from the sun. No other trees stood in the cemetery, and these ones had caused the ground to hump up like when you run your hands underneath a blanket. It had disturbed the headstones, causing them to lean like winos.

"All right, then," Peaches said, and took a deep breath. "Y'all wait here."

"No!" Brendy objected. "Take me with you!"

"That ain't a good idea," Peaches said. "Not all haints leave the boneyard when they wake up. This one...I hear this one ain't the nicest."

"Then maybe you shouldn't go, either," Perry said.

"It's okay," Peaches said. "It's broad daylight. Besides...I gotta go. I just—I just *gotta*. Wait for me."

This was the first time Perry had heard Peaches express true need. Her tone told him that arguing would do no good and that if he and Brendy cared for her, they would do as she asked.

"Okay," Perry said. "We'll wait."

"If I'm not back in half a hour, just go on home. I'll catch y'all up later."

"We'll wait."

Peaches wavered, but Perry held her gaze. Finally, she nodded. As she turned to leave them, Perry wondered how she'd get inside. Like most mausolea, the place had no proper door—just a carved stone slab where one would be. Peaches approached it and stared thoughtfully at it for a moment; then she knelt down and lifted it with one hand.

The structure was actually hollow inside. It wasn't a mausoleum at all; it was a covering for a marble staircase that led down into a blackness so complete that the daylight fell right into it, illuminating nothing. Could Peaches see in the dark?

Brendy slid her arm around Perry's waist and gave him a squeeze.

Peaches turned to look at them over her shoulder, her expression one of fearful resolve. She looked so small and pale against that blackness. She seemed ready to say something, but she turned away and closed the grave behind her.

"I don't like this," Brendy said.

"Me either," Perry agreed.

"We shoulda gone with her. We shoulda. We her friends."

"I know," Perry said. "I know."

——— ❦ ———

Perry didn't know how long they'd stood waiting for Peaches—he carried no watch—but he knew it had been longer than a half hour. For quite a while, he and Brendy had stood together, staring at the fake mausoleum. They'd stepped a few feet from the gravel walkway to sit in the grass and thumb-wrestle. Perry dominated his little sister for a few matches; then, when he feared she'd begin to lose interest, he let her win once or twice. She smack-talked him, telling him that a week from now she'd be bigger and stronger than Perry. So big and so strong that she could put him in her pocket and carry him around town.

"In a week, huh?"

"Not even a week," she said with an exaggerated nod. "By next Tuesday!"

"Girl, you three feet tall."

"Three feet six and one-quarter inches," she said, enunciating carefully. "Dr. Balfour says I'm growing like a weed."

"That's stupid. Weeds are bad."

"Weeds grow *fast*, dummy!"

"Hey, now."

"Sorry. You ain't a dummy, but this is stupid, sitting round here like this," Brendy said. "We shoulda gone with Peaches and now she all under there and we don't even know when she coming out. I *hate* waiting around."

"I hate it as much as you."

Brendy stuck her tongue out. "You just want Peaches to come back so you can think about hugging and kissing."

"Why you gotta be saying stuff like that?"

"Cuz you love Peaches like monkeys love bananas."

Unable to think what else to do, Perry stood up. He hated when Brendy talked like this, but he didn't understand why it angered him so. He felt like giving her a good shove.

Hey, now. Hey.

Perry froze.

"Aw," Brendy said. "Don't say nothing."

Hey, you kids.

Brendy stared up at Perry, wide-eyed, and shook her head once. She pressed her right forefinger against her lips.

A disturbance smudged the air before the mausoleum. It hung there like a graffiti tag, but it was much less solid, less distinct. Perry knew the haint would have been much clearer against the night. He also knew that because the hot Nolan sun still shone down on the day, the haint couldn't see him or Brendy even as well as they could see it.

I know you here. Y'all holdin' up the music.

Perry didn't answer.

Y'all got no business messin' round in here. Ya need to get the hell on.

"Why can't y'all just go ahead and play?" Brendy asked.

"Brendy!" Perry snapped.

Now the spirit knew exactly where they were. It drifted closer, and as it passed through the shade from the trees above the mausoleum, Perry saw a blurry, indistinct version of a youngish man in a red-and-white suit.

Decent folks tryna sleep up in here.

"Listen, sir," Perry said. "We're sorry to disturb you, but we're waiting for our friend. As soon as she comes out, we'll go."

Y'all don't need to be messing round no boneyard.

"I know. But we came with her to make sure she be okay," Perry said. "She down underneath that grave, and we'll leave soon as she comes out."

She what? Now I know you lying. Ain't no way nobody could get down there.

"She's real strong, sir. She just lifted it up and went on down."

Boy, you out your damn mind? Real fear flashed bright in the disembodied voice. *You know who buried down there?*

"Nossir," Perry said, his heart beating fast. "What should we do?"

I tell you what. Against my better damn judgment, I'ma go on down there and get your friend. When I bring her back, you get the hell outta this here cemetery, and don't you never come back, ya heard me?

"Who down there with her?" Brendy demanded.

Nobody you need to worry bout.

The disturbance in the air began to fade. "Mister!" Perry called. "Hey, mister."

What?

"Thanks for bringing her out. We worried."

Brendy had made up a new dance, and she showed it to Perry as they waited. She spread her fingers and held both arms straight down at her sides. Then she went through a series of kicks and knee bends set to no particular rhythm. From time to time, she went up on her tiptoes and spun around, but she never moved her arms.

"See?" she said. "I call it the Jackson Avenue Jig."

"I dunno," Perry said. "I don't think they be doing that one in the club anytime soon."

"They will," Brendy said. "And I'll make a kapillion dollars."

She lost interest in the dance and stood staring at the mausoleum. "Aw," she said. "Nuts. *Nuts!*"

"What?"

"He been down there awhile."

Perry schooled his expression. The worry in the old haint's voice made his stomach ache, but he'd told Peaches they'd wait, and he couldn't send Brendy along by herself. "It's been maybe ten minutes," he said. He hoped his tone was neutral.

"Ten minutes!" Brendy wailed.

"You making me crazy," Perry said. "Just settle down and wait."

"You owe me a dance," Brendy said. "I danced you one, now you make one up."

"We didn't strike no deal," Perry said. "I don't owe you nothing."

"Perry!" Brendy barked.

Perry heaved a sigh. "Fine. Here." He crossed his legs behind him, bent his elbows at his sides, and flapped his hands out at his hips. He jerked his head forward, staring at Brendy with first one eye, then the other. He strutted a bit, jerking his upper half as he moved along, pecking the air with his face. Then he relaxed into a normal stance. "Know what I call that?"

"Pigeon-Pigeon!"

"I woulda called it just 'The Pigeon,' but that—"

Perry bit off the next word as the ground shuddered beneath him. When the tremor ceased, he stood still, waiting, his nerves on high alert.

A deep twang ran through the earth beneath his feet, and then the ground tilted hard. Perry lost his balance and would have fallen if the earth hadn't righted itself immediately. As it was, he stumbled like a drunk.

Before he could shout his surprise, a loud crack sounded from the mausoleum. The front slab came off, fell hard into the walkway, and Peaches charged out, stiff-armed. *"Run!"*

Without a word, Perry snatched Brendy up and carried her as fast as he could. Peaches skidded to a halt before him, and he ran right into her. Without saying anything, she gathered Perry into her arms and carried him and Brendy both as she sprinted for the gate.

As they rushed through the cemetery, Perry twisted round to look behind them. A blot of darkness had spilled from the mausoleum.

At first, it looked like fabric. Like the black ribbons from Mamaw's funeral. But the fabric moved, questing blindly this way and that. A piece of the darkness reared up like a cobra, its tip sharpened to a point, and turned in their direction. It darted toward them, but they'd already moved too far, too fast, and the tendril dissolved in the daylight. As Perry watched, it retreated back into the mausoleum, and Perry imagined he heard a hollow growl of frustration from somewhere underground.

"Peaches!" he said. "What—?"

But he lost his voice as Peaches jumped the cemetery's outer wall.

A split second later, she dropped lightly to the sidewalk outside and let her friends down to stand on their own. She leaned on her knees, breathing hard.

"What was that?" Perry asked. "What happened?"

"Stupid-ass stupid haints messing with my things."

"What are you talking about?"

"My things is my things, and can't no haints go messing with what's mine."

"Peaches!"

Peaches straightened. Perry hadn't realized it before, but she hadn't come out of the vault empty-handed. She held an envelope in her left hand. It read PEACHES in big ugly caps. She ignored Perry as she tore the envelope open and pulled its contents out. She held the paper in both hands, the envelope crumpled in her left, still breathing hard as she stared at it.

"What it says?" Brendy asked.

"Oh, uh-uh," Peaches said. She turned the paper over. Neither side seemed to have been written on. "Somebody in trouble now," she said. "Damn, damn, damn, damn, *damn!*"

"Peaches," Perry said. "Peaches, you gotta focus. Tell us what happened."

"I'ma go back in. I'ma go back in, and that damn haint gonna give me what's mine," Peaches said.

"Go—? You can't go back there," Perry said. "You can't. *Peaches.*"

"They stole my daddy's letter, Perry," she said. "They stole my daddy's letter to me. They can't—I can't—I *need* it!" She shocked them both by bursting into tears. She stared at Perry for a moment, wide-eyed. "Don't."

"Don't what?" Perry asked.

"Don't look!" she said.

"What? Hey," Perry said.

"Don't look at me!"

Peaches turned and ran.

V

JAYL313

Casey drew Ole Girl to a halt and turned off the engine. By now, the sun was setting, and this sector of the Ninth Ward—or was this Bunny Friend?—had not fared well since the storm. Here, the streets were cracked and humped, desperately in need of care. He looked at the scrubby grass and dandelions trying to force their way into the world and thought of what his cousin had said about not belonging.

The one time Casey had felt he belonged anywhere, it had all come apart in the space of a few weeks—first the evacuation, then watching on the news in their Memphis hotel room as the levees broke and New Orleans was left to die. Before the Storm, the city had felt like some sort of alternate universe situated at right angles to the conventional world, but Casey had never believed that was really true. New Orleans was still America, of course. One of its greatest cities. Surely not even a rich, post-dumb faux cowboy like Bush Jr. would consider leaving her to drown. But he had. They had.

Casey shook his head. No use reliving Storm trauma. Across the street stood a square two-story building that reminded him of classic Westerns—though he wasn't sure why. It didn't look like a Spanish mission or a Wild West saloon. No. It was . . . a theater?

Jayl's Jordans crunched on the gravel as he approached. "You ever hear of Club Desire?"

"I thought that was a sex club in the CBD."

"Nigga—!" Jaylon started, but he couldn't help laughing. "Back in the segregation days, this was the *spot*. Everybody who was anybody came through here on the Chitlin Circuit—and a lot of the cats from here in town played on the regular."

Jaylon liked jazz well enough—they'd danced more than their share of second lines together—but he had never been the music obsessive that Casey was. They weren't here for music.

"Yeah?" Casey frowned. "Listen, man. I don't... You know I don't do this no more."

"Relax," Jaylon said. The way he smiled as he did put Casey at ease—made him feel like he'd been silly to think that Jaylon had brought him tagging without telling him beforehand.

Inside, the club was in dire disrepair. Chunks of plaster drywall littered the floor, fallen from the ceiling. Shopping bags, tree branches, and fast food trash lay in piles, having collected here and there like drifting snow. Toward the uptown corner, Casey saw five or six dirty diapers stacked together. His heart sank as he realized somebody must have been living here. The pastel accents on the dirty bundles hadn't even had a chance to fade.

Casey's eyes slid over the sad tableau until some gravitational force fastened like a tractor beam onto his attention. In the southern (not southern—uptown, Casey reminded himself) corner of the club, a mythic scene had been painted in hard, bright colors. Conky, the robot from the old *Pee-wee's Playhouse*, knelt with his boom box face upturned as above him a group of sainted jazz musicians—Jelly Roll Morton, Satchmo, Sidney Bechet, James Booker, Fess—gathered around Buddy Bolden, who extended a finger toward Lil Wayne, Juvenile, Trombone Shorty, Jamison Ross, and Kamasi Washington.

Wait. Casey had been wrong about the light in here. At first, he'd assumed that sunlight must be shining down on the painting from gaps in the ceiling. But there were no holes—none that he could see from here. Outside, the sun had all but set, and there were no streetlights along this stretch of Desire Street. The light shone from the painting itself—and it wasn't because of glow-in-the-dark paint: The haloes around the jazzmen's heads, around the more contemporary musicians' heads, all glowed softly but robustly enough that Casey could see his surroundings even though the open door they'd used to enter was entirely dark. It wasn't just the haloes, either. Juvenile's oversized white T-shirt gleamed as well, as did Professor Longhair's jewelry.

"Wow," Casey said, and as he did, he realized he was speaking as quietly as he would in a church. "What kind of paint you used?" Even as he said it, he realized he made no sense. Paint didn't behave this way. It didn't give off this much light.

Jaylon ignored the question. "Listen, mane. You can't tell nobody about this. Not yet."

"Who would I tell?" Casey asked. "What am I seeing?"

"You know what it is," Jaylon said. "Better than anybody."

Casey's scalp contracted.

"Oh. Hey. *Oh*," he said. "We said we wouldn't. We said we wouldn't do it on purpose."

"I know," Jaylon said. "I know. And I didn't. Not at first. I mean... We couldn't ignore it forever."

You couldn't, Casey thought but didn't say.

"You ready to see more?"

"You quit smoking?"

"Yeah," Jaylon said. "Mostly." He slid a pack of Newports from his track pants and flipped open the top. Casey took one and Jaylon followed suit, then lit both of them.

The second drag made Casey light-headed. He savored the feeling, and the dirty blue taste of the smoke. He was shocked by Jaylon's revelation, but not surprised. Jaylon had kept tagging after he returned to New Orleans. It was inevitable that he'd drift into... whatever this was. If Casey had understood that fact sooner, maybe he'd have gotten back to it himself. But he hadn't—and that was a good thing. Wasn't it?

"All right," he said. "What else you got to show me?"

———❧———

As he followed Jaylon's burnt-orange Jeep, Casey wished they'd just driven together. The thought of riding shotgun with his cousin warmed him. He and Jayl had spent so many nights haunting the city streets in Jayl's old Escort GT, either driving aimlessly or tooling around City Park, halfheartedly looking for the old municipal swimming pool that the white folks filled in with concrete instead of sharing with Black folks when integration became law. Tonight, time had become a silken membrane dividing the present from the past, and he knew for sure that if he could reach from the exact correct angle, he could touch that skin, slick it against his fingertips.

This wasn't the first time Jaylon had shown him something strange. No, the first time was in the summer of 2005, after their first year at UNO. They lived together in a rickety old house on Mandeville Street, and Casey had found a paid internship around the corner at Chez Lazare...

———❧———

June 2005

Chez Lazare was situated inside a converted funeral home at the corner of St. Claude Avenue and Elysian Fields. Casey remembered finding the place after reading *A Streetcar Named Desire* and wondering if this was the very house Williams had described. Next door, Gene's Daiquiris and the po-boy shop were painted a bright Pepto-Bismol pink, but Lazare's front-facing building was a simple muddy gray with dirty white trim.

Casey had just bought a pack of Newports from the Robert's across the street, and Mandisa, the home's executive director, didn't have any work for him right now, so he was just sitting outside sweating gently in his polo and jean shorts.

Patricia, a golden-skinned mixed woman with thick blunt fingers and blurry prison tattoos, sat gabbing with Marjane, a thin Lebanese girl with sharp eyebrows and delicate wrists. Casey loved listening to them gossip and squabble companionably.

"—What did you think, though, Case?" Marjane asked.

"What?" Casey said. "Of what?"

"You read comics n shit, right?"

"Yeah."

"So what about it? What did you think of that new Batman?"

"I mean, it's the best one so far," Casey said. "But there's some shit that don't fit with who Batman is, ya heard? He lets Ra's al Ghul die in the train. Batman wouldn't do that shit."

"I mean, he said, 'Just because I won't kill you doesn't mean I have to save you,'" Marjane said.

"Yeah, but allowing death through inaction goes against the core of his character," Casey said. "Bruce Wayne watched his parents die before his eyes, and he set out on a lifelong crusade to make sure nobody else goes out like that on his watch. Letting the Demon's Head perish—even in a wreck that he caused—is antithetical to Batman's muthafuckin' motivation."

"Well, *damn*," Patricia said.

"I know, right?" Marjane said. She sounded proud, and Casey stretched like a plant in direct sunlight. "I told you. Casey knows all that shit."

"Ay, goddammit!" The shout drew Casey's attention back to the street. A rawboned black woman was charging against traffic. As she crossed the neutral ground into the uptown lanes, a rust-red Mazda 6 nearly clipped her, and the driver leaned on the horn as the car dopplered down the avenue. The woman wore what looked like a long red sleep-shirt mottled with stains and old-school house slippers on her feet. Her braids had come unpinned from her skull, sticking out at odd angles.

For an instant Casey thought he heard more shouting, but if so, it was from far off. When he moved to New Orleans for college, Casey thought he might be overwhelmed by the place—the way it seemed separate from conventional reality. He'd felt none of that, though—not for all that first year. Now, as sophomore year approached, he would have these moments of déjà vu, these little patches of bullet-time where he felt himself drifting against the surface of a giant soap bubble.

The woman's hand on Casey's wrist snapped him back into his body. *"Please,"* she hissed through clenched teeth. "They gone kill me."

"Who?"

"Hey," Marjane said. "Get inside. *Now.*" She pulled at the woman's hips, gesturing with her chin toward the building's doubled front doors.

The woman disappeared into the office, and now Casey *did* hear shouting. A heavy-set bullet-headed Black man and a short, thick woman were crossing Elysian Fields from the downtown side—just as the other woman had.

"Y'all seen anybody running?" the woman called.

The man gained the steps. "Crackhead-ass woman come this way?" he demanded. His voice was flat and hard.

"Who y'all looking for?" Patricia asked.

He turned to stare at Casey. "You seen her?" he asked. "You see anybody?"

Adrenaline brightened his vision, but Casey noticed a bulge in the man's burgundy jean shorts. It *might* not be a pistol, but...

"See who?" Casey asked. "What's up?"

"Our cousin Marva havin' a psychotic break or sumn," the woman said as she climbed the steps. "We tryna find her, take her home. She come this way?"

"I didn't see nobody," Patricia said.

"She inside?" asked the man. "What y'all doing here?"

"This is a place of business," Marjane said. "We work here."

The man grunted, dubious, and went for the door. Nobody moved to stop him as he led his girlfriend inside.

Casey, Marjane, and Patricia waited for a moment in silence. Casey didn't know whether to look at them or avert her eyes. He realized now that he was physically terrified in a way he hadn't been in years.

He felt foolish in his surprise. Crazy niggas were bound to show up at a battered women's shelter once in a while. The real surprise was that the woman on the run came from outside instead of within. Not for the first time, Casey wondered whether he should have gone with Jaylon to get a job down at the beignet stand in City Park, serving pastries and coffee in a paper hat. Interning at Chez Lazare was more interesting, though—and to be honest, the fact that nobody expected him to be at work before ten in the morning had *heavily* influenced his decision.

The double doors opened again. Mandisa Russell stepped outside followed by the man and woman. Mandisa was a round, muscular stud with a skin fade and neck tattoos from her days in the Hollygrove projects.

"—I get it, though," she was saying. "Y'all concerned. Believe me, we see her come through, we let y'all know. I got ya cell number and errythang."

"Didn't mean no disrespect," the woman said.

"Don't tell me," Mandisa said. "Tell my folks out here."

The man dipped his bullet-head and frowned. "We didn't mean nothing," he said in a chastened tone that made Casey wonder what Mandisa had said to him inside. "We come on strong 'cause we worried."

"You good," Casey said, reflexively.

The man held Casey's gaze for a moment, then seemed to find what he was looking for. He took the woman's elbow and led her back down the front steps. Casey watched them go back the way they had come.

Mandisa was the first to pull in a whooping breath. *"Well!"*

"Yo," Patricia said, and shook her head.

"Got her out the back before they made it inside," Mandisa said. "Ioknow what the fuck that was, but we need to beef up security." She made a point of finding Casey's gaze and holding it. "You good?"

"Yeah," Casey said. "Yeah, I just...I never seen nothing like that. I'm from the suburbs."

"Up there in Baltimore, right?" Mandisa said.

"Catonsville, Maryland," Casey said. "Yeah."

"If I give you the afternoon, you gone come back tomorrow?"

"Oh, no doubt," Casey said without thinking. Instead of scaring him away, the incident had proven to him that the work they did here truly mattered.

On his way back to his LeBaron, Casey checked his Razr to see three missed calls and a text from Jaylon.

PRICE IS RIGHT.

Casey sucked his teeth. That meant he should grab his gear and "come on down."

Jaylon must have scouted a location in the park and wanted to know what Casey thought before they returned to it by night. But no—what kind of location would Jayl need Casey's approval for? He pulled into a spot by the Peristyle, an open, columned pavilion designed as a site for dance parties in the early years of the twentieth century. The structure reminded Casey of a perfect scoop of sherbet. He loved its lines, and the fact that it had been designed for pure enjoyment.

As he rounded the back of his Chrysler, he saw Jaylon trudging wetly from the direction of the café. Sweat stained his short-sleeved white button-down. His bow tie hung loose and his white-and-green paper hat dangled from his left hand.

Jayl's Escort was parked a few spaces down from Casey's Le-Baron. As he reached it, Jaylon craned his neck in his cousin's direction and rolled his eyes theatrically. He gestured with his chin to let Casey know he wouldn't need his gear. Casey slid into Jayl's passenger seat and they headed out to Marconi Drive. To their left, the buildings of the community college sat sleeping in the heat.

As Jaylon drove, Casey recounted the events that had him off work early.

Jayl hummed low in his throat like their grandmother. "Ain't *that* some shit," he said. "You can always come work at the Morning Call."

"This is the whole point of Chez Lazare," Casey said. "I should've expected some shit to jump off sooner or later."

Jaylon sucked his teeth. "Couldn't be me."

When Jaylon turned right down Taylor Drive, Casey knew where they must be headed. Here, the breeze held better sway than it did in the Marigny. Jayl's car AC was broken, but the perfumed air slid through the interior and almost made Casey forget the danger he'd faced earlier in the day.

When he was little, Casey had taken City Park for granted—it was just a cool place New Orleans families would cook out, visit the art museum or the little Storyland theme park. In those days, he'd been unaware of the park's vastness. It was significantly larger than Central Park in New York City. The fact that much of it had been abandoned when the golf course had fallen into disuse meant that the park was largely an undiscovered country. If New Orleans felt like an alternate-reality banana republic hidden at the bottom of the country, City Park was the treasure secreted in one of its socks.

Jaylon parked at Pan American Stadium, and together, they struck out on foot. They hadn't been back to this location since Jayl had started work at the café, but this little clubhouse was one of Casey's favorites. Last time they were here, he had used it to test out a couple characters: Bee Sharp, a Pam Grier type with an Afro and bug-eyed sunglasses whose arms were covered in a swarm of bees, and her archnemesis the Hanging Judge, a wizened, hateful man in judicial robes and a powdered wig who commanded an army of mutant pigs in SWAT gear.

Casey's heart sank as they reached the low, broad concrete building. Someone had erased the Judge. Bee Sharp hung at the center of the wall, gritting his teeth as he projected the swarm from his right arm at a blank patch of wall where the villain should have been. He—wait.

"What...the fuck...?" Casey said aloud.

Sharp was positioned wrong. Casey had painted him standing over the Judge, flexing in triumph as he drove his right foot, Bruce Lee style, into the Judge's sternum. Not only had the Judge been eliminated from the scene, it was almost as if Bee Sharp was—Casey shook his head. It was silly, but it really did look like Bee Sharp was reacting to the Judge's escape.

Removing the art was one thing—the city was full of self-righteous dickheads who felt street art contributed to the moral decline of New Orleans—but this was something else. To come behind Casey and repaint his figures...It was an insult so grave that Casey was almost more impressed than offended.

"...What...?"

"I came over here on lunch to see if we might want to tag the other side and found your mural like this." Jayl sucked his teeth. "Don't make no sense."

"Why would...Who would do this?"

"Mane, I'm confused than a mug. You ask me, it looks like that nigga *left*."

Casey flinched. He hated the idea, and even more, he hated that he'd been thinking the same thing. He had the distinct feeling that if he were to look away from Bee Sharp right now, when he looked back something significant about the painting would have changed. His position, his facial expression...*something*.

"That's not funny," he said slowly.

"Naw," Jaylon said. "It ain't. But the real question is, what is we gone do?"

"Ioknow," Casey said. "I mean, whoever did this is . . . good."

"Fuck that shit," Jayl said. "You do *not* mess with another nigga's tag."

"I know that," Casey said. "I know, but . . ." He couldn't say the rest: *What if that's not what happened?*

He didn't realize until he and Jaylon were headed back to their apartment in their separate cars that when he had first drawn him, Bee Sharp had been a woman.

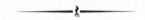

August 2018

"I got invited to this festival in New Zealand couple years ago," Jaylon said as he fingered a set of keys on a fat ring. They stood before the old beauty supply store at the corner of St. Claude and Elysian Fields. Casey hadn't been over to this part of town since he got back, though he'd come close—the busiest part of Frenchmen Street was only blocks from here. "It was one of those times when you can *feel* your life changing. When it's like a door is opening inside you, and you know you don't quite understand what's up yet, you know?"

Casey laughed wryly. "I do. I do."

The joy of being with Jaylon again mixed with the dark feeling of Casey's unease. Jayl was a grown-ass man. He could take care of himself—and had since he'd come back to town alone. If what he'd made at Club Desire didn't frighten him, should Casey be frightened for him? But was that what this was? Was Casey frightened for his cousin or for himself? He swallowed and looked away. How could he talk about this to Jayl?

"I didn't sleep for three days after I got home, and at the end I was delirious. That's when I figured it out. And that's when I painted the piece at the Club. Took me eight hours."

The shop was a long low building covered in tags. Looking at the riot of colors, Casey recognized a murderer's row of talent from the Gulf and beyond. Jayl unlocked the shop, ready to lead Casey inside, but Casey's train of thought derailed as a man with dirty white-boy dreadlocks zipped past on a double-decker bike. He'd never seen a bike like that, and questions crowded into Casey's mind: How are you supposed to stop your bike when you're that high up? What did the man do at traffic lights? The light on the corner had just changed, so if Casey had known to look, he might have seen then. Where were these people coming from? Who were they? The man's tattoos were blurry, and his clothes seemed like they'd been treated to communicate a sense of wear, like a hobo Halloween costume on an elementary school child. He wore a pair of ballet flats.

Casey opened his mouth to say something, then deflated.

"Nigga, you don't even know!" Jayl said. "Before I left on my trip, I saw a white motherfucker walkin' a purple dog."

"Oh uh-uh," Casey said, incredulous.

"Nigga, I thought I was watching cartoons!"

They both laughed hard.

"Wait," Casey said. "Figured what out? That glow effect?"

Jaylon's expression grew solemn. "Well," he said. "I'm finna show you." He stopped short. "Maybe—nah. Come on in here."

Casey had expected to find the place a wreck—but then why would Jayl have brought him here to begin with. The shop's interior was meticulously clean. Work tables lined the walls, and here and there canvases stood on easels or leaned against the walls. Everything Casey saw was in Jaylon's style, so this space must be his alone. And he'd been *busy*. The splashes of color reminded Casey of fireworks displays or botanical gardens. The air seemed to sing with beauty, with raw creativity.

There was a vibe in here, Casey realized. A hum, almost. He thought briefly of the Magic Shop at Disneyland and the family trip they'd gone on together when they were ten. Was he dissociating?

He followed Jaylon toward the back of the shop where stood a covered canvas ten feet wide. Jaylon stopped short for a moment, frowning. Was his mind racing the way Casey's was right now? Why would it be if he was taking all this in stride?

Without a word, Jaylon pulled the fabric away.

For a moment, Casey didn't understand what he was looking at. It was balloon caps against a flat gray background. But no. It was ... The stylized letters of the tag seemed to breathe and strain, but instead of being painted onto the background, they projected from it into the air.

Like a hologram, Casey thought. But that wasn't it. Holograms had an irreality to them that set them at odds with their surroundings. Not this. The tag—JAYL313—simply projected out from the surface into the air before it.

"—see it, too," Jayl finished.

"What?" Casey asked. He wanted to glance at his cousin, but he couldn't. The tag wouldn't let go his gaze.

"Right before I uncovered it, I asked myself what I would do if you couldn't see it, too."

"This ... What is this?" Casey asked.

"It's a tag."

"It's not ... *on* anything."

"It is and it isn't," Jayl said. "When I roll the canvas across the room, the tag goes with it, so it's anchored or something, you know? That's that shit I don't like ..."

Casey felt as if he stood in two places at once. One of him was here with Jaylon, and the other stood in an alien landscape that his life would become. Seeing the tag made him feel a bitter pang of loss. Had he wasted his life? Wasted himself? With great effort, he spoke calmly, trying to roll with all this, incorporate it into his world without becoming something less than human. "It's 3D?" he said. "You figured out how to ... I don't know. Wait. What don't you like?"

Jayl sighed explosively. This was a sore subject. "It's still *on*

something," he said. "I want it to stand up. I want it to...I want it
to exist on its own."

"That's impossible."

"Sure." Jayl shrugged. "But so are a lot of things."

Casey's scalp tingled, his face was hot, and an electricity shivered from the tips of his fingers up to his forearms. "Do you know
what this means?"

"I think so. A little," Jayl said. "One thing I do know is it means
we need to talk about what happened back in the day."

Casey swallowed. He felt his brows knit in a frown.

"I mean with the Judge."

"I know what you mean," Casey said.

"Then you remember," Jaylon said tonelessly. "That shit *happened*."

What bothered Casey wasn't so much that the world he'd
understood was being taken away, it was that Jaylon was caught
up in it. If it had been just him, in the old days, he might have—
he might have— He didn't know what he would have done.
But it didn't matter: He and Jaylon had promised to protect each
other. He'd quit drawing and painting because it had gotten too
weird. He'd feared that once the weird crept into his life through
the slightest gap, it might begin to influence everything. It might
make him—and Jaylon—into people Casey couldn't recognize—
wouldn't want to recognize.

"I want you to watch me make one. Make it with me," Jaylon
said. Casey realized now that Jayl might have been speaking for a
while, and that most of what he'd said Casey had missed. At least
he hoped he'd missed it.

"Not tonight," Casey said. "Not—I need to sit with this, okay?"

"I ain't told nobody else," Jaylon said. "Only you. For a reason."

"I know," Casey said. "I know. Just..."

"You're a better tagger than me."

Laced with panic, Casey's laugh spiraled up toward the studio's
ceiling.

"Case—"

"Jayl, bruh," Casey said. "Listen. I love you. I'm your dog. *Truly.* But you were right—This shit is *crazy* crazy, and I need time to ... to even take on what you just showed me. Let me think on it before you pitch me this or that. Please."

Jaylon reached into his mass of dreads and scratched his scalp as he watched Casey with eyes that were just a little too wide. Feverish. "That's ... fair ..." he said slowly. "I guess—ah—you want to head out, or ... do you wanna play Madden for a while? I got the new one ..."

Casey wanted nothing more than to hide from the world in his bare apartment right now, but he couldn't leave before reassuring Jaylon that they were still cool. If they could do something normal for an hour or two, then maybe he could shake this feeling. This feeling that he'd soon be forced to abandon his cousin. Again.

"Aight then," he said. He hoped the words didn't sound as forced as they felt. "I got Ravens, baby!"

VI

OLD KIDS PRETENDING

There was no catching Peaches. On his best day Perry wasn't the fastest runner, and *nobody* could keep up with Peaches at full speed. He watched her recede into the distance, keeping pace with the cars rushing along the avenue.

"We gotta find her," Brendy said.

"What...? What just happened?" Perry's voice sounded thin and childish in his own ears. An awful fluttering sensation had lodged in the center of his chest. He tried to rewind the scene and replay every word Peaches had said before fleeing.

They stole my daddy's letter, Perry. They stole my daddy's letter to me.

Peaches had never mentioned a mother or a father. She lived alone in her house save for whatever stray animals she'd taken in at the time. Six or seven dogs, five or six cats, countless geckos, chickens, and some time ago her great white horse, Alphonse, had come to stay.

But of course Peaches had parents. Everyone did. So where were they? Perry had heard of orphans who'd lost both parents in the Storm, but if her folks had been taken from her, how was Peaches still getting letters from her daddy? Or... or was that why they'd gone to the boneyard? Was Peaches's daddy writing letters from... from the Other Side? The thought wrinkled Perry's forehead.

Brendy was still yapping at him, pulling at his blue striped polo. "Okay," he said. "Okay. This is what we gonna do..."

"What?" she said. "What?"

"She gotta come home sometime, right?" Perry said. "She gotta come back to her house. Them animals need feeding, and she...and she needs somewhere safe to rest. So...so we'll go there and wait."

Brendy let go of her brother's shirt and just looked up at him. He couldn't read her expression. "But...is she okay?"

"I don't know," Perry said. "If she ain't, we'll help her. That's what we do."

"She was crying," Brendy said. "Peaches don't cry."

"Listen, Brendy," Perry said. "Maybe...maybe you and me think some things about Peaches that ain't necessarily so."

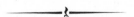

Peaches was strong. There was no doubt about it. One time, Perry and Peaches were walking home from Hansen's Sno-Bliz, just the two of them. Brendy had been sick with the flu that week, so she couldn't come run the streets as they normally did on weekends and after school.

After missing the Tchoupitoulas sky trolley, Perry and Peaches had waited and waited for another. In the end, they'd decided to walk and set out, unhurried, sure they could catch the next car a stop or two up. Of course, things hadn't worked out that way. Anytime they took a particular path somewhere, they never went the same way back.

Tchoupitoulas was quiet, especially for a Saturday, but there was no mystery as to why. Before they'd even left the house, Perry's father warned them to watch out for graffiti. "WWL's Paint Report says it's pretty heavy up there," he'd said. "I'm sure I don't have to warn you to steer clear."

"We will, Mr. Junior," Peaches said, wide-eyed and sincere.

Perry's father suppressed a scowl. Peaches insisted on calling him "Mr. Junior" instead of Mr. Graves.

"Well, 'Mistuh Graves' your grandaddy name," Peaches had explained once, when Brendy asked her why.

"No, it ain't," Brendy said. "His name is Daddy Deke."

"Yeah, but people who don't know him call him Mr. Graves outta respect."

"I guess..." Perry had conceded.

"So there you go. That's his name. And your daddy's name is Mr. Junior cuz he Deacon S. Graves *Junior*. Besides. He likes it."

"He does not."

"Yeah, he do," Peaches said. "He just don't know it. He *likes* having a name only I call him."

"...And don't dillydally," Perry's father had warned. "I don't want you running into any P-bodies."

Perry shivered. Paintbodies. They weren't any more dangerous than zombies, but they were far more disruptive—snarling traffic and strewing trash with their unending parades.

Of course, graffiti tags were the scourge of Nolan drivers. Since the Storm, somebody had figured out a way to paint graffiti not just on surfaces but onto the very air, and their loudly colored signatures, figures, and stylized mottoes would drift on the breeze for days and days until they either were cleared away by the city or faded away on their own. Or that is, they *would*, if it weren't for P-bodies.

Perry had learned both at home and in school that it was best to steer clear of graffiti. If a person were to walk through a tag, he'd find himself disoriented and dizzy, an unpleasant tingling sensation rolling through him in waves until the graffiti sickness passed. Perry himself had seen a man walk through a tag and begin vomiting flower petals. Folks in Nola referred to that nasty business as the Color Rushes.

But some people actually *liked* the feeling they got from walking through tags, the weird things that happened to them inside and out—so much so that they cared for nothing else. They forgot all about their wives, their children, their friends, their jobs, instead wandering into parades searching, night and day, for more tags. And after one walked through enough tags, certain permanent effects began to set in, and a person became a P-body.

By the time they reached Valence Street, passing at least five tags along the way, Perry and Peaches had lost interest in the trolley. One passed overhead, humming softly to itself, and they ignored it. Once they'd crossed the street, Peaches stopped, hands on her hips, and cocked her head. "I smell 'em," she said. *"Nasty."*

"Who?" Perry asked. "Uptownaz?"

Peaches shook her head. "Gangbangers smell like weed and too much cologne."

But by now he smelled them, too. Their rich and complex stench—Perry detected notes of armpit, booze, tobacco, and urine—preceded them by several blocks, at least. It must have done, because Perry heard no music or shouting.

"I wanna watch," Peaches said suddenly.

"What?" Perry asked.

"I wanna watch 'em pass."

"Watch them—? Why would you do that?" Perry asked. "How would you do that? They'll trample anything in their way. Even you."

"You know the safaris in City Park? You know how they set up them things—them hidey places—so they can watch the ducks and the kites and the giraffes and shoot at 'em without the animals knowing?"

"...Yeah."

"I can make one right here on the street, and they won't be able to get at us."

"You want to make a blind?" Perry said. "We don't have time. Just gathering the sticks and grass would take—"

"Don't need no sticks. Or grass," Peaches said. "This ain't the park. We gotta blend in."

"How?"

"Wait here," Peaches said. "I be back directly."

Excited by her own genius, Peaches twirled away, half jogging, half dancing up Valence Street. She stopped at the first car she came to, a little red hatchback parked on the curb at Valence and Annunciation. She cupped her hands around her eyes and leaned in to stare through the tinted windows. Satisfied, she knelt down and rolled the car onto her back.

Perry's mouth went dry. This was hardly the first time he'd seen Peaches do something a girl her size shouldn't have been capable of, but this was by far the heaviest thing he'd seen her lift. She stooped slightly, but from the way she positioned herself, wobbling a little, taking one or two running steps in one direction, then another, he realized that it wasn't the weight that bothered her, it was balancing the car on her back. She seemed to find a grip that worked for her and jogged toward Perry with her prize.

"Isn't that somebody's car?" he asked.

She let it fall right at the corner, bouncing a little on its tires. Its rusty red butt pointed toward the river. "Don't worry," she said. "This old thing ain't been driven since the Storm. After the parade, I put it right back where I found it."

"How does this help?" Perry asked. He could hear the parade now, the horns and drums, and the off-key singing of the marching P-bodies. They'd be in sight before long.

"This our— What you called it?"

"A blind?"

"Right. This our blind," Peaches said. "I show you."

She tried to open the front passenger-side door and failed. She sucked her teeth, then pulled the handle again. The door came open with a crunchy sound of protest. She reached in, grabbed the top of the backseat, and pulled it down. "Get in!"

Perry hesitated, then climbed into the car. Its interior smelled as moldy as the rotten old newspapers in Peaches's house, but all in all, it wasn't so bad. For one thing, he was pretty cozy in here, lying on his belly, getting dust all over his clothes. He heard a skittering sound and wondered if there were waterbugs or spiders in here.

That thought skated right out of Perry's mind as Peaches climbed in next to him. Her smell filled the enclosure, earthy, a little dark, slightly stronger than she'd ever smelled before. "You smell..." Perry said.

"Shh!" Peaches said. Then, "You mean I stink?" she whispered.

"No. Not bad. Like...I smell you, though. You smell like outside and like...I don't know."

"It bother you?"

"No, it— Don't worry about it."

"I swum yesterday."

"Yeah. You don't smell bad. It's just...you don't smell like you used to."

"Hush," she said, then licked the pinky side of her fist. She reached up and rubbed the dusty back window of the car, letting the daylight shine through the clean space. "When they get real loud, we be able to look at 'em through there."

"I didn't know you could do that."

"What?"

"Pick up a car," Perry said. "I didn't know you could pick up a car."

"It's just a car. A itty-bitty one."

"Yeah, but—how come you so strong, anyway?"

"Why you always gotta be axin' questions all the time?" she said. "We supposed to be quiet."

"Spider-Man got bit by a spider, and Superman crash-landed. How come you're so much stronger than normal folks?"

Peaches made a rude noise. "There ain't no such thing as normal people. Anybody pay attention to anything know that."

"But you're *really strong*."

"Perry. You ever try to pick up a car?"

"...No."

"Then how you know you can't?"

He had no response to that.

"You know what your problem is? When a grown-up tell you something can't be done, you just believe 'em. Don't you know there ain't even no such thing as grown-ups?"

"What?"

"There ain't," she said. "They's all just old kids, pretending. Now, keep *quiet*."

Perry did as she asked, but what Peaches had told him made his head hurt. He knew she was at least as smart as he was, but sometimes the things she said made no sense. No such thing as...? Old kids pretending...? That couldn't be true. Grown-ups were grown up. They knew what they were doing. The city—the *world*—couldn't just clatter along with nobody in charge. If Perry's father was just an old kid, then how could he be so good at math? Perry had seen the man make instant calculations—adding up how much things cost, how much money to tip in a restaurant—that Perry felt he'd, at the very least, need pencil and paper for until the day he died.

They could hear the music now. It sounded like jazz if jazz could be played...sideways. All the notes seemed stretched into the wrong shapes. The horns, the piano, and even the beat of the drums. The sound made Perry's skin cling tight to his bones, and little cat feet of terror walked across his back. They shouldn't be here, and Perry had no idea how, when the time came, he would find the courage to look.

"It's okay," Peaches whispered.

Perry tried to believe her.

After a few beats, Peaches lifted herself on her elbows. "Aw. Aw, man," she said.

Perry wavered a bit, then levered himself up to look.

He'd heard all about the P-bodies before, but never from anyone who'd actually seen them up close. Everyone in Nola knew it was best to make yourself scarce when the P-bodies were on the march. Well, they were *always* on the march, but there were only a few krewes, so it was easy enough to steer clear.

Perry had always imagined them as inhuman monsters, wizened and made ugly by the effects of the paint, but they looked healthier than he expected. Somehow he'd also imagined them as naked—and in the large mass of them, Perry thought he saw maybe one or two naked ones, sunburned and paint-streaked—but most of them wore costumes cobbled together from common household items, ordinary street clothes, and the kind of novelty masks you could find in any of the tourist shops on Decatur or Canal. All their costumes were spattered with layers upon layers of paint. Some of their coloring was so thick, so caked on, that it actually did make them look inhuman—but Perry could tell those were the very oldest P-bodies, who had been marching the longest. Many of them wore feather boas and beads, and they danced along without rhythm—their movements didn't even match the bizarre sideways jazz that surrounded them. They herked and jerked like chickens, turning or swaying their heads without ever taking their eyes off the nearest graffiti tag. One of them reared back his head and belched a plume of purple fire into the air above him.

One tag had blown up onto the sidewalk and was so badly slanted that Perry was unable to read it from here. Its edges had frayed with age, but it must still be a pretty good one. The lettering was no one color. Instead, it was a confusion of blue, orange, green, and pink, constantly shifting between hues.

Three P-bodies walking in the front reached the tag. They started jostling each other, fighting for space. Each one wanted to be the only person to walk through the graffiti, but all three made it. The paint clung to their clothes, and they seemed to blur, melding with the floating colors, until they snapped back into focus, more vivid now, realer than real, as if, while the world around them was 3D, they had an extra dimension. They howled like apes. The one on the right shook his head, and multicolored confetti poured from his ears. The one on the left grinned an impossibly large grin, and his teeth had become piano keys. Glowing pin-wheels appeared in the middle one's eyes, and he staggered, drunk on magic, tripping up his companions, who elbowed him in their irritation.

Perry's scalp tingled. He ducked down again, shaking.

"I can't see any more," he said. "It's too—! It's crazy."

Once the parade had passed and the day had regained its eerie stillness, Perry and Peaches climbed out of the car. Perry's muscles ached from clenching, and his sweat smelled worse than usual. He felt weak—like a shadow of himself.

"Why did we do that?"

He hadn't asked Peaches, but she answered anyway. "We needed to see. We needed to know."

"Why?" Perry asked.

"We gotta know everything we can find out about the city, Perry. It's important."

She watched him, but Perry found it impossible to return her gaze. Peaches reached out and touched his chin lightly, tipping Perry's face to meet hers. "Your parents, Daddy Deke, your whole family . . . do they ever talk about why things in Nola is the way they is? The zombies, the haints, the trees growing Mardi Gras beads?"

". . . No."

"I really did sail the Seven Seas," Peaches said. "And even if I hadn't, I seen the TV. There ain't no place like Nola. Not in all the world."

Perry knew there was nowhere else like his city, but he'd never been anywhere to know for sure. Still, Peaches's words struck a chord with him—and not just because she told the truth. He was only dimly aware of it, but her vehemence, her strength, helped him see clearer, stand taller. "Yeah," he said. "Yeah, you right."

Peaches spoke slowly now, choosing her words with great care. "Perry, Nola is different because Nola is *important*. We have to know everything about it because we need to be able to protect the city when the time comes."

"What time?"

"*The* time. The time that always comes."

"What do we gotta protect it from?"

"Ioknow, Perry, but you know I'm right. Anyplace, any*thing* this important, somebody always try to mess with it sooner or later. And I don't love nothing or nobody like I love this city, ya heard me?"

It's you *I love*, Perry wanted to say. But the words were too big. They couldn't fit through his throat.

"Okay," she said. "I put the car back now."

Still unable to speak, Perry just nodded.

"You done good, baby," she said. "Thank you for that."

Perry and Brendy walked in silence. At first they'd planned to catch a skycar, head back uptown, but no trolley cast its shadow across their path.

It wasn't that unusual. The cars ran on their own unpredictable schedule. Most times, you could catch one every ten minutes or so, but other times an hour, two hours might pass with none to be had. One day, thinking of Peaches's warning that they needed to know everything they could about the city, Perry had called the phone number for the Ride Line posted at all the stops. The phone had clicked, someone picked up and yelled into the receiver, *"Hey dere, baby! Didda wah didda, wahdidda, doo!"*

"Hello?" Perry said. "This the Ride Line?"

"Hey dere, baby. Hey! Heyyyyy! Didda—!"

Perry had hung up and never called again.

Now Perry and Brendy had reached the 610 overpass. Perry intended to head over to North Broad and see if they could catch a car there. If not, he'd see what he could do about a taxi. He had only a few dollars on him, but he had a stash of dollar bills and quarters in his bedroom at home that would probably cover the expense.

Perry felt a tug on his arm and realized that Brendy had stopped walking. He turned. "Hey—" he began, but Brendy just pointed.

Perry turned back to see what had stopped his sister in her tracks. A familiar shadow lay on the street, darker than the shadow of the overpass rumbling above them. Even before he smelled the cigar smoke and alcohol, Perry knew what would happen next.

Doctor Professor's piano resolved into view, and the spirit himself followed close behind.

Perry had already been sweating from the summer heat, but now he was aware of it. He stood rooted, staring, just watching as the Doctor turned to look at him through his big dark glasses. He was dressed differently from the way he had been last night. Today he wore a black fur hat like a Russian in a spy movie, and instead of the purple suit he wore a blue-gray shirt with Boy Scout patches sewn onto the shoulders and a pair of matching slacks. He seemed thinner than he'd been last night as well, and—Perry noticed it all at once—he wasn't playing a note.

Hey, now, said the ghost. His mouth didn't move, but Perry heard his hoarse half croak even more clearly than he would have if it had sounded on the air.

This is it, Perry thought. *This is what Peaches was talking about.* He looked all around, as if he'd find her hiding in plain sight.

It's you I'm talking at, baby. You and the lil girl. What y'all names is?

Brendy let go Perry's hand, and before he could hold her back, his baby sister stepped forward and curtsied. "My name Brendolyn Eunice Graves."

Graves, Doctor Professor said. *Uptown Graveses?*

"Yessir."

Thass a good family, baby. He laughed softly to himself, nodded. *And you? What your name is, little man?*

"Puh-Perry. Perry Graves."

Think I knowed some of y'all's kin when I come up dancin' in the clubs. Where your friend at?

"You mean Peaches?" Brendy asked. "We don't know. She runned off."

"Brendy," Perry said. He had begun to recover himself. "Sir,

Peaches had to—she's not with us right this minute, but if you need us to—if you need us to deliver a message, we're her closest friends. We can—we can make sure she hears what you have to say."

Word for word, baby. Every one.

"Verbatim, sir," Perry said. "I've got an excellent memory."

Come closer, Doctor Professor said. *I got a lot to say, and ain't no reason to sit here in the way of traffic while I says it.*

Brendy crossed to him immediately. Perry wavered for a beat. It was as if his legs belonged to someone else. He wondered idly what Milo from *The Phantom Tollbooth* would think of all this. Milo wouldn't question it. Milo would move right along, his boredom giving way to wonder. That thought comforted Perry enough to lift his paralysis, and he went to stand beside the piano.

Up close, he noticed a strange electrical hum—almost like the sound you hear when a guitar is plugged into an amplifier, before the player strikes the first chord.

Thass magic, baby, pure and simple.

"What magic?" Brendy asked.

Jazz, baby, said the ghost. *Potentest sorcery in all of Nola. Y'all ready now?*

"Nuh-no," Perry said before he could stop himself. "But...but let's go."

Put your hands on Mess Around. Touch her anywhere you want.

Perry and Brendy did as they were told. The glittery gold wasn't just paint—it was a crust, built up from countless celebrations.

Don't let go, now. Not till we get where we goin', ya heard me?

Perry just nodded, having lost his voice again.

"Right," Doctor Professor said aloud, and began to play.

Perry watched the keys as the old man struck the chords. He played hard—Perry had always known it, but his own piano lessons told him something else. He'd heard others play the Doctor's songs, but coming from their hands, the notes always seemed to be missing something. Now Perry understood, a little, what made Fess's playing so powerful: He struck the major and the minor

chords at the same time and played a heavy walk-up from one
chord to the next, trotting his fingers along the keys. It was more
than that, though. Somehow, at the same time, he was playing the
bass, the horns, and the drums as well.

He seemed to start the song in the middle, but Perry couldn't
be sure. It wasn't one he'd heard before.

So long!
So long!
So long . . . !

This time Perry's legs didn't feel compelled to dance, but his
body moved anyway, swaying awkwardly, keeping time, as he
kept his hand pressed against the Mess Around.

Seeeeee you later after while!

The song ended with a flourish, and Perry blinked, amazed.
"Where we—? What?" he asked.

"We here, baby," Doctor Professor said.

But Perry wasn't sure where "here" was. They were on a stage
in what looked like an enormous nightclub. There seemed to be no
ceiling—or the ceiling was painted to look like a vast starscape, with
nebulae, constellations, and even comets moving through the black.
The stars seemed so near that Perry felt they could fall at any moment,
descending to burn the dance floor.

". . . It's empty," Perry said.

"Ain't empty," Doctor Professor corrected him. "All the greats
is here. They playing right now. Buddy Bolden blowing a solo like
you wouldn't believe. But that music ain't for living ears."

"Like in the boneyard?" Perry said. "The music for the dead?"

Fess shook his head. "That music for the earthbound. The dead
who ain't climbed up the Ladder. This here—it's the Music of All.
The Jazz Beyond Jazz. Thass why you cain't hear it or see it played."

"You talking like people now," Brendy said.

"It's the magic," said the Doctor. "It gets good to me when I'm out and about, and if I open my mouth, I gotta sing. Songs is powerful and wild, so they gots to be used a certain way. So I speaks without speaking, if you know what I mean."

"I don't," Perry said. He didn't want to, either.

The Doctor eyed him. "You got talent in spades, baby, but I ain't so sure music what you talented for."

Perry opened his mouth, but words had left him again.

Doctor Professor rose from the piano and gestured. A drink appeared in his hand. He took a quiet sip and grunted his approval. "Now, listen," he said. "We ain't got a lot of time. I brung you here because I need y'all's help. Y'all know what the Great Powers is?"

"That's the City Musicians," Brendy said.

"Magicians," Perry corrected.

"You both right, baby. Magic and music the same thing. Music is what keep Nola hummin'. It's what makes her the city she is. Now, them Great Powers, they all under me. I keep 'em in line, and I keep 'em from fighting amongst theyselves. It ain't because I'm better than they is, or because I play better. It's because I been tasked from On High to power the city. I composed thirty-two songs to keep everything running, and them songs is awake and aware. The most powerful ones got they own personalities. They likes and dislikes. 'Tipsy Tina,' 'Walk Dem Blues,' 'First Chief,' 'Curly Girly,' 'Mean Ole World,' 'Ballhead Betty,' 'Jailbird Stomp,' and 'Cain't Get Right Blues.' Them eight is the most powerful, and I uses 'em to keep thangs in line. But they been stole, baby."

"Stolen?" Brendy said. "How do you steal a song?"

"Can't be done outright," Doctor Professor said. "First, you gots to make it think it's something else. Something finite. Then you gots to trick it, on account of you can't tell a song what to do. A song do what it wanna. Somebody figured out how to do that and made off with nine of my babies."

"Who?" Perry asked. "Who took them?"

"That's the thing right there," Fess said. "Even if I knew, there ain't much I could do bout it. Not directly. I am alive, and I exist, but I don't exist the same as you. Everyone and everything abide by certain laws, and the law says my interaction with the physical world got to be a certain way. That's what I need y'all for."

"You want us to find out who has them?" Brendy asked.

"Don't nobody has 'em," Fess said. "Them songs can't be held. It don't make no difference who took 'em, neither, because can't nobody do with 'em what I can do. I need you and your friend to bring them songs back to me so I can keep the city hummin'."

Doctor Professor fell silent, letting the information sink in.

Perry's mind raced. He could feel his thoughts jostling to make room for the new information. He looked at his shoes, frowning. *I'm here right now*, he thought. *Me. This is happening.* He wondered how many kids—how many human beings—had stood where he stood at this moment. He spoke again, slowly, piecing the words together as they came to him. "I . . . I seen one. I saw one just today."

"What?" Brendy asked. "Where?"

"You did, too," he said. "On Elysian Fields. The crazy lady marching down the street? That was no lady. That was a song."

Doctor Professor nodded. "You got it, baby. Susan Brown," he said. "She the walkinest girl in town."

"Yeah," Perry said, warming to the idea. "That's right. 'Walk Dem Blues.'"

"Seems to me, I picked the right man for the job."

"You picked Peaches," Perry said without thinking. "All we can do is help. But I have a question."

"What you wanna know?"

"You said nine of your songs were stolen, but you only listed eight names," Perry said. "Who the other one is?"

A shadow passed across Doctor Professor's expression, but it was gone so quickly that Perry thought he must have imagined it. "Thass a little test for you, baby. You said you got a memory for words. I threw that in to see if you notice."

Perry did his best to school his expression. "I'll talk to Peaches directly, see if she'll take your quest."

"She'll do it," Brendy said brightly. "Us and Peaches, we like this!" She showed the Doctor two crossed fingers, then considered and added a third.

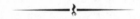

It was raining when they returned to the world, and Jackson Avenue was empty of traffic. Perry and Brendy stood with both hands against the Mess Around as Doctor Professor played and sang:

Mama was a seamstress
She sewed me my blue jeans
My daddy, he was a gamblin' man
Down there in New Orleans—
Yes he was . . . !

Fess kept singing and spoke at the exact same time. "Now, let go, baby. Doctor Professor got places to be."

Thunder cracked overhead, but it seemed to matter as little as the rain that soaked Perry's body and clothes. It was a warm rain, the kind you could dance and play in without catching cold. Doctor Professor didn't seem to notice the rain at all, and as Perry watched the elderly man, he realized that none of the drops touched him or his piano. Maybe for the Doctor the weather didn't exist at all.

He's just as real as we are, Perry thought, *but he's a different kind of real*. It was like the old folks said at church. Doctor Professor was in the world, but he was not *of* the world.

The first time he tried, Perry couldn't let go of the piano. His hips shook from side to side, and he knew he looked silly, but his body didn't care. With an extreme effort of will, he commanded his hands to release, then pulled Brendy away.

"Sorry bout that, y'all," Fess said. He'd already begun to fade away. "Ain't used to no passengers."

"That's okay!" Perry shouted over the music.

"See y'all later, then," said the Doctor as he segued right into another song.

Gee, but it's hard to love someone
When she don't love you-u-u-u . . . !

And then he disappeared.

Perry leaned on his knees, thunderstruck. The music still rang in his blood, and he didn't think it would ever fully leave him. He wondered dimly what that meant. He cared a little more about the rain now, but only a little.

"Come on, baby," Brendy said. "Walk it out, walk it out, walk it out!"

"What?" Perry straightened.

Brendy held her wet face up to him, beaming as if in sunlight. "I feel it, too," she said. "But you and me, we got *work.*"

"Work," Perry said. "Right. Okay. We'll check in at home, then we'll go find Peaches." He held his sister's hand as they crossed the front lawn.

Before Perry could reach out to touch it, the doorknob turned in its collar, and the front door flew open. Their mother stood there, her face a mask of worry. "You're back?" she said. "Is Daddy Deke with you?"

"Daddy—?" Brendy started.

"What?" Perry asked. "No. Why? What's wrong?"

"Yvette?" Perry's father called from deeper in the house. "Is that them? Is he with them?"

His mother turned, swaying a little on her feet as if she couldn't decide which way to face. "No, it's—it's just the kids."

Their father stepped out of the kitchen. "Inside," he barked. *"Now."*

"They haven't done anything wrong, Deacon."

"Neither of you are going anywhere until further notice. You kids just go wherever whenever, and—and—!"

"What did we do?" Brendy asked. "Did we do—?"

Perry cut her off. "Please. What's going on? Why is everybody so upset?"

Their father paused. Something about the way the light of the house shone behind him made him seem smaller than he should. He pressed his hands against his face, and fear soured Perry's belly as he realized their father was fighting for calm.

"Police came by this afternoon," their mother said, her voice flat. "They found Daddy Deke's car, still running, sitting empty at the light at St. Charles and Washington. They think...they think because he's old, he got confused and just...just wandered off."

"Know-nothing sons of—!" Perry's father began, then caught himself. "There's nothing wrong with his mind."

Perry felt the inverse of that same feeling he'd experienced when he realized he had seen Susan Brown marching down the street. It was as if he stood at one point in his life, looking across a gap in the minutes to see another point from a new perspective.

"No," he said.

"Perry," his mother said.

"No—*listen to me!*—somebody took him. Someone has taken Daddy Deke."

Now the rolling thunder overhead and the noise of rain hitting the roof mattered much more than they had before. It seemed to Perry that they were the only things in the world.

VII

BREAKFAST ON THE MOON

Perry went to bed that night certain that he'd be unable to sleep, but after a few minutes he drifted into dreams. Earlier that night, once Perry and Brendy were accounted for, Perry's father had called on every family member and family friend over the age of fifteen and set out to scour the city for Daddy Deke. Perry didn't say anything as he watched his father shrug into his raincoat and grab his car keys, but he knew Daddy Deke would not turn up tonight. Someone had taken him, was holding him, and Perry wasn't sure how he knew, but he was certain that the same person who'd tricked Doctor Professor's songs into leaving the Mess Around had kidnapped Daddy Deke and was holding him for—not for ransom. For what?

Lying in bed, he tried to imagine what had happened. When Perry was younger, Daddy Deke would read to him and Brendy before bed every night. Some nights, especially during summer, Perry would find himself too tired to sleep after running around all day. Eventually, he asked Daddy Deke what to do about it.

The old man had rubbed his chin, squinted a little, and shifted in his chair. He had dimmed the overhead light even before he started reading, and now the strongest illumination in the room came from Perry's old night-light, plugged into the wall by his bureau. Daddy Deke's shadow fell across Perry's chest, and Perry reached to touch its velvet smoothness.

"Well, baby, seems to me," Daddy Deke said, "you could just make you a memory and follow it into dream."

"What do you mean?" Perry asked.

"Well, just because something ain't happened, or ain't happened to *you*, don't mean you can't remember it. All you gotta do is just think real hard about how it *woulda* happened. You just imagine it in your mind's eye and watch real close. Then you got yourself a memory. Once you make it real enough to keep on without you concentratin' so hard, well, usually it turns itself into a dream."

"Can you show me how?"

"Well, sure," Daddy Deke said. "First, you gotta relax. Relax real good. Let your eyes close, and breathe nice and slow, you dig?"

"I dig." Perry did as his grandfather instructed, listening to the quiet tide of his own breath.

"Now think of something. Anything. It can be something happened to you, like the last time we went to Jazzland, or it can be something that happened to somebody else or that never happened at all—like the time we ate breakfast on the moon."

"Breakfast on the moon," Perry said, and laughed a little.

"Right. And you just think of every detail. What the moondust smelt like. Who you was with. What the light looked like falling from the shining half circle of the Earth hanging up there in the black sky of space. You see it?"

"I see it," Perry said. "It's so—I didn't know Earth could shine like the moon."

"Ain't it something?" Daddy Deke said, and cackled softly to himself. "Now think about the tablecloth we eating on. The real nice china the Moon Lady done set out before she got to cookin'. The way the moonjuice tasted when you gulped it down, and how much lighter you was than you are when you go walkin' round town...And now you sort of...let go. Let the moon breakfast remember itself."

The Moon Lady saw Perry's empty plate and slid three more little blue mooncakes onto it. She smiled, and her mouth was full of stars. Perry stared at her, amazed.

Daddy Deke sat on the other side of the table, squeezing Brendy's Afro pouf and making her squeal. Somehow, his disembodied voice still spoke from elsewhere. *Then, after while*, he said, *you ain't gotta concentrate no more. You dreaming, baby.*

The next morning, Perry was too full of mooncakes to eat his breakfast.

The next time Perry tried the memory trick, he decided to imagine something else that hadn't happened. As he was getting ready for bed, he realized he had forgotten to study for his spelling test. He knew some of the words just fine—spelling wasn't hard—but there were a couple he found tricky—like *lightning*. Was the one without the *e* the one that stabbed through the sky during storms, or was that the one that described the process of an object changing color? For a little while, Perry was irritated with himself. He didn't want to get a C or even a B, if he could help it. He decided to remember himself studying. To remember looking over the words, tracing them with his fingers, and reading off the letters one by one. Before long, the dream took over, and the words started to squirm on the page—but by then, Perry already knew what he needed to know. He came away with an A.

Tonight, Perry imagined himself standing on the front lawn of Daddy Deke's house, around the corner on Brainard Street, watching as his grandfather glided past him toward his beautiful old Comet. Daddy Deke loved that car, and so did Perry—its glossy doubled headlights, the toothy grin of its front grille. Deke turned the key in the ignition, and the car roared to life. Alvin Robinson's groaning voice coiled out of the car's speakers, backed by heavy bouncing bass, smooth guitars, and ticking drums.

That's the reason why I stroll away and cry.
Blues grabbed me in the midnight, didn't turn me loose till day.

Blues grabbed me in the middle of the night, ain't turn me loose till day.
Didn't have no mama to drive them blues away . . . !

Perry stepped through the front passenger-side door to sit ghostly in the seat beside his grandfather. Daddy Deke backed out of his driveway onto Brainard and rolled across Jackson Avenue before turning left up Philip. He stopped just before the intersection with St. Charles, then turned his signal on and eased the car forward, looking to the left to check for traffic and graffiti. Satisfied, he turned right and started sailing uptown.

It was bright out, and simmering hot. Daddy Deke kept the air conditioner at a full blow, and Perry felt its chill from a remove. He didn't realize it, but he had tumbled into sleep without relaxing his concentration. His muscles untensed, his breathing evened, and the vision crystallized around him, realer than real.

"They can hold my body, but I go where I wanna and I do what I do, you dig?" Daddy Deke said.

I dig, Perry said. *It's dug.*

"Can't nobody stop me talking to my grandbabies."

Where are you? Who took you? Anything you can tell me will make it easier for us to find you.

Daddy Deke stopped for a red light at Louisiana.

"Don't come lookin'," he said. "Sumn else going on—somethin' sinister. I got a job to do but damb if I can remember what it is."

Haints are stealing things. One of them stole from Peaches. A letter from her daddy. I think it's the same one stole you!

The light turned green, and Daddy Deke guided the car onward.

"No," he said. "At least I don't think so. This trouble bigger than any before. This ain't just a afternoon adventure, you dig?"

It's serious.

"More than 'serious,' baby. This life-and-death, this one. And not just for you and yours. For all of us. For all Nola."

Perry's belly felt full of shadows—as if he'd eaten so much night that it had made him sick. He had intended to pass Doctor

Professor's message to Peaches, but he had also intended to warn her that the old haint was not to be trusted—tell her that maybe she shouldn't help him at all. But dream or no dream, the more he talked to Daddy Deke, the more convinced he became that seeking out Doctor Professor's songs would also mean finding Daddy Deke.

But why would anyone want to hurt the city?

"Not everybody live in Nola in love with Nola, ya heard me? Hate is the mirror image of love, and it's a powerful thing."

The light was green at Washington, and they sailed right through.

"I been here so many years, baby. I been here such a long, long time."

You don't have to leave. I made this memory. You can stay as long as you want.

"He can't know I'm gone, baby," Daddy Deke said as they approached Napoleon. The light turned from yellow to red, and Daddy Deke began to apply the brakes. "He can't know I'm talking to you. We don't want him ready when you come."

Who can't know? Who's got you?

"Can't say his name, baby. He'll hear me for sure, and I can't risk him finding you with me."

Daddy Deke—

He stopped the car, idling it before the light. "You and Brendy and Peaches. All y'all children and grandchildren, you are my joy."

Wait!

"Quiet now."

A blue shock of fright ran from the edge of Perry's forehead to the soles of his feet. He wasn't ready for this. Invisible, he had turned in his seat to watch Daddy Deke's face. Now he saw something there he'd never seen before—fear. But not just fear—fear tinged with a sort of tired resolve.

Perry had to clap his hands over his mouth to keep from screaming as the rear passenger-side door opened behind him.

An oily hiss filled the car, and it took a moment for him to realize that the sound was a voice. "Whatever you say," Daddy Deke

said. "I come quietly. Just promise me one thing: You leave my—
you leave my family alone."

This time, Perry understood the answer.

YOU THINK YOU CAN DEAL WITH ME? YOU KNOW WHO I'M IS?

"Promise!"

The voice laughed. Perry felt its hot breath on the back of his
neck. He began to sweat. He could feel his living, breathing body
lying at home in his bed. He felt it stir. He felt it open its mouth to
cry out, and in the dream he held his mouth again, desperate for
quiet.

I HEAR YOU TALKING TO SOMEBODY, OLD MAN? YOU WANDERIN'
IN YO SLEEP?

"I ain't been nowhere," Daddy Deke said. "Couldn't leave if I
tried."

Perry felt his mind striving to imagine the owner of the awful
voice and fought the image, trying to keep from seeing it. Whoever this was must be all teeth and throat.

DON'T BE TRYNA DEAL WITH ME, BABY, said the voice. YOU COME
ON OUT THIS CAR, OR I PAY A VISIT TO YO KIN THIS VERY NIGHT.

The worst thing about the voice was how untroubled, how
utterly calm it was. All it did was state facts, and when it spoke, the
facts were never good.

"Go near 'em and I'll kill you my damn self."

WILL YOU NOW? The voice laughed again. HOW EXACTLY YOU
GONE MURDER YOU A SONG?

"Stack—!" Daddy Deke started, but a flood of darkness washed
into the car's interior. It was a darkness so inky, so black, that Perry
thought it would drown him. He shook, clenching his eyes and his
teeth, but he could feel a scream climbing through him from the
bottom of his feet. Before long, it would reach his throat, and he'd
have to let it out. He only hoped that once he started screaming,
he'd be able to stop.

———※———

Deacon Graves Jr. slid his jacket off and let it crumple on the back of an antique chair. His wife, Yvette, sat on her side of the bed anxiously kneading her own hands. Ordinarily she'd ask him sweetly to hang it up, maybe mention that the maid was on vacation. Tonight, though, she just watched, making a mental note to hang the jacket once Deacon had fallen asleep.

"No sign?" she asked.

"Nothing," he said.

Deacon's eyes flicked to the LED screen of the alarm clock sitting on the bedside table. "It's half past three."

"And you got work in the morning." Deacon had spent years working on rigs out in the Gulf, but nowadays Shell had him in an office working to track and refine their procedures.

"Should I call in?"

"You know what I think," Yvette said. She drew a breath, preparing to argue, but as she did, Yvette realized there was no argument in her—no strength for locking horns. The plain fact was that sometimes, people simply disappeared. Her own mother had gone missing one day when Yvette was young, and it had been hard, but eventually she gave her mother up for lost, shut all her anguish and hope in a little room inside her heart. It wasn't time to do that with Daddy Deke—not yet—but there was a resignation inside her that worried her, made her feel as if she were betraying her husband, her children.

"Yvie," Deacon said. "She's a little girl. A wild-ass little girl."

"She can help. You've seen her in action."

It was true. Weeks ago, Deacon had been working late in his office when the building began to shake and rumble. At first he'd thought it was a bomb attack—but then he'd seen Peaches streak past his window carrying what he learned later was the dumpster she'd used to capture the little girl with the fireworks.

"There's no denying her abilities," Deacon said. "She's like something out of a comic book—but she's still a child. She thinks like a little girl. She has the emotions of a little girl. Brendy and

Perry would follow her anywhere, but our kids are normal, Yvie. They're brave, they're bright, and they're wonderful, but we can't look to them when we're in a bind." He looked away, swayed on his feet, then crossed to sit on his side of the bed. Shirt, shoes, pants came off, and he lay down in his boxers and his socks to stare at the pocked surface of the bedroom ceiling.

"I've been thinking on it all night," Yvette said. "This trouble feels different. What if Perry's right and somebody did take Daddy Deke? What if you can't find him because he's being held somewhere?"

Deacon had an effortless smoothness about him that made Yvette's heart flutter, but exhaustion had withdrawn that smoothness to rest beneath his skin. He was lovely, still, but he also seemed small and hard—like a pebble.

"I'd be a fool to ignore the possibility," he said. "But if it is true, if something bigger is going on, that means we need to keep the kids safe."

"If they the only ones can fix what's wrong, keeping them out of it won't keep nobody safe." Yvette took a breath, held it, then let it out as a sigh. A disturbance waited at the edge of her memory— something wanted to bubble up into her mind. Someone had told her something once—about the city? About Daddy Deke? She felt the basic shape of the knowledge, but it was resolving slowly—too slowly to be of use right now.

"Now," she said, her speech slow and distracted, "you need to go to work in the morning. You know your team don't run right without you."

"I gotta look," Deacon said. "I gotta find…" But before he'd finished speaking, exhaustion carried him off into sleep.

She knew there would be no sleep for her tonight. There was too much to consider, options to be weighed.

The telephone shrilled from the bedside table. Yvette stared at it, wondering who would call this late.

But she knew.

Divided from herself, Yvette watched herself reach for the handset, pick it up.

"Well, hello, honey. How are you?" said a familiar voice on the other end.

"Muh-Mama?" Yvette asked. "Where are you? Where you been? Are you coming home?"

Now the memory resolved. She saw her mother's face, smooth and ageless, her eyes serious. *One day a storm will come. It will take everything we've got to protect ourselves against it. When the hour arrives, I'll remind you of your duty.*

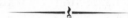

Abruptly, Perry sat up in bed. He covered his face with his hands and spoke softly to himself. "You're here, not there. You're *here*, not there." But the thought held no comfort.

When Daddy Deke had been taken, he had experienced something similar to what Perry had seen, all by himself, with no one to witness or protect him. A lump rested in Perry's chest. While crying might have dislodged the blockage, Perry felt as if an unseen hand had reached into his heart and turned off the waterworks. There were no tears to cry.

By this time of night, the moon had risen to silver the city, and its light splashed like milk through his open window. Perry's bedroom fan hummed away, sucking hot air from the room to blow outside. Just as Perry decided he'd need to wake Brendy and head over to Peaches's house in search of his friend, he realized she was already here. He couldn't see her, but he smelled her, and he wondered why she hadn't waked him from his nightmare.

"I woulda woke you," Peaches said softly, "but it seemed like the dream you was having was important."

Now Perry saw her. She sat in the rocking chair Daddy Deke had given Perry when he turned eight.

"It was," Perry said. "Daddy Deke's missing. I think he—I think he just contacted me."

"People straight conniving in this town," Peaches said. "Taking things don't belong to them. Now they taking *people*?"

"There's more," Perry said. "It's not just Daddy Deke we looking for. Somebody stole Doctor Professor's songs." Perry explained what Doctor Professor had told him and Brendy.

"Damn," Peaches said. "Awright. One problem at a—"

"I think it's all the same problem, though," Perry said. "I think—I think the same person stole them is the one who took Daddy Deke."

Peaches watched him, unconvinced.

"Okay, so you know that feeling when you outside playing and clouds get in the way of the sun and everything seems to . . . *shift*?"

"Sure," Peaches said.

"Well, that's what I'm feeling right now. Something is changing in the city, things are getting darker, and I can't prove that the song-stealer and the kidnapper are the same, but I feel it. I feel it on my skin."

Peaches's expression softened. "I know what that feel like."

Perry opened his mouth again, only to find himself flustered speechless. He hadn't expected Peaches to agree with him—in fact, he'd been counting on her to explain why he was wrong—that none of this was as bad as it seemed.

"Them songs belong to Nola," Peaches said. "They all of ours."

"I think it was a song took Daddy Deke," Perry said." I think it was 'Jailbird Stomp.'"

"That song about the wino? You think he could get it together to grab somebody?"

"Maybe if somebody else told him what to do," Perry said. He was on shaky ground now, feeling his way through these ideas. "The thing in my dream—in my vision, though—it wasn't nothing like Jailbird. It was— That song ain't scary, you know? Maybe . . . maybe the songs *change* the longer they're away from the Mess Around. Maybe they're so convinced they're people, they become more like us. Like the worst, craziest people."

"Yeah, maybe," Peaches said. "How 'Jailbird Stomp' go again?"

Perry opened his mouth to sing and faltered, confused. "I know this one," he said. "I can't even count how many times I sung it."

But how did it go?

He could almost hear the music in his mind. *Almost*. Perry shut his eyes tight, reaching for the lyrics. "'In the foggy...the...' No. That ain't right. I *know* I know it."

"You usedta did," Peaches said. "But the song ain't there for you to sing. It's out there somewhere, snatching folks out they cars."

"That would be *bad*," Perry said. It was one thing for songs to escape from the piano to gallivant around town, but if they had gone rogue, that would make their job *much* harder. "This song knows it's a song, too. I heard it say."

"Maybe they ain't all like that, though," Peaches said. Rocking softly, she pressed her right fist against her hip and tapped her left foot as she considered. Her attitude was so grown-up that Perry wasn't sure how he felt about her at that moment.

"Listen," she said. "First, we find Jailbird and Daddy Deke. He family. But we can't do nothing till morning."

"Why not?"

"Because number one, you mostly still asleep. You musta been tired than a mug when you laid down."

Now that she mentioned it, Perry could tell that even the vividness of his vision was not enough to keep him awake till morning. "What's the other reason?"

"What?"

"You said 'number one,'" Perry said. "That means there's more."

Peaches stopped rocking and sat forward, elbows to knees. "We can't just leave in the night," she said. "If your folks look in and find you gone, they'll blame me. And they'll be right. I don't...I can't have that right now."

Perry had become dimly aware that there was something his friend wasn't telling him. He sensed it, though, baking from her like heat from a stove. Should he ask her? What would a good friend do? All Perry could think to say was her name: "Peaches."

"Yeah."

Perry took a settling breath. "What...? What happened at the boneyard?" he asked. "I never seen you so upset."

This time, Peaches watched Perry so long that he didn't think she'd answer him. She left the rocking chair and crossed to the bed to sit with her back to him. Nothing seemed different about her, but the grace of her movements, their...their fluidity...amazed Perry, made him feel as if he was noticing something forbidden.

"My daddy," Peaches said. "He traveling. I travel with him— Well, I usedta done. We was on a boat way, way out. The boat sunk, and we got separated. He told me...he told me he'd find out where I gone and he'd write me letters till he could come get me."

"Did he?"

"Yeah," she said. She lifted her left leg and reoriented her body toward Perry. He felt a little less embarrassed this way, but only a little.

"Only they don't come to the house," Peaches said. "I gotta find 'em. So I looks for them around town. That's...that's what I do most of the time if nobody need nothing. Each letter has a clue to where I can find the next one, and the last one, it said I find it in one of the barbecue pits in City Park. But it wasn't there. All I found was chicken bones."

"Like a pile of bones?"

"No, like a skeleton," she said. "All the bones. Head-bone. Everything. It was a message."

"From a haint."

"Thass right. So I axed around, found out only one haint use the Yardbird Sign. And that was him buried in that grave. He took my daddy's letter, and that's why I can't find the next one, and I... I don't get to write back. Daddy never in the same place twice. One week he in French Polynesia teaching cannibals to break-dance, and the next week he in Australia helping buffalo learn to drive. His letters... they all I got of him right now. I nuh-*need* them."

"You never mentioned him before."

"I know," Peaches said. "I'm sorry. I know I shoulda. I just... Some things are hard to say."

"Yuh-yeah," Perry said. "They are."

"Listen, I know I ain't really told you what happened at the boneyard. I promise we talk about it, but I just gotta—I ain't slept in about a week."

"That's okay," Perry said. "Sleep."

"—And," she said. "And they's things you ain't tell me, neither."

His chest tightened. "What you mean?" But he knew.

"Why you changed schools like that. Brendy don't know. Nobody know."

"Because I don't— Because I can't do magic."

"Really?"

Perry opened his mouth. He wasn't sure what would come out of it. He focused on holding himself in the present as danger loomed on the edge of his mind. He understood that life could become a series of perils and frights, each close on the heels of the next, and he did *not* want that.

He shook his head, mute.

Peaches touched his shoulder. "Hey," she said. "It's okay. You okay." She paused. "Can I...?"

"What?"

"Nothing." She turned away again.

"You want to sleep here?" Perry asked. "You can have my bed, and I'll sleep on the floor."

She turned back to him again and opened her mouth. She seemed to try to say something and failed. Together, they sat in silence, then, slowly, Perry got up to make way for his friend.

VIII

NEGROES AND FLIES

Downstairs, Brendy was just finishing setting the table. Perry's daddy had already headed out for work, so it would just be the four of them this morning. Still, Brendy set an extra place for Daddy Deke, and seeing the plate flanked by the flatware, the napkin, and the juice glass created a storm of conflicting emotions inside Perry. No matter how crazy things got outside in the city, home was still home, but how could that be when Daddy Deke was missing?

"Peaches!" his mother called from the kitchen.

"Ma'am?"

"Come on peel these potatoes and dice 'em up for home fries."

Unable to think what else to do, Perry followed Peaches into the kitchen, where his mother stood wearing her apron. She bent to check the biscuits and nodded, satisfied.

"Perry, I peel, you dice," Peaches said.

"How big?" Perry asked.

"Like keys on a computer," Perry's mother said.

Peaches grabbed two russet potatoes and squeezed them right out of their skins. She handed them off to Perry and he got to chopping. Perry lost himself in the familiar motion. If potatoes could be peeled and chopped, then things couldn't be so bad.

The next couple potatoes Peaches stood up on end; then she snapped her fingers, and the skins fell right off on the cutting board.

"Girl, you magicking them potatoes?" His mother looked at Peaches over her shoulder with only the merest shadow of sadness in her expression.

"Naw, Miss Yvette," Peaches said. "I don't know no magic."

———— ⸙ ————

"So, Mama..." Perry said as he used his last bit of biscuit to mop up the yolk from his eggs. "We was thinking we might go out today, if that's all right with you..."

Perry's mother set her coffee on the table before her. "I won't keep you in suspense," she said. "I don't want to let you go. I don't want to at all"—she bit off the last word and picked up her knife, standing it on its back end—"but I'm raising y'all to do right just like my mama raised me, so..."

Perry held his breath. She had to let them go. She *had* to.

"I will let you go," she said. "But there's some business we gotta get to first."

Perry and Brendy shared a look.

"First of all, y'all need to tell me what went on yesterday."

"*Oh,*" Brendy said. "Well, you see, what had happened was—"

"I said 'tell me,' Brendolyn, not 'fib something up.'"

With her mouth hanging open, Brendy looked to Perry for help.

"I don't know, Mama," Perry said. "The way we play, if we tell you what happened, it might not make sense."

Perry's mother took a deep, irritated breath. "Now, I already told you that as much as it pains me, I'm letting you kids out my sight today," she said, "so you will explain to me what happened or you can stay shut up in your room, ya heard me?"

"Okay. I got you," Slowly, haltingly, Perry explained all about his meeting with Doctor Professor. He started out trying to tell the story in terms his mother would understand, but somewhere in the telling, he gave up and began relating events exactly as they had happened.

"So that's what's going on," he finished. "That's why Doctor Professor appeared the other night. The city's in danger. And I think—I think the same person who stole the songs stole Daddy Deke."

Perry's mother sucked her teeth. She frowned into her coffee mug as if she expected it to add something to the conversation. "You mentioned that last night," she said. The darkness in her tone confused Perry. "Do you think it, or do you *know*?"

That was not at all the question Perry had expected. He was still a little shaky about whether it was Jailbird who had captured Daddy Deke, but this question was easy to answer.

Peaches stopped shoveling scrambled eggs into her mouth. "Perry know," she said simply.

"I mean, I do," Perry said. "But how can you—? Why would you believe me?"

"I didn't raise you to lie," she said. "If you're saying Doctor Professor's songs were stolen and he wants you and Peaches to get them back, then that's what's going on. I don't have to like it, but I know truth when I hear it."

"Then how come you always get on me for fibbing?" Brendy asked.

"Because I don't want you to get used to lying. I don't want you to get good at it and have your lies sound like truth. That's no way to live." She paused, shook her head. "This city. I love it, but, baby, sometimes I don't like it."

She gazed into her mug again, but it remained just as silent as it had before. "So the Great and Powerful Fess has charged you with this mission."

"Peaches, really," Perry said. "But, since we got separated, he asked me to let her know what was going down."

"That's not what you said before," his mother countered. "Now, think. Did Fess say he wanted *your* help?"

"Yes," Brendy said. "Yes, he did!"

Peaches frowned thoughtfully. "I guess anybody who know me know we a package deal."

"But he gave you no weapons or tools."

Perry hadn't thought of that. "He didn't . . . I mean . . . Peaches is strong as anything."

Perry's mother sighed heavily. "Lord. Magic and spirits, and . . . *negroes and flies!*" She shut her mouth, visibly working to keep calm. Perry just watched her, amazed.

"All right, then," she said. "Clear the table and meet me in the living room."

Perry entered the living room to find his mother sitting in her red leather wingback chair. Her hands lay in her lap, crawling over each other like cats play-fighting. Perry had never seen her so worried.

"Sit," she said. "And pay attention. You'll be running the streets soon enough."

As far as Perry was concerned, this time it *would* be soon enough. Perry found it hard to concentrate with Daddy Deke out there somewhere menaced and alone, but he also knew there was danger out there for which they must heavily prepare.

Perry, Brendy, and Peaches sat on the sofa opposite the television. Brendy kicked her legs impatiently as Perry's mother bowed her head in prayer. Her attitude made it hard for Perry to pretend they were about to embark on a normal adventure. It made him think of darkness, of a figure in dirty robes and a grimy powdered wig. He shut his eyes against the memory.

Mrs. Graves sighed explosively and looked up at them. "Well," she said, "my mama called me on the telephone last night."

Perry's mouth fell open. Daddy Deke's wife, Mama Edna, had died in the Storm, and Perry had never known his mother's mother, Lisa.

"The Graveses are not an especially musical family," his mother said. "But there is more to magic than music, and on my side, there have been Wise Women. My mother was the wisest of them all, and the Lord took her before any of you were born. She went out running one morning, and all they found was her clothes. Our family, the police, everybody searched and searched, but I knew what had happened. The Lord *swept her up*. She never did die, she just...went on..."

Perry felt the same way he did when he got in trouble at school and had to wait for his father to come home from work and announce Perry's punishment. It wasn't that his mother never spoke of his maternal grandmother—but any mention was slight, offhand. Perry had always assumed that his grandmother had simply died, but this...? It made Perry wonder whether he was the person he'd always assumed himself to be. If magic ran in his family after all, was there any point resisting it?

"Before she went, she used to talk to me about you. All of you. She knew you well. She told me never to confine you if I could help it, and she told me that you would be some of the most talented children alive. Perilous, the moment you were born, I knew Mama Lisa had told the truth. When I held you in the hospital room, you kept twisting around to look and reach for nothing. Like there were other people in there with us that I couldn't see. I knew from that day that you were different."

Different. Different. *Different.* Perry shook his head, swept the word from his mind. "Like, there was haints?"

Yvette's expression was impossible to read. Looking at her made Perry think of his favorite shot from *The Neverending Story*. The moment when the Sphinx begins to open its eyes, ready to blast Atreyu for failing its riddle.

"Your birth was a special thing, and I do believe it was attended by spirits," his mother said. "That's why we got you those piano lessons. You sense things other people don't see or hear. If you had a gift for sorcery, who were we to do anything but encourage it?"

Perry's heart sank just a little. He and his teacher, Mr. Yaw, had believed Perry might be capable of magic. Still, the learning was slow. Each song he played was a faltering thing, a collection of notes instead of a graceful whole. Mr. Yaw said music was like that sometimes. That you had to work for it, find an understanding, instead of waiting for it to occur to you like a bolt from above... But then magic had failed Perry when he needed it most.

He shut the memory down before it could fully resolve in the theater of his mind. It wasn't so bad this way. Knowing he'd never cut records or use his music to light the Christmas decorations along Canal Street made him feel a pang of stifled longing, but with a little practice it had become easy to ignore.

"What about Brendy?" Perry asked. "Is she different, too?"

"I'ma grow up supastrong like Peaches," Brendy said.

"If anybody could, it's you," their mother said with a smile. She wrung her hands gently, then disengaged them to press the fingers of her right hand against the bridge of her nose. Now Perry saw how exhausted she was. Had she slept at all last night?

"I don't know how to equip you," she said, "but that's not up to me. I..." She trailed off, frowning. Then, "Peaches," she said, "I got something I need to say to you."

"Don't worry, Miss Yvette," Peaches said quietly. "I know how you feel."

"Well, I need to say it." She paused. "Peaches, as a—as a *mother*, it's hard for me to see you living with all those animals in that big old house. The only reason I haven't invited you to come and live with us is that I—I wouldn't be able to stand it if you told me no. You're always welcome in this house whether you find Daddy Deke or not."

"I find him," Peaches said.

"Well, I been round and round about this with Deacon, but I do believe that we must use every resource available to find my father-in-law. Now, Peaches, you think you can find him, bring him back?"

"I do."

"And if my babies go with you, you can keep them safe?"

"Always, Miss Yvette."

"I'd go with you, but somebody's got to be here in case Deke turns up on his own. I've got some vacation days, so..." With that last, she seemed to address herself.

"You gots to get some sleep anyhow," Peaches said. "I understand what you tellin' me, though, and...and it mean a lot. But I'm happy in my house. I'm free."

"Okay." She stopped and bit her lip.

Horror welled in Perry as he realized his mother might burst into tears.

The seconds ticked by, and then she took a breath. "Okay, then. Okay. Well. Brendolyn Eunice Graves. Stand."

Brendy sprang to her feet and cut a quick twirl. "Awwww, shucks!" she said. "Come on with it, mama!"

"Perilous Antoine Graves. Stand."

Perry was certain that he could no more rise from his seat than he could detach his own head and basketball-dunk it like Anthony Davis, but his body took over for him. He stood.

Perry's mother beckoned them closer. Now Perry got a better look at the motion of her hands in her lap. She wasn't just fidgeting, she was executing a set of precise movements with her fingers, drawing her hands together and then apart several times.

"I thought you didn't know magic," Perry said quietly.

"I don't," his mother said, but her hands didn't stop working. "This is...When I worked at the call center, they gave me a paragraph of Spanish to say whenever I got somebody on the line who didn't speak any English. Lo syento. Todo nwestro personaale que obblah Esponyoll—It's the only Spanish I ever learned. I could say it well enough to be understood, but I didn't know Spanish..."

She held her right hand before her, palm in, the thumb and forefinger pointing up. She curled her third finger into a hook and clasped it with the third finger on her left hand, which she held palm down, with the thumb tucked strangely underneath.

"This," she said, "is the one spell I know. The one every woman in our family has known for generations."

"What's it do?" Perry asked.

His mother pulled her hands apart, and as she did, a seam appeared in the air before her.

"It opens the Way."

"The way to what?" Brendy asked. Her voice frayed at the edges, but Perry couldn't tell whether she was frightened or excited.

"Let's—!" Peaches began.

"No!" Perry's mother cut her off. "Not you. Them only. You'll have to wait here with me."

Perry hadn't considered that Peaches wouldn't be allowed to go wherever his mother was sending them. All this magic, all these revelations about his family and his ancestry, had been bearable because Peaches was nearby, ready to catch him if he fell. Watching his mother conjure a door in the air made Perry feel as if the sorcery it had caused him such pain to set aside was still active in his life—active in ways he'd never known or understood.

"Mama," he said. "I don't think...I can't do this!"

"You can," she said. "You will. You *are*!"

Something like a heat devil rippled in the air around them. Perry heard a groaning noise, as if the air itself was under tremendous stress. His mother was wrong. He couldn't do this. He couldn't. *What if the Judge found out?!*

Something shoved Perry—hard—from behind. He heard a sound like hundreds of voices gasping, shocked, except *backwards*. Almost before he could take any of that in, a series of explosions ignited right before his eyes—or no. The bursts weren't in front of him, they were inside—cooking off against the interior of his skull.

Somewhere, everywhere, enormous bells tolled. The din was stunning.

Perry opened his mouth to scream, but before he could, the

sound receded. He pitched forward into red sand, as if he'd been tripped. Laughter took flight like a flock of birds.

Perry rolled to his feet and wheeled in search of the laughter's voice. About twenty-five yards away, a woman sat in a cheap lawn chair positioned on a flat red stone outcropping jutting up ten feet above the beach. And it *was* a beach. A mountain rose to Perry's left, and to his right the red sand plunged into lapping waves. A black stone stairway ascended the mountainside. In the other direction, away in the distance, the water was the bluest blue Perry had ever seen—bluer than the sky. So blue it wasn't just a color, it was a *sound*—a low, clear, sustained note that rang all around. Perry had to fight to keep his attention on the moment at hand, instead of letting his eyes drift closed and just *listening*.

He had questions, he felt sure—or at least he should. Oh. Right. "Did you push me down?" Perry called.

The woman pointed theatrically to herself, made a face, and shook her head. Her nose was large and sharp and her hair was wild and dark, forming a glossy mane. Her skin had a greenish undertone, and she wore what looked like track pants and a baggy hooded gray-and-black tunic that seemed as if it had been woven by hand.

"Who are you?" Perry demanded. "What is this place?"

"I'm Touride," she called back. "But you can call me Denkine! This is the Canaries!"

Perry blinked, surprised. "As in the Canary Islands? Way over by Spain?"

Denkine shrugged elaborately. "Who's to say?" she said. "But you better get a move on, habibi. Low tide's coming soon, and half the inn will go."

Perry opened his mouth. He wasn't sure what to ask first, so he parsed the exchange for the most important ideas. "So, uh, I need to go up, then, right?"

"Unless you're ready for a swim, I'd say so!"

The stairway was steep and long—so long that Perry couldn't see where exactly it led—but he reasoned that if he climbed high enough in time, he could rest if he had to before going on…wherever.

"Are you coming too?"

The woman shook her head. "No need! I'm a statue when we sink!"

Perry didn't bother asking what she meant. He knew she'd probably just pull a face and roll her eyes at him. "Nice to meet you, Denkine!" he called, and started up up up.

Brendy felt the cold before she knew where she was. She opened her eyes and blinked. She knew only that she had crossed a great distance very quickly, and that she had heard the sound of thousands of bells, ringing, their sounds stacking and stacking until they were a cacophony that filled the world and dimmed her memories. But now she stood at the corner of St. Charles and Jackson. The near side of the street had been shut down to traffic. On the neutral ground, several families had set up tents. One had a barbecue grill and a table full of fixings. They had a boom box, too, blaring "The Wobble" at top volume.

Groups of people strolled, unhurried, headed uptown or downtown, and a toy vendor pushed his shopping cart with its racks of cheap plush toys and party favors, waiting for someone to stop him and buy something.

Brendy's heart swelled, and an electric joy thrilled through her. Mardi Gras, baby! She thrust her little fists into the air and cut a couple quick dance steps on her toes. She scanned the crowds. Perry and Peaches must be here somewhere. This was their usual spot, after all. On the downtown side of St. Charles, some white folks had set up ladders to elevate themselves or their children high enough to catch beads and throws from the parade floats. Maybe it was a good idea for Brendy to get some height herself. After all, she remembered dimly that she was here looking for something. Chances were, it was a parade throw.

What day was this, though? Was it Mardi Gras day itself—when the Zulu parade rolled with its black-faced and grass-skirted riders? Or was it one of the other days? It must not be a weekday, because the parades wouldn't start until nightfall, so there wouldn't be this many folks in place while the sun was still—

"Hey," someone said.

Brendy turned to see a bigger boy standing over her. He wasn't much older than Brendy, she felt sure, but something about his face—the set of his mouth and the darkness of his eyes—made him seem much older than he looked. Dark, wet-looking curls piled atop his head. He had a nice chin, too . . .

"You landed wrong."

"What? What you mean?" Brendy couldn't help but shake her booty a little bit. "The Wobble" had given way to a brass-band version of "Casanova," and she felt like keeping still would be a crime on par with bank robbery.

"I mean this is the wrong part of town. I trapped it for you, but it's in the Bywater. I can't carry it myself."

"The thing I'm here lookin' for," Brendy asked. "That's what you mean?"

"Yes," the boy said. "If I don't get you to it in time, they'll add to my sentence."

"Your sentence?" Brendy said. "You in trouble?"

"Look, it's a long story, but we've got to *go*." He pointed in the direction of Jackson Avenue.

Brendy considered for a moment, then shrugged. "Aight, then," she said. "But what your name is anyhow?"

"Scander," the boy said. "Scander Nuñez. What's yours? Do you remember?"

"Of course I do," Brendy said. "My name Brendolyn Peachpie Thunder-lightning Potato Chips Graves. Pleased to make yo acquaintance."

"Likewise," Scander said, and together, they started through the crowd.

OR DIE TRYING

Perry wasn't sure how long he'd been climbing. The daylight seemed a little different now—or was he imagining it? That deep blue sound still rang everywhere, but its pitch had shifted—it seemed higher. Was it because of the altitude? Eventually, he'd have to look to his left—over the drop-off. He wasn't particularly afraid of heights, but he'd read about the Imp of the Perverse, and the idea of his body urging him to plunge to his death made him think twice about taking a look.

He felt a weary sort of relief as he came to another stone landing—this was the sixth he'd seen so far, and by his reckoning, the landings were a hundred or so yards apart. This one was different from the others in that it included a marble bench to each side—one tucked up against the mountain, and the other near the edge of the cliff—about eight feet apart. They looked as if they'd been carved from the living rock rather than fashioned and set here. The legs went straight down into the stone below.

Perry took a seat on the mountainside bench. Now he felt a tingle in his legs, almost like they wanted to twitch. He wished he'd put on shorts instead of jeans…wherever he'd come from. Why couldn't he remember where his journey had begun? He frowned as he tried to recall the faces of his family. He saw them clearly enough in his mind's eye, but he couldn't remember their names. The forgetfulness didn't alarm him, and he thought that must be a function of the quest—because he felt sure he was on a quest, though for what, he had no idea. Someone must have told him at some point, but either he hadn't listened or the quest had dulled that memory, too.

Maybe, Denkine's voice sounded close to Perry's right ear—as if she sat on his shoulder whispering. Perry was too tired to look round for her. *It could be you never knew and finding out is part of the mission.*

"What is this place?" Perry asked. "Where am I?"

I'll explain, but you gotta keep climbing. Low tide is no joke.

Perry couldn't think what else to do, so he rose and resumed climbing. "Will you tell me who you are?"

That part is kind of hard to explain. I used to be a lot of people. I used to be a god. I am still, but I used to be, too.

"Which god?"

Tanit, Denkine said. *Of the Phoenicians. Ever heard of me?*

"Sorry, no," Perry said, embarrassed. "I know the Phoenicians, though. From the Bible and from Hannibal and the elephants."

Hannibal, Denkine said. *Now,* there's *a name I haven't heard in ages. Anyway. You probably have the Canary Islands on your Earth? Or you think you do—and they're just islands.*

"We think—?" Perry stopped short. That sounded like another trick. "They're islands," he said. "In the Mediterranean."

Okay, well, sometimes an island has an up side and a down side, and the two sides are in two different worlds. Because there are worlds and worlds and worlds.

"Then what are these Canaries?"

Eggs of the World Serpent. She left them here forgotten, so they're just floating in the sea. Most of the time, the eggs are about two thirds out of the water, and people live and work on them and do their thing—like run an inn or an airport or whatever.

Finally, Perry looked out to sea. The water was heartbreakingly blue. Away in the distance, he saw what must be an airport resting beneath the waves. He saw its control tower, its runways, and its main terminal—even an empty parking lot, airplane hangars, and runways. In size, it was midway between Armstrong International and the Lakeside Airports. Perry stopped walking to stare.

Oh, no you don't, Denkine said. *No time: run run run* run*!*

Perry broke into a run, and his legs seemed to carry him impossibly fast. The stairs blurred beneath him, and he wasn't sure his feet touched them at all. He understood now that there was a serious chance that he wouldn't make it through this quest alive. He was impossibly far from his home, from everything and everyone he knew, streaking up a set of stone steps carved into—into what sounded like a colossal dragon egg while a goddess spoke directly into his mind.

Perry tripped on a stone and tumbled into grass, breathing hard from exertion. Had Denkine given him super-speed? He rolled onto his butt and took a look around. He sat on a grassy circular lawn bisected by a marble pathway, which led up another short flight of stone stairs to a sprawling villa surrounded by a covered porch.

I was a little worried about you for a second there, Denkine—or was it Tanit?—admitted. *I thought maybe they sent a normal human.*

"I am, though."

You're what?

"A regular human," Perry said. "I'm smart, I guess, but there's nothing special about me."

Perry, Denkine said, exasperated. *I got news for you . . .*

Perry scowled. "Oh, come on."

As Perry watched, the mountain rumbled, almost as if it had indigestion. The sound built and built until the air was full of it—and Perry wouldn't have been able to make himself heard above it even screaming at the top of his lungs. He climbed to his feet, bone weary, but ready to run again if he had to.

It wasn't until the mountain began to sink that Perry knew

he had climbed to safety after all. Within no more than five minutes, it had descended into the sea. Very carefully, Perry walked to the edge of the path and looked down. He could see the mountain down there, resting beneath the waves. His stomach turned over.

Perry glanced back at the villa as Denkine opened the front door and stepped out. How had he mistaken her for human? Her physique still seemed compact, if a little skinny, but she was roughly eight feet tall, and she wore a circlet of flame around her head. Her tunic—Perry wasn't sure it was made of fabric, the way it shone and billowed in the wind—stretched down to her hips, where she wore what Perry thought at first must be a layered skirt, until he realized that it was actually broad-legged pants.

Perry, she said. Her "voice" brimmed with kindness, with patience, as she closed the distance between them. *Some things aren't worth holding on to. Why do you wish so fervently to be normal?*

"I don't know!"

Do you think Peaches could love a normal boy?

Perry couldn't answer. He couldn't say the word. He bowed his head and pressed his left fist against his forehead, struggling. Fat tears rolled down his face.

"Hey. Hey, now."

Perry opened his eyes to find that Denkine had become human again. Her small right hand rested lightly on his shoulder.

"We can't just *give* you things," she said. "Your minds are too small. Too brittle. You have to stretch your understanding to wield these weapons."

Perry opened his eyes. "I'm just—I don't think I can," Perry said. "I'm a human boy."

"You're stretching, though," she said. "You could have died back there."

"Would you have let me?"

"Doesn't matter," she said. "You didn't. Now. Come."

Together they ascended the steps and crossed the verandah to the villa's circular wooden front door. Denkine opened the door, gestured with her chin.

Perry had read once about the quietest room in the world. It was in Minnesota, and it was so quiet, so still, that humans could hear nothing but the workings of their own body. The villa's interior was hushed this way. Perry heard the ticking of his heart, the soft hiss of his own breathing, the noise of his own blood.

Should I take off my shoes? he thought.

Yes, Denkine answered. *Where you're going, they'll only weigh you down.*

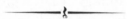

"I know how this looks," Scander said as he unlocked the driver's side door of a car that looked to Brendy like a baby shoe. "But nobody here seems to mind me driving. Anyway, I'm good at it, so don't worry."

He unlocked Brendy's door, and she didn't hesitate to slide into the passenger seat. She rarely got to ride up front in a car, as those seats were usually reserved for her parents. Now it crossed her mind that she was entering a stranger's car, but the thought didn't worry her as much as she thought it normally would.

"How you got your own car when you just a kid?" she asked. She was impressed, but didn't intend to let on.

"I seem like a kid to you?" he asked. "I figured if you were magic enough to cross the Water, you'd probably have the Sight."

"I see sumpthin', but I dunno," Brendy said. "I'm not magic."

"Oh," Scander said. "You're one of *those*."

"One of what?"

Scander shrugged as he turned the key in the ignition. "Look, it's none of my business, but in my experience, it's not a good idea to resist the Call."

Brendy wrinkled her nose. "No wonder they lets you drive," she said. "You sound like a grown-up."

"You say that like it's a bad thing."

"Grown-ups are dumb," Brendy said. "But maybe you one of the good ones. Seems like you helpin' me out, anyways."

It was clear now that even in this little baby-shoe car, Brendy was too small to see over the dash. The situation frustrated her, but she resolved not to let on about that, either. Even if he was a man that looked like a boy, Scander carried himself with grace and dignity, and she didn't want to seem like a baby in his eyes.

"So where we going?" she asked, wiggling her legs as Scander turned on the heat.

"I'm not sure what you're after, and I don't think you are, either, so we're headed to the Asking Tree. It'll give you a riddle, at least, and if we can solve it, we can get you your talisman or whatever."

"'Tha Asking Tree,'" Brendy repeated. She bugged out her eyes and rolled them.

"Yeah, it's...I mean, it won't be as easy as it sounds."

"Why not?"

"Well, it's Bacchus Sunday and it's after noon, so she's almost certainly drunk."

When Brendy got out of the car, she felt like the wind was trying to blow right through her. She hugged herself and shivered. She hoped she could finish up fast and go back...somewhere.

A strange voice slanted through the cold of the afternoon:

I cry inside to know you're gone
Don't know where you went or for how long
Come back come back come back to me doll
You done me wrong
I'm passing small.

The voice was deep and rich, but to Brendy, it sounded like a woman—maybe even someone she'd recognize if her head wasn't so fuzzy. As she searched her dim memories, she nearly forgot the chill.

"Hey," Scander said, interrupting her musing. "Take this." He had pulled off his crimson-colored hooded sweatshirt and now handed it to Brendy.

She thought about refusing to take the fleece, or at least asking if he'd be too cold, but instead pulled it over her head. It was a little big, but only by a couple sizes. "Thank you, Scandy," she said, and batted her eyelashes him.

Scander seemed caught off guard. He reddened and inclined his head a little, searching Brendy's face. As they regarded each other Brendy understood that the brightness in Scander's eyes was a raw red sadness.

"So…" she said quietly. "You gone tell me how you a kid and grown at the same time?"

Scander shook his curly head. "That would bore us both to death. Just…listen. When I was your age, I crossed worlds. I had grand adventures. It's hard to know until the traveling and fighting and magic are done how much they change you. So hold on to yourself."

"Don't you worry none bout that," Brendy said, and hugged herself again. "I always got me, ya heard?"

Scander smirked in spite of himself. "Come on," he said. "She's in here."

The house was circular, built from big stone bricks of varying sizes. Once they passed down the little curved alleyway leading to the oblong front door, Brendy got the impression that this structure had been here far longer than the rest of the city. An ageless weariness baked from its surfaces, but there was something sweet about it that made Brendy feel a swirl of emotions similar to the ones she'd felt looking into Scander's sad, haunted eyes.

Inside the house, the singing was louder, clearer, but Brendy couldn't parse lyrics. The whole house was constructed around an enormous live oak whose trunk was broader than most of the houses on the block. Its branches reached this way and that like dancing limbs. It reminded her of the octopi she'd seen at the aquarium, but instead of eight tentacles, it had arms and arms and arms that sprouted stiff paddle-shaped leaves in a riot of colors. Some were black with an iridescent oil-slick sheen, others were a truly metallic gold, some a gleaming silver, and some colors seemed like only hints to Brendy, as if their frequency lay beyond human sight. It was still winter outside, but in here there was a breathy warmth, and the air smelled sticky and green, like pine sap.

To Brendy's right stood a short staircase leading up to another curved platform, and to her left, a wooden ladder bridged a longer gap between floors. It was almost as if, instead of being built, the house had been gathered against the tree the way Brendy gathered dresses against her body. A keen understanding pierced her heart: She would remember this place only in dreams because the knowledge of it didn't belong in her world.

The voice had finished singing and now spoke a little too carefully, its *T*s and *G*s like little pinpricks of sound... *That one? That's a favorite. Willie "The Lion" Smith wrote it in his sleep and forgot by morning. I always hoped he'd come see me so I could sing it back to him.*

"Come with me," Scander said, and took Brendy's hand again to lead her up the stairs. "Tree!" he called as they walked. "I'm back, and I've brought a friend. She has questions!"

Questions? said the disembodied voice, but as it did, the light pulsed and the tree's branches flexed slightly. *It's Bacchus Sunday, my baby. This my off day.*

"This is a special case," Scander said. By now, he and Brendy had climbed to the next floor and crossed another broad landing. Instead of curving past the tree's trunk, this one had a jutting platform leading directly to a carved smiling wooden face as wide as a garbage truck was long. Its eyes were closed, and when the tree spoke the carved mouth didn't move. "She crossed the Water to meet you."

Fine, fine. Show her to me, at least.

Scander nudged Brendy from behind. She stepped forward and curtsied at the tree's sleeping face.

The tree gasped, and now its face grew animated. Its eyes flew open and its mouth formed a perfect O of surprise. *Why, it's you!*

"Yessss!" Brendy hissed. "Wait. Who I'm is?"

Brendolyn Wayminute Aubergine Tangeriffic Timbuktu Hot Cheetos Liberry Whispers Graves!

Brendy giggled. "Guuuurl! Where we met?"

One of my flowers made its way to you, and you cared for them beautifully! Ask away! Shoot!

The tree's face settled back to sleep, but it seemed different from Brendy's own. Brendy used her face *all the time*, for talking and looking, showing emotion. The Asking Tree must use hers only when she was especially excited. That made sense, in Brendy's estimation, since trees must not need faces—she didn't remember ever seeing a tree who had one.

"Well, okay," Brendy said. "Let...me...think."

What you want to know?

"Ah. Okay. Um," Brendy said. She struggled to phrase the question in a way that wouldn't make her sound stupid. But she wasn't stupid, she was just *young*. Daddy Deke always said, *Ain't nothing wrong with not knowing long as you willing to learn.* "What I'm doing here, anyhow?"

Great! Grand! Wonderful! Superb! Do you want a big answer or a small one?

"Big, then little?" Brendy said. "Or no: little, *then* big."

You are here to retrieve a weapon that will aid you in your quest to save your city.

Now it was Brendy's turn to form her mouth into an O. "Thaaaaaat's right!" she said. "Yay! Yes! Now what's the big answer?"

Inside you lives a light that your loved ones will need if they are to save your city. They don't just love you, they need your cheer, your warmth, and your humor to meet their trials.

"*Oh,*" Brendy said.

Have I disappointed you?

"Naw," Brendy said. "It's just…I mean, I *been* knowing that. Scandy said you'd have a riddle for me."

As it happens, I do have a riddle for you, but it's not the kind you're expecting.

"Oh, word?"

The tree laughed low and throaty. *Yes*, she said. *Word.*

"What you got for me, then?"

Hold out your hand.

Brendy thrust out her right hand and clapped her left over her eyes. "And close my eyes?"

You don't have to close your eyes.

"They're closed! They're closed!"

Something small and hard dropped into Brendy's palm. She opened her eyes to see a pebble about the size of a marble and shaped like a kidney bean resting on her hand's wrinkle. "What…? What this is?"

That's the riddle, my baby.

"But it's a rock, though."

It was passed down in your family from Wise Woman to Wise Woman until Nola was born and it was brought to me for safekeeping. I knew some-day one of you would return to collect it.

She tried to speak calmly but she heard herself shout the question. "I'm a Wise Woman?"

I don't know, the tree said. *You have a Way about you, but you might be something greater still.*

"Oh," Brendy said. She sucked her teeth. "Well, damn. Uh. So this rock what I came for?"

Yes.

"Then how I get home?"

The tree shivered and opened her mouth. Instead of forming an O, it stretched open wider and wider until Brendy saw the corridor of its throat stretching and stretching toward a distant glow. The tunnel seemed even longer than the tree was wide.

Brendy laughed, nervous, and took a closer look at the tree's lips. One thing she didn't see was teeth. Maybe that meant the Asking Tree wasn't offering to eat her up. Wait. A question. She should ask a question.

"It's safe for me to go in there, right?"

In the way that you mean, yes, but very very difficult.

"And that's the way back . . . where I came from?"

Yes.

"She's telling the truth," Scander said. "If she takes questions, she always tells the truth."

"Ohhhhkay," Brendy said slowly, then brightened. "Wait. Tree!"

Yes?

"How you get all drunk?"

Every Bacchus Sunday morning, citizens come into my house and take turns pouring beer wine and spirits into my soil. I spend the day drinking it and singing and it is the best thing.

Brendy raised her eyebrows. She didn't know what to say to that.

"Another satisfied customer," Scander said, and held up his hand for a high five that never came.

"All right, all right," Brendy said. "I gotta hurry. Can't waste time."

Scander frowned, then seemed to decide against mentioning whatever was bothering him.

"Boy, what?" Brendy asked.

"Time doesn't pass where you live," Scander said. "So, really, you have all eternity."

Brendy felt hot and cold all over. *"What?"*

A caught look appeared on Scander's face, and then he laughed hard. "Psych, you're mine," he said. "I got you *good! Look at your face!"*

The hot-cold feeling didn't recede. Brendy wanted to ask Scander what he'd meant, but she had the feeling she'd been gone a long time, that she'd better get back . . . wherever.

She pushed her worry aside. Of *course* time passed there. She dimly remembered being younger, smaller—but only as dimly as she remembered everything else about her life.

Slowly, she approached the Asking Tree's open wooden mouth, her rock—*just a rock? Really?*—held tight in her fist. She looked back at Scander one last time. He looked smaller, and even sadder, than he had before. What if he hadn't been kidding...? Then she could always come back and ask him later.

"Okay," she said. "All right. Sing me a song and I'll go, Tree."

Boyyyy I knew I knew when we first met
Always gonna love you don'tcha never forget
You got me runnin' and a-hidin'. Got me hidin' and a peepin'!
But I'll always come home
Always come home to ya, yeah!

The tree went on singing as Brendy climbed over her wooden bottom lip and started down her throat.

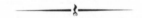

Denkine led Perry through a large, high-ceilinged kitchen and touched a disguised panel on the wall beside the stainless-steel refrigerator. The appliance glided out of its stall and rolled silently to the left. Now a doorway stood revealed. Perry followed her through it and down a short flight of steps where a dormant torch stood nestled in a sconce on the wall. She grabbed the torch and it flared to life. Then they started down, down again.

"Perry, you're so smart," Denkine said. "You've such a curious mind. What you need to understand is that there are situations where orderly, rational thought won't help you. When you won't be able to ask the right questions because the answers can only come in the language of spirits."

Perry hoped Denkine wouldn't see him shake his head at the idea. Now the smooth walls had given way to rougher stone as the stairway curved down the rocky wall. Perry smelled stone, moss, lichen, and far below, water...?

What was the point of climbing so high only to descend again? And hadn't Denkine said these islands were eggs from the World Serpent? Shouldn't there be a titanic fossilized embryo in here?

"Perry," Denkine groaned. "We came up the mountain but we're not going down *inside* it. We're somewhere else."

"Do you have to read my mind all the time?"

"I'm trying to help you, munchkin."

Perry swallowed and walked silently for a time as he turned her words over in his mind. He looked over his shoulder again to tell Denkine her words made no sense. Instead of a woman or a giant following behind him, Perry saw a six-foot pillar of holy, blazing fire. The light abraded his mind, threatened to scour his consciousness away.

Perry barked a shout and pressed his hands over his eyes. He still saw the fire this way, but maybe it wouldn't kill him. Maybe—!

Perry blinked, disoriented. Denkine was grasping his shoulder tightly with her free hand and shaking him as she held her torch in the other. "Hey. Hey!"

"What what what what?"

When she saw he had returned to himself, Denkine stopped shaking him.

"I don't know where I am," Perry said. "I don't know where I am, and I'm going to die here."

"Yes," Denkine said darkly. "You very much will—unless you *get it together!*"

They resumed their descent, but Perry wasn't sure for how long. It felt like forever—*Forever and a day make a month of Sundays*, some dear remembered voice sounded in his mind, but Perry couldn't remember its owner. Eventually they came to a smooth-edged grotto whose walls and ceiling dripped with slime and mineral deposits. The stone platform on which they stood slanted abruptly down into a kidney-shaped pool of wine-dark water. Perry kept looking from the pool to Denkine's face as she held the torch, waiting. If she was fire herself, why did she need the torch? Was it for Perry's benefit?

He suspected what was supposed to happen next, but he couldn't bring himself to believe it. "Are there... animals in there?"

Denkine's face softened. "I know this is hard for you, bibi," she said. "I'm sorry I snapped. Of *course* you're afraid. Fear is useful most of the time, but people like you—"

"People—? What—?"

"*Heroes*, Perry. Heroes are the ones who push past their fear and do what needs doing!"

"...How?"

Denkine sighed. "I don't...I don't know. There must be as many ways as there are heroes."

Like Hannibal. Perry clamped down on his worry and his fear. Before he could change his mind, he turned and ran for the water. He peeled off his polo shirt in what felt like a single motion. He took a big breath, pressed his hands together, bent, dove.

Breaking the water sent an electric shock rattling through him, but it was warm—at first. Eyes closed, Perry swam down until directions stopped making sense to his body. He opened his eyes and saw a glow far below him. Was the light purple, or was its color neutral and the purple from the water through which he swam?

Something brushed against Perry's thigh, bringing with it a terrible cold. Perry swam faster. It seemed a bad idea to look around for whatever had touched him. In books and movies, it was *always* a bad idea. He kicked his legs and imagined he was Prince Namor swimming toward a sunken kingdom. A moment, then another. Another, and Perry's lungs began to burn. The cold was worse now, and the Imp of the Perverse was with him. It was a little tickling voice at the back of his mind saying, *You're not cut out for this, boy. You're no hero. Just breathe in. Breathe in as deep as you can and drown. Save yourself the misery...*

Perry gritted his teeth and swam on. The dark voice changed tactics.

How far have you come by now, do you think...? Maybe you can make it down to that treasure or whatever it is, but ain't no way you'll be able to swim back up. Why not just...drown? Better to drown than let the dead hands take you...

That last thought terrified him. He was as frightened as he'd ever been. Beneath the waters of an alien world, swimming for his life with no idea how he'd survive.

The glow below had intensified, and Perry wished it hadn't. The water around him was alive with severed arms, hands, fingers writhing and whipping like swarming fish. Higher up, only one or two had come close to him, but now they closed in. They grabbed at his shorts, snatched at his ankles. For every one that fell away, two others found purchase and kept it. They pulled at him, slowing Perry's swimming to a crawl. Every touch sent cold needles lancing into Perry's flesh.

Terror was a bright black globe at the center of his skull. The more Perry fought to ignore it, the larger it grew. He swallowed, forcing the terror out of his braincase and down his throat to his belly. That stilled his panic some, allowed him to think again.

Perry frowned and cocked his head, the grabbing hands and limbs momentarily forgotten. He'd drawn close enough now to see that the thing he swam toward was not a treasure chest but a steamer trunk. He'd seen it before, he felt sure. He considered everything that had happened since he appeared on the beach. Had he walked past it in the inn somewhere?

No. It was from Before. He'd seen it in his own world.

Perry's spirits buoyed. He swam harder. The dead still grabbed at him, but now that he thought about it, Perry realized that none of them had kept hold of his wrists, his ankles, his actual body. He considered struggling out of his shorts, but there wasn't time. He swam harder, faster.

Perry reached the trunk and struggled to pry it open. He didn't think how badly he needed to breathe. He didn't think about the constrictive pain in his chest begging to be replaced by anything, if not air, then water.

The trunk refused to open. Perry's vision had begun to dim even in the trunk's glowing light. *Don't breathe in don't breathe in don't breathe in there's no air.*

Or, you know . . . do. Just let it happen . . .

Perry tried to scream. Water rushed into his open mouth. The fingers pulled at his hair now. At his skin. Enraged, Perry punched the trunk's lock as hard as he could. Before he knew what was happening, a powerful suction took hold of him. Perry fought to swim the other way, but when he turned his head, he saw that the disembodied limbs had gathered together to form a leering compound face whose eyes rolled madly in their sockets. Its jaws worked silently, laughing its triumph.

A rush of frothy water carried Perry swiftly away, and without meaning to, he breathed in, whooping, knowing he'd failed, knowing that this was what it meant to die trying.

He hadn't even found the talisman, the weapon, he'd come here to retrieve.

Barry Obamz

Casey awakened in a sweat. The room was as hot as it was dark, and the darkness was complete. He lay still for a moment, trying to let his speeding heart calm. Something brushed underneath the mattress. Casey thought of whales or dolphins surfacing from the ocean depths, then diving back down in quick succession. The idea calmed him a bit until he realized that his mattress lay on his bedroom floor.

Dog's under the bed. Someone had spoken the words aloud. Was it Casey? Why was it so damn dark in here? And the heat wrung beads of sweat from Casey's forehead. He felt as if he sat in a little vacuole pressed upon by the seething alien night. The darkness had a weight, a shape, volition.

Fear sickened Casey's stomach. The thing under the bed—impossibly under the bed—humped up again. God damn it.

I don't have a dog! Casey tried to say, but his voice hid in his chest. He touched his solar plexus and felt the wet bandage there. He knew somehow that he'd had top surgery, but it didn't take. His breasts would grow back any day now. His body was betraying him—again.

With his left arm, Casey propped himself up. He'd been wrong about the bed. It wasn't a mattress on a carpeted floor—it was a hospital bed. The thing underneath it was a dog after all—but that wasn't any better.

"I don't need you." Ximena's voice. "I need—"

No. Not Ximena. Casey had left her back in Baltimore. Then— he realized now that he must have left the apartment's front door unlocked when he went to bed. Someone—a woman—had wandered in from the street.

She stood in front of the bricked-up fireplace. She wore her hair wrapped up in a fringed scarf, and her wrinkled face was mostly nose. She must have been the one who'd spoken.

Darkness still reigned, Casey realized, but somehow it failed to touch the homeless woman. Casey saw her clearly, as if she'd been lit by a ring light. Casey tried to call out to her—or he tried to scream. He wasn't sure. His breasts were back now. His mind raced. Did he have a binder here? Could he find one before work?

The woman was speaking a language Casey didn't know. He recognized the word "cabeza," he thought, but that was it. The rest was too fast, too rough, choked by decades of phlegm and tobacco smoke.

He smelled cancer, that sickly-sweet funk that had been everywhere on the oncology floor at Johns Hopkins—

Casey forced himself awake. Breathing heavily, he sat up and tried to collect himself. Without thinking, he tapped his forearms with opposite hands, touched his neck, his scalp. He waited a beat, still breathing, and brought his hands to his chest. No bandage. No blood. He fell back against the mattress, whooping his relief.

For a moment, he just lay with his hands covering his face. When he checked his phone, he saw that it was 6:15 in the morning— another ten minutes and his alarm would ring.

His panic had receded enough that Casey was able to observe it without being swallowed. That woman. He didn't want spirits in his house. He didn't want bodiless spirits in his house. The only one welcome was his grandmother, and he doubted she'd ever contact him.

Jesus.

Jesus, God.

He thought of the Hanging Judge and had to admit—it could have been worse.

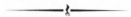

A thunderstorm had come through while Casey slept, and the morning was unseasonably cool. A thick fog filled the city as Casey ventured out early. The way it lay on the ground made him feel as if he lived in a hidden kingdom.

Casey told himself he was stopping by the Walgreens on St. Charles before work to pick up a sketchpad—which was true—but he knew as soon as he stepped inside that he'd be buying a pack of menthols on the way out. He had started smoking as a freshman in high school when a heavy, dark-skinned girl with a gap between her front teeth had held him in her lap and taught him how to drag for real instead of smoking for show. When he thought back to that night at the party— he couldn't remember anymore whose party it had been—Casey found it hard to regret picking up such a filthy habit.

The *William Tell* overture blared nonsensically as Casey pulled Ole Girl into the lot. At the cobbled intersection of Felicity and St. Charles, an elderly homeless man stood playing the saxophone. The way he frowned and rocked made him look lost in the music, but every note was out of tune. That, combined with the idiot classical music, added to the dreamy irreality of the morning.

The old man sounded like he might have been hot shit once upon a time. Casey wondered if he was some unsung session musician who had cut records on one of the city's small labels before the crackdown in the seventies drove so many venues and musicians out of business.

He caught a glimpse of himself reflected in the glass of the automatic door and for a moment didn't recognize himself. His fade would need a touch-up soon, but it was his eyes that bothered him. They looked hollow, ringed with a darkness that reminded Casey of the raccoons running free in City Park. That nightmare had done a number on him—but it wasn't just that. He'd had trouble sleeping long before his terrifying dream. Jaylon's tag rose up in his mind.

The image had been at the back of every thought he'd had since he saw it. The wonder was that he could think of anything else.

He didn't know what to call the phenomenon yet. The…anomaly. Something about it seemed blurry in his mind—as if it couldn't quite contain the memory. Casey sucked his teeth and shook his head.

Casey didn't like any of the sketchbooks, so he picked the cheapest one and grabbed himself a pack of pencils. As he marched up to the cash register, he saw that a line had formed. He checked the time on his phone and saw that waiting would be no problem. When he took his place at the back of the line, he recognized the man standing in front of him.

"Hey," he said. "Foxx King!"

Foxx leaned his whole upper half back as he looked over his shoulder. "Who's askin'?"

"I'm Casey," Casey said. "I saw you at Three Muses last week."

Now King turned around, shuffling backwards a little as the line advanced. "Hey, yeah, I remember you," he said. "You was right in front, vibing."

"I'm still thinking about that set."

"Oh, word?" Foxx said. "That was a hot one…" He glanced at Casey's hands, and something changed between them. Before, his demeanor had been friendly but reserved, but now his eyes lit up, and it was as if they'd stepped over some invisible threshold together. "Sketchpad, huh?" Foxx said. "You draw?"

"I'm rusty these days," Casey said. "But yeah. I used to bomb all over town before the Storm."

"What your name was?"

"C4S3," Casey said.

"Just your government name?"

"The A is a 4 and the E is a 3." His face heated slightly. "I was a kid."

"You was good, though, wasn't you?"

"You know," Casey said. "I think I really was."

"Why you stopped, then?"

Casey opened his mouth to say "Katrina," but of course that wasn't true. "It got away from me," he said. "Got scary."

Foxx shrugged with his whole body. "Wise old man told me once that if you scared, you headed in the right direction."

Casey didn't have a response to that.

Later, when he slid back into the driver's seat, he felt a hum inside him, similar to the singing of a crystal goblet when a wet fingertip is drawn along its edge. Was that what Foxx had noticed in him? Was that why their conversation had changed? He thought what H. T. would say: *Man, you think too much. Just relax. Just be.* If he learned to relax would the hum in him rise or recede...?

As Casey pulled out of the lot and headed toward work he remembered the indecipherable speech he'd heard in his dream. Was it possible to dream in a language you didn't already know? He had a habit of making decisions unconsciously and noticing later. When, exactly, had he decided to start sketching again?

He scowled, not at traffic, but at his own thoughts. It felt painfully narcissistic but he couldn't help connecting his decision with the visitation in the night—for it felt like more than a nightmare. Casey never had responded well to threats.

"Niggamancer," he said aloud. Then, *"Fuck."* He'd forgotten the cigarettes.

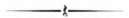

Casey sketched idly throughout the workday. As he made his prospect calls and firmed up his task list for the coming weeks, his right hand moved whenever it was free. At first it was kiddie shit: That fat angular *S* whose origin nobody seemed to know, heavily shadowed geometric shapes popping out from the page. Superman and Batman's insignias. He even tried his hand at a Ninja Turtle. That one turned out well enough once he stopped thinking about the Mirage or Archie comics and improvised his own style. When he was done, Raphael growled from the page, brandishing the middle fingers of both mutated hands while his trademark sai rested in his belt.

Casey thought he'd feel more the first time he dared to draw a figure again. He was proud enough of his work, but the drawing was just a drawing. It seemed to bear no relation to the strange works Jaylon had shown him—or to the misbehaving mural from before the Storm. Looking at it, he felt himself relax.

When he cold-called Baker Ready Mix to solicit a donation for the school, he spoke breezily and authoritatively about the high school, its mission, and its programs. Soon enough he was on the line with Arnold Baker himself, discussing just how much the school could expect from him before the third quarter closed in September.

When he got back to his apartment that evening and flipped through the sketchbook's pages, he found an image he didn't recognize—painstaking detail rendered in pencil and blue ink. It was a black woman—not quite Ximena—her hair was twisted into Bantu knots, a style Ximena had never liked—and the image had been carefully composed to communicate motion. The woman's eyes appeared over and over, floating above her face to mark where she had inclined her head, cocked her neck, cast her gaze from side to side.

Looking at it, Casey couldn't help thinking of Jaylon's impossible tag. Of art spinning out of control, taking on a life of its own.

"No," he said aloud as he stood just outside his kitchen, the lights still off. "My life is my life."

But was it?

Casey's phone trilled in his pocket before the thought's wicked edge could lacerate his mind. He answered without looking, hoping it was a telemarketer or political campaign. "Yeah."

"I did it," Jayl said.

"Oh shit." Cold fear walked up Casey's spine.

"Nigga, come look!"

December 2015

There was a lot of talk in New Orleans about which restaurant made the best fried chicken. Casey had never truly understood the controversy. He loved Willie Mae's Scotch House best of all—it was a medium-sized spot on St. Ann in the Treme with white siding and dark green trim—and the chicken there was batter-fried golden brown. Truly delicious—but to pronounce it "the best" didn't seem right.

When Jaylon picked Casey and Ximena up from the airport on the Tuesday before Christmas, Willie Mae's was their first desti-nation. As Casey slid into the passenger seat of Jaylon's Jeep, Jayl nudged him with his elbow. Casey knew what that meant—he approved Casey's choice of partners.

As they took their table in the back dining room, Casey took a good look at his cousin: Jayl looked well cared for. He'd never been ashy—not in public—but now he was better moisturized. He looked like a more expensive version of the cousin Casey knew.

"You looking good, baby," Casey said.

"Aw, thank ya, cuz. You too—and you ain't told me you landed you a solid *dime*." He beamed at Ximena.

That was something Casey had always loved about Jaylon—a lot of hood niggas exhibited a stone-faced stoicism, but Jaylon was always expressive—larger-than-life without being obnoxious.

Grinning, Ximena mimed a few model poses.

"So what's up?" Casey asked. "Lemme guess—you won the Powerball and you need help spending all that money."

"Mane, you know I ain't got no hunnid mil," Jaylon smiled, shook his head. "But...I *did* get a grant. From the Strandelf Foundation."

"Oh shit!" Casey said. "For real?" He'd seen their annual grant as he prospected for education funding: seventy thousand dollars.

"I've heard of them," Ximena said. "They're...*big*."

"Welllll, yeah," Jaylon said. "It's the Big One. That's one reason I wanted y'all to come out for Christmas," Jayl explained. "I got the call about the grant the same day I met Barry."

"Barry who?" Casey asked.

The waitress appeared to pour water and take orders. Casey went with the three-piece, dark, with sides of mac and cheese and butter beans. He might even get a slice of cheesecake to go—for his money, it really *was* the best in town.

When the waitress withdrew, Jaylon picked up where he'd left off. "Barry Obamz, y'all. I met the President of the Whole-Ass United Muh Fuggin' *States* here."

"Nigga whaaaaat?" Casey asked, then blushed. He tried not to throw that word around in public.

"You met Obama?" Ximena said. "When? Tell *everything*."

"Bout four months ago," Jaylon said. "Shit was crazy. I knew he was in town, and when me and my boy Von got here, I saw all these FBI-lookin' cats with macaroni earpieces hanging out. They wasn't, like, *at attention*, though, and I figured if Barry was coming inside to eat, they woulda patted us down or some shit.

"We was sitting right here at this very table, and Von got up to hit the head. Well. That was when Mistuh POTUS just glided into the room. I swear, it was like my nigga had skates on. So as soon as he comes in, errybody in here rushes him. Except me. I'm a big dude, so I figured I'd stay where I was at and just watch. He had a crazy crazy vibe. You remember when Charlie Murphy said Rick James had a aura? Mane, it was like that.

"So he's shakin' hands and shit, and I'm sitting here with my picked-clean chicken just grinning at him across the room, and all the sudden, he zeroes in on me and crossed the room. He parted the crowd like it was water. He held out his hand to me and he was like"—Jaylon slid into a note-perfect Obama impression—"'Uhh, what's your name?'

" 'Jaylon, sir. Jaylon Bridgewater.'

" 'Jaylon Bridgewater. It's great to meet you. You've got some great taste in chicken.'

"And he walked out that door." Jaylon gestured with his chin to the back exit. "When he walked out, this *shout* rose up from the neighborhood. I ain't heard nothing like that since the Saints won the Super Bowl."

"*Damn*," Casey said.

"I know, right? Von came back out right after he was gone, and I felt so bad for him. And then—"

"Oh my God," Ximena said. "There's more?"

"Yeah, so on my way home, I called Aunt Manda and told her what happened, and she was like, 'Soon as you get home, write him a letter and send him a painting to the White House. Something small, but get it in the mail, and mention meeting him in your note.' So I did that shit."

"You sent him a painting?" Casey asked.

"Sure did," Jaylon said. "And a one-page letter about what his, ah, presidency means to me. And last week, I got a answer." He paused. "You know, I'm sure it's a canned response. He might never have even seen the painting—but maybe he did, and I guess that's enough for me. I memorized the card as soon as I saw it:

"'Thank you for your gift. It was such a nice gesture, and we were touched by your generosity. Your thoughtfulness reflects the extraordinary kindness of the American people. More than anything, please know that your kind words and support for our shared values motivate us each and every day. We wish you the very best.' And he and Michelle both signed it..."

"That's..." Casey said. "That's powerful."

"It is," Jaylon said. "Same day I met him, I sent my letter and the painting—it was a portrait of Mookie where his clothes and the background are modern, but Mookie is all street. Always street—and as I was getting back to the cut, my phone rang, and that was Tanks from the Foundation telling me my application was approved." He fell silent for a moment, looking down at his plate. "It took me a long time to figure out what it means."

"What?" Ximena asked.

Jaylon smiled, and his eyes were damp. "Just...It's the biggest thing that's ever happened to me. Meeting Obama was just part of it. I turned a corner. So...so it turns out I'm not wasting my life..."

———————❧———————

August 2018

Dread pooled in the pit of Casey's belly. When he'd first read Jaylon's text it had been a little trickle inside him, but now it threatened to take over his whole body—keep him from pressing Ole Girl's pedals.

Casey's stomach flipped, weightless, as he saw a thick black plume of smoke rising to the north of I-10. It was too far away to tell for sure, but it looked as if it issued from Jaylon's workshop. But that made no sense—Jaylon had some flammable paint in there, sure, but this looked like the kind of chemical fire you might see coming from an oil refinery.

His fears were well-founded. The shop's heavy doors had been blown off their hinges and lay twisted on the neutral ground amid a shower of broken glass and debris.

Casey parked hastily and got out of the car without bothering to close the door. He wavered for a moment, staring at the column of smoke and thinking of the Ten Commandments. Then he broke into a run.

As he reached the neutral ground, something slammed into him from the left. A man had attacked him, dragged him to the ground. Casey fought, hammering with his fists.

The man cried out, shielded his head.

"Get off me! You let me the fuck—*!"*

Another explosion shook the world. It seemed to rattle something in Casey's head, because even lying on his back in the grass, he felt an awful dizziness. A wave of force rolled over him from the ruined studio space, and Casey felt like the earth was about to open up and swallow him whole. He wished it would.

The white man who tackled him was sitting up now, shaking his head. *"You can't! You can't go there! You can't go in there, man! I'm sorry! I'm sorry! I'm sorry! I'm sorry!"*

Casey held his head as a scream tore its way from his throat. He thought just clearly enough to hope he wouldn't remember any of this.

THE DEAD TAXI

When the starting pistol fired and the gate slid up, Caesar Macklin shivered. All day he'd felt an eerie, weightless vibration in his chest and hoped he knew what it was. Today was the day his luck turned, when he finally won enough to cover his debts and then some. One way or another, this was his last bet.

The handlers dove out of the way and the camels exploded out of their starting positions, their two-toed feet pounding the dirt. Without meaning to, Caesar shot to his feet. Beer sloshed from his transparent cup to splash the old woman sitting on the next riser down, but Caesar barely noticed. The crowd roared, and he howled his camel's name, *"Fillllllllayyy Gumbooooooooh Ya-yaaaaaaaaaaaaah!"*

Caesar spilled the rest of his beer down the front of his sport shirt as Gumbo Ya-ya pulled into first place, spurred by the whipping of its robot jockey. Time elongated like a hank of saltwater taffy.

"Yes! YEAAAAAAH!" Caesar screamed. Now he felt as if he'd left his body. He saw himself at the far end of a blazing golden tunnel thrusting his crumpled beer cup in his hand.

He blinked, and quick-cut, he lay with the riser digging into his back. An enormous Black man with eyes so blank he looked like a statue bent over him, glaring into Caesar's face as he held the barrel of a gun to Caesar's chin. His excitement turned to terror, Caesar thought he might already have loosed his bowels.

CAIN'T GET RIGHT, growled the man. GOT A FRIEND I WANTCHA TA MEET, HEARD?

With his free hand, the man snatched the front of Caesar's shirt and lifted him easily from the seat, keeping the gun's barrel trained on Caesar's face. He knew he'd been watching for something. He knew something important had been happening, but as he stared into the black circular space, he couldn't remember what it had been. He clenched his eyes shut.

The scents of stale beer and turned earth and summer sweat disappeared, replaced by those of mold and dust and piles and piles of books and yellowed paper.

THIS HIM?

yes o yes it is cant get right indeed

FOUNT HIM AT THE FAIRGROUNDS JUSS LIKE YOU SAID.

is he sleeping passed out from terror

BREATHING LIKE THAT, HE PROLLY AWAKE. JUST SCARED IS ALL.

open your eyes dear ditty tune unless you prefer to lose your limbs before you die

Caesar forced his eyes open and the bottom dropped out of his belly. Raggedy streams of paper hung from the vaulted ceiling above him, and a terrible white grinning face hung above him like a rotten moon. One of its eyes was shut, its lid sunken as if the ball had gone, and the other was red and mad and glowing. Its throat worked, and for a moment Caesar had no idea what was wrong with it, but then he realized—the thing had swallowed something awful, wriggling, horribly alive, and it fought to keep from vomiting whatever it was straight into Caesar's face.

"Pluh-please!" Caesar stammered. "I—I—I can get it for you. All of it. Just don't— Don't! *Please*."

hail and welcome friend said the wraith. tell me what do you believe your name to be

"Suh-suh-Caesar Macklin, sir. I can guh-guarantee, whoever you lookin' for, I ain't him."

you aren t the one or you can get the money which is it caesar macklin

"Buh-*both*!" Ceaser's voice broke. "Whatever you want! *Please!*"

He didn't hear the shot that killed him.

The wraith bristled like a feral cat and stretched its mouth into a hateful yellow square. imbecile youve shot him youve killed how dare you

YOU THE KINDA CAT LIKES TO PLAY WIF HIS FOOD, BUT THAT DON'T DO NOTHIN' FOR ME.

The wraith hissed and rippled, turned briefly away to spit a moccasin onto the carpeted floor. For a split second, the serpent lay still; then it began to slither away.

mister Shelton said the haint, it is through the enactment of my plan that we will be liberated from our prison so never do not ever interrupt my interrogation again understood

The spirit and the big man glared at each other for a moment.

Then, finally, ION WORK FOR YOU, DIG? WE PODNAHS.

yes partners just so those were the terms we established

GLAD YOU REMEMBER. I'D HATE TO HAVE TO REMIND YO ASS. His stony glare softened some. DID KILLIN' THIS ONE WORK LIKE WE THOUGHT?

The wraith lifted its blade of a nose to scent the air. i believe so yes i believe youll find when you investigate that the races at the fairgrounds and the speechless mules and horses are all gone

Stagger Lee grinned mirthlessly. THEN WE RIGHT ON TRACK. I'LL GO GET THE NEXT ONE.

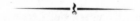

Miss Yvette stood barefoot in a cold rain. She was running from something, she knew. An unseen pursuer that seemed to be not just behind her, but overhead as well. As she hurried across muddy ground, a cold gathered in her feet that she was sure she'd never get out. She—

Thunder cracked overhead, and cracked again.

With the rain falling so hard, she could barely see, but when she squinted she could make out shapes in the twilight. Pine trees, or giant, heavily skirted women standing at regular intervals. They were too big to notice her. They didn't care what was happening. They just—

That thunder. That damn thunder, she—

Yvette jerked awake. Peaches sat on the sofa across from her, knees drawn up so that her feet—they were clean, thank God—rested on the surface of the royal purple cushion. "What was that?" she asked.

"The kitchen," Peaches said. "I think they back."

Carefully, Yvette rose from her chair and tested her balance. She was still bone weary after her first spell in Lord knew how long, but she no longer felt ready to collapse under her own weight. She crossed through the dining room to the kitchen with its pale yellow accent tile and black-and-white checked floor. The refrigerator hummed pleasantly away and the cabinets stood closed. A muffled scraping clatter came from the broad bottom cabinet to the left of the doubled sink, then the battered enamel stockpot Yvette had inherited from her mother edged open the door and fell to the checked floor. Its lid rolled off and across the kitchen until it met the stove's warmer drawer and clattered unsteadily to a stop.

Soon after, Brendy climbed out to stand wide-eyed in the kitchen. She wore a smudged red hooded sweatshirt Yvette had never seen before. "It's winter here, too?" she said.

Now that her daughter mentioned it, Yvette realized it was cold—and not the pleasant chill from the AC set to seventy-three degrees. It couldn't be warmer than sixty-eight in here. Brendy rushed to her mother and Yvette bent to squeeze her tight. Tears swam in her vision as she smelled the cocoa butter grease on the girl's little scalp. "Welcome home, sweet pea," she said. "Thanks for coming back to me." Then, "Where's Perry?"

Brendy spoke into her mother's breasts. "Ioknow," she said. "He musta gone somewhere else. I met a tree but all she gave me was a rock."

"Can I see?"

Brendy didn't respond right away—she seemed to need a little more closeness—but finally she pulled away far enough to lift the stone up on her palm.

Yvette shivered as her eyes fell on it, and it was an effort for her to speak at normal volume—she wanted to whisper in hushed tones for fear of disturbing the thing. "I see... Go get cleaned up and meet us back in the living room, heard?"

Brendy pursed her lips and narrowed her eyes momentarily at the little thing. "You hold it for me?"

Yvette shook her head. "It's yours," she said quietly. "Guard it with your life."

Brendy grunted softly as if she'd rather not share what she thought of that. "Okay, rock. I show you around!" She scampered out of the kitchen, then darted back at full speed to throw herself at Peaches.

As the older girl wrapped her arms around Brendy, her eyes closed and all the tension all but left her face. "Girl, I was *worried* worried."

"Pssssssssht," Brendy said. "Baby, I'm from Central City!"

They unclasped and she hurried away again.

Now Peaches looked troubled again. "I thought they was together."

"So did I," Yvette said, "but Perry will be back directly." She didn't add that if Brendy had retrieved the Rock, there was no telling what Perry would bring with him. The situation must be worse than she'd feared.

After a beat, Brendy's shout rang down the stairs: *"LORDA-MERCY THIS NEGRO IN THE BATHTUB, SLEEP!"*

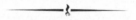

Perry sat up hard, coughing. The water—! The water was still on him, still around and in him! He stopped short, blinked. It took him a moment to realize that he was somewhere utterly familiar. From the blue flowers on the shower curtain to the heavy wooden vanity and the medicine cabinet suspended above it, to the open door and Brendy standing halfway into the hall, watching him with wide eyes.

Perry tried to speak and lost his voice in another coughing fit. He crawled onto his knees and spat a gout of water directly into the bathtub drain. He'd lost his shirt. A brief flash of memory came to him, pulling his shirt up and off before diving into water... *somewhere.* For a moment the memory threatened to resolve, then shuddered and blipped away completely. "I couldn't get it," he said. "I failed."

The noise of feet sounded on stairs, but Peaches appeared before it ceased.

Perry shut his eyes, shook his head. "I didn't get it."

"Uh, Perry..." Peaches said. "I think you did, though."

Perry opened his eyes and frowned. A giddy tingle raced from the crown of his head down the back of his neck when he saw a hank of rough brown fabric clasped in his left fist. With effort, he loosened his grip. His mouth worked without sound for a moment, then, "Brendy, where you got that hoodie?"

He and his baby sister stared at each other for a beat, shocked. Her only answer was a theatrical shrug.

Now their mother appeared behind Peaches in the bathroom doorway, wide-eyed and breathing hard. Her gaze locked on the something in Perry's hand and her face paled. "Perilous," she said, but she didn't take her eyes off it. "Thank God."

Perry shook his head. "I thought I died," he said. "What is it? What's this?"

"I don't know everything," Perry's mother said, "but I can tell you a thing or two. Brendy, you can use the master bathroom. Both of y'all get cleaned up and put some fresh clothes on, then come to the living room. Come on, Peaches. Let's get out their way." She turned and started back down the hall.

Peaches lingered for a moment. Her expression was difficult to read, but when she smiled, Perry knew all he needed to.

———————— ⸹ ————————

Perry's mother sipped her tea and hummed absently in her throat. When Perry had descended the stairs, freshly showered-up and dressed, she'd had a tray ready, complete with tea and honey for each of them and a little dish of lemon slices. Now, instead of using the couch and the chairs, Perry's mother sat on the floor, her thick legs stretched out in a vee, and the kids arranged themselves to face her, cross-legged, on the thick blue-gray carpet. Perry's potato sack—for what else could it be?—sat spread before him, and Brendy's bean-shaped pebble lay before her. She glared at it fiercely with her arms crossed over her belly, then cleared the expression away before anyone besides Perry could notice.

Perry lifted his cup and breathed the steam. He wondered idly how long they'd been away.

"You done good," Yvette said. "Both of you. I'll explain what I can, but first I must tell you of your fourth-great-grandmother, the Wise Woman Kadiatou. She was powerful indeed. By the time she was sixteen, she could *crack* the earth just by stamping one foot. But one day, slavecatchers stole her husband and her baby boy."

Brendy took a sharp, hurt breath.

"Kadiatou wept and wailed and tore her clothes, but that's not all she did. She went after them. She found the place where they were last seen and walked around it three times, until slavecatchers grabbed her and carried her to the coast. There, they loaded her aboard a big-bellied ship with two hundred other African folks. Chained together and terrified. They set sail.

"Before they'd gone far, lightning split the empty sky like God's own finger saying, *THERE!* The slave ship sank, and everyone on board went with it. Your fourth-great-grandmother, too. But instead of drowning and sinking to the bottom, they were rescued by a squadron of soldiers with gills and fins and black-black skin."

A chill spread across Perry's chest.

"Queen Abla Pokou had pulled the slave ship down into the

depths. She was tall-tall, and her skin was even blacker than that of her soldiers. Black-black and spangled like the night. She ruled the kingdom of Grand Lahou, down beneath the ocean waves.

"The kidnapped people rejoiced, and the kingdom rejoiced with them. Everyone sang and danced beneath the waves. The celebration lasted forty days and forty nights, and at its end, Queen Pokou called the kidnapped people before the throne. She asked them, 'Now that we have welcomed you to the Land Beneath and celebrated your rescue for forty days, what would you thrice-blest people do? Who among you would return to your homes?'

"One hundred men and women stepped forward, saying, 'Yes, O Queen. We would return to our homes and to our peoples who mourn our loss that they might smile again and rejoice our return.'

" 'Go, cousins,' said the Queen, and gestured with her sacred Orb. When she did, those one hundred returned instantly to their homes to live in peace for the rest of their days.

"And the Queen Abla Pokou said, 'You others, what would you do? Would you remain here in Grand Lahou, honored among our people?'

"One hundred men and women stepped forward, saying, 'Yes, Most Gracious and Fearsome Queen. We would remain in Grand Lahou, revered as treasured citizens.'

" 'So be it,' said the Queen. 'As sons and daughters of Grand Lahou, you will remain with us as full citizens of the Land Beneath. You will marry the greatest and most beautiful among us and bear Lahouan children to live and thrive for untold generations.'

"A great cheer rose up, and those one hundred danced from the throne room. The festivities resumed to last another forty days and forty nights, for the lost were now found, and were home at last.

"But the Queen was troubled. Worry knitted her starry brow. Nine of the kidnapped people had chosen neither to return to their homeland nor remain beneath the waves. Queen Pokou said, 'You remaining nine. You would not return nor would you remain.

You do not dance for joy. Why are you still unhappy after all we Lahouans have done for you?'

"'O great Queen Beneath the Waves,' cried your fourth-great-grandmother, Kadiatou, 'My heart is heavy. My home is no home without my husband and my infant son. Neither is Grand Lahou, for they are not here. I'll find no peace until I see them once more.'

"The other eight wailed and lamented their agreement, saying, 'Our loved ones have been stolen and carried across the sea. How can we rejoice? We must travel on and be reunited in life or in death.'

"And the Queen said, 'I know where your loved ones have been taken. The lands you speak of are harsh and full of evil men. Pain and violence are its meat and bread, and tears of the innocent water the crops. If you travel there, you will surely die.'"

Perry clenched his teeth. He knew about Slave Times. He'd learned both at home and at school how for generations, white folks had enriched themselves through the blood and pain of Black people. For Kadiatou to travel to America in those days... The Queen was right. Only death and torture waited for her there—whether she found her family or not.

"'It is true what you say,' Kadiatou told the Queen. 'But just as my homeland is no home at all without my husband and child, my life can hold no joy without them. If seeking them in that far-off land will kill me, I will perish knowing that I have tried.'

"The Queen saw that Kadiatou and the rest of the Last Nine would not be dissuaded. 'If you would journey on, so be it. But do so armed with powerful weapons to aid you in your quest.' Two enchanted weapons were given to each of the Nine. Wise Woman Kadiatou used hers to rescue her husband and her son and they lived free for the rest of their days."

"She found them?" Perry said. "She did it?"

The idea of anyone—even a Wise Woman—rescuing her kidnapped people from the plantation... He could almost see her. The fine darkness of her features. In the theater of Perry's mind, he saw her raise the sack in her left hand. She opened her mouth to speak, and—

"Yes," his mother said. "But that's a story for another time."

"Aw, nurtz!" Brendy said, and clapped her hands over her mouth.

Perry's mother cracked a smile in spite of herself. "I know," she said. "And it is quite a story, let me tell you . . ." She paused. "Perilous. Stand."

Perry picked up the sack and did as he was told. It felt like an ordinary thing, just an ugly old bag like so many he'd seen before at the farmer's market.

"Perry, this bag has been passed down in our family since your fourth-great-grandmother received it from the Starry Queen. For generations, it's been hidden elsewhere for safekeeping, and now you've recovered it." She swallowed. "Perry. Perilous. It is *exceedingly* powerful, so—so be careful with it, *please*." She hesitated again. "I don't know what all is inside it, but it might be connected to the other weapons of the Last Nine. *Reach in*."

In that moment, Perry felt like more than a single boy. There was a crowd inside him, jostling and squabbling. Some of him wanted to do as his mother told him, but others screamed at him to throw the sack to the floor, refuse it. Curiosity was a bright burning pinprick in Perry's chest. He was on the verge of something terrible, but after the story his mother told, how could he refuse?

Perry opened the bag to look inside. He saw nothing at all. It was not that he saw an empty bag; it was that inside the sack, he saw Nothingness itself. It was a black, light-drinking void impenetrable to his eyes.

Holding the bag with his right hand, Perry reached in with his left. He reached down and down, first up to his shoulder, and then stuck his head in as well, sweeping his hand back and forth in search of something. His fingers closed on what felt like a length of wood, and images flashed in his mind.

Perry stood in the throne room of a grand Egyptian palace, gripping a staff in his left hand. The pharoah in all his glory stared, unimpressed, as Perry cast his staff to the stone floor of the throne room. When it hit, the staff hissed and writhed, and—

He let go of the staff, breathing hard.

"I told you to be careful," his mother said. "Don't open the Clackin' Sack unless you need to use it. But there's something else."

"What?" Brendy barked.

"The sack is not just for pulling things out. It's for putting things *in*. Anything. Anything at all. All you have to do is open the sack and say these words: 'Clickety-clack, get into my sack.'"

"And then what happens?" Perry asked.

"Then anything you command will get into your sack."

"...Anything?" Peaches asked.

"Anything."

Terror darkened Perry's mind like the shadow of a predator bird. He tried not to consider what he'd seen. What his mother was telling him made Perry want to dig a hole, climb into it, and pull the hole in after him. He felt exposed. Exposed in a way he'd never wanted to be since...since he'd switched schools.

The life he wanted was slipping away. He didn't know how long he'd been away, but assuming this was the same day he'd left, this was only the second day of their quest. He could already feel his spirit bowing under the weight of new knowledge. At this rate, a week from now Perry wouldn't be able to drag himself out of bed. He sat down again before his legs could fail him.

"Brendolyn Eunice Graves. Stand."

Instead of jumping to her feet, Brendy rose slowly, like an old woman. Perry's mother motioned Brendy closer. "Brendy, Mama Lisa told me about the device you retrieved. It is vastly powerful, but its control cannot be taught."

Brendy held up her stone and squinted at it. *"Great!"* she said falsely.

To Perry, Brendy's rock looked like nothing but a mildly interesting pebble you might find lying in the grass. It didn't even look substantial enough to cause trouble for a lawnmower. He knew how Brendy thought: Whenever they played, she insisted that rules be applied equally to everyone involved. She had a wild streak, but fairness was her compass, and when that value was violated, she was liable to explode—provided she could do so on her own terms, and in a time and place of her own choosing. A stranger might not see it—even a loved one might miss it—but her face seemed less expressive than usual, which told Perry she'd put on a mask. She must be *furious*.

"Mama Lisa told me it only looks like a rock. According to her, this object is at least as powerful as Perry's sack."

"If it ain't a rock, then what it is?" Brendy asked lightly.

"It's—honey, I don't know," Perry's mother said. "My migraines kept me from getting very far in my training. I've only got a couple spells and using them is buku costly for me. Otherwise, I'd ask it myself."

Brendy swallowed hard. "Oh—okay, then," she said. "Yes. Wonderful. Thank you, Mama." Her face slackened even more.

"I know you're disappointed. I wish Mama Lisa herself was here to explain."

"That's okay," Brendy said, raising her eyebrows a little too far—selling too hard. She was getting angrier by the minute. "I love my rock. It's better than Perry's dumb old bag, anyway." She wavered, then resumed her seat next to Peaches.

"What about the cold?" Perry asked.

His mother pursed her lips and nodded. "That's one more thing that ain't right in all this. I think you're right—that whoever took Daddy Deke took the songs or tricked them into running away. I think they're trying to change the city, take its power away, and whatever they're doing is working. Y'all need to get out there and find them songs."

"And Daddy Deke," Brendy said.

"One will get us the other," Perry said grimly. It sounded like the kind of thing the Blue Marvel would say as the Ultimate Avengers mobilized against a new threat. Who was stronger, he wondered—Peaches or Miss America?

Peaches stood. "Aight, then," she said. "Y'all heard y'all mama."

"Do you need me to drive you?" said Perry's mother. "How y'all getting where you going?"

Peaches shook her head. "Cain't drive where we headed," she said. "We need us a dead taxi."

"Do y'all understand the risk I'm taking by letting you go?" she asked.

"I—I think so," Perry said.

Yvette shook her head. "You don't. You can't. Just—you're all part of my heart, so please *please* look after each other."

"What's a dead taxi, anyway?" Brendy asked as she, Perry, and Peaches waited outside in the fog. Her voice sounded brittle and deadly calm. Perry knew she was about to snap, but he had no idea how to avert an outburst—or what to tell her when it came.

Her question was fair, though. Perry didn't understand the concept himself. Peaches spent a lot of time on her own, and she seemed to know a lot more about dead folks and haints than Brendy or Perry did.

Folded small, his magic sack rested in the front pocket of his jeans. What bothered Perry even more than Brendy's barely-suppressed rage was that Mama Lisa must have been mistaken. Perry *never* should have received the sack. He wasn't ready for such a responsibility, and he never would be. He tried to think of the incantation he'd been given to use and failed. The words wouldn't sound in his mind—not because he had forgotten them, but because even to think them—let alone say them—would be for Perry to admit that his life could not be what he wanted...But what did he want?

He knew that his resistance had something to do with the

Terrible Thing that had forced him to switch schools—the voice that wasn't his that sometimes sounded in his head—but he sensed there was more to it. He felt it when he thumbed through his parents' photo albums, saw pictures of them at their wedding in City Park, dancing beneath the Peristyle, or at Skate Land in Metry, laughing hard as they held each other upright...He wanted photos like that when he grew up, photos of him and Peaches. But if he ran from his responsibilities, all that would be swept away. His cowardice would mark him just as starkly, just as indelibly as some sorcerous mantle.

Desperate for distraction, Perry watched the girls. Peaches wore her usual raggedy dress, but Brendy wore a puffy white winter jacket over her blue-and-white polka-dot dress. Perry himself wore a bright blue hoodie over his T-shirt. He had left it unzipped when he came outside, but now he drew the zipper up to protect himself from the chill. He tried to feel good about the weather— after all, the fog spared the city the heat of summer—but it was clammy and bothersome. More than that, Perry knew it was silly, but he worried that when the fog burned away, it would leave behind a neighborhood different from the one he knew. He imagined the streets and buildings whispering in the murk, conspiring to confuse the common citizenry.

"It's a taxi that take you to the Dead Side of Town," Peaches said.

"Brendy," Perry said. "I'll trade if you want." As soon as he spoke them, he knew that his words had brought Brendy's outburst closer rather than staving it off.

Brendy grinned a plastic grin. "Peaches," she said, "would you please tell your friend ain't no way I'ma trade my inheritance for his stupid-ass dusty-ass bag?"

Peaches raised her eyebrows, saying nothing.

"Brendy," Perry said.

Brendy crossed her arms, still grinning. "Please explain to your friend, Peaches, that I done said what I said."

"Damn, Brendy," Perry said. "Why you gotta act like you didn't get nothing?"

Once again, he knew he'd made things worse. *Here it comes*, he thought.

Brendy pivoted to face him. She planted her feet, balled her fists, and let Perry have it. "Why I gotta—? Why you always gotta act like my feelings don't mean nothing?" She clenched her fists at her sides, screaming at Perry with the full force of her voice. "You always get the best toys and the best everything cuz you older and you a boy! You get to fix the fishes and all I do is chop the damn salad! *You ain't no better than me, Perry!* You ain't no more important than *I* am, Perry! You just a gawky-ass little kid scared outta his damn mind, so good luck saving the city with your stupid old dusty bag!"

"Baby, y'all gotta keep it cool," Peaches warned.

"Tell Brendy!" Perry said. "*Brendy* needs to keep it cool! And you know what? *You can't blame me for this!* You can't blame me for something some old haint decided! This ain't my fault!"

"Oh, ain't it?" Brendy yelled. "Because it surehell *feel* like your stupid fault, Perry! You lucky I don't whup your ugly ass right here in the street!"

Peaches stepped between them and held them apart. "Now, listen," she said. "We got work. We ain't got time to stand here woofin' in the street. Y'all need to cool out, or best believe I will leave y'all ass right here and handle this my damn self."

Brendy reached around Peaches to stab a finger in Perry's direction. "You supposed to be my big brother, Perry, but you *left* me! *You left me at Dryades all by myself!*"

Now that it was out, Perry realized this was what had been hovering, unsaid, around them for months.

Peaches raised her eyebrows and got out of Brendy's way.

Perry's heart sank. "I don't—! I didn't—!"

"Because you couldn't play piano? That's some *bullshit* right there, Perry!"

"You don't know nothing about that," Perry growled. "And I *will not* get into this with you."

Brendy paused, seemed unsure what to say.

"I don't even want the sack," Perry said. "I *hate* it. You think I want pictures of fucking *Moses* in my head?"

"Pictures of—? What?" Brendy said.

"I don't—I don't know," Perry said, and realized all at once that he was crying. Once again he felt that crowd of selves inside him, all squabbling, every one saying something different. Too many. The chorus made his brain feel hot and wrinkled his scalp.

"In books and movies, magic adventures are *fun*. But this don't feel fun, it feels heavy! The only reason I'm glad to have the bag is because I don't want nobody else to have to use it. Especially not you, Brendy. I need you to stuh-stay happy."

"Negro, all I got was a rock! A *rock*!"

"Brendy—!"

"I don't wanna fight with you bout this, Perry." Brendy sounded tired, much older than she was. "You say this ain't your fault, and you probably right. But it *feels* like your fault, and I get to be mad at you awhile if I wanna."

"You don't get to be mean to me, though."

"That's true," Brendy said. "I can be mad without being mean. So. Anyway. Whatever." She brushed some imaginary dirt off her right shoulder.

Perry turned away from the confrontation and tried to shut out the shouts and murmurs inside him. That hot-brained feeling was still with him. He hardly felt the chill wet of the fog.

Moses? Was that who he'd been when he touched the staff? The name had just tumbled out of him when he was yelling, and he wasn't ready to reflect on what he'd seen. He didn't feel ready to reflect on much of anything.

"Okay," he said. "Dead taxi. Peaches. You called it already? I hate this nasty-ass fog."

"You don't call the dead taxi," Peaches said. "It just show up when it supposed to." She raised her eyebrows as she studied her grimy fingernails. "...But I tell you what, Brendy," she said. "You might be mad about that rock of yours, but it *smell* like magic. Smell more magic than Perry's sack, and Perry's sack *reeks* of hoodoo."

Brendy smiled sadly. Perry wanted to take her in his arms, but he knew she'd explode again if he tried.

Even as he had that thought, Perry heard hooves clopping down the street. The sound didn't seem quite right to him, though. It sounded—not dishonest, not exactly—but like it was *pretending* to be hoofbeats so as not to worry anyone. Perry paused, ran that thought back through his head, trying to understand it.

Instead of emerging from the fog, the mule and carriage appeared all at once. But that wasn't a mule, and that wasn't a carriage. Perry was sure of it. The driver sat in front with the reins, and Perry felt that he, at least, was more or less what he seemed—a shabbily dressed man a few years older than Perry's own parents.

"*Ou vous allez*, baby?" he asked, addressing Peaches.

"Department of Streets," Peaches said.

"*Montez*," said the driver. "Juneteenth Street and Tabbary Way."

As Perry looked on, Peaches climbed into the carriage and reached down to lift Brendy aboard. He paused, unsure.

"It's okay," Peaches said. "I promise."

Perry nodded, then swallowed and climbed on up.

Seldom Traveled by the Multitude

September 2018

Casey sat in his office, locked in a prison of hurt. He hadn't bothered turning the lights on when he arrived that morning, and now dark clouds had brought a premature twilight to the city. He barely noticed. He didn't notice much these days.

When he was eight or nine, Casey had fallen terribly ill. A tickle in his throat started the sickness like sparks in kindling, and Casey disappeared into a haze of pain and fever. At some point, his tonsils had been removed. He remembered floating with his back against the ceiling of the hospital room, looking down at himself.

What stayed with him most from that episode was the feeling that he rode a wave of wrongness, of discomfort. He felt as if he'd been tubing down the Bogue Chitto, but the currents that carried him were choppier and more treacherous than they'd ever been on the river.

After Jaylon's death, Casey felt washed out of himself again. The thought of Jaylon's death in some sort of chemical explosion should have bothered him more, but it still didn't seem real. At first he knew he was in shock, but it had been weeks now, and the scenario didn't feel any more convincing than it had that night.

His life became a series of fragments, islands that swam to the surface of his mind whenever the pain receded enough for Casey to remember himself. The sound of his own screams haunted him. He heard them clearly over and again throughout the day as he sat in his office doing nothing, as he rode the streetcar aimlessly uptown. Their sound seemed to live in his bones. He saw himself talking to NOPD detectives as they explained that while the investigation was still ongoing, they were prepared to rule out arson.

He saw himself sitting on Uncle Trev and Teedy Manda's plastic-covered sofa, trying to stay in his body as they shared a bottle of Bas Armagnac after dinner.

Work receded into the haze. Casey went through the motions, turning out grant copy, conducting meetings and calls, meeting with the school leadership and the Board of Governors. Doctor visits. Shots. Telephone conversations with his brother and his parents.

Nigga, come look!

Every time Jaylon's last words occurred to him again, he heard them in Jaylon's voice instead of seeing them in their little gray bubble against the white text screen. *This* was what he'd been afraid of all along. The way his art had begun to misbehave before the Storm had communicated a sense not of vitality but of extreme volatility. If a painted figure could escape from its surrounds and go—where?—then anything could happen. Jaylon had seemed excited by the prospect, but as they discussed the situation over blunts and beers, a cold dread had stolen over him. When Katrina forced them to evacuate, he'd felt the Storm itself was not the cause, but was somehow *connected* to the strange behavior of his art—and not just his paintings. His sketches had started acting weird as well. Figures would change positions, or entire pages would appear that Casey didn't remember drawing. He'd stopped smoking, stopped drinking, and finally, stopped drawing.

But now he was sketching again—even after Jaylon's death—and he asked himself over and over why. Why was he still putting pencil to paper if it was this dangerous? No answer came to mind, but there was something in the silence. Some other, silent self whose motives Casey didn't understand. Was that the same version of him who drew the sketches Casey didn't remember, or did those somehow come from outside him?

Casey swallowed hard and his vision swam with tears. They didn't spill over this time. He picked up a pencil and opened his sketchbook, flipped through looking for an empty spot and found none. He blinked, surprised. When had he filled this thing?

He shut the sketchbook and looked at its cover. This was a different book than the one he'd bought at Walgreens weeks ago. The paper was of a better grade, and the pages, crowded though they were, were larger: 9" x 12" instead of 5.5" x 8.5". So he'd filled up his old book, bought a new one and filled that up, too, then forgot all that in a haze of grief?

Casey pulled up his Amazon account on his office PC and took a look at his order history. This sketchbook was part of a three-pack. One by one, Casey looked through the drawers of his heavy institutional desk—very possibly an antique of the Rabouin days—but found no other pads. Panic was a physical mass sitting on his right shoulder, ready to unspool and cover Casey's face like a plastic bag.

Fuck this. Casey left his desk and headed out of his closet and down the tiled corridor to the school's front office. Ms. Phyllis sat at her workstation comparing figures on a printed sheet to the ones on her computer screen. Ms. Rolonda was on a call, massaging the bridge of her nose as she listened to something she didn't want to hear. Casey reached for his glasses before he remembered he'd worn contacts today.

Rolonda looked up at him, silently asking what he needed.

Casey gestured at the closed frosted-glass door to Dr. Pullen's office. She waved permission.

Casey knocked and sidled inside when he was bidden. The office smelled of furniture polish and pine cleaner.

"Our star player," Pullen said, grinning. Broad-shouldered and dark-skinned, he appeared to be in his mid-forties, but from hints dropped in conversation, Casey thought the man must be fifty, at least. "What's up, Mr. Ravel?" He pronounced it like the composer's surname instead of Casey's own: *Ravvle.*

He hadn't prepared an excuse. He stood dumbly for a moment, then simply said, "I'm done with work, and I'd like to go."

"Will you be back for tonight's meeting?"

"No, I—no. I'm having a hard time. I'll be back in the morning, but I need—I need tonight. My cousin."

Pullen's expression darkened with concern. "You only took a couple days off when it happened. I didn't think you should come back so soon, but your work's been impeccable."

"Uh. I—thank you?" Why was it a question?

"Mr. Ravel, can I ask you something?"

"Sure."

"Why did you take this job?"

Casey opened his mouth, frowned his consternation. But he understood after all, and he didn't care how his answer sounded. "I needed to come back to New Orleans. I felt led."

"Called?"

Casey sucked his teeth. "I don't know. It didn't seem that profound. I lived here for eighteen months before Katrina, and I guess I wanted—I guess I needed to ... to find what I left here when I evacuated."

Pullen looked as if he wanted to ask another question.

"I don't know if I found it," Casey said. "Jaylon—my cousin—died so soon after I returned, and everything has been about that. It feels like it always will be."

"I know what that's like," Dr. Pullen said. A shadow rested behind his kind brown eyes. "It feels that way, but ... eventually, it recedes—a little, at first, and then so much it surprises you. Makes you feel a little guilty, even." He cleared his throat. "Take the time you need. As long as you're meeting deadlines, you don't have to be here all day. We'll let you know when you're needed."

"Dr. Pullen—"

"Kendrick."

Casey's grief was deep—so deep that he felt lost in it and knew part of him would never emerge back into the world—but he still felt a pressure to explain, as if someone might accuse him of malingering. Thinking that way angered him, made him feel stupid, trapped like a forgotten action figure in a discarded toy chest.

"I don't—Kendrick. I'm not all right. My—Jaylon. He was like a brother to me."

Eyes clouded with thought, Dr. Pullen pressed the thumb-edge of his right hand against his upper lip for a moment. "My uncle Leonid was like my father," he said. "He disappeared in the Storm. His house wasn't flooded. None of his things or his money were missing. Just him."

The admission came as no surprise. The city was full of stories like these. Friends and relatives who had died or disappeared in the aftermath of the Failure, enough negative presences to alter the flow of history.

"That's—I'm sorry. How did you . . . how did you get past it?"

Dr. Pullen's gaze drifted to his office window. "I haven't."

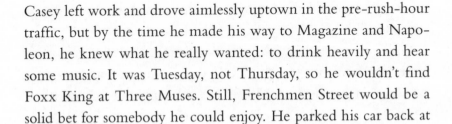

Casey left work and drove aimlessly uptown in the pre-rush-hour traffic, but by the time he made his way to Magazine and Napoleon, he knew what he really wanted: to drink heavily and hear some music. It was Tuesday, not Thursday, so he wouldn't find Foxx King at Three Muses. Still, Frenchmen Street would be a solid bet for somebody he could enjoy. He parked his car back at the apartment and summoned an Uber to take him on.

As his driver's shiny Nissan carried him across the elevated stretch of I-10 on its way to the Elysian Fields exit, Casey gazed out at the city gliding by and noticed something new: Someone had renovated the roof of Circle Food and opened a rooftop bar. From here, Casey saw a pavilion for use as a bandstand, tables, chairs. The entire floor looked green, like someone had lined it with Astroturf.

Casey signaled his driver, a stout dark-skinned woman with kind eyes and tight cornrows. "Hey," he said. "Change of plans."

One thing Casey had always loved in New Orleans was the little details that got by him. He heard a lot of things through word-of-mouth talking to strangers as he waited in line or ran some minor errand, but he had *not* heard that Circle Food was open again—and certainly not that they had a bar upstairs. He saw why when his Uber pulled into the abbreviated parking lot on St. Bernard Avenue—the supermarket was still closed. It looked like someone might be doing some work inside, but there was no signage about an opening date. As the Nissan zipped away, Casey wondered whether he'd made a mistake. How would he find his way to the roof?

That didn't matter, he reasoned. From here, Frenchmen was an easy walk. One way or another, he'd pass some time and do his best to forget his troubles. Casey headed for the front doors and was surprised when they whispered open to admit him. What he saw inside was weirder still: instead of the grocery store's interior, he saw a green stairwell leading up. He grunted softly and went for it.

It wasn't turf lining the stairs after all. It was grass. It wasn't the look of it or feeling it beneath the soles of his loafers that made Casey admit as much; it was the smell: Fresh and green, it smelled like spring afternoons Back East, when Casey would lie barefoot in his yard, staring up through the branches of the cherry tree that stood beside his childhood home and watching the clouds pass lazily out of sight as lawnmowers droned up and down the neighboring yards.

When the scent hit him, Casey paused his climb, his left hand resting on the rail. He worried for a moment that he might cry. Teeth clenched, he slid his phone from his pocket and texted H. T.

I'm walking up a flight of stairs that shouldn't
be here. WYD?

He didn't bother waiting for an answer. He didn't need one. The familiar action of texting his brother was enough to calm him, keep him from feeling washed away by whatever this was.

Upstairs, the understated piano music sounded both floral and aquatic. Two or three couples sat at tables, nursing drinks and talking easily to each other. No signs displayed the club's name, but iron tables and chairs stood here and there in the grassy lawn, and a circular double bar stood to the left of the stage. Casey approached it and asked the broad-faced little woman waiting there for a single-tall White Russian with a spritz of cola. Back in Northampton, they'd called it a Smith and Wesson, but elsewhere he'd heard it referred to as a Colorado Bulldog.

He took his seat and started drinking as he half listened to the man on the keys. "Oh shit," someone said. "I didn't know it was like *that*."

Casey smiled in spite of himself. "Foxx King," he said. "Let me buy you a drink."

Foxx frowned, confused. "Bartender took your money?"

Casey realized he hadn't actually paid. "No," he said. "I guess not."

"Good," Foxx said. "I be back directly."

Casey had just enough time to himself to wonder why he kept running into the musician. And why here? Even after what had happened to Jayl, that first set Casey had seen was never far from his mind. He thought he might have dreamed about it more than once.

Foxx returned with a drink of his own—a Bloody Mary or something like, with a garden of olives and pickled vegetables bursting from the glass.

"First time here?" he asked as he took a seat in one of the low, broad wrought-iron chairs. For the first time, Casey noticed the Roman numeral for 10,000 tattooed on the back of Foxx's hand, and some Arabic script on that same arm.

"Well, yeah," Casey said. "I had no idea the place was here until I saw it from the highway."

"You do art, though, right?" Foxx said. "Must be you ain't nothin' nice."

"I mean, I'm all right, I guess. My cousin is..." he trailed off. Grief was with him again, an unwanted guest sitting at the table.

"What you gave up?"

"What do you mean?"

"Two ways to slip into a place like this for the first time," Foxx said. Something hard rested in his eyes. "Back in the nineties, I worked for the State Department. Suit. Tie. Errythang. Tunis was my first post overseas. The night my baby girl died, I walked out my villa and into a club across the street wasn't never there before. Before that, music was a hobby."

Grief and terror rested cold at the center of Casey's chest. It made him very still, as if one wrong move would spill the sensation beyond its bounds.

"Is that real?"

Foxx laughed, his eyes still hard. "Real as real, bruh. But is it *true...?*"

He paused, fell silent. Casey knew he should say something, but his voice had left him. This grass. He couldn't stop thinking about it. The lawn they sat on was beautifully manicured, but how could that be, exactly? Did they clear out all the furniture every few days, trim it with lawnmowers? He couldn't imagine they did. Who was *they*, anyway? Casey's drink tasted fantastic. Like the quintessence of a Colorado Bulldog, and he hadn't paid a dime. Could Jayl's death have allowed him entry to this place?

The other man's eyes softened just a little. Casey imagined him as he might have been twenty years ago—his hair neat, black instead of salt-and-pepper, wearing a gray pinstriped suit and a red paisley tie. State Department.

"There's places all over this world only Artists know. That only we can access. You ain't thought it was weird that the locked doors opened for you and instead of the store you saw the stairs leading up here?"

"I mean, of course I did," Casey said. "I just figured there was a rational explanation."

"*Did* you, though?" Foxx said. "Or did you just roll with it...?"

Casey didn't answer. Of course he hadn't tried to reason it out. Why bother? If it wasn't possible, it wouldn't have happened. Except this wasn't the first time he'd seen something impossible in New Orleans.

"So you're telling me this place is here for me because I draw?"

Foxx shrugged. "That's prolly it," he said. "Mostly. Anything unusual happen to you recently?"

"My cousin died," Casey said. "In some kind of explosion. On—on—on—at his studio. On Elysian Fields."

"Jaylbird kin to you?"

Casey went still again. "You know him?"

Foxx grinned. "Nigga was famous wasn't he?"

"Is that how you know him?"

Foxx showed his palms. "Welllllllll, not exactly," he said. "I didn't know of him till after. His passing caused a stir."

Casey gripped the lip of the metal table. "What kind of stir?"

Foxx's face turned serious as he considered. "Aight, you know what pops a balloon when you stick a needle in it?"

"The needle."

"Not so!" Foxx said. "Don't take my word for it, but if you stick a perfectly clean needle through the skin of a latex balloon, that balloon will not pop. It'll just get a hole in it. That's what death is usually like. Jaylbird's death, though, it was dirty. It caused a rupture. So we noticed."

"Who is 'we'?"

"The answer to that question ain't gone make any real sense to you right now," Foxx said. "I'm not evading, I'm just telling you. You ain't ready."

"Ready for *what*?" Casey asked. He was still holding the table, his grip hard enough to hurt. He was sick of walking through this hall of mirrors, collecting scraps of information that amounted to nothing. Worse than nothing.

"You done started down a long strange road to somewhere you've never seen before."

An image popped into Casey's head. He remembered one of his early trips to New Orleans when Uncle Trev had taken him and Jaylon to see a revival showing of *Wattstax* at the Valiant Theatre. The Bar-Kays' performance had electrified Casey. In their blond wigs and silver suits, they'd looked like superheroes or spacemen. Black astronauts tearing up the funk. "'It's been said many times and many places...'"

"'...That freedom is a road seldom traveled by the multitude,'" Foxx finished. "Yeahyouright. We got *lots* to talk about, bruh. I hope you wearing your drankin' pants tonight, because we getting into bottles and bottles."

Casey felt the dark pit of a mysterious future yawning before him. The compulsion to return, Jayl's glowing paint and his barely-anchored tag, the spirit in his own apartment whispering in an unknown language. He felt like it was all reaching critical mass, that the world around him was forcing him to be another way when he wanted to be one way. If a clean needle could pass through a balloon's skin without popping it, then Jayl's death was dirty indeed—and not just for him.

He remembered the day he told H. T. that he was interested in girls, not boys. His brother had leaned against the kitchen island in their parents' house, listened as Casey blurted his confession; then all he said was "All right, then."

At first, Casey thought his brother hadn't understood. Or that he'd known the truth for some time and had just been waiting for Casey to tell him. In time, Casey came to understand that H. T. had taken Casey's admission and put it through a series of rapid-fire tests, then come to the conclusion that the information had no bearing on their relationship.

He envied H. T.'s ability to make decisions this way. He never seemed to agonize, to second-guess himself—for all that he was still ready to alter his thinking if the situation called for it. For Casey, every decision needed to be considered and reconsidered along with the decisions branching from it. It was exhausting.

What if Foxx King was just messing with him? What if somehow all this was in Casey's grief-addled head? What if there was a rational explanation to the disappearance of the Hanging Judge, all those years ago? What if what it what if what—?

Stone-faced, he sipped his drink. "I'm listening. But I got a serious question for you first."

"Get at me."

"Are you trying to scare me?"

"Bruh, *yes*," Foxx King said soberly. "You *should* be scared. You should be muh fuggin' *petrified*."

Casey awakened in stages. His dreams had been all chaos and tangled limbs: running from the police after tagging a wall somewhere in a city that was both New Orleans and Baltimore, and maybe Northampton, as well. Swallowing hot stones to keep them from falling into the wrong hands and burning his fingers, his throat, the inside of his belly. Ximena—or her shadow—looking out the observation window of a moon base or a space station.

Here in New Orleans—at least for musicians—"dead" ain't exactly a fixed value, dig?

Casey hazily remembered a grassy rooftop bar somewhere in the Treme, and drinking with Foxx King. But there were no such bars in that neighborhood. All the rooftop places were in shiny newly renovated buildings in the CBD or the Warehouse District.

You say ya cousin died—and maybe he did. But even so, he might still be around, and I heard a thing or two bout that, me.

The darkness of the apartment was nearly complete, as broad and thick as cola syrup. Groaning, Casey sat up and realized he'd fallen asleep on the couch and not in his bed. He didn't like the way his home looked. It was fully furnished now, which strength-ened the impression that the darkness was hiding something. Casey looked over his shoulder at the rectangle of deeper blackness standing beside the kitchen.

Jayl stood in the doorway, watching him.

When Casey's eyes met Jaylon's, his cousin stabbed a finger toward his mouth and *howled*.

Casey snapped awake breathing hard. He sat for a moment, trembling, trying to force himself to look back at the doorway by the kitchen—to see that there was nothing and no one there.

Maybe it's because we leave pieces of ourselves imprinted on the air—or, in y'all's case, on paper or on walls—but if what we make is powerful enough, we can be suspended Between before fading completely. If you got something to say, you can find him. You can tell him y'own self. But you gone have to let your spirit lead you.

Instead of looking at the space where Jaylon's image had appeared, Casey collected his wallet, keys, and phone from the coffee table and headed out.

Religion When I Die

Last May, a few weeks before school ended, Perry had awakened to find a note from Peaches on his bedroom nightstand: *POOL AFTER SCHOOL, BABY!* it read in her swooping scrawl that was neither print nor cursive.

It would be just the two of them today—Brendy had dance lessons that afternoon—so as soon as school let out, Perry jumped on the 91 sky trolley, heading toward the natatorium in City Park. The windows had been fogged opaque by the tension between the air-conditioning and the almost-summer heat outside. Droplets of condensation beaded all over the car's red exterior and made it look as if it were sweating from exertion. Inside, a trio of elderly ladies coming from the Tchoupitoulas Walmart squawked and gossiped, filling the car with the scents of candy lozenges and pressed-flower perfume.

The day before, Mr. Yaw had changed his approach to Perry's piano lessons and given Perry a small keyboard to practice on. About the size of a shoebox, it fit easily into Perry's book sack. The idea was that he would take it out and practice his fingering and chords whenever he had the chance. That way he could practice at home without his folks investing in a real piano before Perry's aptitude for sorcery revealed itself.

Mr. Yaw was a white man of medium build who stood just over six feet tall. The strangest thing about him, in Perry's opinion, was his bearing. At times, he seemed stiff and formal, speaking from somewhere low in his throat, his voice squeezed tight as it traveled up and out.

"I'm not sure what the issue is, but this is what worked for me as a boy," he'd said. "Having a way to practice idly until the motions became natural to me. Wasn't long before I was locksmithing on an amateur basis."

Hearing that had made Perry hopeful. There was something about locks that he found compelling. Being able to manipulate their interior mechanisms by playing this or that simple tune— even such modest magic would make Perry proud.

As the skycar scooted along above Esplanade Avenue, Perry sat with the keyboard balanced on his right knee and played chords with the volume off.

The trolley glided past the entrance to City Park with no stops before the turn on Orleans. It paused a couple times after the turn, but Perry stayed on until it turned again and descended to the street out front of Delgado Community College. Perry disembarked, ignoring the vibrations at his feet. Something about Delgado had always seemed weird to him, but nobody else had ever said anything, so it was probably all in his head.

Perry headed into the park, his keyboard hanging from his left hand, swinging along with his arm. He loved the smell here. There was always a little algal must in the air, but instead of smelling moldy and gross, it smelled *alive*. The oaks and magnolias joined hands overhead as Perry followed the familiar path toward the pool. He walked automatically, musing over how good it would feel to cut the water with his hot brown limbs, and how school was almost almost almost over.

That was why it took him so long to notice something wasn't right. Perry slowed down as he realized that the light was wrong. It was only 3:30, but out here it looked as if night were about to

fall. The sky was cloudless but dim and exhausted, and the trees...
the magnolias, the oaks, the willows, the cypress trees all looked
dead and bare. Even the Spanish moss looked washed-out and
withered. Perry thought of that scene in *The Wizard of Oz* where
Dorothy and her friends stumbled into the wrong part of the forest
where the trees threw apples at them.

He made his way into a clearing before he stopped and turned,
trying to get his bearings. He saw no landmarks he recognized, no
signs that he was even in the park anymore. Beneath his feet, the
asphalt bike path had given way to a beaten dirt track without Perry
noticing. He was...he was *lost*.

In the distance, Perry saw a figure standing by what looked like
a well. From here it was hard to tell, but Perry thought it might be
an older white man. "Hey!" Perry called. "Hey, excuse me!"

Something about the way the figure's body responded made
him think calling out had been a bad idea. Its body tensed, vibrating with attention like that of a hound. Perry almost expected to
hear a howl or bark.

Fear fell on him like a wet blanket. He tried to turn around, or
at least halt his approach, but his body paid him no mind. It carried
him closer to the figure, and closer still. Barefoot, it wore grimy
black judicial robes with a soiled powdered wig that had slipped
back on its skull to show its stubbly scalp. Its face seemed translucent white, and its skinny bare legs were dirty, badly scratched by
brambles or stickers.

You people and yer goddamn jungle music, it said. *No home-training...!*
Its voice was raspy and ragged, like it had shouted itself hoarse at a
Saints game.

He was still roughly twenty-five yards from the judge, but he
could hear it whisper just the same. *Him*, he told himself, *it's a*
him. *It's not an* it, but he knew that wasn't true.

Just a-drummin' and a-hollerin'. Ya dirty up the place and vandalize.
Paint yer little mess over the statues and the walls.

Perry hadn't painted anything, but terror broke against his breast to spread across his core, a gelid web. A hollow tremor ran through him as he realized that the Judge wore a noose around its neck. Its frayed edge hung down like a necktie or a severed tongue. Its face wasn't just unnaturally pale, it was made-up like that of a clown or a mime, and its cheeks were comically rouged. At first, Perry thought the Judge wore dark lipstick, but it seemed more like it had ingested something rotten and thrown it back up. A ragged black stain ringed its mouth and ran down its chin.

It stood next to a well. It was a broad, stone-built structure that rose to the Judge's waist. As he drew near, Perry became certain that it was the *well* pulling on him, not the Judge, and certainly not his own two feet. What if it kept dragging him and dragging him until Perry went over the side, and—?

Two large rough sacks lay at the Judge's dirty feet. Had they been there before?

"We wanna integrate! We want equality!" Now its voice was high and mocking. *But ya live like scum, like animals. Without us to keep you in line, ya kill up yer own selves.*

This was a dream. Perry had fallen asleep on the skycar and he was having a nightmare.

Moving jerkily, like a poorly operated marionette, the Hanging Judge—his name sounded in Perry's mind, as if something outside him whispered it—stooped to grab one of the large bags lying on the dead grass and heaved it over the lip of the well. More sacks appeared, a pile of them. The judge grabbed two more, one in each hand, and threw them in as well. Perry realized now that the bags were big enough, lumpy enough, to hold human bodies or remains—not full-grown people, but kids, at least. Boys.

It's only right. I only do what I got a right ta do.

Now he was about five feet away from the Judge. His legs were still, and his feet didn't touch the ground. Perry hung suspended before him, his arms stretched to either side. The worst thing about the figure was not its ratty, disheveled wig or torn and dirty robes—not even the pallor of its face or the rust-brown substance that stained its fingers and palms. It was the eyes. The eyes were very human—bloodshot, utterly insane, but *human*—as if this were no evil spirit or malevolent haint, but a man. A man who barely saw Perry, but hated him just the same.

Eyes locked on Perry's, the Hanging Judge reached into its robes and withdrew an object. Without looking away from Perry, it tossed the thing into the well.

A foul exhalation rushed out, the dark, red-brown stench of blood and human shit. A thrum ran through the ground beneath Perry's feet, and the well trembled, belched a tongue of flame. Acrid smoke poured into the air, rising in a column up, up into the dimming sky. Just looking at it made Perry's eyes water. Hot tears rolled down his cheeks.

Something about the smoke seemed *wrong* to Perry, and gradually he realized what it was: There were faces and bodies in the smoke. Distended and pulled out of shape as they rose into the sky and dispersed. One face rolled its hollow eyes in Perry's direction as it went, its mouth pulled into a moan or a scream of anguish.

Perry cut his gaze from the smoke back to the Judge, as if that would relieve his terror. The Judge was bigger now. Before, it had been the size of a normal man—under six feet. Now, it was seven feet if it was an inch, its dirty, blackened teeth clenched as it glowered at Perry.

You don't need to know who I am, it said. *That ain't none of yore concern. All you need ta know is that if I burnt ya alive right here and now, wouldn't nobody in the world miss yer Black ass.*

"Don't!" Perry shouted. "Don't burn me! *Please!*"

Ask real nice, said the Judge. *Beg!*

"Please!" Perry wailed. "I didn't do nothing! I'm not a vandal or—! *I didn't do nothing wrong!*"

Too late! Too late! crowed the Judge. *Yer mine! Miiiiiiine!*

Perry forced himself awake to find the trolley headed back uptown. It reached Carrollton and turned left from Orleans, gliding back toward Esplanade. Perry had missed his stop. The old ladies were gone now—so was everyone else. He was alone in the trolley except for the driver. His keyboard had fallen from his lap and lay at his feet, smashed as if it had been thrown from somewhere high. It didn't matter. It had done him no good.

The next day, Perry asked his parents to transfer him to a different school—one where he could focus on STEM—and discontinue his piano lessons.

He couldn't explain his reasoning to anyone else—maybe because it wasn't a matter of reason. He knew that if he told Peaches about his dream—he resigned himself to call it that, though he was dead certain it had not been a dream—that she would have gone looking for the Hanging Judge, intent on teaching it a painful lesson. Perry didn't think the Judge could best Peaches in combat, but that seemed beside the point. The episode had opened a fissure in him, a red and angry wound that refused to heal. Sometimes Perry would find his attention wandering toward the memory, playing along it like fingers along a scar—except it wasn't a scar, it was still raw, and it ached with a pain that felt as if it had always been with him.

It would do no good to beat the Hanging Judge even if Peaches could get her hands on it. The Judge simply *was.* It was a fact of life, and the sooner Perry learned to live with that, the sooner the pain would become dull and bearable.

More than a year later, he still felt this way, and he'd never told a soul.

———————— ❧ ————————

The carriage ride was long and dreary. By now the fog should have burned away, but it stood thick as soup, resolute. Every so often, a landmark swam by—the low, salmon-pink Wm. B. Allen building on North Rampart Street, the Rock'n'Bowl from Mid-City, and Cooter Brown's, that bar on the end of St. Charles. Perry resolved to just stop looking—the sights weren't making any sense.

What if the fog ain't in the city? Perry wondered. *What if it's in me?* He shook his head, irritated by his own willingness to upset himself. He considered reaching into the sack for something that would banish the fog or light the way, but the idea sickened him.

Eventually, the fake-clop of the mule's hooves gave way to the blunter, mealier percussion of hooves against dirt, and they left the haze behind.

The ride had taken less than an hour by Perry's reckoning, so it should have been broad daylight, but the sky above the carriage showed indigo, as if the sun had just bedded down for the night. Streetlights burned with flames instead of filaments, casting dim and buttery light onto the neighborhood. This street looked like Bourbon or Frenchmen, but longer, with clubs and bars standing three and four and sometimes more to a block. Each one produced a riot of sound—jazz clashing with zydeco, clashing with blues, clashing with soul. People walked, stood, talked, drank all along the sidewalks and in the streets. Every race, creed, and color seemed represented—Black folks, white folks, Asians, Hispanics, actual Indians, even what Perry thought must be Australian Aborigines. There were even animals—pigs, goats, pelicans, giant nutria, even a crab or two. Perry saw a P-body disappear into the crowd as the dead taxi pushed slowly through.

Zombies were out in force, standing stock-still on the corners or shuffling to and fro. As they rode by, one zombie wearing a tux with tails passed another in what must have been a mix-and-match Mardi Gras costume (a sailor's hat with a pirate's blouse, puffy genie pants, and cowboy boots) and the Mardi Gras zombie waved while the fancy one just twitched his shoulder and moaned a greeting.

The taxi turned down another street corner—Perry was too busy staring at the zombies to read the sign. He saw zombies often enough, but he'd never seen any dressed so wildly or with so much personality. Bounce music poured out of a club's open front door. The drums and bass stuttered as the lyrics barked into the street.

Keep it keep it keep da body clean
Keep it keep it keep da body clean

Keep it keep it keep it keep it
Keep it keep it keep it keep it
Keep it keep it keep it keep it
Keep—

As the music receded behind them, the block began to change. The clubs and bars gave way to large gated lawns and austere mansions lit by dirty orange light. As they passed a grand old place with a brick-and-ironwork fence, Perry saw a haint stepping out onto the sidewalk. This was the first time Perry had seen a haint by night, and he was amazed at the way the ghostly white woman shone in the dim.

She paused outside the gate and looked over her shoulder. Another haint, a distinguished-looking Black man whose hair was dusted with gray, stepped out and took her arm. The two of them danced to nothing, dipping down the sidewalk.

"Pie Lady, Pie Lady!" someone sang. The voice was a high, sweet contralto, and now that he thought about it, Perry realized he hadn't heard it in months.

"Oh no!" Brendy said. "Pie Lady dead?"

"Maybe," Peaches said. "But maybe not. We here, and we ain't dead. Maybe haints need haint pie."

"Pie Lady, Pie Lady!" The Pie Lady turned the corner. She was tall and rawboned, and before her she pushed a wheeled aluminum cart full of pies. She looked whole and solid to Perry, but he supposed she could have been recently zombified.

"Pie Lady!" Brendy shouted as they clopped past. "You still alive?"

"Sure am, darling," Pie Lady called back. "Better tips on this side of town. They give me *gold*! *Pie Lady, Pie Lady!*"

"Aw," Brendy sighed. "I miss her."

"The thing about the Dead Side of Town," Peaches said, "is that it ain't just for haints and zombies and like that. It's for everything in Nola that passed on. So all the buildings here is ghosts of buildings used to be on the live side. That might not even be the real Pie Lady. Maybe she left Nola, and the city decided it wanted to remember her."

"Buildings have ghosts?" Perry asked.

"Everything do," Peaches said.

"And wait," Perry said. "You're telling me there's haints of people ain't even dead?"

"It's complicated," Peaches said. "I don't know if I'm explainin' it right. Ask Mr. Larry about it and he'll tell you."

"Is that who we're going to see?"

As if on cue, the carriage slowed to a stop. "Department of Streets!" the driver called over his shoulder.

Peaches reached into her pockets and retrieved a $45,000 hell note. "Keep the change, baby," she said as she paid up.

Perry descended first, then helped Brendy down. As he lowered his sister to the cobbled street, in his peripheral vision Perry saw the carriage as it really was. It was a hearse like the ones they used at the Majestic Mortuary on O. C. Haley, but the top of it had been sliced clean off to expose the seats to open air. Instead of regular car wheels, the carriage had big fat tires like on a tractor or a monster truck.

But that wasn't all: Just as Perry had thought, the "mule" was something else entirely. It was only a skeleton, but it wasn't composed of mule bones, either. It looked like a six-legged cross between a spider, a giraffe, and a dragon. Fire rested in its mouth and eye sockets.

Perry clenched his eyes shut and heard the rattle of bones as the creature swung its head his way. Something dry scraped the side of Perry's head. Had it—? It had. It had *licked* him! What kind of creature had a bony tongue?

"Bahomet!" the driver barked. *"Lèches pas!"* He snapped the reins, and the carriage moved on.

When he was sure it was gone, Perry opened his eyes and turned to stare up at the Department of Streets. The building stood nine stories high. It reminded Perry of the Cabildo in Jackson Square, but pieces of it seemed blurry and undefined, as if they hadn't quite decided how to look. The third story jutted out above the entrance, supported by great white columns, and a well-kept patch of cobblestones stretched from the dirt street to the main entrance.

"Well," Peaches said. "We is where we at."

"Why would the Dead Side need a Department of Streets?" Perry asked.

"Why wouldn't it?" Peaches said with a shrug. "Every city gotta have a place you can go to and find out everything you need to know. Here in Nola, this is it."

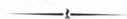

The building's interior was dark. The tiled floors seemed to be black and white with green and gold trim, but with the lights so low, Perry couldn't be sure. The corridors curved this way and that, lined with heavy wooden doors. Most stood closed, but some hung ajar and others stood entirely open or absent, offering nothing but a blackness akin to that within Perry's Clackin' Sack.

Perry had expected to see people working here, just as they did at his father's office in One Shell Square, but no one was around. Maybe nobody was in charge of the streets after all. And who was in charge of Nola, anyway? Perry had seen the king and queen on TV, but now that he thought about it, he wasn't sure whether they really ruled anything, and he knew there was a mayor and even a governor. How could there be so many official personages and nobody home in what, it seemed to Perry, should have been an important departmental office?

As always, Peaches walked unconcerned. She seemed to know where they were going, so Perry didn't worry. Much. Brendy must have worried, though, because in the gloom she reached for Perry's hand and held it tight. He tried to read his sister's body language, but she didn't speak or look his way.

They reached an open doorway beneath which a dim spill of golden light seeped into the hall. Peaches knocked on the frame.

"Mr. Larry!" she called. "It's Peaches! You back there?" The volume of her voice seemed somehow profane in the stillness of that abandoned building.

An answer came back, stretched upon the air. "...Come on back!..."

Peaches led them through a room where dusty books, sheaves of paper, and stacks of accordion folders stood columned, reaching for the ceiling. Many of the stacks were so high that they looked to Perry as if they'd collapse at the slightest provocation. The air in here smelled of learning and neglect. Perry thought of all the potholes and graffiti tags in town and felt he understood a bit more about Nola than he had this morning.

They threaded their way through the maze to find a tired-looking, gray-haired white man standing over a scale model of Nola, complete with a length of the Missus Hipp, and sky trolleys suspended above the streets. He wore a faded blue dress shirt unbuttoned at the collar, a brown-and-gray striped tie, and red suspenders. A great big mustache hung over his upper lip, but he didn't wear a beard. His steel-gray hair stood up in corkscrews, and bags stood out under his eyes. His right eye was a clear and piercing blue, but the left one looked strange to Perry, even in the watery light of the room. It looked almost as if the eye were a fake, carved out of wood and popped into the socket.

"Mr. Larry, these my friends Perry and Brendy," Peaches said. "Perry and Brendy, this Mr. Laf-ca-dee-o Hearn. I said it right?"

"Yes, darling," he said. "But you can call me Larry." His voice was soft and smooth, like oiled leather, but there was something foreign about his pronunciation—a funny little lilt that Perry couldn't place. Clearly, he was from Away—especially with a name like "Lafcadio." Perry didn't even know what country it was from.

Mr. Larry turned to smile down at Brendy. "And aren't you the sweetest little thing?" He looked like the sort of man who didn't smile often, so his smiling now counted double. "Brenda is your name?"

"Bren-*dee*," she corrected.

He turned to fix Perry with a one-eyed stare. He looked like a giant bird. That thought made Perry feel as if his eyes were being deceived again, the way they had been by the fake carriage and the not-a-mule. Mr. Larry wavered just a little in Perry's vision, but then his image snapped back more vivid than ever. Looking at him made Perry feel less than real.

"And you're Perry?"

"Yuh-yes sir."

He took Perry's hand and shook it firmly. "Well, I am just pleased as can be to make your acquaintance, young sir."

"Mr. Larry know everything there is to know about the city," Peaches said. "And what he don't know, he know how to find out."

"I've inhabited these environs many a year," Mr. Larry said. "A long, long time." Something in his voice reminded Perry of Daddy Deke, and before Perry could close it off, a surge of emotion washed through him.

He shook his head, took hold of himself. Mr. Larry was talking, and Perry felt he should listen. "...first came down from Ohio, I wrote regionalist articles about the goings-on down here," he said. "New Orleans captured my heart the first time I saw her."

"Nuh-owlians?" Brendy said. "What that is?"

"He just call Nola that sometimes," Peaches said with a shrug.

"New Orleans is a different city," Mr. Larry said. "Much like this one, but sadly lost to time." He bowed his head, staring at the floor. The way his neck bent reminded Perry of the ostriches at the Audubon Zoo. *Maybe he's crazy*, Perry thought, and immediately he felt ashamed.

Mr. Larry looked up and made what was almost a smile. "Forgive me," he said. "The mind wanders. For one as old as I, there is a wealth of memories to riffle through. Peaches, darling, tell me about your latest adventure. What's this I hear about you hunting songs?"

How does he know about that? Perry thought, suspicious. But if Mr. Larry was as in-the-know as Peaches said he was, why wouldn't he?

"Just one song for now," Peaches said. " 'Jailbird Stomp.' You know it?"

"We think—*I* think Jailbird kidnapped my grandfather, sir," Perry said. He immediately wished he'd kept his mouth shut, but he wasn't sure why.

"I see," Mr. Hearn said gravely. He rubbed his smooth white chin. "Of course I know the tune you mean," he said. "Let me hum a few bars, see if I can entirely recall...

"Now, let's see . . . 'Just a visit . . .' 'way up in that . . .' 'I see the way . . .' Ah. I got it." He raised his arms, took a sliding step with his right foot, and spun under the vaulted ceiling. He sang as he bowed his back and shuffled his feet:

I just pay my visit
Don't live here no full time
I'm gone back home directly
Let the sentence fit the crime.

As soon as the first verse began, Perry recognized the song that had escaped him the last time he tried to sing it. This was it, exactly right, and Perry wondered how Mr. Larry knew it when the song was out running the streets.

I walk on down these dirty streets
With worn-out shoes upon my feet
They call me a jailbird, they call me a junker
They just jealous because I'm free!

Piano, drums, and bass. A horn section tooting quietly, waiting to open up for the solo. The smells of booze and tobacco unfolded into the air, and Perry could almost see Jailbird, in his rumpled suit with his tarnished silver watch chain hanging from his pocket.

On his head, he wore a fedora that looked like it had been sat on during a sky trolley ride.

Fear coiled in Perry's belly, but he felt it from a remove. It could be, he reasoned, that the music was sweeping him so swiftly along that he didn't have time to fear the magic—but it was more than that. He felt stronger than usual, more solid. Why should he fear his own breath? His own blood?

Perry sensed other people standing with them in the room. It was like the room had become a club, and Perry stood among the crowd. He felt an elbow bump his head. *Sorry bout dat, little man.*

You good, Perry said silently.

I'm just paying my visit
I don't live here no full time
I'm gone back home directly
Let the sentence fit the crime.
HEY!

Raucous applause filled the room. After a beat, Perry realized that he, Peaches, and Brendy were hooting and clapping by themselves. "That's it, baby," Peaches said. "That's it right there!"

"Yeah," Perry said. "Yeah. Now I'll know him when I see him."

Mr. Larry raised his eyebrows. "You *saw* him?"

Perry paused. Mr. Larry's expression was one of simple curiosity, but Perry sensed that he was missing something. It seemed to him that there were a right answer and a wrong answer to the question, and he wasn't sure which was which. What he was sure of, however, was that he had no intention of mentioning the Clackin' Sack or Brendy's rock to Mr. Larry. Those things were none of the old man's business. And if they were none of his business, then neither were the other ways in which Perry or his sister were different.

"Well, yeah," Perry said. "Just from the way you sung and danced. That's Jailbird all over."

"Yes, well," Mr. Larry said slowly. He stared his bird-stare again, this time at Perry, "No harm done, I suppose. I'm sure we were all caught up in the moment…And I did do my best to capture Jailbird." He paused and took another breath so deep that Perry thought he'd burst once more into song. Instead, he spoke. "So. Let's review what we know from the lyrics."

"He was born up in the jail," Brendy said.

"That he was," Mr. Larry said. "That he was. So from that, we're meant to understand that Jailbird feels he belongs in Angola. He thinks of it as his true home, and he's never far from it. So a man going to prison very soon likes to enjoy himself while he can."

"So he lookin' for booze and maybe some women," Peaches said. "But he ain't got no money."

"No money, sure," Mr. Larry said. "But this is Nola, and there's one thing spends better here than money."

"Favors," Perry said with a nod.

"Yeahyouright," Peaches agreed. "Why else would a song like Jailbird wanna mess with Daddy Deke? He doing a favor for somebody. Somebody big. So if he drinkin' on somebody dime—somebody shady…"

"I know where *I* would go for that kind of enjoyment," Mr. Larry said.

"Da Cut," he and Peaches said in unison.

"What's Da Cut?" Brendy asked. "Where it is?"

"My dear, you just may find out someday when you're older," Mr. Larry said. "No one under the age of twenty-one is allowed inside. Alas."

"Don't worry," Peaches said. "We'll get in."

"Now, Peaches," Mr. Larry said. "I'm offering you information from my stores, but not so you can run off and do something rash. You'd do better to contact the City Magicians."

"Mr. Larry, I got a job to do," Peaches said. "I gotta protect this city and get all them songs back where they belong so Nola can keep on rockin'. Now, you know I'd go to the grown-ups if I could, but they ain't never listened to me before and they ain't like to start now. I'ma get that song with or without your help. Now, if you don't wanna tell me nothin' no more, that's your decision, but I sure could use the knowledge you got."

Mr. Larry watched Peaches, frowning, for what seemed a long time. Then he looked down and away. "Needs must," he said with a sigh.

"Aight then," Peaches said. "So tell me this: Which room in Da Cut got the biggest bar, the loudest music, and the loosest women?"

"That would be the Velvet Room, my dear."

The dead taxi that floated up to the curb outside the Department of Streets was different from the one that had brought them here—it was a United Cab without wheels. Perry, Peaches, and Brendy piled into the backseat while the driver, a slightly built zombie in a patch-work blazer, sat in the front, holding a copy of the *Times-Picayune*. She seemed to be reading it, but she had no eyeballs, so Perry wasn't sure.

When he first saw the zombie, Perry had wanted to hold out for another ride, not because he found the cab or its driver especially creepy but because he had always assumed that zombies must smell pretty bad.

It turned out he was wrong: This zombie, at least, smelled just like the dining room at Dooky Chase—like fried chicken and okra, and hot sausage and good, good apple cobbler—so Perry realized there was still an awful lot about zombies and the dead that he just didn't know.

Instead of a not-really-a-mule pulling it through the haze, a glowing ball of phosphorescent light preceded the cab. All it seemed to do was illuminate the haze, but that, and shelter from the clammy fog, were enough to make the return to the land of the living much more pleasant.

"That Mr. Larry something else," Brendy said as the dead taxi glided through the haze. "He slick."

Perry agreed, but he kept his mouth shut, knowing that Peaches would protest. It wasn't so much that Perry thought Mr. Larry was a bad guy; he just didn't naturally trust people he didn't know—especially white people. Peaches, on the other hand, seemed to see the good in everyone until or unless they proved her wrong. It was all right—even admirable—for her to conduct herself this way, in Perry's opinion, because her physical strength and invulnerability allowed it.

"Oh, he ain't slick," Peaches said. She sat in the center of the backseat with one long leg folded underneath her. Her toes dug into the carpet at the bottom of the car. "He just know a thing or two about a thing or two. And he know how to talk to kids."

"What you mean?" Perry asked.

"Well, he sweet and nice and everything," Peaches said. "But you know: most grown-ups is fake nice. Mr. Larry talk to us like we people."

"Is that because he down with kids, or because he down with Black folks?" Brendy asked.

Peaches shrugged. "Prolly both. I think he was married to a Black lady once. I seen 'em together in a picture."

"Lots of white folks married to Black folks," Perry said.

"Yeah, nowdays," Peaches said, "but the picture was all old-timey. Like from Slave Times."

"Wait. So he a ghost?" Perry said. "He look like a real person."

"Haints is people, too, Perry-berry-derry-larry," Brendy said.

Perry blushed and suppressed a grin.

"I dunno," Peaches said. "I mean, he *smell* like a man, and I can hear his heartbeat. But...I dunno. They's more to people than haints and living. Think about it—the P-bodies, they ain't dead, but are they really alive? I mean, *really* really?"

The dead taxi drew to a halt. Perry peered over the front seat as the driver grabbed a mouthpiece off the dashboard and spoke into it. "Ooooah," she groaned. "Oooooooh. Urrrrrrrgggh."

A polite, British-accented voice sounded from the car's speakers. "Your destination has been reached: Dumaine and Moss Streets."

"Oh, all right, then," Peaches said. She peeled off another big bill from her roll and handed it to the driver.

"Unnnh, huh-huh, braaains mRRRRRRUgh!"

"Thank you ever so much. How much change would you like?"

"Thass okay, baby," Peaches said. "Buy yaself something nice."

"Unnnh, huh-huh, gggguh-hruuugh. Urrrrgh."

"Thank you ever so much. Have a long and wonderful life!"

Perry opened his door, and the kids piled out onto the street. "Man," Brendy said. "Zombies is crazy."

Before bidding them good luck and seeing them off, Mr. Larry had explained Da Cut and its history. "Some time ago, a team of what I suppose one would call extraterrestrials lost control of their vessel. This conveyance was not so much a flying saucer as a massive circular structure composed of a single piece of black glass. It came down in Mid-City, cutting a swath of destruction from nearby the racetrack to the Bayou Saint John. Historical records say it sat there, sticking out of the water like some mad modernist sculpture, smoldering, for some time, causing a record-breaking winter heatwave.

"Gradually, it sank into the bayou until the water covered it over, where it lies to this day. One night some years later, a drunken businessman by the name of Creighton Durrant fell into the bayou and found that in spite of his extreme inebriation, breathing the bayou's waters failed to end his life. He awakened at the bottom with ribbons of sunlight streaming down into the waters, which had for many years been filled with the murk and filth of city run-off. Not only did the bayou seem much cleaner after the crash, and the waters entirely breathable, he was able to see that the crew of the spacecraft had opened a panel in its side and fled.

"As it turned out, there were many rooms inside the craft full of alien gewgaws and artifacts, and as he wandered from chamber to chamber, Mr. Creighton hatched a plan. He would return with a crew of contractors and convert the place into a novelty establishment where patrons could experience the thrill of underwater intoxication. After striking a deal with the kings of the various fauna that called the bayou home, Mr. Durrant opened Da Cut to great fanfare. These days, it's taken on a somewhat seedier aspect—for one thing, it is the only establishment willing to serve not just animals and the deceased, but P-bodies as well."

"You mean P-bodies do something besides parade?" Brendy asked.

"Rumor has it that they do indeed." Mr. Larry paused to load his pipe and lit it with a long, thin match. Dirty puffs of smoke trickled from his mouth and nostrils, and he squinted at them through his little cloud. "What's more," he said, "P-bodies are not the strangest creatures to be found in Nola proper. The bar also plays host to High Nutrias, Megaprawns, and Grand Crawdads—among other things."

"What other things?" Perry asked.

"I'll let you find out for yourself," Mr. Larry said, "but I'll say this much: The P-bodies have paraded for far longer than most anyone realizes. Those parading now are not the same ones who first began, which raises the question: Once a P-body parades long enough, walks through enough graffiti, what becomes of him in the end? What are paintbodies really after?"

"What?" Brendy asked. "Tell us!"

"Mr. Larry in onea his moods," Peaches said with a roll of her eyes. "It ain't important. And if it *gets* important, we find out ourselves."

CLICKETY-CLACK

Casey Bridgewater sipped his coffee and set it back down on the counter. He pressed his right palm against his forehead and drew it slowly but firmly down his face. Doing this told him that his face was still there, even if it was so numb it felt like some thief had made off with it while he wasn't looking.

He had spent the night arguing with his girl Naddie. Every time he thought he'd drift off to sleep, she prodded him awake with another question or accusation. Casey'd had to head into his first job at 8 AM with next to no sleep and then go straight on to his second gig, working the counter at the gas station across from the fancy apartments at the end of Esplanade Avenue.

The day had been cool and foggy for the most part—which was good, because the Food Mart's air-conditioning was on the blink again. Mr. Satcherie said he'd do something about it, but there was no telling when or if he'd make a move. Casey sat behind the counter in his black-and-blue uniform shirt, sipping coffee and counting the seconds until 8 PM, when he could walk out of here and head home to be yelled at some more.

And now the radio was on the blink, too. WWOZ sounded like two different stations—one playing Dr. John's new record from start to finish, and the other interrupting it with static like a bickering spouse.

Casey grabbed his pen and filled in some letters in his crossword book. Of course: *jihads* was the perfect six-letter word for "Arabic struggles." As his pen skritched across the page, a few bars of piano—*definitely* not Dr. John—rang out, and the lights of the Food Mart blinked off, then back on again. Right after, a medium-built man in a faded gray hoodie jangled into the store, his hood all the way up, walking in a hurry. If Casey hadn't known better, he would have thought it was raining outside, but by now the fog had burned away, and the darkening sky was dry as baked ceramic.

Casey moved on down the line of crossword clues, but he had stopped reading. He made a show of frowning at the page, but really he was looking toward the back of the store, where the man in the hoodie stood holding a jar of queso dip, staring at it intently.

In queso emergency... Casey thought, and almost giggled at the pun.

It seemed like the lights had never come back on in the far back of the store, where cold cases stood against the wall. That section of the Mart was lost in darkness that shouldn't have been there. Still, Casey took it for an optical illusion. After all, the back of the store seemed much farther away, much darker than it usually did. Lack of sleep could make a man see things, Casey knew. Of course, he'd never started seeing things without missing at least twenty-four more hours than he had so far—

"Gimme this."

"What?"

Casey's vision had skipped. One second, he'd been peering at the darkness clotted in the back of the store, and the next, the man in the hoodie was standing before the counter, glaring down at him. The jar of queso lay on the counter between them.

"Gimme this," said the man. His right hand lay hidden in the front pocket of his hoodie, and something else in there pushed against the fabric, pointing in Casey's direction. "Gimme this and gimme what you got in the register."

Casey felt as if he stood up to his chest in deep water. Time seemed to slow to a trickle of seconds, and each of those seconds was now much more important than before. Casey was keenly aware of the sawed-off shotgun beneath the register, and he was also keenly aware of what a gamble it would be to bend down, arm the thing, raise it, and shoot. A lot could happen in those few seconds. An awful lot.

"All right, cuz." He held up his hands, palms out. "I'ma reach down and open the till *real* slow, ya heard? I give you what's in it, you can take what you want and go on. Everything is cool."

When the shot rang out, Casey thought he'd been hit. His hands leaped to his chest, and he pressed them there for a moment, even as he realized he'd seen the hooded man bounce forward against the counter and then slump down to the tiled floor.

Casey was more frightened now than he had been when he realized the hooded man's gun was on him. Another man stood before him now—at least it *could* be a man, Casey thought. He honestly wasn't sure.

He was dressed to the nines in a blue-and-white striped suit with what looked like a ruffled white silk scarf at the neck instead of a tie. He looked like a time-traveling pimp. He wore an old-timey purple hat—sort of like the ones Dr. Watson wore in the old Sherlock Holmes pictures. Still, even dressed all fancy, there was an amazing physicality to him. He looked capable of any movement, any exertion, and the Colt .45 dangling from his left hand seemed almost an afterthought. What bothered Casey most, though, what made him wonder whether the thing standing before him was a man at all, was his face.

As a young boy, Casey would sometimes go into his parents' bathroom and keep the light off, cracking the door just a little as he stared at himself in the mirror. At first all he saw was a poorly lit silhouette watching him, but after a while, the muscles in his eyes would relax, and the image would change. A monster face would appear, and Casey imagined that it represented the worst aspects of himself. Casey had always felt that if he was able to identify, to physically *see* the worst wrinkles of his character, then they couldn't hold so much power over him.

Tonight, Casey realized how wrong he'd been. It wasn't the worst parts of *himself* he'd seen in that mirror. It was something else entirely. It was this thing that had appeared in his workplace and just *ended* the twitchy robber.

"Wh-what can I do for you?" Casey asked. It was all he could think to say.

FIVE DOLLARS ON PUMP THREE, BABY. The man's mouth didn't move when he talked. His voice seemed to sound somewhere inside Casey, instead of traveling through the air of the store.

"Puh-pump three? Sure." Casey waited for the man—the thing—to hand over the money.

YO LIFE AIN'T WORTH FIVE DOLLARS?

At first Casey didn't understand the question. The sharp-dressed man seemed to operate on a different wavelength—one where the fact that he'd just shot a man in the back and that same man now lay at his feet meant less than nothing.

He tried to remember what the pimp had said. Something about five dollars. Casey's life— Oh. Right.

"Yuh-yeah. Of course." Casey glanced out the window and saw no cars at the pumps. He keyed the transaction in anyway, and when the register opened, he pulled the last five from his wallet and put it in the till. That was his trolley money. He'd be walking home tonight.

SEE YOU LATER, BABY—OR NEVER, IF YOU LUCKY. The man grinned. His mouth was full of gold and jewels.

Casey spoke to himself in his mother's voice. *Don't even look. Just turn your head. You don't want to know what that Negro finna do.*

Casey couldn't help it.

He watched the strangely dressed man step out of the Food Mart and cross to pump three. He pulled the nozzle from its cradle, took off his purple hat, and paused, almost as if he knew Casey was watching. Casey's mouth fell open as the man fit the nozzle in his mouth and began to swallow.

Eventually, he finished drinking and put the nozzle back. Then he reached into his suit and withdrew a metal cigarette lighter. He held it up to his mouth and exhaled a gout of flame. He nodded, satisfied, and turned on his heel, walking toward the bayou. Casey watched as he stepped into the water and disappeared.

Casey knew as soon as the man had gone that he, Casey, would not work another second at the Food Mart. He would go straight home, call the police, and tell them about the robbery—although he wasn't sure what he would say. *Something pretending to be a man shot the robber to death before he could kill me. Then it started breathing fire and walked into the water. Send the SWAT team. Send errybody.* It sounded crazy—and not regular-old-Nola crazy. It sounded for-real-schizo-that-never-happened crazy— Had Casey lost his whole-ass mind?

He grabbed his Yankees ball cap, fit it on his head, and left the Food Mart forever.

To Perry's right stood half a house. Set back from the street behind a beautiful wrought-iron gate, it boasted a wraparound porch lined with modern-looking columns. At some time in the distant past, the house had been cataclysmically sheared in half. Its northern side stood fully intact, but the southern side, the one facing uptown, showed open rooms. One of them looked like half a dining room— a dark wooden table stood on two legs, two and a half chairs positioned around it. Perry wondered about the people who lived there. Had any of them lost part of themselves when the spaceship rolled through? Did the family really have 2.3 children? Hastily, Perry abandoned the thought. He didn't like the idea of half people having to go about their lives like everything was just fine.

The scar left behind by the UFO's passage stretched on for maybe a mile. Now that he thought about it, Perry had seen the scar from the sky trolley without knowing what it was. He tried to imagine a giant black-glass alien ship slicing through the city the way the giant pizza wheel rolled toward James Bond's privates in that one movie. It must have looked, sounded, smelled like the end of the world.

"That's it," Brendy said. "I wanna meet a alien *right now*."

"Aliens is just foreign folks from even farther away," Peaches said with a shrug. "Anyway, we got work. Perry, I want you to repeat the plan to me just like we said."

"All right," Perry said. "So I go in and I ask for my daddy. I get upset and I start raising hell, really make myself the center of attention. I don't stop until whoever working there takes me to the Velvet Room to see my daddy—who ain't really my daddy at all, but Jailbird."

"And?" Peaches said.

"And I gotta make sure to kick up enough fuss that you and Brendy can sneak in. Y'all make y'all way to the Velvet Room, and I come along behind you. Then once we're in there, I call out Jailbird's name, say the Words, and scoop him up. Then we get ourselves thrown out, and we go find Doctor Professor."

"But what about Daddy Deke?" Brendy asked.

"Well, once we get Jailbird to Doctor Professor, Fess can make him tell us where Daddy Deke at," Peaches said. "Then we come up with another plan to get him back."

"Bet," Perry said.

"I need to know one thing, though, Perry," Peaches said. "When the time comes, you gone be ready to use that sack?"

Perry felt stung by the question—mostly because he kept asking himself the same thing and coming up without an answer.

A wave of sound and smell broke over Perry as he stepped into Da Cut. The aroma of the place was so intense that Perry had a hard time picking out scents. All he knew was that there were good ones and bad, and that some of the smells were entirely unfamiliar. The sounds of at least three different songs—punctuated with the sibilants and gutturals of speech, the clinking of ice, the sounds of billiard balls colliding—warred with each other, presenting an overall impression so tangible, so *there*, that Perry felt as if he could have touched it.

It wasn't just that he was standing beyond the threshold of a starship that made Perry feel light-years from home; it was also that Da Cut looked even more alien than the cantina from *Star Wars*. The front room was cavernous—so much so that Perry thought maybe the place was bigger on the inside than it was without.

At first Perry thought the club was lit by giant bulbous colored lanterns, but he realized after a beat or two that the lanterns were ticking slowly across the ceiling, crashing into each other in "mid-air," and crawling over each other in slow motion. They were giant lightning bugs with big, fat glowing butts. Perry couldn't be sure of their size—the room was so large and the ceiling was so high that the bugs could be the size of Peaches's dog Karate, who weighed exactly fifty-six pounds.

A haze of roiling smoke hung above the tables and the three bars, but the smoke was not just one uniform color. Colors coiled around one another, swirling and eddying, and sometimes disappearing into nothing before being replaced by new clouds. Perry hated the smell of cigarette smoke, and he'd never liked the look of it, either, but there was a certain beauty to these clouds. Perry tried to think how one would smoke underwater, and imagined the smoke must come out in bubbles that people blew. But if you're breathing water, then there are no bubbles coming out your mouth and...and the smoke wasn't smoke at all, was it? It was more like strands of colored water threading together.

And then—! And then there were the bar's patrons. A six-foot mustachioed catfish hovered by a table to Perry's right, and seeing him reminded Perry once again that he was actually underwater, that he was on the bottom of the Bayou Saint John. Still, the utter absence of physical distress as Perry stood locking eyes with that giant fish made him feel taller, stronger, and more capable than ever before. Was this how Peaches felt all the time? The hardest thing to get used to was the way the water pushed on him. Every so often, a current would rush by—the weaker ones tickling his fingers or brushing lightly against him, and the stronger ones pulled or pushed with such force that Perry had to tread water just to stay in one place. How did people ever get used to this?

A high nutria about four feet tall and with orange buckteeth the size of playing cards swam over to Perry, kicking his back legs. "What it do, podnah?" he lisped. "Thomething you need?"

"Yeah," Perry said. "I'm looking for my daddy. He in here somewhere, and it's time for him to come home."

"Who your daddy ith?"

"Jimmy Dean Hebert Jr.," Perry said.

The nutria didn't even bother pretending to search the crowd. "I don't know nobody by that name," he said. "He mutht be thomewhereth elthe."

Perry tried not to let on, but as he conversed with the nutria, he kept his eyes on the catfish as well. Up till now, the fish had been nursing a transparent sack filled with amber liquid held with one of his antennae, and now he rested it on the table, watching Perry as keenly as Perry watched him.

"I know he in here," Perry said, addressing the catfish more than the nutria. "I seen him jump into the bayou yesterday. You let me talk to your manager."

"Hey, now," said the nutria.

Perry raised his voice and flailed his arms. "I said I want to talk to the manager! I want my daddy back. All y'all do is trick people! You keep 'em liquored up so all they do is gamble and play pool!"

At the edge of his vision, Perry saw a shock of carrot-colored Afro glide by. His first instinct was to pause his yelling until he knew Peaches and Brendy had not been detected, but to do so would have been falling down on the job.

Perry could feel himself losing steam, but he knew a surefire way to bring his performance home. He thought of Daddy Deke. He thought of his grandfather held somewhere, scared, alone. He thought about how badly he wanted the old man returned to him. Immediately, Perry felt a dizzying surge of rage.

"You give me my daddy back right now. I'm down here underwater, and I just want my daddy home. He got a squashed-up hat, squinty brown eyes, greasy hair, and a wrinkly plaid suit, and I *know* somebody seen him just tonight."

"Now, look," the nutria growled. His lisp had disappeared. "I got things to do. I can't be bothering with no little kid. You can't come in this joint—you too young. Yo mama wants your daddy home so bad, she can come on down and get him her damn self."

"Where the manager at?" Perry demanded. "Why don't you let me walk through and point him out? Then you toss him right out, and I take him home!"

The catfish swam over and nudged the nutria gently with its flank. "Listen, Barry," it said, its antennae twitching. "I seen this kid's daddy in the Velvet Room. Lemme take him back there so he can get on out and leave everybody alone."

The nutria's shoulders sagged in defeat. "Papa Nguyen, you methin' up my night," he said. "Take the kid back and you rethponthible for makin' thure he and hith daddy get on outta here."

"Aight, then," Papa Nguyen said. "Swim after me."

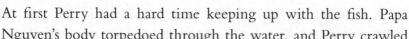

At first Perry had a hard time keeping up with the fish. Papa Nguyen's body torpedoed through the water, and Perry crawled along in his wake. As they left the large front hall, though, Papa Nguyen seemed to realize that Perry was much slower and somersaulted to face the boy.

"You best hang on to my left fin, baby," he said. "They's some crazy rooms between this one and the Velvet, and you liable to lose your way."

Perry hoped Peaches and Brendy had made it through okay. Cornering Jailbird on his own seemed like a losing proposition. He reached out to take hold of Nguyen's fin. It was slimy but not gross, cold but with a living warmth beneath the chill. *This is what a fish hand feels like,* Perry thought. But the thought didn't really make sense. Papa Nguyen used his antennae in place of hands.

Now their swim became a flight. As they left the grand hall, Papa Nguyen rolled in the water, and the rooms streaked by. Perry had no sense of down or up as the rooms whorled past, a mess of glowing colors, glittery stars, and neon beer and liquor signs. Perry caught sight of a graffiti tag in the shape of a woman, rippling on the current. From the way the tag moved, it looked almost as if it were holding a conversation. But wait. It—she?—was. A living tag moving on its own? What—?

They streaked on.

"Here we is, baby," Papa Nguyen said. He stopped so abruptly that it seemed like he must have applied some sort of internal braking system. Perry thrust out his legs, certain that he'd sail right into the bar, but Papa Nguyen wrapped an antenna around Perry's left arm and stilled him in the water.

And there he was. There was Jailbird, realer than real, sitting half-slumped over the bar. He was just as Perry had imagined him—if Perry *had* imagined him—when Mr. Larry sang his song. His wavy, greasy hair floated in the water above his head, and his wrinkly suit looked a bit better underwater, but his hat, which sat on the bar before him, still looked squashed-up and sat-on. He pinched a cigar between the first two fingers of his left hand, and as Perry watched, he lifted it in slow motion and took a pull. He took a puff, threw back his head, and let two underwater smoke rings sail toward the ceiling.

Perry hardly saw the rest of the room. He understood dimly that somehow they were upside-down, that if he could see clear through the club, he'd see the surface of the water rippling below his feet. He hoped Peaches and Brendy were in position by the door. He knew he was about to depart from Peaches's plan, and he wondered whether it was because he was unprepared to use the magic bag burning a hole in his jeans pocket or because he was just too angry to stick to the script.

A zombie stood behind the bar, serving drinks. He handed one to a blue-skinned lady with too many arms, then turned to Jailbird. He groaned.

"Thass right, baby," Jailbird slurred. "One mo' 'gin."

"This your daddy, boy?" Papa Nguyen said, gesturing toward Jailbird.

Perry ignored him. "Jailbird. Look here."

Jailbird's back straightened, and his head wobbled on its stalk. He braced his right hand against the bar and turned himself the wrong way.

"Not there," Perry said. "Other side."

Perry, Peaches said, throwing her voice. *What you doing?*

Perry trembled. The anger he'd let loose to cement his performance in the club's front room had grown beyond his control. He was so mad he could hardly speak. He'd have to force the words between his teeth. It disoriented him badly to learn that he must have been this angry, this upset, ever since Daddy Deke went missing, and that somehow, sometimes, he was able to just put his rage aside.

"You look me in the eye, Jailbird," Perry growled.

Jailbird turned to fix Perry with his watery yellow stare. His gaze didn't seem to focus fully, and Perry knew the man—the song—was seeing him through gallons and gallons of booze.

"My name Roscoe Jankins," Jailbird said. His voice was a thick, wet croak. "Don't know no Jailbird. What you want wif me?"

"I. Want. Him. *Back*," Perry said. "Give him to me, and I let you go. Take me to my granddaddy right now, or I put it on you."

"Put what on me, baby?" Jailbird slurred. "If you looking to buy me a round, I thank ya kindly. If you ain't, you ain't no use to me. Don't need nothing. Don't need no . . . don't need no 'lijun or nothing else."

A commotion swirled through the room. Perry realized only later that he had moved. He had drawn the bag from his pocket and lunged through the water to yank Jailbird from his stool, but everyone had turned to look at something else.

One of the bottles sitting on its shelf behind the bar exploded. Distracted, Perry turned to look at the cloud of amber liquid. He turned back to scream at Jailbird, ready to demand the truth, and saw that Jailbird looked away, toward the entrance of the room.

A man stood inside the doorway, holding a gun in his left hand. He wore a blue-and-white striped suit and an old-timey purple hat. His eyes glowed, but his expression was deadly calm. Peaches stood before him, and from what Perry could see, she had knocked his gun hand as he shot and made him miss his mark.

"... What?" Perry said.

The man opened his mouth and vomited a cloud of fire.

Perry lost sight of Peaches as the flames engulfed her. He saw Brendy dive away from her, frantic to avoid the fire.

"No. Oh, God." Perry wasn't sure who'd spoken, himself or Jailbird.

"Save me, Jesus. Save me. Hide me, Lawd. Oh, God!" That was definitely Jailbird. Hearing him cry out broke Perry's paralysis.

"Brendy! Peaches! Jailbird Stomp!" Perry knew what his next words would be. He was about to say the most awful thing he'd ever said in his life. Worse than the F-word, the B-word, or anything else.

I can't, he thought. *I say them words, I'm not me anymore.*

When he heard them, it was from a remove, as if someone else were speaking.

"Clickety-clack, get into my sack."

The water seemed to disappear from the room. For a moment, Perry felt whole and dry, and a strange lightness settled in his limbs. He knew then that up until this moment, he could have lived. He could have been a boy, played with his friends, loved his family, and gone to school. But not now. Now he was a sorcerer.

He had heard of such people. Figures who could reach behind the seams of the world to manipulate nature or objects. They weren't like the musicians, they were something darker, meaner. All Perry had wanted from life before he quit piano was to magick little things for folks—turning on lights, opening locks whose keys had been lost...not *this*. Certainly not this.

Jailbird had disappeared. Perry had already lost track of Peaches and of Brendy, but now the first gust of flame had cleared, and the fire-breathing man had fixed Perry with his awful gaze.

BABY MAGE, he said without moving his mouth. WHO DONE GAVE YOU WHAT YOU GOT?

"You," Perry said. And as he said the words, he knew he wouldn't be understood. "It was *you*."

BRING JAILBIRD BACK OUTCHEAH. IT'S TIME FOR HIM TO DIE. YOU BRING HIM OUT FORE I SHOOT YOU DEAD AND ROAST THE FLESH RIGHT OFF YO BONES.

"Perilous Antoine Graves," Perry said.

I DON'T PLAY, BABY. BEST BELIEVE.

"Clickety-clack," Perry said. "Get into my sack."

The man—the thing—the song—aimed. It aimed and it shot, and Perry watched the bullet leave the gun. It sailed calmly toward him, ready to kiss him between the eyes. Perry felt the weight of the water around him, the weight of the sky above the water, the weight of space upon the sky. He was at the bottom of everything, circling the drain, ready to pour out into nothing.

Well, that's it, I guess, Perry thought. *For ten whole seconds, I was magic.*

And then...?

And then nothing.

And then black.

Just black.

AUNTIE ROUX

Casey wasn't sure what he was expecting when he returned to Club Desire. Earlier that day, he had taken a step he'd been working up to without realizing it: He'd sketched Bee Sharp again. This time, Sharp was emerging from a hole in the paper, his bug-eyed face a mask of grim resolve. Instead of drawing him in the Marvel house style of the seventies and early eighties, Casey went for a little more realism. His musculature was light, his shoulders on the narrow side, and his Afro had been plaited into cornrows.

That motion effect had emerged again. Casey had employed it almost unconsciously, but once he noticed it he leaned in. He wasn't sure how much control he had in all this, but he knew what he wanted, what he needed. He missed the wildness of creation, the feel of its mechanisms. It had been so long since he thought about it, but he had enjoyed dodging cops and rival taggers, the scritch of graphite on paper, the sizzle and smell of paint rushing from its can. He had to ask himself: If his art was becoming something that shaped the world, that behaved in impossible ways, was that so bad? He had worked so tirelessly to exert control over his own life, over his body, that he'd forgotten something important: some of his best discoveries had come to him when he let go and just clung for dear life.

But what if it brings the Storm?

Casey growled softly to himself. In times gone by, he would have chided himself for thinking so magically, for connecting ideas and events that had nothing to do with each other. The impression that the Storm was somehow connected to the weird things that happened with his and Jaylon's art was only that—an impression. He couldn't ignore it, exactly, but there was no point in letting it run his life.

He finished his sketch and stared at it, waiting for ... something. He didn't like the way Bee Sharp's head was inclined to the left. He looked like he was listening for something. Casey stared hard at the page and willed the figure to take the pose he wanted. When it began to happen, the air of the room took on a hollow, breathless quality. As if it was waiting to be filled or broken. Sharp's head tilted back, and his eyes—or were they sunglasses—appeared a little more faintly at intermediate points in the motion. For a moment, Casey had wondered if it was like a watched pot, if he needed to look away for the drawing to move—but no, there it was. Some small part of him wondered if he was hallucinating, but that voice was tiny, weak. He knew.

Waiting for night was the toughest part. He wanted to bust out of his apartment and run the streets with his gear, find the nearest blank wall—but there was only one place to go. One place where he knew for sure that his familiar world touched something *other*. So he distracted himself with video games until sunset, then got going.

So far out of the way, he was unlikely to catch any flack while he scouted the location, looking for the best place to put the mural. He wore gray-black jean shorts, a black-and-gray camouflage Henley, and a pair of black Chucks. He'd rummaged through the box of paints he'd moved with him ever since evacuating—he'd brought them to every new place, knowing that they represented his old life, something he'd forsworn, but that he still might need them someday. No. That wasn't true, he'd known he needed them, that even if he was unwilling to use them, he needed the strange energy that radiated from them. He'd used it to keep going, to light his path. The path that had led him here, to this moment.

That was why he brought the things with him for what should be a simple scout.

Foxx King's voice returned to him: *First place to look for him would be in his work. His livest and most powerful, heard?*

But Jaylon's mural was gone. It wasn't removed or painted over, it was just absent, as if it had never been. Something about seeing the wall in the light cast by his portable lantern—so pocked and scarred that nobody in his right mind would want to put up a mural here—enraged Casey. He started working feverishly, not even stopping to check his sketch.

Casey felt it happen the moment he finished Sharp's face.

He hadn't even begun filling in the outline of the lettering in his name, but a ripple spread from the wall and broke over him, knocked him backwards onto the lantern. With a crunch the light winked out and darkness rang like a shout.

The energy surrounding him was neither hot nor cold, but he recognized it as the same power that had surrounded him when he willed the sketch to change its position. The dark air danced with it, and even though he could see nothing at all, Casey was terribly aware of the trash, debris, and detritus, the vermin hiding and peeping among the rubble, the cast-off garbage and the wall, the wall, the wall where Bee Sharp's invisible face had turned to gaze down at him.

Suddenly, Sharp was gone. Casey still couldn't see him—his eyes were only barely beginning to adjust to the near complete blackness threatening to drown him—but he knew it just the same. Now the door through which he'd entered the ruin was visible away to Casey's left. A silhouette appeared there.

"Who's there?" Casey asked. His voice cracked.

You know who, baby.

"Foxx? You followed me?"

If it helps, I spose.

"I broke my lantern. I can't—I can't see."

Can't you?

Casey *could* see. His surroundings were just as visible as they would be by daylight, lit by a moon that must have emerged from the clouds. The figure at the door was still just an outline, becoming more visible by the second. Casey looked hastily away. "I'm looking—I'm looking for Jaylon. They—he's supposed to be dead, but they—they never found his body. Not even a scrap of him."

Heard. Lemme ask around see what I find out. And thank you.

"For—for what?"

Now, Casey clenched his eyes shut. *Don't say it,* he thought. *Don't don't don't. I'm not ready!*

"For helping me." The figure paused. "Out."

Casey didn't answer. His eyes were still shut, and now his hands were plastered to his face. That rippling energy was still around him, bathing him, tickling his skin. Then, as with the flip of a switch, he lost consciousness.

Yvette Graves told her husband over the phone that she'd let the kids go out on their own while he was away at work. The manufactured calm that he'd cultivated since his father went missing disappeared from his voice, replaced by a full-blooded shout. *"Woman, have you lost your mind?"* he'd bellowed into the receiver. *"Now I gotta look for them too? You can't just—! You can't just let them go wherever whenever!"*

"Now, listen, Deke, I know you upset, but you gotta hear me on this," she said. She had called and explained the situation to him as best she could because she knew that if he came home to find the kids had gone, he would have been even more frightened, even less understanding than he was now. Deacon was used to musical magic—everyone in Nola was. It kept the streetlights running, powered the electricity in their homes, and kept the trolleys in the sky. Slowly, over time, Yvette had told him about the Wise Women of her family, revealing a darker seam of sorcery that ran through their world. He'd been reluctant, at first, to allow Perry to take piano lessons, but Yvette had convinced him that it was a safer, less demanding alternative to the sorcery she'd tried to learn.

When Perry had come to them, clearly upset, and demanded to transfer to a different school, Deacon couldn't hide his relief. He had explained to Yvette that their son wanting to be a normal boy made it ten times easier to protect him, give him space to thrive. Yvette argued that they needed to question Perry, or take him to a psychologist who could ferret out the reason for their boy's change of heart. Deacon hadn't liked that idea at all.

"Yvie," he'd said, "if he was sick, if he was hurt, I'd be all for it. But what he's asking us is utterly sane. Why would he want a session spot at the Sewerage and Water Board, or an apprenticeship at Young Money with all those gangbanging rappers? I'm not saying we should let him switch because it's easier, but I know in my bones it'll be healthier for him in the long run."

Yvette couldn't help remembering her own lessons. Mama Lisa had started early, teaching her small spells at home: heating bathwater, helping to weatherproof their house on South Lopez Street, keeping the house plants healthy—but by the time she was ten, Yvette began having migraines. Magickal workings only made the pain worse, and finally Mama Lisa had had to concede that Yvette wasn't meant to be a Wise Woman after all. When the lessons ended, the migraines had disappeared, and an enormous weight had lifted from her shoulders. How could she deny her son that same relief? Mama Lisa had told her before disappearing that Perry had a sorcerous destiny, but she'd failed to predict her own disappearance. So...maybe she'd been wrong.

The night Doctor Professor appeared out of season, Yvette had seen her babies dancing in the street and felt a pang of regret. What if she'd made a mistake?

She shut her eyes against the memory. "They're with Peaches," she said. "She'll keep them safe if anyone can." She thought it best not to mention that the children were armed or how they'd got their weapons.

By the time Deacon arrived home that night, Yvette felt ready to explain. Leaving aside her telephone conversation with her dead mother, she would instead focus on how proud she and Deacon should be that their children cared so deeply about their family and their city.

When Deacon's car purred quietly into the driveway, Yvette positioned herself in the hallway outside the kitchen, where she had a full view of the front door and its stained glass. She took a breath as her husband's key scratched in the lock and held it as he stepped inside.

"Aw, honey!" she said without meaning to. She couldn't help it; her husband looked ten years older than he had this morning. His shoulders, usually squared with confidence, sagged in his jacket. He looked like an overgrown little boy. It occurred to Yvette then that, in some ways, that's exactly what he was. What they all were—children stumbling through the world, bowing their shoulders underneath the pressures of responsibility and fear.

"I'm only here to change clothes," Deacon said. "After that, I'll go out and look."

"Deacon. Deke."

"I'm sorry I lost my temper. I just—sometimes I feel like we're up to our eyeballs in crazy, and we've got to stick together, because...because what do we have if we don't have each other?"

"We have—"

Yvette's voice stopped in midsentence as a snatch of song rang out from the kitchen. It was a high, sweet alto: *"My first name is Yve-e-e-e-tte!"*

Yvette answered without thinking, *"Y-V-E-T-T-E!"*

Yvette turned as Mama Lisa stepped out of the darkened kitchen, and they sang together:

Cuz that is my name, and it can't be tamed
There just ain't nobody like me!
And my first name is Yvette!

It wasn't much of a song—Mama Lisa had adapted it for Yvette from a church hymn neither of them remembered. She had used it to teach her little girl to say and spell her first name, but as Yvette grew, they had held on to it, singing snatches every now and then. Every time they did, a tingling warmth spread through Yvette's body, and she felt as she had when she was a toddler and her mother would rub Yvette's belly and fold her against the comfort of her mother-ness. Hearing and singing the song again, Yvette felt five years old: small but fiercely alive. Safe. Protected. Joy and relief coursed through her, and her knees wobbled as she stood.

"Thank you for your apology, Deacon," Mama Lisa said quietly. "My baby girl shouldn't be spoken to just any kind of way."

Now Deacon *sounded* like a little boy. "Mama Lisa?" he asked, his voice cracking high in his throat.

"Yes," she said. "Here I am."

The strangest thing to Yvette was that now, fully grown, she was physically larger than her mother. The woman was small boned and dark-skinned—five feet tall if she was lucky—but her influence on Yvette, the bond between them, was so strong that whenever Yvette thought of her mother, whenever she saw her mother in her mind's eye, she towered.

Yvette tried to speak, but the only thing that would fit through her throat was a sort of pained babyish squawk.

Yvette rushed to her mother, grabbed her off her feet, and squeezed the smaller woman with a force that surprised even her. She clenched her eyes shut, and for a moment there was no hurt, there was no danger, and no questions came to mind. Mama Lisa's warmth, her solidity, soothed an ache Yvette had harbored quietly for all the years of her mother's absence.

After some time, when she was ready, Yvette set Mama Lisa back on the linoleum floor and just stared at her.

"Don't goggle at me like that," Mama Lisa said, smiling slightly. "I'm not a two-headed dog."

"I don't understand," Deacon said. "Where have you been?"

"Away," Mama Lisa said. "I didn't want to go, I didn't mean to leave, but it was time."

"Where?" Deacon asked. "Where?" It was as if that was the only word he knew.

"I'll explain later if I can," Mama Lisa said. "I promise. Right now, Yvette and I must go to Congo Circus. Stay here. Don't leave the house. Lie down and rest. The children will be back before long, I promise. The two of us will return even before they arrive. Now, tell me what you are to do."

Deacon opened his mouth and just stared at the small woman. "I'm to— You want me to stay here. Try to sleep. The kids are coming back soon? Are they?"

"They are. They're unharmed. Peaches has kept them safe."

"What about my father?"

"He'll be found before long, but not by you," Mama Lisa said. "Yvette and the children need you here."

"Is he...?" Deacon couldn't finish the question.

"Dead? No. He's imprisoned. Captured by the rebel song."

"That's what Perry said," Deacon said. "He said someone stole my father."

"You two have done well with him. With all of them," Mama Lisa said. "Go upstairs, shower, and sleep. We have a lot to talk about when the children arrive."

Casey Bridgewater finished his torrent of words but did not close his mouth. It hung open in the post-midnight darkness of the bedroom, and while his sobs made no noise, he could tell from the wetness against his cheeks and palms that he was crying. This weeping reminded him of the way he had cried as a young boy—when his voice would leave him and he would wail without sound into the uncaring air.

Naddie rested her small, sincere hand on his left thigh and sat silently until Casey could speak again. He breathed in her scent— honey and melons—and let it calm him.

"That's why I was so late coming home," he said. "I had to walk here cuz I gave that monster my last five."

He lay in the depression at the center of the king-sized bed they shared, both hands covering his face as if even the late-night gloom was bright enough to hurt his eyes.

"I'm glad you're okay," Naddie said softly.

"I'm not okay," Casey said. "And neither is Nola. Something bad's going on."

"You really think so?"

Casey paused to examine the fluttering unease at his center. It had been so long since he had felt anything like it that the sensation was almost unrecognizable—but it was the same guttering orange flame of anxiety he felt anytime he saw on the news that a storm was headed through the gulf. Storm coming. Storm coming. Wind, flood, fire, and—

"I know so," he said. "I know it."

He didn't know how the thing he'd seen at work was related, but he knew there was some connection he was too ignorant to parse.

Naddie's fingers grazed his wrist, then closed around it. She pulled his hand gently away, and he moved the other himself. In the darkness, his girlfriend was little more than a collection of shapes—her red-blond hair shining in the streetlight that crept into the small room from the blinds on the east window.

"You're safe," she said.

"We gotta get out of here. We gotta *go*."

"Go where?"

"I don't know," Casey said. "I don't remember. Grand Isle, maybe? Somewhere."

"If you really think something bad's about to happen to the city, we should tell Auntie Roux."

"What she gonna do for us? She don't even tell fortunes no more."

"No. She doesn't. But she knows Doctor Professor."

"Doctor—? She don't know him. Nobody does. He's like a— Is he even a person? I never seen him."

"He's real," Naddie said. "And if something's wrong with the city, he needs to know."

"And you wanna go over now," Casey said bitterly. "I don't even know if I can leave the house."

"What do you think that man—that thing—you saw is doing down in the bayou?"

"Nothing good."

At least they didn't have to walk this time. He sat in the passenger seat of Naddie's car, watching the city scroll by as they made their way from Gentilly, headed for the French Quarter. Naddie swerved to avoid a graffito, and not for the first time since they'd left the apartment. There was more of it tonight than usual. Casey had seen four or five tags at least on his way home. That overwhelming sense of something big and bad and wrong with the city returned to him again, and Casey shut his eyes against it. It felt as if the night were a bubble of soap and the pressure from outside could easily destroy it.

Naddie guided her little white Bug off Esplanade and onto Rampart Street. *It's okay,* Casey told himself. *It's fine. Everything's going to be fine.*

The houses on Rampart Street stood mostly silent. Here and there, orange light flooded through doors and windows, adding its glow to the streetlights that splashed over the car. No other vehicles were out at this hour, which, to Casey, seemed more than a little strange. Casey breathed his relief as he saw the open doors of the Powder Room. When he had lived in this neighborhood, it had been his favorite bar—and if it was open and serving, then things couldn't be so bad.

They reached Armstrong Park, and Naddie found a parking space outside the Ninth Circle. She drew the car to a halt and made to go off alone.

Casey had made it clear in the past that he was extremely

uncomfortable around Auntie Roux. He didn't understand her magic, her bizarre personality, or honestly, her importance to Naddie. That fluttering in his chest told him what to do—he *had* to go with her this time instead of waiting in the car. He felt like he'd been waiting in the car all his life.

Casey unlatched his seat belt and climbed out onto the street. Naddie paused, and they shared a look across the car's roof. From here, Casey could smell the caramel apples and cotton candy of the Square circus, and the steamboat calliope piped up from the Missus Hipp. Until just now, Casey hadn't realized how much he'd missed its strange no-song.

"Let's do this thing," Casey said.

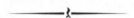

Even at this hour, the circus was still going strong. Ninja clowns sparred just inside the gates of the park, and fortune-tellers in poet's blouses and pirate hats waved their hands, selling silly predictions to people from Away. Here and there, a giant crawfish, a nutria, or a zombie sat selling trinkets or rubbing the rims of crystal glasses, adding glassy hums to the sound of the pipes. The entire scene reminded Casey of one of the old Jacques Cousteau specials, where the Frenchman drifted through a drowned garden full of jeweled fish and tubeworms like feather boas. Casey had always wondered what kind of music could be heard down there.

Naddie reached for Casey's hand, and together, they made their way toward the circus's grandest tent. It was a broad, lacy structure striped in lavender and white. It smelled of cinnamon and oils from far away.

Inside, the sound of the circus died away, and an atmosphere of peace pervaded the scene. At the center of the tent, instead of a pole, a statue, weathered beyond identification, raised its cornet toward the sky. A pelican sat preening on the statue's shoulder, and as the light shifted just a little, Casey realized he could see through the bird. He'd never seen an Animal haint, had no idea such things existed—but why wouldn't they? If nutrias, crawfish, and gators lived lives and did business, why would all that activity cease at death?

Auntie Roux sat at a kidney-shaped table, holding the hands of a heavyset light-skinned woman with short hair and perfectly arched eyebrows. Another darker woman sat by her, and watching them, Casey couldn't tell which was the older.

"Now we ready, babies," Auntie Roux said. "Our final piece of information is here." She looked up at Casey and smiled. "What it do?"

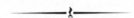

Auntie Roux swore she was five feet tall, but Casey had his doubts. She was perfectly proportioned, so she must not be a dwarf, but Casey was certain that if she rose from her seat to stand at her full height, the top of her head would barely reach his shoulder.

Instead of proper jewelry, she wore rubber bands inset with sequins and plastic stones—the kind of things you could buy out of dispensers at Rouses Market for ten cents a pop. Wind chimes hung from the fringes on her puffy sleeves, and jingle bells lined the hem of her diaphanous skirt. Roux was given to broad, flowing gestures, so most of her movements were accompanied by music.

Her complexion was difficult to process. In low light it looked a bit yellow, but having rarely seen her by day, Casey wasn't sure how she would be categorized by anyone interested in race. Her hair was a rich royal purple, locked into dreads hung with puka shells and hammered brass crescent moons. Faded blue tattoos stood out on her face—crosses, diamonds, moons, and even a Star of David or two. Two bright spots of color stood out on her cheeks, making her ageless face both childish and comically wise.

As always, she was attended by a squadron of sewing moths— little diamond-shaped squares of fabric made from the sewing together of two triangles—who flapped their tips, wheeling around her to chase each other or dart toward bystanders before zipping away. No one but Casey ever seemed to acknowledge their existence—to the point where Casey was unsure anyone else could see them.

In his dealings with Auntie Roux, Casey had heard her say little that made any practical sense—not that she blathered about spirits, fates, or symbols. Most of what she said related to cooking or sewing. Casey would nod and smile at her advice, just like everybody else. He wondered whether he was the only one who simply humored her.

"So," Auntie Roux said. "Ladies, you have stirred yo gumbo just right! Arming dem children was the best decision you coulda made. But no mistake, chits and chitterlings, it ain't through the strength of arms that they gonna prevail at last. It is through the clearness of dey voices and the purity of dey affections."

"Roux," the dark woman said. "Settle down and talk straight for a change. I taught you better than this. My daughter and I need your skills. Where are my grandbabies?"

"I can locate and contact anyone or anything in this world," Roux said, speaking more clearly and with more care than Casey had ever heard from her, "but I have checked and double-checked and checked again, and they are nowhere to be found."

The other, heavier woman rocked back in her seat and took in a deep breath, as if ready to shout.

"Yvette," the darker woman said sharply. "Hold on. This isn't the first time they've left this world."

"They are nowhere to be found among the living or the dead," Roux said. "In which case, they must be elsewhere entirely. I don't know where they at, but I know someone who might. Fess can tell us what we need to know."

"Good," said the dark-skinned woman. "It's time I had words with that one."

"You're not the only one. My Naddie and her boy have news he needs to hear."

"We do?" Casey asked. "I do?" He hated the way he sounded—ignorant and out of his depth.

"Tell what you come to tell, boy," Auntie Roux said.

Casey told his story. This time, he took his time, taking care with every detail as well as the sequence of events. All eyes rested on him, and nobody liked what they were hearing.

"This is worse than I thought," the dark woman said. "You produce that old haint right now, Roux, and I'm going to tell him about himself."

"But—" Casey began.

"I will call and he will come," Auntie Roux said, "but best you remember his value to us all."

"Roux."

"Wait a minute," Casey interrupted. "What's going on? Somebody gotta tell me something."

"That wasn't a man you saw," the dark woman said. "His name is Stagger Lee Shelton. Way back when, he murdered a man named Billy Lyons in an argument over his Stetson hat, and the dealing of death got good to him. He started off killing anybody who did him dirt or disrespected him, and he moved on to killing other things—animals, words, days of the week. With the power of his gun, he was even able to murder ghosts."

Casey opened his mouth.

"Don't interrupt. You asked and I'm answering. Now. The only way the Wise Women were able to stem the blood-red tide of Stackolee's murderous intent was to immortalize him in song. His essence was drawn out of the world to reside in what for many, many years was a harmless tune, but it seems it ain't so harmless now. He's out on the street killing again, and it's Fess who's to blame. Does that answer your questions?"

"He— Days of the week?" Casey asked.

The dark woman ignored him. "Roux. Summon him!"

Rocking in her seat, Auntie Roux began to sing.

A Day Gone Come

July 1922

Verret's Lounge was a modest little bar at the corner of Washington and Baronne. Its interior was all dark wood paneling and velvety green carpet. These days, Deacon Ravel spent most of his nights there when he wasn't running errands or delivering messages for the Family. Tonight, the large industrial fan they used to cool the place was out of commission, so he'd stripped to his undershirt while he shot pool, drinking copiously and dipping out now and then for some fresh air and a smoke. The place smelled like a locker room.

Deacon put the six in the corner pocket and mopped his brow with the bar towel Linc the bartender had lent him earlier that night. He thrust his chin at his cousin Learned and stepped aside while the heavier man eyeballed his next shot.

When he turned, he almost collided with Weeby Jackson, a clean-cut teenager who walked with a limp. Weeby was still fully dressed, but beads of sweat stood out on his forehead. The set of his face let Deacon know that the boy was determined to ignore his discomfort. "Gotta visitor, Mr. Deke," the boy said. "Said to tell you it's Dip from the Waifs."

"Send him round back."

"Consider it done."

The back courtyard was lit by green glass floor lamps that spouted halos of dirty dim bulbs. Two bare wooden picnic tables stood to Deacon's left, but back and to his right was a floral-printed canopy under which sat a low couch and two folding visitor chairs. Dipper stood waiting in powder-blue slacks, a damp pinstriped suit, and a blue-and-white striped vest.

"Sit, sit, Negro!" Deacon said as he strode past to the couch. "Ain't no job interview."

"No interview, naw," Dip said. "But serious just the same."

"Well, that don't sound good," Deacon said. He hated that things had come to this, but at least Dipper seemed to understand the gravity of the situation.

"Ain't here about trash pickup this time round," Dipper said. "You might say I went ahead and took it out myself."

"They's been a bit of buzz in the old beehive lately," Deacon said. "Cain't say it's the good kind."

"I'll give it to you straight," Dipper allowed. "I been summoned. Problem is, I ain't sure what I'm walking into if I come like I been told."

"Well," Deacon said. He glanced at Weeby standing stock-still and stone-faced outside the bar's back door. "Weeb. Bottle of VO and a couple glasses, then make yaself scarce, heard?"

"Yezzir," Weeby said, and pivoted crisply away.

"I thought it was handled," Deacon said. "Legs was broke and messages was sent. But then you mixed it up with some white boys over in Gretna? Six or seven of them and one of you?"

"I ain't proud," Dipper said. "That one didn't go the way it shoulda."

He paused as Weeby returned to set the bottle and glasses before them. When the boy withdrew, Deacon poured them each a couple fingers.

"Le chaim," Dipper toasted, and they drank.

"Five of them boys dead as Latin," Deacon said. "And that's the problem. You shoulda kilt 'em all. The other one telling crazy stories about a ten-foot nigger with a scream that kills."

Dipper's expression brightened a little. "Well, that don't sound like me a tall…"

"Not to nobody don't know nothing," Deacon said. "But the Powers ain't exactly enthused if you catch my drift. They discussing punitive measures."

Dipper's face fell. Carefully, he lifted his glass to his scarred lips and drank. "Drastic measures?"

"They's voices in your favor," Deacon said. "But my advice is hand over that cornet and beat feet awhile. Let things blow over. That way the calls for banishment lose they teeth."

The corners of Dipper's mouth sagged. He looked sick. "You know I can't," he said. "You know I can't part with the horn. I swore a oath."

"Use your head, baby! How you think that's gone sound to the Kid?"

"We could cut," Dipper said hopefully.

Deacon's scalp tightened. "Nigga, you cross horns with the Kid, you *die*. You ain't seen the kind of sorcery that motherfucker will put on ya. Now, this ain't coming from me. I talked to Jelly Roll, dig? He will honor your service by allowing you to leave without barring your return—provided you stay gone a good long while."

"But—"

"But unless you turn over the horn, ain't nothing nobody can do. If that white motherfucker remembers wa'ant no nigger shouting, he was playing a horn, that spells trouble don't none of us need."

Dipper fell silent, considering. Then, "What about the Karnovskys?"

There it was, Deacon thought. That was the same spirit that had gotten Dipper into trouble to begin with. If he'd been alone when the Klansmen attacked, he wouldn't have employed such deadly force—not to save his own skin.

"Off-limits," Deacon said. "They'll be under the Powers' protection indefinitely."

Dipper sagged, relieved. Deacon saw now that the question bothered his cousin worse than he'd realized.

"I can't give you the whole thing," he said. "It'd violate my oath, and I could never safely play another note. But. I'll give you the mouthpiece right now if that will settle it."

Deacon sipped his whiskey and took a moment to savor its familiar burn before he answered. This was what Jelly Roll had demanded when Deacon went before him to plead for Dipper's life. It had been a gamble to ask for the whole horn, but if he hadn't, Dip wouldn't have been willing to part with even this much of it.

"The Powers gone be pissed," Deacon said. "But I might can smooth it over."

Dipper nodded sadly. He stood, and calm settled over him and his eyes swam shut. Without opening them, he gestured quickly and the blazing trumpet appeared in the air before him. Its shine lit the courtyard like a frozen flash of lightning.

Deacon shut his eyes as Dipper reached for the instrument.

For another moment, his vision showed red, and when he felt the light recede, he opened his eyes. Dipper held the gleaming mouthpiece in the palm of his hand. The rest of the horn had gone back where it came.

"Deke."

"Yeah," Deacon said softly.

"I'ma turn this over to you on one condition."

"Being what?"

"Show it to the Powers. Let 'em know you have it and that I promised I'd go for good—but don't turn it over. *You* keep it."

"Me?" Deacon said. "I ain't played since the Home. What I do with it?"

"It ain't for you to use," Dipper said. "But a day gone come."

A day gone come. Deacon rolled onto his back and tears ran down to his temples. Was it here, though? Had the day finally come? *Lord,* but he hoped not...

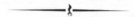

So this is death. The words sounded faint and calm in Perry's mind, and he was impressed with his own cool. He felt himself falling, falling through a blackness so profound that he couldn't be sure whether his eyes were open or closed.

He tried to open his eyes—or he tried to try. He imagined the curvature of the earth and clouds upon clouds piled below him and decided that if his eyes were closed, they should stay that way a little while longer.

I know what's happening, Perry thought. *I've been shot, and this is me falling down dead.* That must mean that time had slowed even more than it had when the evil song had fired its gun, and if it slowed any further, Perry might hurtle like this forever. He wasn't sure how he felt about that. He enjoyed the absence of gravity, but he hated that feeling of waiting for something else to replace it.

Something damp touched Perry's right arm, and he knew he must still have a body. He had suspected that his body had been riddled with bullets, damaged beyond repair, and that he had stepped out of it, tripped, and fallen. He wondered briefly where he would end up after all this. Had he been good enough to get into Heaven? He was sure he hadn't been bad enough to get into Hell. He'd never done anything truly wrong.

...Except for messing with the Clackin' Sack.

Except for saying the Words and trying to use the sack on himself and his friends.

Shouldn't he be afraid? Perry decided that he must be terrified, but his terror must have become too much for him, and his body had been too small to contain it. Somewhere nearby, it too fell through nothing and nothing, unable to rattle Perry's bones.

Well, in that case, Perry wasn't afraid after all, was he? And if he wasn't afraid, he might as well do something.

"*Brendy!*" he shouted in the darkness.

Now he felt his heart beating in his chest. It was faster than normal, but not out of control. *Ba-bump, ba-bump, ba-bump*, going like a metronome. Perry counted four, five, six . . .

Then, away in the distance: "Waaaaaaaugh! Perry! Where you iiiiiis?"

"*Don't know!*" Perry bellowed. "*Close! I can't see nothing!*"

"I'm faaaaaallling!"

"*Yeah!*" Perry shouted. "*Me too! Where Peaches at?*"

"I'm sorry I got mad! I don't wanna die!"

"*Brendy! Where Peaches at?*"

More wetness. This time the sensation enveloped Perry, dampening his skin, clothes, and hair. Had he passed through a cloud of some kind? He smelled salt. It reminded him of the sea aroma Perry had smelled when his family had taken a boat trip out onto the Gulf. Perry pushed the thought away. Memories were no good to him. What was important was right now, and moments from now.

The wetness passed, and Perry fell free again. He could feel himself drying rapidly, but somehow he wasn't cold.

He could hear Brendy sobbing. She must be crying big little-kid tears, because he heard her crying better than he'd heard her calls.

"Brendy," he called. "*Everything gonna be oh! Kay! You gotta answer me now, you hear? Where? Peaches? At?*"

"I gots her, I think. I think I'm holdin' her hand. The fire hit her! She burnt!"

Now Perry offered a silent prayer. This one was different from any he'd prayed before bed or during church. It came from a part of him that barely understood words. It poured from him as a feeling, and as it bubbled up through Perry's consciousness, he translated it to himself. *Please, Lord, please.* Please *let Peaches be okay.*

And then because it seemed that ship had sailed, *Please let her live. Just let her live, Lord, and I'll care for her till she's better.*

Peaches was the only person who would know what to do right now. Without her guidance, Perry felt worse than lost. What would she do if she found herself falling and falling through nothing? Change direction? That wouldn't work. How could Perry even be sure that he was falling down and not up? The normal physical laws didn't seem to apply. He thought of what Peaches had told him about grown-ups, about how they were just old kids pretending, making things up as they went along. The idea had horrified him, but maybe something in it could aid him. Maybe he should just…make something up. He couldn't see how doing so could make matters any worse.

"*Okay!*" Perry called. "*All right. You got her. So I count to three, then we stop! Falling!*"

"We gonna hit!" Perry couldn't tell whether it was a question.

"*No!*" Perry shouted. "*I count, and then on three, we go somewhere else where we ain't falling, aight?*"

"Where we go?"

"*Anywhere with solid ground! If I ain't there, I come find you. Stay with Peaches!*"

"What about Jailbird?" Brendy asked.

"*Oh, we got some things to talk about,*" Perry said, and the stone in his voice surprised him. "*If he ain't there after we count, I find him. I promise.*" Then, "*You ready?*"

"Ready!" she called. She sounded almost hopeful.

"*One!*" Perry shouted. "*Two! Three! GO!*"

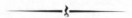

The transition was so perfect and so complete that Perry forgot all about falling and darkness. He forgot years and years, and he was small again—not so small he couldn't talk, but small enough that if he spoke, he'd have to struggle to make himself understood.

He sat in a church pew. His legs were so short that they stuck out straight in front of him, not even dangling over the front of the pew. To dangle his legs, Perry would have had to scoot forward on his booty. He fidgeted, scanning the sanctuary.

From here all he saw were backs of necks, backs of heads. Grown-ups sat in their Sunday finery as a preacher blustered about the straight and narrow. Perry reached for his mother's arm, pulling at her flesh, but she pulled away without turning. Perry wanted her to look at him. He wanted her to say something, to shush him at least, or glare at him to behave.

Perry squinted at the woman, willing her attention.

"Saints, I tell you true," said the preacher. Her voice stretched out on the perfumed air, and it seemed to bend as it hung, changing to become more familiar. Still, it was a voice Perry had never heard—at least not in waking life—and he recognized it the way he would beautiful music played by expert hands.

"All it takes is a little consideration. All you gotta do is listen real careful to that Still Small Voice, and it will tell you everything you got to know."

Perry had heard that voice somewhere, all right. In his dreams? Not in the ones he built himself, and not in the surface dreams that had him jousting dragons or freeing his brother pirates from space prisons, but in the secret dreams, the ones that played out on a mental stage fully removed from Perry's own unconscious mind. The ones dreamed not just by him, but by everyone all the time, the dreams that people wander into and out of without remembering in daylight.

"The Kingdom is within all of us. We know right from wrong. You know right from wrong. You know because the Lord knows within you, Perry."

"What?" Perry asked.

"Let us lift our voices, church!"

The congregation rose to their feet, and Perry's mother rose with them. Still, she didn't look around at him, and Perry had begun to doubt her identity. Maybe he shouldn't be trying so hard

to get her attention. Maybe she'd be upset with him if she ever did
turn.

I was standing on the corner
Down in old Saint Louie Town
And my dog started barkin' at two men
Who was cussin' in the dark

The song's opening bars filled Perry with dread. *Please don't*, he
tried to say. *Don't sing that song. It's a bad one.*

It was Stagger Lee and Billy
And both men been drinkin' late
Stagger Lee say he threw seven
Billy swore that he threw eight

Perry tried to argue with the congregation. *You don't understand.*
If you sing his song, he's here. *If you sing it, he* knows. *He's not like the*
rest.

New connections flashed like lightning across Perry's brain,
brightening and dimming so quickly that his consciousness
couldn't hold on to them. He ceased his arguing, listening intently,
hanging on every lyric. He concentrated, trying to remember as
closely as he could, to file it all away.

Now, Stagger Lee shoved Billy
And he drew his forty-five
Said, Billy, you in trouble
You ain't leavin' here alive
Aw, Stagger Lee!

The singing died away, and raucous piano music rose to the fore.
The pianist pounded the keys, and a saxophone began to scream.
The two instruments dueled each other in a graceful tug-of-war,

rising and falling and tumbling together like raptors warring over a mouse.

I'm Stagger Stagger Lee
I'm Stack Stack O Lee
Y'all know just what you seen
I done shot that Billy down

As the church band played the last few bars, Perry scrambled to stand in his pew and roared into the noise. The howl that rushed out of him was one of anger and triumph, and Perry hadn't known such a cry existed within him. Feeling it in his throat brought tears to his eyes.

Even as the tears spilled down his cheeks, Perry's surroundings began to dissolve. A lump clogged his chest.

"No!" he called. "Tell me why! I want to know why he took Daddy—!"

But the image faded, and blackness reigned again.

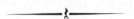

The little room smelled of black mold and damp concrete. One lightbulb hung, naked and grimy, from the center of the ceiling. Deacon Graves Sr. knew he'd been dreaming, but he could remember only a couple details. There had been a bar, a cousin or a relative. A bright light. He sat on the hard little cot where he spent most of his time and tried to comfort himself with the thought that he was still alive and kicking. Stagger Lee could have killed him easy as breathing, and yet here Deacon was. That meant Stag must need him for something.

Deacon had seen Stag only once since the powerfully built man had shoved him through the room's narrow doorway—and Deacon wasn't sure whether that counted. He'd been asleep, dreaming of his grandson, Perry, and Stagger Lee had appeared out of nowhere, just as he had in real life, and dragged Deacon back to waking.

But had Stag just appeared? Was that how it had gone? Deacon ignored his hunger and the aching in his swollen knees and thought back to his abduction. He'd been idling at the light, and then all of a sudden Stagger Lee was there, pulling him out of the car. But—

"The radio," Deacon said aloud.

Stagger Lee had first appeared as a column of black smoke rising from Deacon's dashboard speakers. He remembered frowning at the sight, trying to make sense of it. Deacon hadn't smoked in years and years—and never in his prized Comet. At first, he thought the car's cigarette lighter must be on the blink. But the smoke had expanded to fill the car's front seat. Deacon had seen eyes suspended in the cloud, glowing, glaring murder. It wasn't until after the smoke began to speak that Deacon realized that it had become a man.

Well, not a man. Not exactly.

And that was when Deacon had recognized the apparition for Stagger Lee. Who else could he be? It didn't matter that Stagger Lee was just a old blues song. Didn't matter that songs were songs and people was people and couldn't no song put on a pair of wingtips and go walking round town. Deacon had known exactly what was happening, and he did his best to shield his family from whatever magical goings-on had brought this nightmare into the daylight.

Thinking fast, Deacon had used some of the little magic he knew. Without stopping to listen to what Stagger Lee wanted, Deacon belted out a couple of familiar bars:

I thought I heard Buddy Bolden say
Funky butt, funky butt, take it away!

Stagger Lee hissed as if he'd been burned. OLE MAN, he said. YOU HUSH UP THAT SINGIN', YOU KNOW WHAT'S GOOD FOR YOU.

"More where that come from," Deacon said. "I ain't afraid to die. I'll put it on you sumn fierce. Now, what you want with me?"

Stagger Lee's expression softened some. ASSOCIATE O MINE NEED YO HELP. YOU DO AS MY ASSOCIATE ASK, TELL IT WHAT IT NEED TO KNOW, NO HARM NEED COME TO YOU . . . OR YO FAMILY.

"My family?" Deacon said. He opened his mouth to sing again.

NEGRO, YOU KNOW WHO I'M IS, AND YOU KNOW I SHOOT YOU DEAD AND QUESTION YO GHOST. HOW YO FAMILY FEEL BOUT THAT?

Deacon envisioned a room in the Majestic Mortuary. He saw new fissures carved into his son's face. Saw his daughter-in-law wet eyed and keening. Saw his grandkids looking to the older folks for sense. He wasn't afraid to die, but he sensed that he had entered this life on specific business—business that he had not yet finished, couldn't finish if he died again too soon. He didn't examine the thought any further than he had to.

"I come quietly," Deacon said, "long as you stay the hell away from my people."

DON'T BE TRYNA DEAL WITH ME, BABY, Stag said. THE DEVIL DEALS, AND HE AIN'T GOT NOTHING ON ME.

So Deacon had agreed, and the next thing he knew, he was drawn into a shining whiteness. For an instant, he heard what sounded like every song ever written, hummed, or played colliding in a white-noise din, and then there he was, in the dingy little room. He reached into the pocket of his slacks for the mouthpiece he carried everywhere he went, but he had stashed it in his car. Fingering it always gave him some comfort even though he had no idea how he'd acquired it or why.

So there was nothing to do but wait.

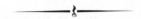

Perry was nothing and nowhere. He was a loose net of awareness hanging against an unrelenting void. He even missed the sensation of falling. He waited for what seemed a long time, and he couldn't help but think about what was happening to him. Was this what sleep was like? Did people experience something like this every single night and promptly forget upon waking?

He felt a stirring somewhere in the depths of his consciousness. His nose began to tickle a bit. It was not so much that his senses began to awaken; it was that an environment began to form, bringing with it stimuli for Perry's senses to read.

He hoped he liked whatever the next place was. The church had been all right, he guessed, but Perry hoped that this time, wherever he went, Brendy and Peaches would be there with him. Together, they'd decide what to—

Water rushed into Perry's mouth and nostrils. He swallowed quite a bit of it before he knew what was happening. He experienced a quick, razor's-edge moment of disorientation in which he knew two things: the first was that this water was not breathable like that of the Bayou Saint John, and the second was that the worst thing he could do right now would be nothing. If he thrashed with all his strength, he *might* just break the water's surface and reach the air he needed.

With a strangled shout, Perry threw himself upward, hardly swimming at all. It was as if he grasped the water and pulled it down past his head. Perry broke the surface, sputtering and coughing. He thrashed around, trying to locate the shore.

"Buh-BRENDY!" he screamed.

"Perry drowning!" Brendy shouted. "Rock! Bring Perry over here!"

It was as if someone had stuffed a flock of pigeons into a cannon and then fired them all, unharmed, into the air. Perry heard a flapping of wings, a bizarre cooing sound, and then Brendy's voice again. "Right! Bring Perry!"

Perry felt himself drawn up into the air and swept to his right like a dry leaf carried on the wind—and this wind smelled of smoke and herbs. Almost immediately, he felt grass beneath him and realized that a drizzle fell from—well, from *up*. Perry could not locate any sky. He closed his eyes. He'd known that his little trick, if it worked, would get them out of their predicament. It had worked—or he thought it had, but they were still lost.

"Here Perry!" Brendy crowed. "I do good?"

"Why you talking like that?" Perry asked, eyes still shut.

"What say?" Brendy asked. Then after a pause, "He wants to know why you sound so funny. *He* talk funny. He talk people. You talk all broke up like baby talk! Well, here Perry. Alive. I know he alive. Thank you. You live in my rock? Not understand. I told my rock to do something, then you came. You live in the rock...?"

She went on like that for a while.

Once Perry had recovered a bit, Brendy's chattering began to grate on his nerves. "Stop!" he said. "Hey. *Hey.* You okay?"

"What say? I'm fine, Perry. How you is?"

"I'm okay, I think," Perry said. "I'm alive. Where's Peaches?"

"He talk funny make no— She right here, laying down."

Perry sat up and opened his eyes to find himself surrounded by a golden fog. He could see no sign of water, but from where he sat in the coarse, scrubby grass, he could see his sister in her blue-and-white polka-dotted dress standing over Peaches. He had no idea what had become of her puffy winter jacket.

"Aw," Perry said. "Aw, no." His body failed him momentarily, but then he raised himself onto all fours and crawled over to gather Peaches into his arms.

He wouldn't have thought it possible, but she'd been badly burned. Some of her skin had been charred by the blast, and her dress was in sooty tatters. It looked, in places, as if it had fused with her flesh. As he drew her to himself, the thought occurred to Perry, bright with panic, that he shouldn't be touching her. She needed doctors. A hospital. But *what* doctors? *What* hospital? If the doctors had to shave her skin or cut her open, would their instruments be strong enough?

"Perry!"

Perry held his friend tighter and felt something constrict inside him. It was as if his heart were shrinking, collapsing on itself.

"Perry!"

He clenched his eyes shut and his teeth hard enough to make his forehead throb.

"Perry!" Brendy shouted. "Tell him down!"

"What?" Perry was stunned to hear Brendy continuing her ridiculous talking game. He thought she must be coming unglued, but some tiny doubt suggested he might be missing something, and it was that doubt that kept him from flying into a rage.

"You gotta put her down," Brendy said. "You can't be holding her like that when rock do rock thing, okay?"

"What?"

"You gotta put her down or the hoodoo get you, too," Brendy said. "Hear me?"

"Of course I hear you," Perry said.

"How hear? Put her down, then, okay?" Brendy said.

Perry stopped short again. Something wasn't right, and it had begun to dawn on him what it was. Brendy's voice had sounded twice, and in his mind he'd divided her words—one set sounded the way Brendy always sounded, if a little upset, and the other sounded strange. Babyish.

If she was playing a game, it was a strange one where she'd learned somehow to say two things at the exact same time—because the normal speech and the baby speech had overlapped more than once.

"Brendy," Perry said. "Is someone else here with us?"

"...Yeah," Brendy said. "Rock here with us."

"Who...? Who is Rock?"

"My friend that live in the rock I got," Brendy said. "It's a haint."

"What 'haint'? What means?"

By now, still holding Peaches, Perry had turned to watch his sister. As soon as he saw what was going on, his mind rebelled, trying to edit his vision for sense: Two of Brendy stood side by side. Both were dressed exactly the same, even down to the patent-leather Mary Janes. First, Perry's vision dimmed one figure, then the other. The more Perry looked, though, the more he picked out a subtle difference between the figures, not of form, but of attitude. The Brendy on the left stood with its arms hanging limp at its sides, and...and its feet didn't quite touch the ground.

"It means a ghost. Like the spirit of somebody dead," said the standing Brendy.

"No haint," chirped the levitating Brendy. "No man woman child. *Div*."

"What's Div?" Brendy—the real Brendy—asked.

"*Div* Div."

"Okay." Brendy didn't seem to understand any better than Perry did. "But you can help Peaches?"

"Brendy help help. Brendy tell."

"That is the solidest haint I ever seen," Perry said, amazed. "Your rock haunted as hell."

"Well, *duuuuuuh*," Brendy said. "Thass what I been tryna tell you!"

"No haint. *Div*."

Very carefully, Perry lowered Peaches onto the grass. He backed away. "Okay," he told the haint. "Do it. Fix her."

"What say?" asked the floating Brendy.

Brendy shook her head. "It can't understand you, Perry," Brendy said. "*I* gots to tell it."

She didn't turn her head to speak to the spirit, and Perry wondered whether Brendy could see it at all.

"So tell it."

"All right, then," Brendy said. "Do your thang!"

"Tell," said the ghost. "Tell name. *Bilipit*."

"What?" Brendy said, and this time panic marbled her voice. Perry understood his sister's untroubled attitude was a front, employed to keep Perry and Brendy herself from going to pieces.

"You have to—I think you have to command it," Perry guessed. "Like on *I Dream of Jeannie*."

"Like a wish?" Brendy said.

"No. Like a command," Perry said, talking quickly. He let the words just pour out of him, speaking only slowly enough to order them. "Like when you told it to get me out of the water. Like that. You have to *order* it to do what you want."

"Rock! Make Peaches not burned no more!"

Nothing happened.

"Tell name," said the ghost. "Tell name *Bilipit*. Tell name!"

"You gotta command it by name," Perry said. "Its name is Billy Pete."

"Billy Pete!" Brendy barked, and her voice gained both volume and echo. "Heal Peaches Lavelle of all her wounds! *This I command!*"

He had just enough time to remember that final phrase from *G.I. Joe*, then that exploding-bird sound filled the air again. Perry jumped back with a startled cry as Peaches's body burst into flame. His hands flew up to cover his face, but before he could shut out the sight, he realized the flames looked wrong, somehow, almost as if...

...As if they were burning backwards.

Perry's hands fell to his sides, and his mouth drifted open.

When the last of the flame died away, Peaches was whole and sound. She lay sleeping on the grass, and not so much as a singe darkened her hair, her skin, or her dress. Perry had never seen anything so beautiful.

Perry knelt next to her and very slowly reached out to lay his left hand across her forehead.

"Peaches?" Brendy asked.

"Yeah?" Perry said. He'd felt his lips move, felt his vocal cords thrum, but it still took him a moment to realize he had spoken.

"Peaches?" Brendy said. "That you talking out of Perry?"

"Yeah," Perry said.

A wave of panic swept across Perry's chest. He began to sweat.

"Peaches, it's time to wake up," Brendy said. "We gotta figure out how to get back outta wherever this is."

"...Naw," Perry said. "Naw, I ain't doing that right now. I'ma just lay right here, sleep."

So Sharp

Back at Da Cut, Stagger Lee watched the Baby Mage fade from sight, leaving behind nothing but a shadow. He bowed his head, took a breath, and considered. Fire still burned in the pit of his belly, undiminished by the water inside and all around him. His lungs expanded and contracted, puffing little gouts of smoky flame from his nostrils, and he wondered why they came so fast. Dimly, he remembered the sensation of exertion, what it felt like to run, and how it cut his breath and made it jag as it came and went.

Was he tired? Out of shape? No, this was something else. The fire burned in his belly, but something else burned with it. It was...? Anger? Frustration. It was frustration. He had focused his will, he had acted, and he'd been thwarted by a gang of children.

The Velvet Room stood mostly empty. Chairs and tables lay overturned by fleeing patrons, and the stench of fear hung thick in the room. The dead bartender stood slack-jawed, bottle still in hand, staring at Stag, a body without a soul.

Without thinking, Stag raised his pearl-handled .45, sighted, and shot. The bullet struck the zombie square between the eyes, sailed on through his head, carrying bits of skull and gore in its wake. The corpse swayed on its feet and went down, never to rise again.

Stag had expected the kill to calm the burning in his gut, but it didn't. Not at all. He couldn't remember a time when he'd settled on a murder and had it taken from him. The girl who'd knocked his wrist and queered his aim was likely dead, but the fact that her body was nowhere in evidence, and that Stag would be unable to watch her spirit leave it and kill her ghost as well, filled him with an emotion that, while it was not alien, came from so far in Stag's past that it seemed to belong to another life, another self, entirely.

Stagger Lee crossed to the bar, inhaled, and vomited a wall of flame that ruptured every bottle on the shelf. The more flammable liquors went up as well, and instead of watching them burn, Stag whirled and went about his business, stomping through tables and chairs. There must have been a hundred tables, four, five hundred chairs, but he smashed every last one to kindling, then used his fire breath to set them burning as well.

The Baby Mage had looked him in the eye. He had spoken to Stag as he would have to a mortal man. Stag thought he'd seen a trace of fear in the little boy's eyes, but terror should have overwhelmed him, driven him to his knees to beg for his life.

He remembered Jailbird's whining. *Save me, Jesus. Save me. Hide me, Lord. Oh, God!*

Stag had felt nothing as he watched the fear cast its shadow over Jailbird's wrinkled brown face—a lion of the Serengeti wouldn't have cared, and neither had Stagger Lee—but the way the little wizard had looked him in the eye and answered his question without a quaver: *You. It was you.* Stag cared not at all that the boy's words had made no sense. What he hated was that the child had been able to find its voice to do anything but beg.

Stag broke the last table in two and turned to survey his handiwork. The only piece of furniture left whole in the room was an upright piano set against the black glass wall. If Stag had known it was here before he'd come in, things would have gone differently, to be sure. Now he wished he could destroy it, but he needed the instrument. He flipped the cover off its keyboard and drew his left hand across the ivory.

The Velvet Room faded from sight.

Moments later, Stagger Lee found himself before another piano. This one was a baby grand, and there was no water in this room. The ceilings were high, but dust lay thick on the carpet and the drapes. Cobwebs hung like party streamers, and wan golden light shone through one of the high windows where the drapes hung slightly open.

YAKUMO, Stag called, and his voice echoed in the empty room.

The darkness trembled. Now, not even the golden streetlight shone to illuminate Stag's surroundings. The darkness pulsed once, then breathed, and then drew itself into a familiar shape.

It was mostly the form of a man, but legless, and it hung at the center of the circular room. A faded, tattered robe draped its rail-thin body, and its skin was icily pale. Its head drooped to the side. Its bloodshot right eye bulged, while its left eye was missing entirely. Its gray hair flowed to its shoulders, and looking at it, Stagger Lee wondered, not for the first time, whether it was male or female. Its body rippled, and it made quiet swallowing sounds that made Stagger Lee nervous.

what news stagger lee it whispered. Its voice sounded like the wind chasing dry leaves across a city sidewalk.

YOU DONE STEERED ME WRONG, YAKUMO, Stag told it. JAILBIRD WAS WHERE YOU SAID HE'D BE, BUT THEM OTHERS WAS ALREADY THERE.

i said they might be i told you what to do if they arrived

THASS RIGHT. KILL 'EM ALL. WHAT YOU AIN'T TOLD ME WAS THAT ONEA DEM KIDS WAS MAGIC.

The haint's outline turned hard and angular. magic you say how so

KID WAS MAYBE TEN YEAR OLD, BUT HE HAD HIM A MAGIC BAG.

yes Yakumo hissed. yesss indeed where is the bag now

BOY WITCHED HISSELF AND HIS FRIENDS INSIDE IT ALONG WITH JAILBIRD.

what and what became of the bag

DISAPPEARED SAME AS THEY DONE. YOU SAID THEY WEREN'T NO TROUBLE. YOU SAID THEY COULDN'T PUT UP NO FIGHT. THEY DONE TOOK MY KILL AND FLED MY PUNISHMENT. I WANTS—I *DEMAND* SATISFACTION, YAKUMO. WHAT ELSE BOUT THESE KIDS YOU AIN'T TOLD ME?

The haint turned this way and that, absently rubbing its clawed hands together. think carefully the bag they disappeared into it

Stagger Lee felt—not bothered or nervous, but...wary. His rage didn't seem to upset or worry the spirit at all. He wondered what would happen if the two of them tangled, and he honestly didn't know. Maybe he should shoot this ghost on general principle. WHAT I SAID?

and the bag disappeared with them

THASS RIGHT. WHO THEY IS?

ha ha haaah laughed the ghost. it hardly matters now theyll never be seen again find the other songs and kill them all soon we will be free of this accursed city

That strange old emotion flooded Stag again. He felt it come, marveling as it sped his heart and filled his lungs to bursting. Now he knew it for what it was: rage. BUT THEM KIDS, he said. YOU SAY THEY AIN'T SHOWING UP AGAIN. BUT IF THEY DOES? WHAT THEN?

then do what you do best lee shelton   kill them kill them all

"LEE SHELTON"? Stag said. WHO THAT IS?

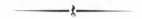

November 2018

No word had come to Casey since the night he'd passed out in the abandoned nightclub. He'd taken the highway past the Treme a couple more times, and only once had he seen the rooftop bar above Circle Food. The other times, the roof held its normal collection of boxy metal and concrete structures—inert engines for the HVAC system and the store's cold cases and freezers, Casey assumed. Instinctively, he avoided Frenchmen Street and he didn't run into Foxx King anywhere else—and more importantly, nobody who was definitely *not* Foxx approached or contacted him.

And how could he? Casey had given the apparition no cell number, no email address. It had no earthly way of getting a hold of him.

Casey grimaced at the unfortunate choice of words as he locked up his office, ready to head home for the night. This late, the building reminded him of a leftover movie set—which was not far-off: Various productions shot regularly at the International School. He jogged across the parking lot to Ole Girl—not because he was worried about being waylaid by some mysterious figure, but because he'd skipped lunch this afternoon to finish a proposal to connect the Foreign Language and International Affairs classes with the State Department's Youth Mentorship Program.

His phone chirped before he opened his car door. Casey sucked his teeth. His phone was almost always on silent for this exact reason. Trying not to think what he was doing, Casey drew the phone from his slacks and checked the message.

COLISEUM SQUARE. 7.

It came from an unknown number. Easy enough to ignore.

Casey checked the time. It was a quarter till. He opened the car door and sat in the driver's seat with the door open. He retrieved a Newport from the forgotten pack in the center console and lit it.

When he finished smoking, he was no closer to a decision. Night had closed like a lid over the city, and the parking lot lights cast a dirty sodium glow that reminded Casey of a season in decline. Idly, he stared at the rack of blue rental bikes parked outside Rouses on Baronne Street. Slowly, he shut the door and started the car.

By the time he turned onto Prytania, Casey had to admit he'd been kidding himself. How could he stay away? How could he even consider it? Given these rarified circumstances, what sort of coward could turn away? He guided the car down Race Street and easily found a parking space. A bit of summer heat had returned to the city, and this soon after sunset, it was still eighty degrees out.

Casey didn't see anyone sitting at the benches positioned around the park's larger fountain, but he knew the place was roughly the shape of an acute triangle. There was a whole other end of the park. He resolved to make a full circuit, and if he found no one and nothing, he'd give up and treat himself to Ethiopian food. Instead, he crossed the street and walked up the concrete pathway to the fountain, then took a seat on a wrought-iron bench that would give him a broad view of the green park lawn rolling away in the direction of Calliope Street.

A breeze gusted past, carrying the scents of raw honey and gardenias. Suddenly, Casey was not alone on the bench. His body tried to balk, but he turned to look at the other man.

Casey sucked in a shocked breath as he saw the bees clinging to the man's lower left arm. Somehow, he thought that detail would be translated into something else—long striped sleeves, maybe? Surely a living man couldn't walk around this way. And yet there they were, buzzing quietly, resting as they awaited their master's commands. But Sharp wasn't their master, Casey knew. He was one of their own, specially empowered by Osun to defend the hive that was planet Earth.

Or at least, that had been Bee Sharp's origin when Casey had first conceived him as a woman. Did it make sense for Osun to empower a man? It didn't matter.

He wore his black-and-yellow striped Afro picked out. He— Casey had sat staring for too long. But the man looked—he *was* sharp. So, so sharp.

"So," Casey croaked.

"Took me a while to get the lay of the land," Sharp said softly, "but I done it."

His skin was darker than Casey had imagined. Darker than

Foxx King's, even. It was what Casey's grandmother would have called blue-black. The park's lights gleamed against its perfectly moisturized surface. And his sunglasses. Casey had imagined them as a pair of black ones like he'd seen Kurt Cobain wearing in a promo photo, but these were different: Instead of lenses and frames they were all one bubble, tapering to nothing as they reached behind Sharp's ears—and those ears were unusually small, like Casey's own. Ximena used to call them "teeny little mutant ears."

"Jaylon was already gone when the studio went up, but where he gone to is . . . complicated."

"What do you mean?"

"Folks saying he got took. Wouldn't nobody say where—and baby, I axed *real* nice."

"So—so that's it? It's a dead end?"

A white woman walked by with a fluffy blond lap dog on a leash. She glanced in their direction and walked faster.

"Not quite," Sharp said. "Came across a cat named Wally Benson. He said to tell the man I work for the Doctor will see him."

"The Doctor? What doctor?"

Bee Sharp shrugged. "Thought it might mean more to you than it did to me."

"Shit. Shit. Okay. Where do I go? When?"

"Benson says the Doctor will send for you," Sharp said. "But look. Some of what I found . . . it's strange than a mug."

Casey looked at Sharp's insect-encrusted arm and waited for him to say more.

"They's another city sharing space with New Orleans," he said. "I can *feel* it buzzing. I ain't really axed nobody bout it—I don't think nobody supposed to know, heard? I feel points, here and there, where the membrane between this place and that is . . . thin. But the vibration I feel is . . . It's sound. And what is a explosion but sound and force?"

Casey frowned, trying to follow. "You think this invisible city is connected to the explosion at the studio?"

"We know that wasn't no normal fire the way that place went up . . . ? And none of the buildings next to it was damaged or even singed. Bang that big, that whole motherfuckin' block shoulda gone up."

"Yeah," Casey said. "I thought about that. Cops told me explosions are unpredictable. You can guess what they'll do, but sometimes they zig when they should zag."

"Sounds to me like five-oh didn't want to admit that they have no got-damn idea what happened."

"Yeah. Yeah," Casey said. "Me too."

They sat in silence for a moment. "What you want to do now?" Sharp asked.

What Casey wanted was to go knocking down doors with Bee Sharp. Question witnesses, threaten violence if he had to—but he knew the feeling came from too much TV and movies. He sighed. "Wait for the Doctor to send for me, I guess."

"You want me to go with you when the time comes? Squeeze the motherfucker?"

Casey shook his head. "Not yet, at least. I'll go alone. But do you . . . do you need anything?"

"My needs is met, baby."

"You sure?"

"Course I'm sure," Bee Sharp said. Emotion roughened his voice. "It's been so long. I thought you forgot me."

"Never that," Casey said. "Never." *I want to see*, he thought. *I want to see your eyes.* But he'd never say so.

For a long time neither of them moved or spoke, but then Bee Sharp scooted forward on the bench and cheated his shoulders until he and Casey were half-facing. He took off his glasses.

His eyes were big, but they fit into his face more or less the way human ones would. Still, they were black, unimaginably compounded. How . . . how could this have come from Casey? He'd never imagined eyes like these.

As Casey stared, he began to notice a tension in the other man's strange face. When a tear spilled down Sharp's sharp black cheek, Casey reached up and wiped it away.

"My God," he said. "My God."

Sharp lifted his right hand, and the bees retreated down his arm. He pressed Casey's hand against his cheek. "...Am I what you wanted...?"

Casey pressed his forehead against Sharp's own, and for a moment, they breathed together. Raw honey, gardenias, woodsmoke, and the change of seasons. The wind slid lightly between the trees, shaking their branches.

"You're so much more," Casey said. "You are everything. *Everything.*"

Bee Sharp began to fade. "I am in you," he whispered. "I am *of* you. I am yours, always. Always."

And then he was gone.

Baby I been too long away
Baby I travel by night
Studying on you night and day
And I hope you feel all right

Her voice began low and quavering—her age might be indeterminate, but to Casey, Auntie Roux sounded ancient. As she reached the second verse, though, the years seemed to fall away. Before long, her voice was as young and smooth as that of Lady Irma.

The sound of a soprano sax unfolded from Roux's throat. Its tone struck Casey to his core, and now he knew why the witch was capable of contacting Fess in the first place. Fess could play and he could sing, but Auntie Roux could sing the sound of the greatest horn ever played—the soprano sax of Sidney tha Great. As the solo stretched on, chords slid in underneath it, and Casey saw the shadow of a piano fade in against the flagstones of the square.

Before long, Fess appeared, sitting at the keyboard, playing and singing right along with all the music of a full band pouring from his mouth and fingers.

"I cain't dance the steps I used to," he sang. "I can't kick or dip or twirl. Now my baby done cast me aside, I'm the loneliest man in this ole world!"

Now his voice joined Auntie Roux's, and they sang the rest together.

> Lord, I do, I do, I do, baby
> I do, I do, I do.
> Without you by my side
> I'm just a-walkin'
> Yes I'm walkin',
> Walkin' that lonely mile.

The music faded into nothing, but Fess stayed where he was, brushing his fingertips across his keyboard. He still swayed, as if in time to some unheard tune. Looking at him, Casey knew that he saw only a fraction of this man. There was more of him elsewhere, and there was no telling what Casey could see if his vision were more refined.

"Henry," Auntie Roux said, smiling. It had never occurred to Casey that Doctor Professor must have a proper name. Roux's eyes were wet now, and hearing her speak, Casey knew all he needed to know about her connection to Doctor Professor.

Ladies, Fess said. *Gentleman. What I can do for y'all tonight?*

The dark-skinned woman rose from her seat. "My name is Lisa Monique Jennings Léandre," she said. "You have burdened my grandbabies with a perilous quest. You have sent them in your name without weapons or resources, and you have withheld crucial information about the nature of their task. It is only out of respect for your position that I restrain my hand. So tell me: What will you do to make this right?"

"Now, hold on a minute there, baby," Fess said. "You got me

all wrong. I was told them children been given some of the most powerful weaponry exists in this world, and that you the one done left it to 'em."

"They had not yet received their birthright when you enlisted them in your cause, but that matters little to me now. What truly angers me is that you sent them on this mission without telling them that Stagger Lee had assumed a physical form."

"Well, that just ain't so," Fess said. "Stag right where he belong, inside my Mess Around. If he was runnin' the streets, I wouldna sent no children after him, and thass a natural fact."

"Fool!" Mama Lisa shouted. "Are you so derelict in your duties that you have no idea what you've lost? This boy here encountered Stagger Lee this very night." She stabbed a finger in Casey's direction, and Casey jumped as if she'd brandished a knife.

"Thass...that's impossible, now, baby. That's just—"

Now Casey spoke up. "It's...it's not, sir. I seen—I saw him. He wore a purple hat, had a mouth full of jewels, and the meanest gun I ever seen. He killed a man right in front of me and then walked into the Bayou breathing fire. He's—you really didn't know?"

Fess looked from Casey to Auntie Roux to Mama Lisa, his mouth hanging open. The helplessness of his expression made Casey feel cold inside. "I gotta talk to the Powers," he said. "They'll know what to do. I didn't—I swear if I'da known Stack was gone, I'da never sent no kids after him."

Mama Lisa drew in a long, slow breath. She'd seemed no taller than Auntie Roux when Casey first saw her, but now she towered. "You consult your Powers," she hissed. "But know this: Your negligence has drawn me across oceans of time to involve myself in this conflict. If any harm should come to my family, you will never play another note."

"I dig what you tellin' me, ma'am," Fess said. "You ain't gotta threaten me none."

"Oh, that's no threat," Mama Lisa said sweetly. "Now, *where are they?*"

"The children? *You* ain't got 'em?" The corners of Fess's mouth turned down as he realized what a stupid question that was. "If they ain't...If you don't...I don't...Let me...I'll find 'em directly and bring 'em to you, ma'am."

"Don't make me come looking for you," Mama Lisa said.

Without another word, without playing or singing another note, Doctor Professor and his piano disappeared.

Mama Lisa sagged with relief and reached up to remove her glasses. She pressed the fingers of her right hand against the bridge of her nose and stood in silence.

"Ma'am—" Casey began without knowing what he would say or why.

"Boy," Mama Lisa cut him off. "Why are you still here?"

STORM COMIN'

Perry tried to move and failed. He could no more stand up or withdraw his hand than he could spit out a squadron of flying monkeys. He would have been afraid, but Peaches was with him, even if her presence had taken on a strange dimension.

"Just a minute, Peaches," Brendy said. She lowered her voice for privacy. "You done good, Billy."

"Need me 'gain?" Billy asked quietly in its borrowed Brendy-voice.

"I dunno. Hang around a bit, and we see, okay? How I get you to come out the rock when I need you?"

"*Haniran sayala alagbara!* Brendy say."

"Haniran see olla alagbera!" Brendy repeated.

"*Haniran sayala alagbara!*"

"*Haniran sayala alagbara!*"

"Yes!" Billy said happily. "Just like!"

Brendy repeated the incantation over and over again as she approached, then stopped as she knelt across from Perry on Peaches's other side. "This shonuff crazy," she said. "Magic bags, magic rocks, and fire under the water."

"Baby, who you tellin?" Peaches-in-Perry said. "This too much for even me. I quit."

"You quit?" Brendy asked.

No, Perry thought. *You can't quit. We need you.* But Peaches didn't seem to hear.

"This too much," Peaches-in-Perry said sadly. "I'm all burnt up. My hair got burnt up. I just wanna go home, feed Karate, make sure Honcho ain't bothering Dudley, and wait for the next letter from my daddy. I can't do that right now, so I'ma stay sleep. Just lie right here."

"Peaches," Brendy said tenderly. "It's scary. It's a lot, even for you. But we gots a secret weapon."

"Oh yeah?" Peaches said. "What that is?"

"Perry," Brendy said matter-of-factly.

"What Perry gonna do if Gun Man come at me again?"

"Oh, well, Perry kill him," Brendy said without hesitation.

Hey, Perry thought. *Hey, now. I don't even know if he can be killed in the first place! I think he already dead!*

"Perry get scared sometimes," Peaches said. "He freeze up. How he gone have my back?"

"We all get scared," Brendy said. "But Daddy Deke told me being brave ain't about not being scared. Being brave about doing what you gotta even *if* you scared."

Perry wanted to protest again, but he had nothing to say to that.

"Girl, you seen how Perry went after Jailbird? He was like a cop show on the TV. He was all, 'Take me to Daddy Deke, or I put it on you!' And, baby, I seen the look in his eye. He wasn't playin'."

Perry's chest swelled a little. Had he really sounded like a cop show?

After the Hanging Judge threatened him, Perry felt as if a door had closed deep inside him. It didn't feel like a normal door. This one felt heavy, old as the Earth itself, and heavier even than the gate to Superman's Fortress of Solitude. He felt as if he stood in shadow, as if laughter and sunlight could still touch him, but that they mattered less. *He* mattered less. Spending time with Peaches—adventuring through the city, or just playing board games or watching cartoons—parted that gloomy haze for him, made him feel as if maybe that door wasn't fully shut. That it might open for him again on some far-off day.

Perry's dream-that-was-not-a-dream made his world, his life, seem small and grimy, but Peaches represented pure possibility for Perry. Maybe there were some things not even she could do, but it didn't matter. She was capable of so much, she was so free, that sometimes Perry thought that maybe he was free, too. Maybe everyone was, had been always, and when they felt chained or trapped it was because they'd been lied to, or they were simply mistaken.

"And then when the Bad Man shown up, Perry turnt around and looked him right in the eye—*after* the Bad Man started shootin'! Looked him right in his *face*, girl! And when the man started breathin' fire, Perry didn't stop to think. He just said his Words and got us right out of there..."

He had read once that knights were not created by the accolade, the tapping of the sword blade on one shoulder and then the other. That the ceremony recognized something that had already happened. Not "We dub this man a knight" but "We find that this man has become a knight." It would be many years before Perry would be able to parse these ideas, express them to himself, but he was aware of them just the same. That awareness felt too enormous to express with language, too secret to share with the outside world.

Brendy harrumphed a little and arranged her legs underneath her. She stroked Peaches's shoulder, but looked Perry in the eye. "My brother ain't perfect, Peaches," she said. "He make me mad sometimes. Sometimes I get so mad, I could spit. And I yell at him, and sometimes I even kick him. But, Peaches, you gotta know. Perry do *anything* for the people he loves. Anything. He loves me a lot. But he love you different. He gets... His voice change when he talk about you. It gets all soft."

Hey, Perry thought. *Hey, now.*

"And when he go too long without seeing you, he get all mopey and grumpy," Brendy said. "Jokes ain't funny to him, and he make this face."

Brendy squinted her eyes, poked out her lower lip, and groaned like a sick bear.

"What face?" Peaches said. "My eyes is closed! I can't see!"

"I show you," Brendy said. "Open your eyes and look."

Perry's paralysis evaporated so quickly that he pitched to his right, balance gone. He rolled onto his back and stared up at the luminescent fog. Away to his right, Peaches burst into helpless laughter. "He do not!" she gasped. "Perry do *not* make that face!"

"Hand to God," Brendy said. "Listen."

The girls quieted. Perry's face burned as he felt Peaches's gaze sweep over him.

"He all embarrassed," Brendy said. "He gone be mad at me for a week."

"Perry. Hey, *Per*-ry," Peaches called in a playground singsong.

Perry didn't answer. He tried not to be angry—he understood why Brendy had said what she said. He understood that any sacrifice that resulted in Peaches rejoining the fight was one worth making, but...but he didn't know how he'd speak to his friend or interact with her now that she had some inkling of the mad boil of emotions that gave him such sweet trouble when she was around—and especially now that she knew those emotions made him even crazier when she *wasn't* around.

Perry covered his face with his hands. He wished they were bigger. He wished they could swallow his whole head.

A deep shiver ran through Perry's body as Peaches's cool dry palm touched his right arm just above the elbow.

Peaches didn't withdraw, but she didn't say anything, either. Then, "Perry," she said. "It's okay. I *like* that you care bout me."

Perry took a breath, lifted his hands from his face. He still couldn't quite look at Peaches. "I don't just care about you," he said. "You don't make me strong."

Peaches grinned so hard that Perry felt the full force of her expression without looking directly at her. "What you mean?"

"You don't make me strong, and—and you don't make me free. You help me remember that I *am* strong. That I *am* free. Always."

Peaches began to laugh. The hand on Perry's arm fluttered against his shirtsleeve like a nervous bird, and she rested her other hand on Perry's heart. He wondered how much effort she had to exert to keep from hurting him with her titanic strength. "That's a lot," she said. "That's so much."

"I know. Too much?"

"No," she said. "It's what I want. It's what I need."

Perry sat up and drew Peaches to him. He wrapped his arms around her and pressed his lips against her forehead. She trembled against him.

"Perry and Peaches," Brendy sang, but her tone did not mock. "Sitting in a tree. *Kay, eye, ess, ess, eye, en, gee!*"

"Aw, hush," Peaches said, but she didn't pull away.

They relaxed, resting in the moment, together in a new way that Perry wasn't sure he understood—that he didn't think he needed to.

"...So what about it?" Peaches said softly after a while. "Where we is, and how we get back to the city?"

Perry barked a laugh. "Baby, you got me!" he said. "Lord only knows."

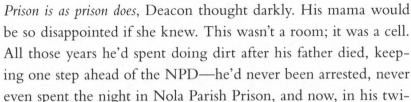

Prison is as prison does, Deacon thought darkly. His mama would be so disappointed if she knew. This wasn't a room; it was a cell. All those years he'd spent doing dirt after his father died, keeping one step ahead of the NPD—he'd never been arrested, never even spent the night in Nola Parish Prison, and now, in his twilight years, he just the same found himself confined. With only a rickety-ass lumpy bed, a dirty square window, a lightbulb, and a hardly working little radio to keep him company.

Deacon pressed his hands against his face and, for just a moment, allowed himself to feel the weight of years and years of living. From time to time he did this to remind himself that he was still alive and that time still passed. He found the ache and the tiredness oddly comforting.

He wasn't sure how long he'd been sitting this way when, out of the corner of his eye, Deacon saw the overhead light flicker off. Deacon's hands dropped into his lap as a viscous darkness filled the cell. He sighed deeply, but he didn't rise or recoil. Where would he go? The ceiling was so low that his only choices were to sit here and see what was what or lie down and stare at the ceiling.

The darkness pulsed like the beat of a baleful heart, and something in it coalesced into a more-or-less human shape. Deacon sensed a tension in it, a wriggling motion, as if the darkness had to work to hold on to itself and that the effort made it *very* angry. A single bloodshot eye swam open, and its gaze fell heavy on Deacon's forehead. He looked the dark figure up and down. Must be mighty inconvenient, not having no legs.

Silence stretched to fill the room, and Deacon waited for the apparition to break it.

The seconds ticked by, then he gave up the game. "All right, then," he said. "You must be Stag's friend he was talkin' bout. What you want with me?"

i have questions for you deacon graves the figure whispered.

"Do ya, now?" Deacon asked. "Got me a few of my own."

we shall trade knowledge for knowledge yes

"Aight, then," Deacon said. "You first."

how long have you lived in this city

"All my life. Born and raised."

except we both know that is not the case

Deacon narrowed his eyes. "What you mean?"

Something tickled at the edge of Deacon's memory. He sensed its importance, but it terrified him. Now was not the time to consider it consciously. He thrust the almost-thought aside.

how many birthdays have you celebrated how long has it been since you laid each of your dear wives to rest what year did you graduate primary school tell me deacon graves

"Listen, Jack, I don't know you," Deacon said. His voice had turned hard, and he spoke with authority. Fear was with him, but so was something else—the simple knowledge that he would not be broken. "You think you can show up like the Haint of All Haints and scare me bad enough to tell you all my bidness, but I done lived a long time. Haints don't scare me none. I'll answer *one* of your questions: I graduated from the Fisk School for Boys in 1913."

tell me then deacon graves how long has it been since 1913 what year is it now

The question shocked him. He felt weaker now, his thoughts scattered. "It's—what year is it? Thass all you wanna know?"

just so   what is the year were you ever young   when you remember your youth do you think of this life in this city or another city similar to this when you dream where are you deacon where do you go

A sick feeling settled in the pit of Deacon's belly. He had thought he'd been doing so well—sitting in this little cell for however many days, mentally composing letters to each of his family members, including his two dead wives. When the haint had appeared, he'd been surprised by his own cool—impressed with his ability to keep it together under stress. But now, with his barrage of bizarre questions, the ghost had shattered Deacon's composure.

"*The hell you ask me that for?*" Deacon demanded. "Errybody know what year it is! You know what year it is! I may be old, but I ain't lost my marbles yet!"

my questions disturb you yes why is that

"It ain't the questions bother me, ya dumb spook, it's *you!*" Deacon shouted. "With your crazy red eye and your no-legs-havin' ass standing in the corner. I ain't answering no questions today. You just get the hell on and leave me be—or let me go. Let me go home. *Let me go! Got*damn!"

answer my questions and we will discuss the terms of your release

Deacon stretched out on the bed, his back to the far corner of the room and the glowering eye of the legless haint. It wasn't so much that Deacon was in pain, or even that he was upset; it was that, suddenly, he was extraordinarily aware of his own skeleton, and now that feeling gave him no comfort. A man his age experiences more than his share of aches and pains on any given day—Deacon's knees had been giving him trouble for years, especially after hard rains—but this wasn't an ache. He just felt his bones. He cataloged them silently: the two small bones in his lower arm, the large bone of his left thigh, the many, many small bones of his hands and feet, and the stony segmentation of his ankles and wrists...

I'm tougher than this, he thought. *Ain't no trivia questions gonna give me fits. I'm tougher.* Tougher. *Tougher.*

And another, quieter thought: *Storm comin'.*

He lay there, his head in his hands, for some time, before the weight of his captor's ghostly stare made Deacon turn over, ready to cuss this haint the *fuck* out—but the room was empty. The dirty overhead light glowed weakly again, swinging slightly back and forth, making the shadows rock like backup dancers.

A tray of food lay on the floor in front of the cell door. The smell of it overwhelmed Deacon, brought a flood of saliva into his mouth. Red beans and rice, garlic bread, and even a praline. So this was Monday? The sight of the glistening hunks of smoked sausage sitting in their gravy... Deacon stared at it for a long time, watching steam rise from the bowl.

He knew he should be suspicious. Any number of things could have been done to that food... but his hunger by far outweighed his common sense. He would eat the food, lick the bowl, and then parcel the praline into chunks that he would allow himself slowly, over time, sucking on each morsel instead of chewing, to make the sweetness last.

Careful to hunch so as not to hit his head, Deacon rose from the bed and crossed to claim his meal. It was the best he'd ever had.

Lord, he thought as he spooned beans into his mouth. *Please look after my grandbabies. Please make sure they all right.*

Casey engaged the parking brake and sat still, watching in the rearview as the shadows of the palm trees splashed across the parking lot behind him. As he and Naddie made their way home, the city seemed as if it had expanded. It was larger and darker now, and its buildings made less sense. There was still too much graffiti out, and the shadows lay in unnatural groupings, as if conspiring together. The city was both dangerous and in danger.

"Talk to me," Naddie said. "I know you're going to say something crazy, but talk to me, at least."

"I haven't been that scared since I was little."

"Of who? Stagger Lee?"

"Of anything," Casey said. "Anybody. Did you hear them? There's kids out there going up against that thing."

"Casey."

"Kids."

"Case."

"This is our city. This is our home." Something yawned inside him. Some dark knowledge that was not quite a memory. He remembered driving, the fender of his blue LeBaron gobbling the road in a driving rain. He felt as if he'd been asked a question and he had little time left to figure out the answer.

"Casey. What are you going to do?"

"I don't know," he said. "But, damn it, I'm gonna do *something*." He paused, staring at his hands on the steering wheel. Then, "Go inside. Pack some bags, and if I'm not home when you're finished, go to bed. I'm going back to talk to Auntie Roux."

Silence stretched for a moment, then, quietly, Naddie opened her door and left the car.

Storm coming.

Storm coming.

Storm—

———— ≀ ————

"Okay," Perry said. "Okay. I've got an idea."

"See?" Brendy said. "What I told you? Perry fix everything!"

Perry, Peaches, and Brendy had talked over their problem for what seemed like hours, but if hours had passed, there was no evidence of it. The luminescent fog still hung thick around them, and the light had changed not one bit. Perry still smelled the ocean, but now, instead of comforting him, reminding him of a vacation he had enjoyed, the smell seemed to taunt him, saying, *Take a big ole whiff, baby. This what the sea smell like! You ain't never going there—or anywhere else—again!*

From time to time, Perry would dream a dream that was beyond his understanding. Once he'd dreamed he was on a giant gas-filled airship that was also Zara's Supermarket, and his classroom at school. His parents had manned the ship's controls as it nosed its way through thunderheads, high above the earth. Perry ran to and fro, fussing with ropes and riggings that he realized only later would be of no use on an airship. As he worked, his parents spoke in bursts, reciting word problems like the ones he did in math class.

"Four-sevenths of the birthday cake was eaten on your birthday!" Perry's mother called.

"Aye, aye!" Perry yelled, and ran toward a valve bigger than his head. He gripped it as hard as he could and sweat sprang out on his brow as he fought to turn it.

Before Perry could budge it, he heard his father's voice: "Two-fifths of the one thousand parking spaces were for cars! When you went to get groceries—!"

"Yessir! Right away, sir!" And Perry went scrambling up a nearby rope ladder, knowing, even as he went, that he was falling behind. He awakened cold and sweating, feeling as if he'd missed something important. The worst thing about the dream was that Perry felt it was trying to communicate something extremely simple, in terms that the dream seemed to consider almost insultingly direct, but which Perry was still at a loss to understand. He still remembered that dream vividly, because the morning after it was the first time Perry found himself wishing he were better—smarter, wiser—than he was.

That was how he felt now as he tried to figure out his situation. How could he lead Peaches and Brendy back to the real world if he had no idea where they were to begin with? This was serious. Everyone—not just Peaches and Brendy, but all Nola—was counting on him. The pressure threatened to crush him, so Perry decided not to feel it.

After sitting cross-legged, like in school, for a terse discussion of their options, the trio found themselves losing steam. They stretched out head to head to head, staring up into the glowing nothing, and Perry suspected he might have fallen asleep for a while.

Now he clapped his hands, trying to energize himself. "Okay," he said. "So we gotta . . . we gotta find Jailbird, right? We find Jailbird, and then once we done that, maybe Doctor Professor show up to come get him, and he'll take us home."

"Oh," Brendy said, clearly disappointed.

"Perry, *we* don't even know where we at," Peaches said. "How would Fess?"

"Because he's magic," Perry said, warming to the idea. "He has magic powers."

"Negro, you and Brendy got magic powers, and y'all don't know shit."

"Well—" Perry began without knowing how he would respond.

"Besides," Peaches said. "Fess on my list."

"On your list?" Brendy said. "Why?"

"Because he lied to us," Perry said. It was the first time he'd allowed the thought to form fully in his mind. "He lied about Stagger Lee. He sent us out to catch his songs without telling us about the worst one of all."

"Stagger Lee," Brendy said.

"Stagger Lee," Perry said with a nod. "Fess damnear got us killed. And he *did* get Peaches burned."

"Musta been some kind of mistake," Brendy said. "Doctor Professor wouldn't do that."

"No mistake," Peaches said. "We gonna have us a conversation, me and him."

"So finding Jailbird won't work," Perry said. "Damn." He raised his arms and let them flop back down at his sides.

"Well, I don't know," Brendy said. "Maybe I should ask Billy to find Perry's sack again."

Much earlier in their discussion, before Brendy dismissed him, she had commanded Billy to find Perry's Clackin' Sack. The spirit had zipped around and around, spouting increasingly frantic gabble, then seemed to tire himself out. He stopped looking like Brendy altogether and became a pillar of smoke. The smoke seemed to have fire inside it, and the fire burned hotter and hotter until Brendy told Billy to go back into the rock and get some rest.

Perry'd had no idea what the limits of Billy's powers were, but he had been certain Brendy's command would get them home. If the spirit could force fire to burn backwards, to unburn Peaches, why wouldn't he be able to transport them from place to place? Perry's mother seemed to think the rock was pretty powerful—but then, she herself had admitted she knew nearly nothing about it.

So it heals people, Perry thought, *but it can't take people from place to place...* That still didn't seem to make sense. After all, hadn't Billy drawn Perry bodily up out of the water and over to Brendy to save him from drowning? But that had been only a few feet...?

"Brendy," Perry said. "That water I was in. How far away was it?"

"I dunno," Brendy said. "I could hear it, but I couldn't see no water."

Well, that was no help. Maybe Perry could go back to sleep and dream a solution to their predicament. The idea was not entirely unattractive, but Perry felt more awake than he ever had. Alert and starved for stimulation. Maybe Billy could put him to sleep, or...

No. Think. What happened?

Perry put himself back in the Velvet Room, locking eyes with Stagger Lee.

"You," he had said. "It was you."

Then: "Perilous Graves. Clickety-clack, get into my sack."

And then the world had gone away.

. . . Unless the world hadn't gone away at all.

"I know why Billy got tired," Perry said abruptly. He realized only after he'd spoken that Peaches and Brendy had been talking together, and now they shut right up.

"The world didn't go away. *We* did." A feeling of relief came over him. The sensation was so profound it felt like an invisible hand lying softly atop him, pressing him into the ground. He imagined himself sinking into the soil, down and down, at peace. A slow grin spread across his face.

"Well?" Peaches said impatiently.

"Man," Perry said. "I was really worried for a minute there. And we gotta apologize to Billy. He started going crazy because *he* knows where we at."

"Where?" Brendy said.

"Negro, *spit it out!*" Peaches said.

The more Perry spoke, the more certain he was that he'd guessed correctly. "Well," he said. "I'll show you: Brendy Graves. Peaches Lavelle. Perry Graves. Clickety-clack, get outta my sack."

The Hidden City

November 2018

Casey stood over the hot bar at Rouses, trying to decide whether to get himself some mac and cheese, some spare ribs, and some collards. Lately, he'd been having stomach trouble. Nothing he ate seemed to sit right. He'd considered a visit to the clinic to get checked out, but he knew what the problem was—waiting didn't go down easily with him.

The only step he could think to take while he awaited the Doctor's summons was to keep bombing. He'd put up tags in City Park, in the Lower 9, on the roof of this very supermarket—but it had been three weeks, and no word came. In his quieter moments, he felt Bee Sharp beneath the waters of his unconscious mind, but the buzz was calm, content, and it pained Casey to disturb the hero just because he'd been too overwhelmed to ask the right questions. Last night, he'd lit candles and incense and sat in a lotus position on his living room carpet.

"Sharp," he said aloud.

The candlelight guttered.

I'm here. You ain't need all these bells and smells to get at me.

"Who is Wally Benson?"

Thass a long story, Sharp said. *He usedta play drums for the Panic.*

Casey frowned. Did Sharp mean the Panic, as in the British Invasion band who had put down roots in New Orleans back in the seventies?

That's them. Nowdays, he reps the Powers. The city magicians. He's like a familiar, dig? Like Renfield in Dracula, but he don't eat spiders or nothing.

At first, Casey wasn't sure how to respond. Finally, he said, "Do you believe he'll put me in touch with the Doctor?"

A brief flash of—was it memory?—lit Casey's mind: It was night, and he levitated above a darkened tile patio, gazing down at an olive-skinned old man who lay among a mess of ripped-apart garden furniture, bug-eyed with terror as Casey's bees buzzed in an angry cloud around him.

Now he knew what Sharp had meant when he said he'd "axed real nice." Good, he thought grimly. That meant Bee Sharp had a proper sense of urgency and was willing to go up to the line without stepping over.

"Let's give him three more days," Casey said. "And if we don't hear from him, we'll pay him another visit."

Sharp didn't respond in words, but a wave of agreement bubbled up into Casey's conscious mind.

Someone bumped Casey's hip. "Excuse me," an older white woman said absently. From her pinched features, Casey could tell she meant no harm—her lunch break was probably too short, and she'd have to eat at her desk. Again.

"You good," Casey said, and stepped back from the bar, his cardboard food box resting open in his hand.

Fuck this. He'd use the bathroom and then grab his car to go... *somewhere.*

He strode past the meat department, through the dairy and freezer section, and hung a left. He stopped short. To his left, a short hallway led to the employees-only warehouse area, and on his right usually stood two doorways. The one on the right led to the ladies' room, and the one on the left led to the men's, but today another door stood between them. One that didn't belong. It was a high, black stone double door with ring-shaped stone handles. It stretched five feet across, and it smelled *wild*. Instead of the slightly pissy, slightly chemical tang that usually wafted from the men's, this door smelled like rain and wood smoke and volcanic rock.

It made him think of Static Shock. It made him think of Jakeem Thunder pressing the plunger on his enchanted pen, his lips parting to say the words.

"So cool," Casey said without realizing it. He grabbed the door's right handle with both hands and pulled. At first it didn't budge, but as Casey strained, a buzzing sound began to fill his skull. A tingle passed from his shoulders down his arms and the door opened easily.

A shiver ran through him as he stepped through. The air here had a different weight to it. It was alive with the hoots and cries of birds or things like birds. A crazed path wound in curves like the Mississippi as it ran up a grassy hill and disappeared. Casey looked up to see a sky lit by stars so bright that it felt as if they were only a mile or so above. Here and there, one star would burst in a glittery shower. Casey wondered whether he was witnessing the death of entire civilizations, whole solar systems, just looking up for a few seconds. Acting on instinct, he turned for a look at the stone door, just in time to see it fade from sight.

"You still there?" he said aloud.

The buzzing sound returned to him for a moment. It was all the answer he needed.

On high alert, ready to defend himself with everything he had, Casey started down the path. Once he followed it over a low hill, the path opened into a circle bordered by a garden full of flowers Casey didn't recognize. He was no botanist, so for all he knew these were perfectly mundane flowers that grew on planet Earth, but among them grew stalks or staffs festooned with feathers and fringe and decorated with animal skulls and bones. As his eyes swept over the scene, he knew before looking who the figure was sitting quietly on a bench, one gnarled hand leaning on a silver-handled walking cane.

"Of course it's you," Casey said. "The Doctor."

The man dipped his head in Casey's direction. He wore a royal purple stovepipe hat and chunky rings on his fingers. "I been held that title a while now, indeed." His voice was an unhurried purr, roughened by years of drink and cigarettes, and God-knew-what else.

"Listen," Casey said. "I'm— I threw your man around a little bit, but I was careful not to hurt him. I don't— We don't want to hurt nobody."

"That's why we talkin' right now," the Doctor said.

"You know where my cousin went?" Casey asked. "You know what happened?"

"I can give a bit of insight into that particular circumstation, yes."

"Where is he?"

"I'm sorry to say where he gone to you cain't follow," the Doctor said.

"You're telling me he's dead?" To hear the sorcerer say so should have pierced Casey with new grief, but something in him rejected the idea—not just that Jaylon was dead, but that Casey couldn't follow wherever he'd gone.

The old man seemed to consider a moment, then rocked a little in his seat. "Sit with me a spell."

Casey crossed to the bench and sat. This close, he heard a hum—like the expectant buzz of a guitar amp just before the first note rang through it. He wondered whether the Doctor could hear Casey's own buzz.

"You come up in the Church?"

"Methodist," Casey said. "Yes."

"Ain't what I meant, but that'll do, I spose," the Doctor said.

"You might recollect that Heaven and Hell are described as being on either side of a abyssal gulf. Now, the scripturists tend to simplificate things so the common mind has a chance of accepting the ideas they relate. It ain't just Heaven on the one side and Hell on the other. There's worlds upon worlds upon worlds on this side, that side, and everywhere in between."

"Like honeycomb," Casey said.

The Doctor nodded. "Quite a bit like, in fact. Now, if ya can capture or imitate the Voice of the Almighty—enough of it, I mean—it's possible to create a sort of pocket inside one of them chambers, divide it from itself, and hide it from something might be lookin' to do it harm."

Casey closed his eyes, took a sharp breath. "Then it's true. There really is another city in the same space as New Orleans?"

"Most absotively, there is," the Doctor said. "And I happen to be one of the ones brung it into being."

"By imitating God's voice."

"We Powers wasn't tryin' to make another New Orleans," the Doctor said. "We was just trying to save our city from the Storm. But when you messin' with that God-power, things don't always go the way you was expectin'."

"And that's where Jaylon is? That's where he went?"

"To the best of my understandin', he musta done," the Doctor said. "It shouldna been possible for him to breach that cosmic membrane, but all us musicians sensed the opening when it happened. We felt the exhalation of power, felt a body pass through. According to the limitations of the working we committed, only sound should bridge the chasm. But I think ya cousin managed it, and I think something made it through with him."

"What did? What?"

"The Spirit of the Eternal Storm," the Doctor said.

—Storm coming—!

"You mean this really does have something to do with the hurricane?"

Dr. John frowned. "It do and it don't. Katrina one of its children, yeah, but the Storm itself is more like—I cain't truly explain its nature to you. Even the initiated struggle to understand. The important thing is this: The Storm has used your cousin's passage to reach across the gulf between Here and There, and it wants to destroy what we Powers created."

Casey wanted to resist the idea, but while he didn't fully understand it, he knew the truth when he heard it. Bee Sharp was inside him, was of him, but he was Casey, too. A drawing, a creature of imagination that Casey had summoned into being. What was Sharp made of? Cells? Molecules? Atoms? He was impossible, but he was also fact. If Casey could create or materialize a man, what could dozens of sorcerers, working together, will into being?

A city. A hidden city.

"So if this storm kills the other New Orleans," Casey said, "Jayl dies too?"

"That is my best understandin'," the Doctor said, "but by my understandin' also, nonea this shoulda been possible in the first place."

"Who else lives there? Even if I can't go there, could I contact him?"

"Son, you already capable of some shit I ain't never seen in my long-ass life," said the Doctor, "but ain't no way. Who lives there? Some folks who fell in there from this side when the working got crazy. Some of them, it's as if the city wanted to hold 'em close, so they Here *and* they There. I think."

"You think?" Casey said. "You're the wizard. Shouldn't you know?"

"I myself ain't crossed from Here to There in some time," said the Doctor. "The way time exists in that place—if ya can say it exists at all—is perplexifying. I see it as through a glass darkly, like the Book says."

"Okay," Casey said. He chewed his tongue for a moment. "Okay. Okay. Okay. Okay. Then teach me what you can, please.

Give me the knowledge, and I'll use it to pull Jaylon back out before the Storm can kill him."

Both men were silent for a beat as Casey's request hung in the air.

The Doctor's laughter stunned Casey. "Boy, you summoned graffiti paintins into real life, and I ain't got the faintest clue how you done it. I seen artistry raised to the level of sorcery many times. I seen reality bent and broke by a sorcerous will. What you done? I ain't never seen that in all my natural days. You wanna learn piano or guitar, I could teach ya—but there ain't even no guarantee you could work sorcery through 'em once you spent the years it would take learnin' to play."

Casey wanted to swear, but he felt like he was in church. The vaulted spangled sky wheeled above him, and the enchanted ground stretched below him. All of this heated his brain, threatened to overwhelm him. He wished he could just explode. That he could just let loose—but now, more than ever, he had no idea what that would mean—especially if whole worlds hung in the balance.

"I ain't sayin' there ain't no way a tall," the Doctor said. "But I am sayin that if there's a way to do what you tryna do, I ain't aware what it could be. None of the Powers are. Music is our language and vocabufication. You and your kin are magicians unlike any I ever heard tell of. Outta simple respect I felt the need to tell you what I know."

Casey stared at the cobbles of the stone path without seeing them. After all this. After giving himself over to this craziness and danger, he'd managed to find and speak to an actual honest-to-God wizard, only to be told he was shit out of luck.

"Don't give up hope, youngin. I may be a sorcerer and a Doctor Professor on the keys, but I am a man standing on this side of the grave. There's more to magic and the multiverse than I could ever hope to see from here. You already done the impossible, so mebbe you'll figure out how to do what you wanna before it's too late. God as my witness, I wish I could help ya."

With some effort, Casey stilled himself. He didn't fit a lid over his rage—instead, he let a memory form around him. A darkened dorm room. A record spinning. Rhythmic syllables that made no sense to him... A sensation gathered in the center of Casey's chest. For a moment it confused him, but then he felt himself being drawn away. "Doctor!" he said hastily. "How do I walk on guilded splinters?"

The Doctor shrugged. "I meant 'splendors,'" he said. "But I sang it wrong one night, and it sounded fonky, so it stuck! Walk in confidence and faith, and mebbe the Way will assemble to meet ya feet."

And then Casey was back at Rouses. In the chip aisle, this time. But he knew the supermarket held nothing he could use.

Casey spent the next day, the next night, sketching. He tried to recall every original character he'd ever created. Bossie Crossie, the gun-toting cowgirl who was literally a cow. Jocus Pocus, the zombie comedian and magician. Xathar Painbringer, the black-skinned hammer-wielding barbarian with the blood-red eyes. Casey made several sketches of each and tried to will them into motion. Nothing. Two nights after meeting with the Doctor, Casey had to concede that his present approach wasn't working. Maybe if he put them all in a mural together, he could—

His phone shrilled, startling him. It was his mother's ringtone. Casey crossed to the kitchen to grab the phone from the counter, then took it to the sofa. "How you doing, baby?"

Casey raised his eyebrows. His mother's question brought him up short. A week or two ago, the answer would have been simple: *Bad. I'm doing bad. Jaylon's dead and I can't figure out how to even begin picking up the pieces.* But a lot had happened since then.

"I guess I'm okay," he said. And the more he thought about it, the more true it seemed.

"We haven't heard from you much since... since the fire," his mother said. "Your daddy and I thought you'd call if you wanted to talk."

"No, I get that," Casey said. "I just didn't know what to say. I mean—most of the time, you tell me to pray or read the Bible, and I just... That never worked for me like it does for you."

"Casey, there is wisdom in the Word. I believe it with all my heart."

He could see her now in his mind's eye. These days, her medium-dark skin seemed creased from use and not age. She wore her hair short, and in the past couple years, she'd given up dyeing it, so now it was a steel gray that Casey vastly preferred to a bottle-black or brown. He thought of her on her daily walks around the Mall or Centennial Lake. He thought of the way her hands hung limp before her while she pursed her lips, deciding what step to execute next in whatever recipe or sewing project held her attention.

When Casey had first told her she thought he might be a boy, she'd said, *But, honey, I don't wear lipstick, either. I don't like the way it tastes!*

"Oh, I know, mama," Casey said. "I don't mean it like that. The thing is, I called to talk to you about something... something we don't talk about much."

In her silence, Casey sensed his mother preparing herself. How would he phrase this?

"...You talk to the dead." It was common knowledge in the family. Since he was very small, Casey remembered his mother recounting conversations with dead family friends, and even a stranger once in a while. Casey had never been what he would call a believer—not in God or religion, and not in ghosts. But he had never felt that his mother was lying or somehow wrong about these... visitations; she didn't like to call attention to them, and Casey had encountered—and endured—enough mental illness over the years to know she seemed utterly sane.

She took a breath and held it for a beat. When she spoke, there was a slight stiffness to her voice. "I don't seek them out. They come to me."

"What about Jaylon? Have you heard from him?"

"You know, I haven't," she said, thoughtful. "Not a word."

"They didn't find him in the wreckage," Casey said. "Do you think...do you think he could still be alive?"

"Casey, I don't see how," she said. "Not everybody comes to me. He might have his reasons."

After his conversation with the Doctor, Casey had no doubt that Jaylon had survived the explosion. That knowledge wasn't comforting, exactly, since Jayl was sealed somehow inside another world, but it helped to know that the craziness wasn't just inside Casey's own head. It was the next topic that Casey found...difficult.

Mostly, when they spoke, he and his mother kept things light. In Casey's teen years, they'd locked horns more than once—his mother had even laid him out once or twice. Now, things were on a more even keel—even if Casey's transition had been nearly impossible for his parents to accept. Would she explode if he said the wrong thing?

"All right," Casey said. "All right." He could tell his mother was parsing his words, trying to read his tone. It must confuse her that Jaylon's death was suddenly so easy for him to discuss. "You know this city as well as anybody..."

"Yeah."

"I don't know how else to say this," Casey said. "But have you ever heard about another New Orleans?"

The one thing Casey hadn't expected was to hear his mother's sharp intake of breath. "Boy, what you mean?"

"Someone...someone I trust told me that there's another New Orleans. Right here. That we can't see it or feel it or touch it, but there's people living there. Some dead and some not."

"Your great-grandfather Deacon mentioned it to me," she said. "I thought he was just— His mind started going after Hurricane Betsy. This must have been in '67 or '68, so I woulda been ten or eleven."

"Daddy Deke died of Alzheimer's?"

"Well, I mean I think so," his mother said. "Around the time I mean, he couldn't do nothing for himself. He lived with us in the house on Kerlerec, and there was a nurse—Miss Dotty—who cared for him. Bathed him and fed him and all."

Her voice took on a faraway tone as she remembered. "I know it was after Halloween because I got into a fight with your Teedy Billie over candy the night before. Oh you know what? It *was* '68 because your Mamaw and Daddy Gerard were both working, and we *were* in the Kerlerec house, and not on—"

"Mom," Casey said. "I need you to focus for me, please. This is important."

"I apologize," she said. Her voice was a little brittle, and Casey couldn't help but smile. "So that morning, I came downstairs after Billie already left, and Daddy Deke was just sitting at the kitchen table drinking coffee he must have made himself. He used to call me his Olive Bush. And he said, 'Well, damn, Olivette. These days, you more like Olive Tree, ain't you, baby?'"

By now her Seventh Ward accent had emerged, which almost never happened unless she was drunk or *very* angry.

"I didn't know what to think. So I said, 'Daddy Deke, you feeling better?'

"And he said, 'Well, they's good days and bad, Olive Tree, and I guess this a good one.' And I sat with him in the kitchen and ate cereal while he drank his coffee, and we just talked for a while.

"And I said, 'Where's Miss Dotty?'

"He said, 'Don't worry yaself none. I don't expect we'll be seeing her again.'

"I asked what he meant, and all he would say is, 'Just a feeling I got,' and then it was time to go.

"I said, 'You gone be all right without nobody here to take care of you?'

"He said, 'I got a delivery to make uptown. I be just fine.'

"I said, 'Uptown? You can't go all the way up there by yaself. What if you get lost?'

"And I remember clear as day. He said, 'Not *our* Uptown. The other one. The Hidden City in trouble, baby, and I gotta do my part.'

"And I went on to school. But Casey."

"Yeah, Ma?"

"When I got home, Mama and Daddy were both there. They told me Miss Dotty had died in the night, and so had Daddy Deke. They looked at me funny when I said he was fine when I saw him. I didn't realize until later he must have been dead when we sat together—that's why his mind was right again—but the thing he said about the Hidden City—I just never thought much about it till now. Dead folks say all kind of strange things."

"So he went to the Hidden City after he died?" Casey said.

"That's what he said."

"But why would...?"

Casey tried to square this with what he knew of the Other New Orleans. If it had been created to protect New Orleans from Katrina, how—? "Wait. You mentioned a hurricane? A few years before that?"

"Oh, yeah. Hurricane Betsy tore New Orleans *up* in '65, baby. Wasn't nothing nice."

The Doctor had spoken of "the Storm," and Casey had assumed that meant Katrina. But Katrina wasn't the only storm ever to damage the city. He hadn't fully understood what the Doctor had said, but maybe the Storm was a sort of quintessential hurricane that was somehow *all* the storms that had tried to destroy New Orleans down through the generations. Now *that* was the type of thing an orchestra of sorcerers might try to thwart using a powerful enchantment.

"You think Jaylon is in the Hidden City?" Olivette asked.

"Yeah," Casey said. "I do. Maybe that's why he hasn't reached out."

He sucked his teeth. His next question was even tougher than the last. "Mama...Mama, things are getting weird."

"Weird how?"

"I don't— Mom, if you don't know what I'm talking about, you're gonna think I'm cracking up."

"There's nothing wrong with you."

Casey stopped short. How could she— When Casey told her he was a lesbian, she'd told him that woman who lies with woman as a woman lies with a man is bound for the Lake of Fire. When he'd failed Chemistry in tenth grade, she'd told him he was lazy, too good to himself, that if he couldn't focus on something beside comic books and weed, he'd never amount to anything. As he thought of these things, he felt no bitterness, no pain—only confusion. If she'd believed those things, how could she believe—?

"Do you hear me?"

"Yes," Casey said.

"What I said?"

"You said there's nothing wrong with me. But you don't— Look. Did I...Did anything weird happen to me or around me when I was little?"

"Who told you? Uncle Trev?"

Casey's skin tingled. "What? Why? What?"

"Did he say something?"

Casey's mouth was dry. "About...what...?"

"You had a lot of imaginary friends when you were small—"

"—And you saw one," Casey finished for her. "You saw one of them."

"You remember?" she asked. "You were only four!"

He didn't remember. Not even dimly. The idea just...*fit*. "The one you saw. Do you know its name?"

"It was the bee man. Shobby."

"Sharpy," Casey said. "Bee Sharp."

"Casey, what's going on out there?" she asked. "What's happening?"

"I can't explain right now," Casey said. "If I tried, I'd only upset you. I have— I think I know what to do. I gotta go. Love you."

"But, Casey, please, please be careful," she said. *"Please."*

PULLING UPHILL

Jerome Holmes opened his eyes and stretched before smacking his alarm clock silent. He wasn't sure whether he'd hit the snooze button or the off button, so he turned his head to check. Damn snooze. Carefully, he picked up the clock, switched it off, and set it back in its place, pleased that he'd resisted the childish urge to bash it to smithereens. It was six in the morning, and Jerome had collapsed next to his wife at three.

He'd been up most of the night preparing for the storm. Yolanda had picked up ice and sandbags while Jerome and the kids boarded up the windows and moved water gallons into the deep freeze.

After the first storm report on WWOZ, he and Yolanda had discussed evacuating—taking the opportunity for a rare vacation, but with the precaution of bringing the deed to their house and their other important documents with them. In the end, they'd decided against it. It had been quite a while since they'd visited Yolanda's family up in Jackson, but...there just didn't seem to be a point. The storm would turn, and things would be fine—just like always.

"Another day," he said.

"Million more dollars," his wife mumbled from her side of the bed. "Leave me some coffee, Romy, hear?"

"Yeah, I hear you," Jerome said.

The bedroom was a mess, but he knew Yolanda would pick up in here if she awakened in time. Otherwise, she'd sleep through her own alarm and awaken in a white-hot hurry, forced to rush off to her job at the doctor's office. This was the year, though—this *had* to be the year—they could stop working for other people. Between the taxicab, the photography, and the car yard, this could be it.

Unless the storm wiped them out again.

Jerome shook his head. Impossible. They'd been blessed last time, and the Lord would smile on them again.

Jerome would have to make himself presentable before heading over to the studio, but after setting the coffeemaker, he shrugged into his bathrobe and headed out back to check on the yard.

The morning was unseasonably cool, but the overnight fog seemed to have let up a bit. The air smelled of drying laundry and cut grass.

Jerome crossed a length of crazy paving toward a wire gate with a curved top. On the other side of it, the car yard lay quiet with sleep, smelling of motor oil and mechanical dreams. "What it—what it—what it dooooooooo, Bossaman?" Cholly called from inside as soon as he sensed Jerome's approach. His voice sounded like an engine trying to turn over.

"Same as it ever was," Jerome called back as he fit his key into the gate's lock. "Quiet night?"

"Quieter than some," Cholly said, appearing on the other side. Jerome's father had cobbled Cholly together from odds and ends, and the robot looked like a walking yard sale. Dinner plates, car parts, various appliances, small and large, with wires threaded through. His torso was a potbellied stove, his head was an old-fashioned ghetto blaster, and his feet were RC cars. The old robot's knees had begun to rust again, and Jerome knew he'd have to oil them up before he turned in for the night—or what was left of it.

"That alley cat had her babies in the trunk of a Datsun," Cholly said. "I left her some kibble and water."

Last week, the elderly tortoiseshell had surprised Jerome by turning up heavily pregnant. Jerome hadn't known it was possible for a cat so old to bear a litter.

"How your eyes and ears?" he asked. "You need new parts?"

"Dey good enough for now," Cholly said. "I hunt up something and replace 'em my own self, me. You got more than enough to do round here."

Jerome shrugged. "If you say so." He grabbed a gas can off the shelf by the gate and nodded to Cholly. "All right," he said. "Let's make the—"

"*Hot damn!*" a child's voice called from somewhere within the maze of junked cars and machinery. "We back, baby!"

"Who's that?" Jerome asked.

Cholly scratched his metal scalp with a metallic skritch. "Dunno, Bossaman. Want me to call five-oh?"

Jerome grinned. "I *am* the police, baby." He took any chance he got to make that statement, even though it was no longer technically true. He'd turned in his badge and his gun some time ago. "We'll go together. But you *must* be getting old, letting vandals past you. This the second time this week."

Cholly stiffened. "Now, listen," he said. "Ain't nobody get by Cholly. I got eyes in the backa my *eyes*."

"Maybe you should build somebody younger to help you out," Jerome said. "Because we got company."

"Brendy!" someone—a boy?—called. "Where you is?"

"Here I'm is!" came the answering call. "We in the city, baby! We back!"

Jerome followed the voices, turning right past a stack of broken washer-dryers and left past a pyramid of TVs. One of the sets had lost its glass, and wildflowers grew inside as if starring in their very own show.

Here, the car yard opened into a dirt-floored clearing, and Jerome saw the boy who'd yelled standing with his back to him, his left hand visored over his eyes as he scanned the higher stacks that stood against the western fence. An old potato sack hung from his right hand. "Hey, you kids!" Jerome called.

A barefoot redbone girl in a grimy red dress with white trim strode out of a narrow aisle full of shelved car parts. She glanced at Jerome and waved, but made straight for the boy. "I hear music," she said. "Close. It's in here with us."

"Hey," Jerome said. "How you get in here?"

A smaller girl in a blue-and-white polka-dot dress danced up to join the other kids, beaming in the sunlight. She seemed unable to contain her high spirits, bopping in place as she grinned up at the sun. Jerome tried to sound stern, but his voice failed him. He barked a laugh.

"Hey, there, Mistuh Man!" the little dancing girl called. "And you, Mistuh Robot! You seen a song thinks it's people?"

"A song that—? What?"

The redheaded girl cocked her head, listening. "I hear her," she said. "She in here, and she ain't alone."

"What in...?" Jerome asked, helpless. He turned to Cholly. "Damn, Cholly, how many people you let in here?"

"Baby," Cholly said, "I don't even know. This *embarrassing*, is what this is."

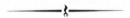

This was an adventure, and this was what adventurers did, Perry reminded himself. The fact that he, Brendy, and Peaches had only just emerged from the Clackin' Sack didn't mean they had time to celebrate, or even to slow down and take stock—the time for that had passed. Peaches had heard another song, and regardless of whether Doctor Professor was friend or foe, they might as well gather up the songs he had set them to find. Perry didn't even have time to marvel at the old robot made of car parts and stereo equipment that stood beside the heavyset man who'd challenged their presence in—what was this place? A car yard?

Brendy danced up, excited but ready for action. Every few

moves she made, she reached into her dress pocket to curl her hand around her magic rock. "Hey, there, Mistuh Man!" she sang. "And you, Mistuh Robot! You seen a song thinks it's people?"

The grown-up had no idea what she was talking about. He turned and said something to his robot. Perry reminded himself to shake hands with the robot before all this was through. He'd seen robots from afar from time to time, but he'd never met one personally.

"All right," Peaches said. "We need a plan. You ready, Perry?"

"Yeah," Perry said, "I'm ready." He was a little surprised to find that it was true.

"She thataway," Peaches said, pointing toward an aisle full of refrigerators and microwaves. "I'ma go up top and flush her out. When she come running this way, you use your sack, you dig?"

"I dig," Perry said. "Which one is she, though? I gotta call her by name to get her inside."

"That's the hard part," Peaches said. "I can't tell from here. Maybe once you catch sight of her, you'll know."

"Well, it ain't the world's best plan," Perry said, "but it's better than nothing."

"Brendy, you back Perry up this time," Peaches said. "If he can't figure out her name to grab her with the sack, you get Billy to put it on her."

"Yeah," Brendy said, still dancing. "But how?"

"Freeze her in place, maybe?" Peaches said. "If you can unburn me, you can freeze her, right?"

"Yeah," Brendy said. "Thass what I do!"

"But what we do about You Know Who?" Perry asked.

"Him?" Peaches said darkly. "I guess once we get her, we call him up and have *words*, you feel me?"

"Right," Perry said. "Break!"

"Break?" Brendy asked. "What you talking bout?"

Perry rolled his eyes. "We was huddled like football players. When the huddle's over, everybody says 'break!'"

"Oh," Brendy said, and now she stopped dancing and put on a serious face. "Okay, then. One, two, three..."

"Break!" they all said in unison.

"Hey," the grown-up said, but his voice sounded even more uncertain than before. "Hey, y'all."

"Not now, Mistuh Man," Brendy said. "We got work!"

Susan Brown strained in her bonds. Her skull ached something fierce. She could feel the skin of her forehead stretched over a throbbing knot of pain. Something cold and hard grasped her wrists, her ankles, but it was more reactive than metal shackles would have been. When she struggled, the material moved with her, expanding or contracting to maintain a cold, implacable grip.

Bound like this, arms above her head, she hung against a concrete wall in what seemed near-total darkness. She wasn't sure she'd be able to see clearly even with the lights on. Twisting her neck to look around sent a wave of sickness roiling from the pit of her belly.

The blunt gray scents of mold and dust mingled and rushed over her in a wave. The sharp yellow taste of vomit splashed into the back of her mouth. With some effort, she swallowed it back down. Throwing up all over herself wouldn't help her get to walking any sooner.

A flash of memory came to her. She remembered marching down Poland Avenue, enjoying the swing of her arms and the rhythm of her steps. Then a sick weightlessness as the big man with the cigarette eyes yanked on her multicolored robe, pulling her off her feet. Acting on instinct, Susan had tried to shed the robe and get back walking, but she was buttoned up tight, even if sweat glazed her limbs. She'd grabbed at the big man's hand, and that was when light exploded across her vision and faded into darkness.

She squinted. Had there been motion in the gloom just now?

She clenched her teeth to keep from shouting as the darkness turned its head. As a blood-red eye opened to glare at her.

it isn t personal it whispered.

She didn't ask what the spirit meant. She sensed a struggle in it, as if it warred with itself. No. There were things inside it, moving frenetically like moles digging in a yard.

free free we must be free at last

Once, as she marched through the Botanical Gardens, Susan had seen thick ropy orange tendrils drooping down from the leaves of a diseased tree. That was what she thought of now as the ghost's pale face opened like a flower. When they touched her, a melting heat spread beneath Susan's skin.

She understood now that her walking days were over and surrendered to the pain.

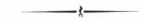

Perry didn't think the grown-up could be dismissed so easily— and he was right. The man's expression clouded, and Perry could tell he was preparing to assert his authority. Perry's mind raced for an explanation this man would understand. Surely there was something. He had a kind, open face, and his voice, even when he protested, sounded like a friendly purr—but there just wasn't time.

As Perry examined him, the grown-up's mouth fell open, and the tension ran out of his body. He goggled, amazed, at a point somewhere over Perry's shoulder. Of course. He must have seen Peaches in action. The way she leaped up the side of the junk heap, beelining toward her target. Nobody could watch her do something like that for the first time and take it in stride. The grown-up would need some time to digest what he'd just seen and integrate it with his understanding of the world. That would probably give Perry and the girls just enough time to execute their capture before he could get in the way.

Which song? Perry wondered. *Which song?* At least they knew this one was a woman.

Perry blinked, and a sensation of vertigo bubbled from his belly as his perspective abruptly shifted. Panic welled in Perry's chest, but he clamped down on it. Whatever was happening right now, he had to let it ride so things wouldn't go to pieces because of him. He could feel the sun on his shoulders and his shirt lying against his narrow back—but he felt those things from a remove, as if he were far away from them. If that was so, how had he gotten here from there? And where was "here," exactly?

Perry stood lightly atop a pile of metal sheeting, staring into the aisle below. He couldn't tell how high up he was, but he was high enough to worry. If he fell from here— Wait. A woman in a tight tank top and painted-on jeans half sat, half lay against a metal rack of dishwashers, smooching with a man in baggy jeans and a blue-and-red diamond-print polo shirt. She ran her skinny fingers over his fade, making wet kissing sounds.

Ew, somebody said.

What? Perry tried to say.

"I gots ya now," Peaches crowed. "You ain't no lady, you a song!"

Startled, the lovers looked up, and for a beat the woman seemed truly stunned. The man was just irritated. "Get on outta here," he said. "We busy."

"Naw," said the woman. "Naw, Leon. I gotta go!" She shoved him off and took off running.

Wait, Perry tried to say as his predicament dawned on him. He should have kept quiet, because this time Peaches sensed his presence. Surprise stole her footing, and Perry's stomach pitched as Peaches lost her balance. She tumbled toward the ground.

Perry returned to himself with a jolt. He felt a fizzing sensation against the vault of his skull. And in just one beat, sweat soaked through his clothes.

"Perry!" Brendy was shouting. "Perry! What your problem is? *She getting away!*"

"What?" Perry asked. "Who?"

"I dunno," Brendy yelled. "But her wig falled off!" She pointed.

Perry whirled to see the bald-headed woman attempt to thread the needle between the grown-up and his robot, headed for the gate. The grown-up still wore a stunned expression, but acting as if on instinct, he stepped gracefully to the left and stuck his right foot into her path.

The fugitive song tripped, went down hard, and now Perry heard a snatch of her music:

She a Balllllllhead Betty—!

"Ballhead Betty!" Perry shouted. For a moment, he forgot what to do next. Then he thrust his sack out before him. *"Clickety-clack! Get into my sack!"*

"Awwwwwwwwww!" the song wailed. While the cry was one of frustration and regret, it was also one of the most beautiful sounds Perry had ever heard. Now it was as if the woman were made of multicolored dust. A high wind blew past her, straight into Perry's sack, and the more it blew, the more it carried her particles with it. In two blinks of an eye, all of her had disappeared.

The grown-up gaped at Perry, wide-eyed and open-mouthed.

Perry gaped right back, equally amazed.

"Well, hell," said the robot. "Guess I need me some new eyes after all!"

"Damn it, Perry!"

Perry shook off his shock and turned back to see Peaches striding his way. Her face was red, and anger brightened her eyes. Perry thought how beautiful she looked, but then he remembered Peaches was mad as hell—at *him*. And why shouldn't she be?

Peaches halted a few feet away, hands on her hips, and glared. "That was *not* the plan!" she said. "That was one hunnid percent grade-A stupid. Whatinhell you was doing inside my head?"

"What?" Brendy asked.

"*This* Negro," Peaches said, "insteada doing like he sposedta standing ready with the sack climbed all up inside my head and damnear ruined everything!"

A chill crept across Perry's back. That was what had happened? He'd ridden shotgun with Peaches? He didn't like the feeling of being divided from his body. Honestly, all his life, he'd thought of himself and his body as one. He knew that church folks claimed that the soul, the spirit, was separate from the flesh, but Perry had never taken the time to consider what that meant. And if—and if Perry had left his body, had he been *dead*? Had his heart continued to beat while he was gone? Had his lungs continued to breathe? These thoughts raced through his mind in a matter of seconds, as Peaches glared her fury.

"I didn't—! It wasn't on purpose," Perry said. He hung his head, but caught himself, looked up again, suddenly angry. "I messed up. Of course I messed up! Why does everybody think I can just *do* this! I told mama I can't do it. I told Brendy I don't want it. 'You can do it. You like a cop show on the TV. You special, Perry!'"

The anger drained from Peaches's face. "Aw," she said. "Perry…"

"That's it?" Perry demanded. "*That's* what you got for me? This ain't games no more, Peaches. This ain't fun! This the real shit, and the bad part ain't that I am *definitely* going to die behind this shit, it's that everybody counting on me and because of me, *they're gonna die, too!*"

"That's not true," Peaches said. "I will *not* let you die."

"It's not up to you!" Perry raged. "This is bigger than you! It's bigger than everybody! I—I—I—We in each other's *heads*, now? I'm just supposed to roll with everything when my body ain't even my body no more? You took me over first!"

A caught expression appeared on Peaches's face. "*That's* what that was?"

"*That's what I—!*" Perry caught himself. He'd been on the verge of screaming at the top of his lungs into the most beautiful face he knew. And for what? What would it change? Everybody was wrong, and he couldn't do this, and everyone was going to die because of it; what would it help to scream and cry about it? Couldn't he just keep on keeping on and hope he was mistaken? The thought didn't make sense to him, but he was afraid to examine it more closely. If it was enough to keep him from feeling he was drowning, that black water was filling his lungs, then he'd just leave it at that for now.

"I, uh . . . I think so," Perry said. "Something like, anyway."

"Oh, *lawd*," Brendy said with a roll of her eyes and a theatrical sweep of her right arm. "Last thing I need is y'all switchin' bodies on me. Magic Negroes is even more triflin' than *regular* Negroes."

"I won't, though," Peaches said. "I won't let you die. You know that, right?"

Perry smiled sadly. "Yeah, Peaches. I know."

Peaches grinned. "I'll pull you uphill if I have to. And you know what yo mama say . . ."

" 'It's haaaaaaard pullin' Negroes uphill!' " they quoted in unison and let laughter take them.

"We caught the song, though," Brendy said brightly once they had taken a beat to recover. "I didn't even have to call Billy!"

"Yeah," Peaches said, her cheer restored, "but that'll be the last one we catch if we keep messin' up like this!"

Perry stuffed the sack roughly in his front pocket and showed Peaches his palms. "I know, okay?" he said. "We gotta be more careful. Especially since me and Brendy ain't used to being magic. I think her rock and my sack, they're still changing us—but—"

"*Butt!*" Brendy crowed.

Perry rolled his eyes and shook his head. "But we are where we at, and what we gotta do is figure out our next move."

"We don't even know what part of town we in," Peaches said, deflated.

"I bet you Mistuh Man know where we is," Brendy said. "Don't you, Mistuh Man?"

All three kids turned to look at Jerome. Jerome himself realized in that instant that he wasn't just shocked, he was terrified. Nola was a crazy place, all right, what with the P-bodies, the zombies, and the bizarre wilderness of City Park, but the madness had never encroached upon Jerome's own property. These kids were younger than his own, and they'd just—!

"You kids," Jerome said. "What you done to that woman?"

"Oh, that wa'n't no woman," the littlest one said. She couldn't have been older than six or eight. "That was a song."

"You know," said the boy. "'Ballhead Betty'? 'Looka there,'" he sang, "'She a ball ball ball ball Ballllhead Betty!'"

"I ain't playing, now," Jerome couldn't hear himself speaking, and he hoped his voice was slow with authority. "I was an officer of the law, and you need to fill me in on what just happened here. Who are you? What are your names? Who was that woman? Where is she now?"

The redhead looked at Jerome with the same expression he saw in the faces of the little gangbanging kids in the worst parts of town. She couldn't be older than twelve, and she should not yet have learned how to make her face close like a fist.

"Don't worry," she said. "We leaving directly."

"You're not going anywhere until I get an explanation," Jerome said. "Then I'll call your parents to come get you."

"Who gone stop us?" the little one asked. "You and yo robot?" There was no malice in her voice. She seemed excited and genuinely curious—and that was what frightened Jerome most of all.

"We don't want no trouble, baby," the redhead said. "Y'all just keep it cool, and we be right out your hair."

Reflexively, Jerome reached for his absent holster.

The kids tensed: The little one reached in her dress pocket. The redhead balled her fists, and veins corded out along her skinny arms. The boy reached for the potato sack sticking out of his left front jeans pocket.

Jerome froze. Time ground nearly to a halt, the same way it had the only time he'd been forced to shoot an assailant. Electricity seemed to course along his limbs. He'd never had this sensation come over him when he was unarmed, and now he felt out of his depth. He concentrated on his expression, willing his mask of control to remain in place. The children glared right back at him, unafraid.

"...Now," Jerome said, acutely aware that he *did not* want to share whatever fate had befallen the woman he'd tripped. "...Now, listen..." What would he say next? What was there to say?

A piano intro split the air, played by no one at all.

"Damn," said the redhead. Jerome felt that if he'd been close enough, he could have seen his own reflection disappear from the surface of her eye. Now that she heard the music, Jerome might as well never have existed.

This is good, Jerome thought. *This is a good thing. Turn around and leave them to whatever this is.*

But...but they were kids, and they were clearly in danger. Jerome couldn't just leave them.

The piano continued to play, its sound filling the car yard and spilling into the neighborhood beyond. A shadow began to form in the clearing.

The redhead shared a look with the boy. "You ready?" she asked.

"Naw," said the boy. "But that don't matter now."

WE STILL HERE

The fog had cleared, making way for the afternoon. First Chief Albert Desravines was running out of options. Sooner than later, he'd have to trek outside the city to ask the Peoples if they knew what had become of First Queen, the Spy Boy, the Flag Boy, and the others. First Chief had searched the whole of the Seventh Ward, and nobody seemed to know nothing about his tribe. Now he stood at the intersection of Canal and Dorgenois and squinted into the sun as he smoothed the feathers that grew out of his arms. His feathers and scales caught the light, turned it, iridescing through a riot of colors.

The need for food rumbled in the pit of his belly. He did not realize it, but as he stood considering, a quiet tune pumped itself out of the stout, hollow quills that jutted from his back. The tune was not loud, but its notes tumbled softly over one another, somersaulting into the afternoon air. When he noticed the music, he grunted—and even that guttural sound was oddly tuneful. *Thass right*, he thought. *Why, I'm the prettiest, me.*

The smell of cooking had drawn him here, but the door to this little place was too small. First Chief glared at it, and the door swung open. He stooped, bending, squatting his long body at the knees and at the haunches, and stepped inside.

The dining room was full. Nearly a hundred heads swiveled on their stalks as First Chief appeared to them, and mouths fell open. First Chief accepted their silent tribute. This was the only correct response to his overwhelming majesty. After allowing the spectators a merciful moment to drink in his splendor, First Chief spoke.

Hey wanna wanna. Hey wanna way.
Heyyyy! Hey, wanna wanna, whatchoo got fo Chief today?
First Chief, me. Bold and feather-proud
Tell Marraine to git it git it
Tell Marraine to git it git it, git it good
Sixty-two inches cross my chest
Sixty-two inches, me
Sixty-two inches cross my chest
And I don't bow but to God or Death!
Lord! Tell Marraine to git it good!

As he recited his demands, First Chief shook his giant crest and the feathers of his arms. They flashed red, blue, yellow, white, black, then green, and the noise of his heart rose through the pipes on First Chief's back, percussing to let his subjects know the seriousness of this matter. First Chief paused, giving the lesser beings a chance to process his command.

One of the subjects, a young man dressed in a purple T-shirt and a grimy apron shook off his expression of blasted wonder and turned to the stout woman next to him. "What...? What is that?"

The woman shook herself out of her own trance. "You must be from Away," she said. "This the Chief of All Chiefs. He say get him some food."

Wanna wanna hey, thass right thass right
I'm the prettiest, me. Prettiest of all

Tell Marraine to git it, git it
Tell Marraine gonna set that jail on fire!

The woman had warmed to her role as translator for the Lessers. "Move! Y'all over there, I'm sorry, but you gots to clear that table. Chief of Chiefs need somewhere to sit!"

"But what he want?" asked the youth who'd spoken before.

"Get him some of everythin. As much as you can fit on a plate. Just put it together and start bringin it out."

Pretty little baby
Pretty little girl
Pretty little thing done right by Chief
Got me riches got diamonds and pearls
Remind me of First Queen, thass no lie.
Don't bow to nobody but God and Death!

The diners at the table the woman had chosen cleared out now, and many other patrons had risen from their seats. First Chief commanded the attention of all, but now the kitchen staff had swung into action, scooping food from buffet trays and piling it on plates. As First Chief watched, the woman set three large plates on a tray and carried them to the table. She set them down, unsure what to do. First Chief regarded her sternly, waiting for her to recover her manners.

The woman bowed, then went down on one knee. "Chief of Chiefs!" she chanted. "You honor us with your presence. A thousand million thanks!"

Pretty little girl rise up rise up
Pretty little girl gonna rise on up
Whatchoo got for me today?
Whatchoo got for me?
Didja tell Marraine to git it good?

The woman stood and pulled out a chair. "Yes, Chief," she said. "This restaurant is one of the best in the city. Is there anything I can do to make you comfortable?"

Chief of Chiefs considered, then took the seat he'd been offered. From his position, he could see the restaurant's broad windows, but while moments ago they had offered a view of the sunny sidewalk and the street beyond, now faces and bodies blocked them, pressed against the glass, staring. There must have been a hundred people looking on, and Chief of Chiefs thought nothing of this. Of course the Lesser Beings sought to drink in his beauty; how could they do otherwise? Chief of Chiefs was prettiest of all.

He lifted a heaping plate of dirty rice and poured it into his mouth, taking it in a single swallow. The drum and cymbal sounds of his heart rattled to express his approval.

"Chief of Chiefs," said the woman, "please forgive me. It is not for me to ask, but why have you come here today? Where are your Spy Boy and your Flag?"

Baby, dontcha know, don't know myself
Baby dontcha know, can't figure it out
Chief of Chiefs him all alone
Lookin' for the tribe he call his own
Sixty-two inches cross his chest
And he don't bow
Don't know how
Where they at, now, where him peoples at?

"Well, I'm from the Seventh Ward, born and raised," said the woman, "so maybe I can tell you what you need to know. What tribe you with, Chief?"

First Chief plucked a stuffed green pepper from a plate of them and popped it whole into his mouth. He let it slide down into his belly, and his heart rattled its approval. When First Chief considered the question, the natural answer seemed that he was with *all* tribes (seeing as how he was the greatest and the prettiest and he had a sixty-two-inch chest), but the question also made him think of piano music, its notes tumbling over and over, and the thought made First Chief uncomfortable.

But why should that be? No jail could hold him, and he bowed to none. He wouldn't know how to bow down even if he wanted to. His knees could bend, but not that way. His knees bent only for dancing. Wasn't he a man?

...But...but *was* he? Men and women crowded the dining room. Many of them had risen from their own meals to ring the room, staring wide-eyed at First Chief as he ate his meal and spoke to this Pretty Little Thing. The men looked so small—the Black ones, the white ones, the Spanish ones and Asians. None of them stood over six and a half feet. First Chief wasn't sure of their measurements, but surely none of their chests approached even fifty inches across. Some of the oldest ones had liver spots standing out on their flesh, or leathery, lived-in skin that seemed ready to tell countless stories. If these were men, First Chief wondered, then what exactly was First Chief?

He stood tall—eight feet if he was an inch, with two great pipes standing out of his shoulders, each one flanked by two lesser pipes. If he chose, he could direct the sound of his heartbeat—the sound of the drum and the sound of the cymbal—through them to make the most beautiful of rackets. His face was black as black—no Black man in the restaurant approached even a tenth of the darkness of First Chief's face—and his teeth were bright red. All these people—when they opened their mouths to stare or yawn, they were pink and soft inside, but First Chief knew that the inside of his own mouth was bright yellow and his tongue was not fleshy pink, but the brightest white. Feathers stood forested on his upper arms, on his shoulders, and of course, on his giant crest, changing color and position to suit his mood. As he considered them, they rose and fell thoughtfully, following the motion of his breathing. While he wore no shoes, First Chief's bright red three-toed claws were much stronger, much tougher, than leather.

He knew his name—First Chief Albert Desravines, Chief of Chiefs, Prettiest, Strongest, Most Formidable in Battle—and he knew what those epithets meant, but try as he might, he could not reconcile them with his surroundings, or the simple physiological differences he observed between himself and others. How had this happened? Had the world changed as he slept? And when had he slept? When had he last eaten?

Fear stole into his mind, and First Chief spoke in a whisper before he could banish his fear with rage or bluster. "I don't...I don't understand any of this," he said, so softly he wasn't sure even the Pretty Thing could hear him. "Something...something terrible has happened."

"It did," said the woman. "But don't worry. The Storm was bad, but we still here."

Perry steeled himself—or tried to. It wasn't long before the bouncing keyboard intro segued into the song itself, and by that time, Doctor Professor's piano had fully manifested. The man himself faded in after, singing loud as his head rolled on his shoulders. For the first time, Perry felt no compulsion to dance, and the absence of that need made him a little sad.

Kick off ya grave clothes, get in line
Baby, dance down the street
Cain't no dirty floor hold ya down
Catch them chords and dig that beat.

Perry didn't know this one, but he liked it. He wanted to hear the whole thing, learn it, hum it as he went about his daily business. *But he's a liar*, Perry thought. *Damnear got us killed.* He thought of Brendy's assertion that there must be some misunderstanding, that Doctor Professor hadn't meant to steer them wrong. But could grown folk—even magic ones—be trusted?

Perry loved his parents, and he loved Daddy Deke. He respected his teachers and knew they meant him no harm...but did that make them trustworthy? If grown-ups were just old kids pretending, could they be trusted even when they meant well? Perry had no idea, and he did not like this line of thinking.

He cast a glance in Peaches's direction, and the sight of her determined frown made him stand a little straighter. The grown-up who'd challenged them had been dancing since the song's first chord, sliding back and forth on his feet, twirling now and again. Even the old robot seemed to dance, creaking unsteadily on his red and crumbling knees. Brendy bopped a couple steps, then looked up at Peaches and Perry and settled down, just nodding her head.

Feelin' fonky and I can't sit still
I done rolled down the mountain
I done climbed that hill
With your rocket in yo pocket
And the gold on your teeth
That rocket in ya pocket
And the gold on ya teeth!

"Well, hey there, baby," Doctor Professor said with a grin as the song went on. "Nice to finally meetcha. I hear you got some thangs belong to me."

"Maybe we do," Peaches said, "but then again, maybe we don't. We got lots to talk about."

Now the music faded a bit, and Perry felt another pang of loss. Doctor Professor withdrew his fingers from the keys. They hovered in the air above the black and whites, and while his grin didn't die, it did lose a bit of its luster.

"Yeahyouright," he said. "We got some thangs need going over. Listen here: I'ma take back them songs y'all hunted up for me and be on my way. Y'all sure have done me proud, but I think I handle the rest my own self just the same."

"Now, wait a minute—" Peaches began.

Perry cut her off. "After everything we went through, you wanna cut us loose? I faced down Stagger Lee himself to capture Jailbird Stomp, and that's gotta be worth more than a thank-you-and-goodbye."

Doctor Professor's fingers stiffened above the keyboard, and a stricken expression appeared upon his face. "You faced down Stag?"

"You durn right he did," Brendy said. "My big brother a hero among men!"

"Why you didn't tell us Stagger Lee was loose and looking for the same songs we was?" Peaches demanded.

"There's levels to this thing I didn't know nothing bout last time we spoke. The city under attack by sumn worse than ole Stag, and I cain't have y'all involved."

"You're scared," Perry said. "You're more scared than we are."

"Listen here," Doctor Professor said, a cracked and weakened sort of authority creeping into his voice.

"Don't give us that," Peaches said. "Don't talk to us like we don't know nothing. We got two of your songs. We got hoodoo for days. You tell us what bothers you bout all this, and we figure out what to do from here."

Fess sighed heavily. "Baby, what bothers me about this is if Stagger Lee got out into the world, then whoever helped him know *exactly* what they messin' with. It's no accident that they endangered Nola—they actively trying to destroy our home for good. They's only one thing could empower them to do that. The Storm."

Perry shivered. He knew the Storm had devastated the city in the past. He saw its memory in the lines on his parents' faces anytime they saw a TV weather report they didn't like. He wasn't sure when it had happened—whether he'd been alive and making memories or whether it had happened years and years before his birth. He'd never heard the words spoken quite the way Doctor Professor did. When he said them, his voice was marbled with panic, regret, and unwanted memory.

"There's got to be something we can do," Perry said. "What if we catch more songs? We've already got—"

"Stag done kilt two already," Doctor Professor said. "And he's looking for more every minute."

"How does he figure out which ones to go after next?" Peaches asked. "How do he make the choice?"

"The Storm must be telling him somehow," Fess said. "Telling him which murders cause what. The first one he got made all the horses and carriages disappear. The one he just kilt disappeared the traffic lights and brought down City Hall. Sinkhole opened up and swallowed it right down."

"My God," Perry said. "Is everyone—?"

"Cars and trucks done wrecked all over town," the Doctor said. "Folks can feel the changes now. They afraid. They boarding up they windows and getting ready to hunker down. And now I gotta find somebody else to help me fight."

"Hold on a minute," Peaches said. "We didn't say we wouldn't find the other songs. Besides—Daddy Deke been took by Stagger Lee. Even if we wasn't willing to help you, we ain't done till we got him back."

Perry frowned. Something Fess had said stuck out in his mind. "You said the Storm is telling Stagger Lee which songs to kill when. How can a storm talk like it's people?"

Peaches shrugged. "How can a song?"

"It ain't the same as a song," Doctor Professor said thoughtfully. "It would need to speak *through* somebody."

A thought occurred to Perry then, but he thrust it roughly away, though even as he did, he knew he was right. Still, it would do more harm than good to say anything until he had some kind of proof.

"Y'all gotta come up off the case, though, baby," Fess said. "I gots me some enemies—maybe one or two I don't know nothing bout. I don't need to be makin' no more right now, dig?"

"What?" Brendy asked. "What that means?"

Now Mr. Man spoke up. "He means somebody in your corner

knows what's at stake," he said. "And they made it clear to this man that his endangering you may have caused him some serious trouble."

"Somebody threatened you?" Perry asked.

"I am Doctor Professor," Fess said. "Can't *nobody* threaten me."

"*Now* he lyin'," Brendy said, wide-eyed.

"We ain't off nothing," Peaches said firmly. "And you best be telling us the truth from here on."

"At least tell us this," Perry said. "The one who threatened you. Was it Daddy Deke?"

"Naw, it was some— Wait." Fess cocked his head, listening to something they couldn't hear. "Hell and damnation."

"What?" Peaches asked. She squinted, listening as well. Perry wondered why, but then he remembered the strength of her senses. "Oh no!"

"Baby, I gotta go," Fess said.

"What is it?" Perry asked. "What's going on?"

Peaches ignored the question. "Take us with you."

"I can't—"

"No time to argue," Peaches told him flatly. "We gone up against him once and came out ahead. You leave us here, and First Chief is good as dead."

Doctor Professor grimaced, uncertain, then: "Grab on to my piano. All of y'all."

Perry, Brendy, and Peaches stepped forward and pressed their palms against the lacquered wood.

Brendy looked at Mr. Man over her shoulder. "You comin', Mistuh Man? Or do you just like to bark at folks?"

Without answering, the grown-up turned away. Perry tried to tell himself he shouldn't be surprised, but disappointment stung him.

Doctor Professor launched straight into the first verse of a song Perry knew well:

Baby, lemme see ya levitate, levitate
Baby, lemme see ya hover on that air

Baby, you as fly as a midnight witch
The way you sweep that broom like ya just don't care...!

The world faded from view.

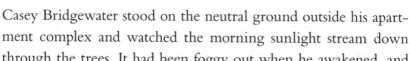

Casey Bridgewater stood on the neutral ground outside his apartment complex and watched the morning sunlight stream down through the trees. It had been foggy out when he awakened, and he'd spent the hazy hours discussing his next step with Naddie. She had done as he'd asked and packed go bags, their most important documents. Since early this morning, they'd had WDSU on the TV, listening to Margaret Orr track the disturbance in the Gulf.

"Austin," Casey had said. "You can go to Austin."

"Are you seriously saying I should go to fucking *Texas* by myself?" Naddie's gray eyes were wide with shock.

"I can't leave yet," Casey said. "I got something I gotta do."

"Fuck that," Naddie spat. "If you're staying so am I."

"Fine—just—! What do we have and what do we need?" He knew they had flashlights, a rechargeable power station, a couple cabinets full of canned food. There must be something he was missing. It had been so long since they'd had to weather a storm together. Hadn't it?

Naddie seemed a little confused herself. "Battery powered fans?" she said. "And batteries. Lots of them."

"Hit up Walmart, okay? But look. Things are going wrong in the city. My cousin Charly says City Hall is gone. It's because of the storm. I know it. I gotta help if I can."

"What does the storm have to do with City Hall?"

"I don't know," Casey said. "I don't understand it myself, but Roux said it would happen before it happened. She knows, and she says I can help. So I have to try. The entire city. Our music, our future, *everything* is in trouble. I might not be able to do much, but I gotta do something!"

"You don't even know what Roux gave you," Naddie said. "You're too afraid to look in the bag!"

Casey crossed to the jeans he'd worn last night and drew a velvet drawstring bag from the right front pocket. Something small and hard weighted it down in Casey's hand. He considered opening it to investigate right now.

Not here! The thought was bright and terrified in Casey's mind. *Not in the house. No hoodoo in the house!*

"She said it could show me where to go," he said. "She said I'd know what to do once I got there."

"And you want me to wait for you, wait here for you to come home and tell me it's all taken care of? *Such macho frickin'—!*"

"I'm supposed to feel bad for trying to keep you safe?" Casey asked. "The whole point of all this is to keep you out of danger! I can't—I can't have you anywhere near that thing I saw. I can't. If that makes me some kind of chauvinist D-bag, *fine*. If you're not here when I get back, if I can't come back to you, then...then at least I know you can handle yourself without me."

"Casey. *Case.*"

His face heated. "I'm going. I got to. Just—" His voice failed him. *Here it is,* he thought. *He's going to cry.*

"What's the difference between being brave and just being stubborn and too dumb to stay out of trouble?" Naddie asked.

"I don't know," Casey said.

"Well, at least kiss me goodbye."

Casey did, but when it came time to disengage, he didn't. They stood together for a long time before he let Naddie go.

Now, standing on the neutral ground, he saw a rippling out of the corner of his eye and looked toward the uptown side of the street. Four different graffiti tags floated up the street: H4INT NOBDDY, CA$$PER, BOOMDOWN, and GRAWLIQZ. He'd never seen so many at once.

He shook his head. He could still feel Naddie against him, and the memory of her helped combat the sense of wrongness, of impending doom, enough that he was able to draw the pouch from his pocket and empty it into his hand.

At first he thought the item was an overlarge locket without a string, and he searched for a seam with his fingers. He held it up to the light, turning it in his hands, and realized that there was no seam where it should open. "Okay, then," he said aloud. "Where we going?"

Someone you must meet, a disembodied voice said from behind Casey and to his left.

Casey was confused. "To help fight the storm?"

Soon.

He felt like a fool. The thought made no sense. "Where?"

Tree Muses.

"For what? For a drink? It's nine in the..."

Silence.

"All right," Casey said. "Take me, then."

Casey Bridgewater winked out of sight.

TREE MUSES

November 2018

Casey didn't think about it often, but if he had to, he could pinpoint the moment he and Ximena began to come apart. His transition had evened out, finally, after what had felt like a second puberty, and Ximena was still busting her ass in grad school at Towson. A blizzard came early that year, muffling everything under its crisp white blanket, bringing life in the DMV to a halt. That same weekend, the head cold Casey had been fighting for the past few days gained the upper hand, making him feverish and irritable.

He *hated* being sick. Ximena brought him zinc, juice, and extra-strength cough drops, as well as a bottle of niacin. "If you really want to burn that fever out, take some of these," she'd said. "Daddy used to give them to me—but I'm serious. It will *burn*."

Casey nodded, croaked his thanks, and drank the whole half gallon of orange juice in what felt like a single pained swallow. He took the niacin and retreated to the bed, sucking on a zinc lozenge until the dark of sleep covered him over like a snowbound street.

Sometime in the night, Casey sat up, burning. Acrid sweat soaked

his side of the bed, and the heat in him was nearly unbearable. A sizzling sound hissed at the edge of his hearing as he held his left hand
before his face. He felt the heat baking off his skin. He felt like the
Human Torch ready to Flame On.

The heat intensified, dancing in the air of the room. Casey
felt the niacin pills resting like hot stones in the pit of his belly.
Was he dreaming this? He remembered picking smooth, glowing
stones from the ashes of an earthen hearth and gulping them down
his throat. A dream? A dream. Somewhere distant, a single bell
rang, and then Casey heard Ximena calling his name, her voice
ragged with terror. He felt a hand in his, larger than his own.
Large enough to swallow him the way big fish eat the little ones.

Then, in the dark, those haunting tones. A carpet of needles, of
metal splinters. All he had to do was step.

"No," he said aloud. "Absolutely not."

The tension in the air snapped, then, with a twang Casey felt at
his core. He fell back against his pillows and slept so deeply that it
felt like being unborn.

The next morning, his fever was gone. He felt like a new man.
He rose before Ximena, cooked a breakfast of pancakes and maple
bacon. Before he was done, Ximena appeared in the kitchen doorway, rubbing her eyes.

"What the fuck, Case?"

"All better," he said. "You got class?"

"No," she said. "They're canceled. Everything's canceled."

"That's what I figured," he said. "So, pancakes, bacon, *Golden
Girls* marathon. Come and get it."

When they ate in front of the TV, Ximena didn't laugh at the
old ladies squabbling together. Every so often she'd hum low in
her throat, instead. Casey didn't realize it for a long time, but that
was the end for them.

Since then, he'd wanted many times to ask Ximena what had
happened. He knew why she couldn't come with him back to
New Orleans—she'd resolved to move to New York, give acting a

real shot—but it was more than that. It had something to do with his bizarre dream of heat and a bell.

He understood it better now, he thought. The dream wasn't a dream—or some of it was and some of it wasn't—but Ximena had seen something alien in him. Something that set him apart. She'd rolled with him through everything else, but this was just too much. He thought to call her, to ask about it, but that seemed unfair. If he did, she would read something in his tone, know he was preparing to take some drastic step. And even if she didn't—what did they have to say to each other now? The pressure to talk to her about his art, about Jaylon's disappearance, about Bee Sharp and Dr. John, would be too great, and she deserved better than to be forced to worry over Casey's sanity—or worse, to know he told the truth and the world was not what she had always believed it to be.

Instead of phoning Ximena, Casey drew all the curtains in the apartment, but too much light came through the living room windows, so he brought in foil from the kitchen and covered them over. He turned the thermostat up to 90, then changed into cargo shorts, a polo, and a pair of Tevas. He fitted his copy of *Gris-Gris* onto the turntable but didn't switch it on. Instead, he pulled up Spotify on his phone, connected it to his smart speakers, and set "I Walk on Guilded Splinters" to repeat.

By the time he ripped open his new three-pack of sketchpads, he'd begun to sweat. He rummaged in his underwear drawer until he found a fleece sweatband to keep the liquid from his eyes. That strange, warm smell of gas heat came to him then, and when it did, he felt a door open in the back of his skull. He took that for encouragement and rushed back to the living room to sit in lotus position and sketch to the music.

The first thing he drew was a hooded figure standing on what he believed must be a forest path. The music fizzed in Casey's skull as the figure turned their head to look over their shoulder. They stopped moving then, and Casey moved on to the next sketch. This one was of Doctor Bong from the old *Howard the Duck* comics. His version was more monstrous, though. More like something Richard Case would have designed for Grant Morrison's run on *Doom Patrol*, but with the suggestion of Mignola's deep shadows. The monster's bell-shaped head vibrated, constantly ringing in sympathy to the music surrounding Casey. Yes. That was the way to go.

Now Casey drew with less conscious thought. Instead of checking the page to see if his figures did what he wanted, he tore out each page and dropped it on the carpet, taking only the barest bit of care to keep them from overlapping. The heat pressed against his slick skin like an angry housewife ironing a dress shirt. He smelled gardenias.

Casey let the sketching, the heat, the music, the scent of his own sweat draw him from himself. He felt that heat in his belly again, that burning heaviness, like he'd swallowed a grill's worth of burning charcoal briquettes. The sizzle rose up around him, the strange tones of the song's central riff, the drumming, the tinging of the bell.

He stood in darkness. At some point, he'd shifted his pencil to his left hand, and he felt its slick solidity against his fingertips. A strange heat played up his forearm to his shoulder. He didn't take the time to wonder where he was. Instead he bent and began sketching a path to walk on.

Bells. Red skies. Animated constellations. A rushing, tideless drift.

One night back at Smith, soon after he and Ximena first met, she and Casey had dropped acid together. In those days, Casey still thought of himself as a lesbian—much to his parents' dismay. An older girl, Tosha, had cautioned Casey about the drug. She sat in her own dorm room, where she sold weed, pills, and hallucinogens to curious classmates, her plum-shaped body situated on a lime-green beanbag chair. The sleeves of her baby-doll dress were flared with lace, and she wore a pair of mauve tights against the bitter Massachusetts cold.

"People say it's volatile and shit, but what they mean is you don't always know what you bringing to it, you know? Sometimes tripping is like jumping into a fast river from *real* high up.

So high you can't see what's on the bottom. Sometimes there's rocks. Sometimes there's little fishies..." She trailed off, smiling. Thinking of those pretty little fish, Casey felt sure. After a beat, she seemed to remember the conversation. "So be careful, you know? Don't be the second-best cliff diver."

"Who's the second-best cliff diver?"

"*Exactly!*" Tosh said. Tickled, she began to laugh.

Casey turned to Ximena, confused.

Ximena combed the fingers of one hand through her mane of curly dark hair. The way the light shone on her, kissing her with brightness as it moved into the world, tightened something in Casey's chest.

"This girl higher than giraffe-pussy," Ximena said.

Tosh giggled some more and then pointed the first two fingers of her right hand toward her eyes, then stabbed them in Casey's direction. "*He* knows," she said.

Casey felt a thrill of anxiety. He felt as if he'd been spied on.

"Whatever," he said. "Ain't no thing."

They dropped in Casey's room and played Mario Kart for a while on his hand-me-down TV/VCR. After what seemed like an hour or two, nothing had happened, and Casey rolled onto his back on his shitty little mattress and let his thick dreads cover his face. "Nothing," he said.

"Boop-BOOP!" Ximena answered.

Casey sat up to look at her. She had fitted fuzzy socks onto her hands and was trying to pull gloves onto her feet. She labored for a moment, confused, then shed a sock so she could use her fingers to adjust a glove.

"*Girl,*" Casey said.

"No, just...you gotta get it," Ximena said. "Look." She got her toes into the glove and looked up at Casey. "I'm *upside-down,*" she said, and beamed at him.

"Oh, *SHIIIIIIIIT!*" Casey said.

And they were off.

Casey remembered the rest of the night as a series of fragments, but he sensed a whole alongside it, divided from the rest of his life into a vacuole of *now*, a timeless, magic bubble that could never be ruptured by the present or future. Casey remembered sprinting down the trail to Paradise Pond, whooping, hands in the air. He remembered playing Connect Four in someone else's common room, shouting "Domino, mother*fucker!*" every time he won a match.

He remembered trying to find a way into the dining hall after some sort of MacGuffin he knew must be stashed there. He wasn't sure whether Ximena was with him the entire time, but he knew they'd spent a significant chunk of time watching *Thriller* over and over and trying to learn the choreography, and then crying into the sunrise, watching Ximena's hands flutter like wind-blown leaves above her head.

That feeling of *emergence*, of new sunlight falling on a different world than the one night had swallowed the evening before, was a small echo of what Casey felt after passing through the Door. A sky so delicately blue, clouds so exquisitely formed that all of it, together, looked like a matte painting. Except the clouds moved, grazing like skyborne sheep, held aloft by an echoing chord of something, of—

Had he been dosed? That old acid trip was the only time Casey had experienced this sense of stillness preceding a chaotic din of impressions, of—of—of—

The clouds were moving steadily toward the west. The air smelled of summer. It was warm out, but not hot. Not for New Orleans.

Casey sat on a metal bench. His heart sank. He shut his eyes against the realization that nothing had happened. He'd had some kind of break and taken off running around town, doing God knew— A figure trudged up the embankment carrying a sodden briefcase. It paused to fit a wet hat on its furry head.

He didn't understand what he was seeing. The man—it must be a man because it wore a sodden green business suit with crimson pinstripes—seemed to be wearing a furry mascot head, or—no, not just a head. Its gloves were furred, as well, and it— No. That was its *face*. Its bright orange buckteeth, its—!

"*Yo!*" Casey shouted.

The creature blinked at him. "You good?" it asked.

Casey bristled like a cat. Part of him ignored the word that thrilled through his mind. It made no sense. It was impossible. It couldn't— Someone had dosed him!

A nutria! A nutria! A fucking talking nutria wearing a three-piece suit!

Before Casey knew it, he was running full-tilt down the asphalt path.

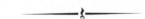

Arms and legs pumping, Casey ran. He hadn't sprinted like this since his freshman year at UNO. He'd run track in high school, but only because he wanted to add discipline to his running when he needed to evade the cops or rival bombers. At first, his body carried him along through muscle memory while his bright and overwhelmed senses flooded his brain with information it couldn't read. Gradually, he returned to himself, and marveled at how well his body still worked. He'd been smoking lately, four or five a day, but his bound chest expanded and contracted confidently as his knees pushed high, the blades of his hands slicing, slicing.

He knew where he was. That was the first realization to penetrate his consciousness. He was on Canal Street, just crossing Rampart. So far, the lights must have gone his way, because traffic had spared him. The facades of the shops and hotels made sense to him. On his right, he was passing that shitty little gym that had always looked suspicious to him—like a mob front, or a—or a—

He nearly stumbled as one of the red Canal streetcars descended from above.

It had—it had been in the air. It had been up above, and it angled its nose up and drifted down. It had no wheels, just bunches of springed metal feet sheathed in black rubber toes that gripped the pavement as the streetcar set down beside a shelter. Casey stopped running and trembled as he watched people and oversized animals disembark. Casey didn't register it until the crowd of commuters had dispersed, but a couple of the figures in tattered suits looked as if they'd been dead a long time. Like—*no.*

Like zombies.

Panic welled in Casey's chest again, constricted his scalp. His legs quaked from terror or exertion—he wasn't sure which.

A hand fell on Casey's shoulder. "Hey, now," someone said. "Hey. Young man?"

As Casey turned to meet the voice he wondered what he'd do if the speaker was another talking animal or undead.

He sagged as he recognized the man he'd always thought of as Umbrella Hat Preacher. When he'd worked at Betsy's the summer before the Storm, he'd seen the man every morning, standing at the bus stop by the Saenger, shouting his Good News through a megaphone. Casey had never bothered to learn the man's name. Instead, he had avoided the preacher as much as he could.

"*You're* here?" Casey asked.

A shadow of confusion swept across the man's broad dark face, then gave way to a smile. "Most mornings," he said. "And you look like you in need, young man."

"I need…" Casey said. "It's too much. There's animals, and— and—"

"Come on siddown with me. Get off ya feet," the man said. He wore a bright red T-shirt untucked at the waist with loose khaki slacks. He looked younger than he should. Squeezed under the band of his umbrella hat, his hair was still mostly black instead of the steel gray Casey had seen on him last week. He looked a bit slimmer, a bit healthier, a bit less tired than he had then.

Casey let the man take his elbow and guide him to the streetcar shelter. Casey realized as the man sat him down that the streetcar had been waiting for them to clear the way so it could lift off again. Watching it go made Casey feel like the last man on Earth. "Fuck. *Fuck—!*"

"What's the trouble?" Umbrella Hat Preacher asked gently. "You don't need to cuss and swear."

Casey's mouth worked. "There's—animals. In clothes. Talking."

"You from Away, ain'tcha?"

"No. Yes. No. I drew a path and walked on it and—!"

"*Oh.*"

The man's tone stopped him short. He seemed surprised, but not shocked. He sounded as if what Casey had said was unusual, but not utterly impossible. He took a seat beside Casey on the corrugated metal bench. "You questing, sounds like."

"What?"

"You ain't came here for nothing, did you? You after something."

"My— Jaylon. My cousin. A wizard. Doctor—? Or maybe it wasn't him—? He said it couldn't get me here, but then I came anyway."

"Ain't the best time," Umbrella Hat Preacher said. "Storm coming. We used to had horses and mules, but they up and gone. The carriages and equipment was just lyin' in the street like they been raptured away. Then the traffic lights and street lights went, and the earth swallowed up City Hall. We in trouble. God wants me to speak on it today."

Casey opened his mouth and shut it. Usually when he heard religious talk, he tuned it out, but Dr. John had mentioned God, had said that sorcery was possible through the imitation of His voice. Casey's own mother often recounted conversations with the Creator, and while he had accepted her speaking to the dead as true without believing, exactly, in ghosts, Casey had more trouble with that—and he hadn't prayed, himself, in years.

"How do you know that?" he said.

"All we can do is ask Him and listen," said the preacher. "Sometimes you can't hear nothing. Sometimes you feel just the smallest urging in the right direction. Sometimes you think you know and you get it wrong anyhow. If you drew a path and walked on it, that's God."

Maybe it was. Maybe— Casey felt in his pants pockets. "I lost my pencil."

"I got one, I think." The preacher leaned over. He had one of those wheeled wire shopping carts sitting next to him. A battered guitar amp sat inside it, his blue-and-white megaphone nestled beside it on a cushion of plastic shopping bags. He retrieved a short golf pencil and handed it to Casey. As he did, their hands touched, and a thrill almost like static electricity passed between them. Both men rested in it for a moment, then drew their hands apart.

"God with you," Umbrella Hat Preacher said softly. "God is with you."

"Okay."

"Brung you this far."

"Thank you," Casey said. "Hey. What's your name?"

"Reverend Keith," he said. "What your name is?"

"Casey."

"Casey Trismegistus. You know what that means?"

He shook his head.

"Great and great and great again. Thrice-great. That's you."

"Oh," Casey said. "Thanks? Thank you."

The shadow of another flying streetcar passed over them, and this time Casey tried to take it in stride, even if it did seem like it was coming down too fast. He stood frozen in place as the shadow abruptly disappeared. He turned, looking back up toward the river. No cars were farther up the line, either. It was as if they'd all just...winked out of existence.

"They done it again," Reverend Keith said. Grief and desperation roughened his voice. "Those dirty murdering motherfuckers!"

"Who?" Casey asked. "What did they do?"

"They took the sky trolleys."

Casey felt cold all over. "Who could do that? *How*—?" But he knew. "The Storm."

Reverend Keith nodded, angry tears streaming down his face. "It's taking us apart piece by piece." With both hands, he swept the umbrella hat off his head, let it fall before his feet. He buried his fingers in his kinky hair and sobbed.

"How can I—?"

The Reverend's recovery was unsettlingly swift. "This ain't your fight. Find your cousin and get him out. *Now*. Walk in faith."

Before Casey could wonder what the preacher meant, the golf pencil throbbed in his grasp. "I will," he said. "I will."

He shut his eyes and drew.

At first Casey thought he had walked back into the real New Orleans—except what was this if not the real city? Instead of burying him under an avalanche of sensory information, the city sizzled quietly, realer-than-real. All the colors, the air itself, hummed and glowed with energy. Casey stood across the street from Favela Chic, with its low blue façade and yellow trim. He'd devoured an order of their meat and crawfish mini pies just last Thursday night.

If there were as many flying trolleys here as there were streetcars in New Orleans—at this time of day, that meant hundreds of people had disappeared. Tourists—were there tourists in the Hidden City? How could there be?—working people, transit drivers...He couldn't think about this right now. Terror was a shadow at the edge of his mind, and if he gave it any attention, it would overwhelm and cripple him.

This early in the day, Frenchmen Street was busier than it should have been. Someone was playing barrelhouse piano to a brisk beat, singing high in his throat like Champion Jack:

Dump 'em on the table, lemme get my fingers hot
Gimme all them mudbugs, gimme all you got
Ain't no ice in my sweet tea and I'm sweatin' through my shirt
But you know that ain't no nevermind, just gimme gimme gimme—!

Whoever it was couldn't have heard about the trolleys. When Casey turned to see where the music was coming from, he stopped short, stunned. Where Three Muses stood in his own city, a barked brown arm rose fifty feet into the sky. From here, Casey could see another arm pressed against it, and at the top, two palms held the club like a serving platter in a restaurant. When Casey collected himself enough to look at the sign above the wrought-iron gate where the bar's front door would have been, he knew there must be a third arm and hand he couldn't see. TREE MUSES, read the sign in angular faux-Greek lettering.

The music came from the bar up there, cascading like falls.

Casey smelled the boil, bright and spicy. If he hadn't already decided, it was a done deal now. Casey stepped under the sign and into a door set where this arm's elbow would begin. The elevator was one of the old kind with the accordion gate, but it seemed fashioned entirely from wood. The smell in here was exquisite— boozy, with a touch of tobacco with all the ugly notes filtered out. With a mix of guilt and nostalgia, Casey thought of the cigar shop over on Royal Street where the Israeli sisters with the big booties squabbled at each other all day.

The elevator stopped, and Casey stepped into the club. This morning's show was lightly attended, but with a storm on the way, that made sense. A couple flies leaned on the lacquered bar, sitting on wooden mushrooms. The pianist sat off to the left, rocking from one song to the next. That wasn't Champion Jack. It *couldn't* be. He'd died in Germany in the early nineties. But he did look like a boxer gone a little to seed. As Casey stared at the man, he started in on "Evil Woman."

Casey didn't know what to do next, but he knew he needed a drink—and maybe a meal. But would they take his—? He froze midway through his turn back toward the bar.

Another Casey stood there, his face a mask of comical surprise.

He had a farmer's tan, his head and arms darker than Casey's own. It seemed to be summer here, after all, so that made— No! *No!* It did *not* make sense!

He was a couple inches taller at least, more heavily built, a bit paunchy in the middle. His cheekbones were Casey's, though, and his hair was a bit rougher—like he should have refreshed his fade a few days ago. Instead of Casey's full beard, this other Casey was clean-shaven. Since he transitioned, Casey had worn a beard to make his manhood obvious, but this Casey passed just fine without it.

…Unless…

…Unless he wasn't passing.

With some effort Casey dragged his focus away from that line of thinking. Regardless of what this cat had going on, he was on a mission. Trismegistus.

The Doctor had said this place was populated by the living and the dead. Casey hadn't realized he meant that some folks here were still alive in— He kept thinking of it as the real world, and he knew that wasn't right. This city was *hidden*, not imaginary, and if Reverend Keith was alive and well in both places, then anyone might be—including Casey.

"So, uh," that other Casey said, his voice thick with confusion and shock, "my compass says your name is Trizz. Trismegistus."

"Casey," Casey said. "Trismegistus is the epithet. I think."

"Where did you come from? How…? *How?*"

"There's another city. It's like this one but not as…colorful, I guess?" Casey Trismegistus said. "No zombies, no talking animals. Streetcars instead of those…flying things." He paused, feeling sick as he thought about what he'd seen. "Do you have a cousin? Jaylon?"

Nola Casey shook his head. "No family here in town. Ain't been home in a while, either."

"Brothers? Sisters?"

Nola Casey shook his head. "Only child."

"Christ. Well. Uh. What's that like?"

Nola Casey shrugged. "It's okay, I guess. Didn't have to share my toys or nothing."

"What kind of money they got here?"

"What?"

Casey gritted his teeth, then pressed his tongue against the roof of his mouth, willing his jaw to relax. "I said, what kind of money do they have in this world? I need a drink."

PERAMBULATIN'

Deacon Graves Sr. knew something was up as soon as he heard the soft click of the door unlocking itself. He waited, certain that one of his captors would enter, but nothing happened. He sat on the edge of the bed, massaged his aching knees, careful not to look at the door. He'd tested it more than once—even spent time beating on it and screaming, to no response. This was a trick and a prank. Stackolee and the Haint of All Haints wanted to see what he would do if he thought he had a chance to escape.

How long you been here by now? he asked himself.

He had no answer. At first, he had thought to reckon his stay by the number of times he slept deeply and for an extended period. What he hadn't counted on when hatching his plan was that the boredom would introduce him to a third state that was neither sleep nor wakefulness but included elements of both. For what seemed like hours and hours, Deacon would lie in bed, staring at the low ceiling until it seemed to shift and flow like the surface of the Gulf. He would watch the whorls and eddies, trying to remember every song he knew. Sometimes he'd hum aloud, and sometimes his voice remained inside him, and just as it became difficult to know wake from slumber, it became difficult for him to divide sound from the memory of it.

My baby she got that velvet step . . . ?

Wait. Naw. That was one version, but wasn't there another that started differently?

Ha. Now he had it:

My baby got them twinkling toes
She dances like a dream!
You might think your girl can dance
But she can't out-step my Ernestine.

He smiled, tested his knees: Their aching had subsided a bit. Maybe a walk would do him good. Of course he wasn't really free, but a jaunt outside before they dragged him back might be just what the doctor ordered. At the very least, it would break the monotony of his predicament. Hell, maybe he'd even get a breath of fresh air.

He rose humming from his cot and sang as he tested the door.

Careful not to make a sound, Daddy Deke pulled the door open just far enough and slipped out into the darkness of the corridor. *We* perambulatin', *baby*, he thought. Thass *what we doin!*

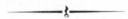

Peaches smelled salt, vanilla, and turned earth. Things seemed to move a little more quickly once Doctor Professor played her and the others out of the car yard—which was just fine with Peaches, because she'd had enough of standing round talking today. It occurred to her that she was about to fight Stagger Lee. The prospect did not frighten her—or it did, but that fright piqued her interest, made her *more* ready to scrap.

Last time, his breathing fire had caught her by surprise, and she'd gone down, burnt pretty good. This time, if he tried to belch up a cloud of flames, she'd knock them right the hell back down his throat.

Hold steady, now, y'all, Doctor Professor warned. *Better stay good and close.*

"Where we is now?" Brendy asked.

Nowhere in pattickler, baby.

Peaches supposed that Fess had not fibbed after all. She had spent enough time observing Grown Folks to know that they sometimes failed to tell the truth even when they weren't lying. Now, though, the old haint was spot on. They were nowhere in particular.

The Mess Around hung above a great and featureless void. Peaches couldn't tell whether the Nothing below them was bright or dark. It reminded her of the glowing blankness of a television screen sitting in an empty room just after it had been turned off.

Just before they'd left the yard, Peaches had heard what must have been First Chief dancing and drumming elsewhere in the city. She'd also heard a dark and oily tinkle of piano music followed by the truncated sound of a single step. In her mind's eye, she saw Stag bloom into being out of nowhere, setting his nasty square-toed shoe on the pavement in the middle of walking. The thought made her clench her fists, squeezing her fingernails into the softness of her palms.

She strained, but Peaches could hear neither song. Fess played a circular snatch of music, walking his fingers up and down across the keys, ascending and descending from chord to chord.

Now, listen here, y'all. I brung us this way 'cause we need some time to figger how we gone handle the present situation.

"Good idea," Perry said, and as he spoke, Peaches found herself paying too much attention to his lips and the way they shaped his words. She remembered the feeling of him against her in that other no-place, the things he'd said to her, and her cheeks heated pleasurably.

Now ain't the time, she told herself. *We got work.* "We ain't got time for this," she said aloud. "I heard Stag gun click. He probably done shot First Chief by now."

I can't do this forever, baby, but we got time, Fess said. *You can't tell because you live in it like fish live in water, but time in Nola ain't what you think. And it don't pass nearly as quick as it seem to.*

"What?" Peaches asked, and immediately wished she hadn't. She didn't want to know exactly what the haint meant. It wouldn't make Stagger Lee any easier to fight. It wouldn't put the songs in any less danger. She looked to Perry and flashed her eyes at him, silently asking him to jump in. Something about this place made her uneasy, and the sound of Perry's voice always helped steady her.

"Doctor Professor, can you hang us in the sky as easy as you're levitating us right now?" His speech was so precise. All his *R*s and *G*s had hospital corners.

Sure can.

"Good," Perry said. "Then I think you should bring us in about twenty-five feet above Stagger Lee. Peaches can drop straight down on him, and then you lower us down to the street. I'll use my Clackin' Sack on First Chief, and then I'll use it on Stagger Lee."

"Do we want him in the bag with the songs we already caught?" Brendy asked. "What if he gets around easier in there than we did?"

"Damn," Perry said. "You're right. I'll use it on First Chief, but Peaches, do you think you can hold Stagger Lee?"

"I can hold him," she said. "I'ma whup his whole ass."

"Okay," Perry said. "If things go wrong, though, I'll use the sack on him, too. Even if he gets around easily in there, there's more songs to endanger outside the sack than in."

Not as many as there used to be, baby, and if we don't act fast, it won't matter none. The city changing faster now. I just felt the trolleys go.

"What?" Peaches said. "Oh no...!" Now Peaches's attention began to wander. Something dark hovered at the edge of her mind, beginning to press in. At first she thought it must be her fear of Stagger Lee, and she knew she could master it easily. Her father had taught her never to let fear control her, stop her from acting in the right. No, this was—Peaches smelled the ocean. And the sound here—a tuneless hum rose up from the Nothing. She could hear it past Doctor Professor's playing. Could her friends?

This was what the darkness must have sounded like in the infinite moment before God spoke the world. The thought made the hair stand up along Peaches's arms. She focused her attention on the hum, trying to listen past it, imagining—or not?—that she heard waves somewhere far below. And was that the rolling of thunder?

The question led her in a direction she didn't like. She remembered the sensation of sodden wooden planking beneath her bare feet and the sight of the vast and terrible ocean reaching out like an angry mama intent on a good smack—

"What?" Peaches said with a shake of her head.

"I said I don't *like* it here," Brendy said.

Peaches knew she must be telling the truth. Her heartbeat sounded loud and jagged—and it wasn't just her. Both Brendy and Perry had begun to sweat. Peaches didn't like their discomfort, but sensing it relieved her just a bit—she was glad she wasn't the only one who hated this Nowhere.

Don't surprise me much, Fess said. *Ain't no mortal been here before. We better get the hell on.*

His playing changed. Instead of the slow walk-up and -down, he thundered into a song Peaches had never heard before.

Listen to me, baby, and listen good!
Get to dancin' honey and hit that flo'
Cuz I ain't gonna suffer no mo' . . . *!*

"You good, baby?" Lyle the bartender asked as he finished cleaning a glass. He was a big, round, light-skinned man with short hair parted in the middle and polished nails.

"I don't know," Nola Casey said. "Yeah. Yes."

"Your friend good?" He nodded toward a sign hanging by the special board. It read, MUSIC ONLY IN HERE.

"I think—Yeah," Casey said. "Why?"

"Cuz whenever there's more than two magicians in a room, shit finna jump off," the bartender said. "You, him, and Jack make three."

"Oh," Casey said. "*Oh.* No. I'm not—" He stopped short. He couldn't be sure his denial would be truthful. Having a compass that spoke in his head and could take him from place to place didn't seem as serious as what musicians did, but he supposed it was more than nothing. "...Can I get a couple sidecars please? Single tall."

"Okay, but I'm serious. Y'all do your business and get on out. You ain't the one worry me, though. That other Negro packin' *heat.*"

Just before he'd left the table to buy drinks, Casey had noticed a faint buzz coming from Trizz. That must be why. He wondered whether he was handling this all wrong. What if Trismegistus wasn't a friend?

Casey put his money down and accepted the drinks without waiting for change. He carried them over to the petrified wood booth where Trizz sat waiting. Casey wasn't sure, but the other man's shoulders seemed a little narrower than his own. It was hard to tell as he sat down, but Casey thought Trizz might be a little shorter, too—but the bartender hadn't lied. It wasn't just the buzz: The air around Trizz was alive with invisible energy. Maybe it was the fact that he belonged to another world. Maybe his being here caused a disturbance of some kind.

He looked like he made money. His clothes were more expensive than Casey's—his diagonal blue-and-yellow striped polo shirt was a genuine Ralph Lauren. His skin and hair were better, too, as if he got styled more often and used product Casey couldn't afford.

"So, uh," Casey began. "If we're the same guy, why are we so different?"

"Your guess is as good as mine."

"And I mean, you're—you're from Away?" Even as he said it, he knew it wasn't right. He himself was a transplant, but this other version of him was from *worlds* away.

"I'm from New Orleans," Trizz said. "I mean, I came here from there...this morning?"

"Listen. I don't know how to— Who brought you here? Was it Roux?"

"I came on my own," Trizz said. "I drew the path."

"So you're magic. *Real* magic," Casey said. "I don't—I don't even know what to ask. My compass told me to come here, but it didn't say why or...or what I'm supposed to do. There's—there's a storm coming. It's trying to kill the city, and I'm supposed to... I'm supposed to help. Use the compass to help."

"I saw," Trizz said darkly. "Before I came here, it made all those flying streetcars disappear."

Casey's scalp tightened. "What? The skycars are *gone*?"

Trizz nodded, staring at his hands. "Maybe fifteen minutes ago," he said. "I think Reverend Keith said something about all the horses and carriages disappearing, and City Hall, too." He sipped his drink. Casey noticed that his elbow trembled. His cool was manufactured.

Seeing that comforted Casey a little. Trizz might be vastly powerful, but he was still human.

"The Reverend says this isn't my fight," Trizz said. "The thing is...my cousin and I might be responsible. Jaylon created an opening when he came here from our world, and I think the Storm came with him."

"The storm in the Gulf?" Casey asked.

"No," Trizz said. "Yes. But not like *a* hurricane. Like *all of them*."

A calm crystalline terror settled like a cape around Casey's shoulders. The other man explained what he knew of his cousin's death. Casey tried to listen, but what his doppelganger said about the Storm stole his focus. What he gathered from half-following the explanation sounded crazy, but what did *Casey* know? He'd seen a fire-breathing gangster song jumping into Bayou Saint John.

One detail stuck in his mind. "Wait. Your cousin's a tagger? He makes graffiti?"

"Yeah," Trizz said. "Why?"

"Well, I dunno," Casey said. "There's always been graffiti all over, but I think there's more lately? Stronger?"

"What do you mean?"

"I mean, they used to clear it out quicker, or there's more of it. It's not usually all over town all the time. But it seems like it gets blown everywhere now."

"What? *What* gets blown?"

Casey was a little frustrated. "The tags," he said. "The graffiti. Come look."

He slid out of the booth and crossed to a broad window overlooking the intersection of Frenchmen and Chartres. One lone tag rippled in a breeze as it hung by the river side of the street. As they watched, someone in a powder-blue VW Beetle carefully guided their car past it before heading on in the direction of the lake.

"Goddamn," Trismegistus said. His voice was full of wonder. "Goddamn. That nigga *did* that shit!"

"You think your cousin the one painting them?"

Trizz didn't answer at first. He kept staring out the window at the tag. From here, it looked as if it read JAY and then some numbers. As Casey watched him, tears brimmed in Trismegistus's eyes and began rolling down his cheeks. He didn't seem to notice.

"He's here," Trizz said. "Somewhere."

"Listen," Casey said.

Trizz cut him off. "I shouldn't have quit."

"What?"

"I shouldn't have quit drawing. I shouldn't have...I shouldn't have left him to do it alone."

"Who? Your cousin?"

"He didn't stop because he couldn't," Trizz said. "It called to him like it called to me, and he couldn't block it out."

"Are you talking about art or are you talking about magic?"

Trizz seemed to recover himself, but he still didn't wipe at his tears. "I quit drawing and painting when my art started acting funny. Jaylon's art got weird, too. We promised we'd stop, but he didn't. If—if—if I'd kept working, if I hadn't shut down, maybe I couldn't have protected him, but I could have— It was *wrong*. I stopped painting because I thought what was happening wasn't natural. But not everything that's natural is right."

He fell silent, still weeping. Casey wanted to take Trizz in his arms, to comfort him; but what would happen if they touched? There was something hard about this other version of himself, and at first Casey had taken it for a stony resolve. It wasn't, though. It was guilt. Guilt and grief.

"My mother said there's nothing wrong with me," Trizz said.

"She's right," Casey offered. "Just look at you." He paused. "Help us. Please. Come with me and help us fight the Storm."

"If there's nothing wrong with me, then there's nothing wrong with you, either."

Casey's head rocked back. "You don't know me," he said. "I've—I'm not like you. I got— Things aren't easy."

"Look, I know," Trizz said. "That's what I thought when I heard it, too. But that's not what she meant. She didn't mean that things are easy for me or that my mind always does what I want or that I don't have problems. What she means is that my problems aren't *me*. They're not the same as me."

"Okay, then," Casey said. "But that's *you*. *I* can't just pick up and go to another world. We *need*—!"

"I didn't just pick up and go," Trizz said. "But I gotta find Jaylon. It's why I came here."

"You got real power, though," Casey said. "You can help."

"I can," he said. "I am. I'm *you*."

"Please!" Casey said. Now he did reach for the other man, but Trismegistus disappeared with a *BAMF* as the air closed in the space he left behind.

First Chief cut a slow turn on the sidewalk outside the Pancake House. He glanced sidelong to his left to make sure Pretty Little

Thing had not been swallowed by the crowd of onlookers gathered to watch him. The woman had agreed to walk with him to the Seventh Ward in search of his Peoples, but first he found it necessary to settle his troubled mind with ritual. None of the Lessers seemed to mind. A few of them even hooted and hollered as he turned and shuffled to his own beat.

He stretched out his massive feathered arms and turned the small feathers on his back and his loin drape to make colored animations of Negroes riding horses, loosing arrows to bring down buffalo, or emerging from their tepees to greet the smiling sun. Those images served to comfort him as they moved to the rhythm of the music that poured from his back. He threw his head back and began to sing:

Heyyyyyyyyy, getcha grass skirt on
And paint up ya face

The crowd chanted back. "Ride on down that Zulu line!"

His broad chest swelled at the response. Maybe things weren't so bad after all. If these Lessers knew the chants, then his Peoples must not be so far away as he had feared.

"I wear my feathers they mighty fine!"

"When I ride on down that Zulu line!"

First Chief cut another turn, and this time he didn't think to look for Pretty Little Thing. He lifted his left foot and bent his elbows, swaying to the rhythm. The crowd before him beamed as if to reflect the sunlight. They looked like sunflowers growing in the field. They looked like magnolia trees dancing liquid in the wind. They—

A hard, dark face appeared above the heads of the people closest to him. With one swift and overwhelming motion, he swept the people standing before him to one side and raised a gun.

Albert stared into the darkness of the barrel aimed right between his eyes. Here was danger. *This* was the fight. He crooked his fingers into claws, ready to rend and tear.

SORRY, NEGRO, said the gunman. THIS AIN'T NO MARDI GRAS.

Hard, fast piano music split the air. First Chief did not hear it fade up from nothing. It just began right in the middle of a chord and started rocking away. Something heavy and fast dropped from above, like a dive-bombing bird, and slammed straight into the gunman.

"First Chief!" someone called, and Albert turned to see who had spoken. He saw the piano now, sitting in the middle of Canal Street, and a boy standing beside it, holding a potato sack.

"Clickety-clack, get into my sack!"

Albert roared his displeasure, but there was something lacking in his voice. He realized too late what it was. He wished he felt otherwise, but part of him knew the truth: This world was all wrong and First Chief was only too glad to leave it.

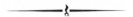

Daddy Deke shut the cell room door softly behind him, pulling it to slowly...slowly...slow. The latch clicked softly, and he sighed, relieved. He tested the door again just to see if it would open for him—after all, what if it was somehow worse out here than it was inside? He wasn't no Institutionalized Negro, but he at least understood the possibility of dangerous-ass bullcrap running round in the Haint of All Haints's Evil Lair.

Evil Lair. Daddy Deke grunted his contempt. More like Triflin'-Ass-Knucklehead Lair.

He depressed the door's handle as slowly as he'd released it, but he couldn't control the final click. He winced as it slapped the air loud as a gunshot. So the door was completely unlocked now, and Daddy Deke could open or close it as he saw fit. Now to find out what was what. He turned to the corridor and saw only darkness.

Damn and a half. The darkness was so profound, so complete, that it was more like blindness than like an absence of light. Well, Daddy Deke supposed it was a plus. At least there were no clues lying around, trying to lead him one way or another. His captors must be manipulating him, but at least they'd given him room to breathe, an illusion of autonomy.

Daddy Deke took a step and his shoes echoed against the floor. He waited. No response. No movement, no sound of Stagger Lee. He took another, waited again. When no response came, his courage grew, and he started walking—not quickly, but without such painstaking slowness. He held his arms out before him, let them quest through nothing, hoping his eyes would soon adjust.

What if he got lost?

Negro, be real, he thought scornfully. *How could you be any more lost than you already is?*

He walked for a long time, navigating mostly by scent. Climbing up a couple stairwells had taken him from what must have been a basement area that smelled of mold and soggy concrete into what might be an abandoned office building smelling of dust, old paper, and, faintly, of oil soap.

By now, he'd been walking long enough to grow hungry. If he didn't find his way out of here, he might just starve. He doubted Stagger Lee and the Haint would let that happen, but what if they wasn't in charge no more? It seemed only reasonable for Deke to consider the prospect that maybe he really had, with the aid of some unknown benefactor, escaped.

It was a possibility, but that was all it was. Deacon Graves Sr. knew better than to embrace the idea. After all, he didn't think he'd left the original building in which he'd started—not unless one of the doorways he'd encountered had magicked him elsewhere—and he hadn't heard a snatch of music but his own since stepping out of his cell.

Slowly, Deacon realized that the darkness had abated some. His eyes adapted just enough to show him a dark-and-light checkered floor and the outlines of doorways to his right and left. He couldn't tell where the light was coming from until he turned down a curve in the hallway and saw a door spilling candlelight into the air. Without stopping to consider, Deacon went straight for the door and let himself into what looked like the most disorganized library he'd ever seen.

It reminded him of the years he'd spent working as a security guard at the Stone Pigman law office downtown—only, the law office took great pains to keep things swank. Here, piles and piles of books stood up from the dusty green carpet. Other books, open and closed, lay atop full shelves, as if whoever was reading them had set them down midsentence to search for something else. Deacon wasn't sure why, but his surroundings gave him the sense of a ransacked house, only in this case, the thief wasn't after money or valuables, he was after words. No. Not words, Deacon corrected himself—*knowledge*.

"That one in front of you there," said a genteel voice. "Is that Armstrong or Bechet?"

He froze. The sound of a normal human voice other than his own was alien after so many days. Unable to think what else to do, Daddy Deke grabbed the book that lay open before him and checked the cover for the title. "This one here's called *Jelly's Blues: The Life, Music, and Redemption of Jelly Roll Morton.*"

"Where is that damned Bechet?"

Negro, run, he thought. *Beat feet! Skedaddle! Get outta town!* But what good would running do?

"I help you look for it if ya let me use your telephone."

Now the owner of the voice stepped into view. He was a white man wearing a rumpled powder-blue suit with sweat stains at the armpits. His salt-and-pepper hair needed combing, and his left eye lay shut. Something about its lid made Deacon think its owner was unable to open it. "Larry Hearn. What's this about a telephone?"

"Deacon Graves—the First," Daddy Deke said. He heard himself speaking as if from another room. His skin tingled. "I need to get ahold of my family, let 'em know I'm alive and kickin'."

"I'm sure we can figure something out."

A silence yawned between them. At first it seemed companionable, but soon Deacon began to sense ice beneath it. He hadn't felt an eerie silence like this since the Great War.

He cleared his throat. "You do that for me, you let me just—just talk to them—and I'll tell you whatever you want to know."

"*Heh.* Why, Mr. Graves, I do believe you've mistaken me for someone else."

"No I ain't," Daddy Deke said flatly. "Whatever game you playin', I'll play along, but I ain't stupid, and I ain't gone play stupid."

"Were I you, given the choice, I'd opt to speak with my dead wives over my living relatives."

"She ain't my wife no more," Daddy Deke said. "We vowed 'till death do us part.' Well, death done parted us a while ago now."

"So the moment she died, your love perished with her?"

"If we gonna be conversatin' like this, I want you to tell me straight: When you say things like what you just said, are you just running your mouth, or are you actively tryna test my nerves?"

"All right," Hearn said. "Why have you come to the city?"

"I don't—I told you. I'm born and raised."

"Born and raised in New Orleans," Hearn said. "But you crossed into Nola after your death. To deliver a message? A talisman? Give me the horn. Do that, and I will spare your life and the lives of your family."

Silence again. Deacon's mind raced. He didn't remember any horn, but something tickled at the edge of his mind, and he let the tickle fade. He'd done so many many times before, but it wasn't as easy now.

"I don't remember no horn," Deacon said. "Honest. But sometimes I dream about another place. Another life."

The ghost took a breath, and even in spite of the turn in their conversation, Daddy Deke wondered if he was right after all. Could this man, who seemed to live and breathe, actually be the Haint of All Haints? He seemed genuinely abashed by his own behavior.

"I spend most of my time alone," he said. "Death separated me from my own wife many, many years ago, and I often wonder whether she still loves me, or..."

"...Or if she stopped loving you when you died."

"Yes. Exactly."

"I never did stop lovin' my Nettie," Deacon said. "I just don't think it's worth reachin' into the afterlife to bother her. If she wanted to contact me, and if she could, she woulda by now, ya heard me?"

Now what light there was seemed to drain from the dim air of the room. Blackness flooded close, surrounded Deacon—but it wasn't the same absence of light he'd experienced as he explored the corridors beyond his cell. This darkness was a presence, not an absence, and instead of a quiet nothingness, it was horribly alive.

Mr. Larry's manner didn't change, but a ragged edge crept into his voice. "What if she couldn't?" he said. "What if she tried and tried, to no avail? What if, even now, *centuries* later, she longs to speak to you, hold you again—but to do so, she would have to do something... *drastic*?"

Daddy Deke's heart skittered wild in his narrow chest, but he tried to keep his cool. "Well, shit," he said. "Then I guess I'd rather she didn't."

Mr. Larry's face irised open. His teeth yellowed and sharpened, and red-orange tentacles unfurled from the flower his head had become. Laughter and an overlapping susurrus of whispers filled the room. Far away, Deacon heard rolling, sizzling thunder and the hiss and pop of hard rain.

unfortunately for us all deacon the first it is not her choice to make whispered the haint. it is mine and mine alone   i say unfortunately because i suspect that an eternity trapped in this perpetually crumbling toilet of a city has driven me quite mad

The orange tendrils danced together for a moment like tube worms on an underwater reef. Then they stiffened, arcing straight toward Deacon's open screaming mouth.

XXIV

Awful Is Me

Peaches wasn't sure whether the world returned to stretch beneath her feet or she and her friends returned to it. What she did know as she looked down was that she was angrier than she'd ever been. Their brief trip into nowhere and nothing had reminded her how badly she missed her daddy and of the no-good thievin'-ass haint who had stolen his most recent letter. From here, she could see Stagger Lee and First Chief both. The bird-man had frozen midstep, elbows crooked, fingers spread, goggling at the muzzle of Stagger Lee's gun.

Peaches Lavelle did not wonder whether she'd be fast enough, strong enough, or bad enough. All she knew was that the swell of emotion in the pit of her belly was rapidly rising up her throat, and she felt ready to breathe her own unforgiving fire. It was a lucky thing that Stagger Lee was up to no good: Peaches needed a focus for her rage, and he would do just fine.

"*Now!*" Perry shouted, and Peaches dived.

For a shining instant, she was weightless and perfect. She moved so fast that she left all her fear, and even her anger, behind. This was how she felt when she dived into Big Lake. With a slight doubling of her thoughts, she imagined herself from afar—an arrow-shaped fish, fired by the Ocean God, straight at the Enemy of Everything.

She hit him so hard that her consciousness skipped. She understood the force of the impact, understood that she was unhurt, but she knew nothing else for a beat. When her vision returned, Stagger Lee was on his back, and she knelt on his barrel chest, with one fist pressed against his throat. The flesh there was as hard and cool as marble, and Peaches wondered for an instant just how strong Stagger Lee really was.

He glared up at Peaches, and the force of his hatred felt like needles on her skin.

It's the gun, she thought. *All his power in it. He ain't nothing but a bully.* "And I chews up bullies and spits 'em out!" she growled.

Peaches smacked the gun out of Stagger Lee's hand, and neither of them looked to see where it went. In fact, Stag seemed to care so little for the loss of his weapon that Peaches had to wonder. Maybe he really *was* bad as bad could be.

Bad or not, nobody liked being punched in the nose. Peaches brought the heel of her hand down on the broad bridge of Stagger Lee's nose, but the bone held firm beneath the blow.

When they'd fallen together, Stag got his right arm between them. Now he used it to lever Peaches off, send her flying. She stumbled past First Chief, fighting to recover her balance, but she didn't stop until her shoulder met the side of a white van parked alongside the Pancake House. The force of her fall stove the van's side in, and she elbowed it out of her way, sent it rolling onto the sidewalk, then turned to face Stagger Lee.

Behind him, Peaches saw First Chief, Brendy, Perry, and Fess moving in slow motion. Perry was opening his bag, making ready to say his Words, glaring at First Chief as if First Chief were the enemy. Brendy was craning her neck, trying to see where Peaches had gone, her magic rock clutched in her little right fist. Fess sat at the Mess Around, his hands moving calmly across the keys. The sound of his music poured like molasses from the baby grand, and its rocking imperative must have cleared the innocent bystanders from the scene.

Ya done done it now, Stagger Lee boomed. I'ma kill ya twice, and I don't need no .45 to do it.

Peaches made a rude noise. "You welcome to try, dummy. You *know* you don't scare me none."

Thass cuz y'ain't too bright.

Peaches rushed him, but Stag was too quick. He crow-hopped toward her and slapped Peaches, harder than hard, across her face. The blow spun her facedown into the street—hard enough to crack the pavement. Hard enough to hurt!

Peaches had never felt a blow hard enough to cause her pain. Until now, she hadn't realized such a strike existed in the world. After all, her daddy was the only one who could hit so hard, and he never would.

The blow scared her, but it thrilled her, too—made her blood roar in her ears.

Perry's voice finally made it out of his throat—but it wasn't his normal speech. It was the hollow boom of his Magic Words. "STAGGER LEE! *WEDE ĀSIMATENYA JONIYAYĒ BEFIT'INETI!*" he roared, and the sound of it made Peaches shudder—as it had every time she heard it. These were not the words Ms. Yvette had given him when she'd told him how to use the sack. She'd said "clickety-clack" something, and Perry had repeated the nonsense phrase. But down in the no-place, when he'd used the sack to return them to the world, that magical African-sounding Hoodoo Speak, that undeniable command, was what he'd spoken into the air—except he'd said it *backwards*.

Peaches turned to watch her enemy disappear, but he stood with his feet planted and his shoulders squared. His image trembled, flickered a bit, but remained whole. He grunted with the effort of staying put, but whatever was keeping them out of sync with the rest of the world was allowing him to defy Perry's witchery.

Now Peaches knew. She knew she'd have to hit Stagger Lee for real.

Before they parted, Peaches's daddy had warned her. She saw

him now in her mind's eye, his stinky pipe clenched between his golden teeth as he stood at the schooner's wheel, staring straight ahead across the vast and deathless ocean.

"You gettin' ta be pretty strong," he said in his gravelly whisper of a voice. "One day you be strong as me. But remember: You can't just go hittin' things and people, baby. Most of 'em, they can't take it. Most times, play-fighting and slappin' get the job done."

"But not every time?" she'd asked.

"Not every time. Sometimes, you gotta hit somebody so he stay hit. You gotta hit 'im for real."

"How I know when, Daddy?"

"You'll know, babygirl. You'll know."

Peaches laughed softly to herself. "Jus you and me, baby," she said. "You ready?"

Stagger Lee smiled, and briefly, the nastiness disappeared from his expression. In that instant, he was startlingly attractive, and he was just as excited for this as Peaches was. BRING IT, LIL GIRL.

Peaches rushed, drew back her fist like a stone in a slingshot. Now she was John Henry, and her fist was her hammer. She drove that steel right past Stagger Lee's guard and into his jaw.

As she threw her punch, Peaches heard a groan—a tortured sound almost like metal bending. When the blow connected, it sounded like a car wreck.

Stagger Lee stumbled hard, almost losing his footing. The expression on his face was one of suppressed shock. At the last split second, he recovered his balance and returned the punch, slamming his fist into Peaches's ribs on her right side.

Peaches had felt pain before—rarely, but she'd felt it. It had hurt when Stagger Lee burned her with his fire, but Peaches had never felt pain inside her body. The punch hurt all through her, and for the first time, Peaches felt her organs—her heart, her lungs, her kidneys, and they didn't like what was happening *at all*. They wanted her to turn and run.

The thought made Peaches see red, and when Stagger Lee swung again, she blocked with her left forearm and stepped back for an uppercut, giving the punch everything she had. Her knuckles connected with the underside of Stagger Lee's jaw, and this time, the air didn't just groan, it shattered, and the Mid-City street disappeared.

———————※———————

Trismegistus stepped onto the street. From here, he could see the tag close-on. It read JAYL313 in bubbly, stylized letters. A bit generic for Jayl, but it was undeniably one of his. After all, who else could draw 3D on nothing at all?

The tag's color shifted slowly within its fat black outline. First it was off-white, then blue, bluer, then, abruptly green. And there were more like this, Other Casey had said. The city was full of them.

He said there'd always been graffiti like this, here. But Dr. John had said... Casey felt a dizzy feeling in the pit of his stomach. He had read once that time was a fiction. That it existed, but that it was imaginary—like a story in a book. That seemed even more true, here. It wasn't that time didn't pass at all, it was that it had a different character than it did in Casey's world. The continuity didn't feel the same. Like Rev Keith and Casey had told him, something bad was about to happen here, was already happening, but Casey sensed that if he'd come here sooner—say, last month? Or even the year before—it would have been *now*, here in the city. That if he came next year, it would *still* be now—or maybe not. Maybe by then there'd be no *here* to come to.

Casey shook the thought away. What did this mean? Jayl was here somewhere, making these tags, but maybe he'd always been here. Maybe he'd been brought here at the moment of the Hidden City's birth, and he'd been here for... Casey asked himself for how long, and he didn't like the answer his mind whispered back: *Forever.*

If Jaylon had already been here, tagging the air, forever, what could be left of him by now?

He wouldn't panic. He would. Not. He couldn't spare the time. On a whim, he reached for the tag, touched it. A mad, fizzing feeling raced from the tip of his right pointer finger to his shoulder. He stared down at the brown flesh of his forearm and watched iridescent scales rise on his skin, only to disappear again, almost at once. This wasn't just the product of some unbelievable painting technique; this was reality-altering magic at least as powerful as Casey's own.

After a moment, the electric sensation faded to pins and needles, and Casey's skin seemed to behave normally again. Flooding the city with tags would require an enormous amount of magical power, even if it cost nothing to maintain them—and this one did look a little worse for wear, its surface blistered in places, and if Casey turned his head a bit, instead of looking 3D, it looked less convincing, like some sort of optical illusion.

Jayl's magic *had* to be related to Casey's own. So, maybe if Casey focused, he could *feel* the tags being made, identify their origin. He took a seat on the curb, resting his arms on his knees, and shut his eyes. The heat. The heat of the day. A cascade of sewing pins falling to a carpeted floor. His grandmother's hands, the soft wrinkles of her skin. Back. His plastic car seat when he was little little. The dim, slightly dingy laundry alcove in his parents house. His mother used to sit his car seat on the dryer while it ran to make Casey go to—

Wait. There was something. A sound so soft, so quiet, it could barely be called a noise. It was like a single sustained musical note played on a ghostly synthesizer. Casey listened to it just to listen, letting his hearing (though he knew this had little relationship to his auditory sense) guide him along it. As if gliding over water in a canoe, hanging a finger over the side to skim, just a little, across the surface... The sound broke for a moment, resumed.

Casey opened his eyes. That was it. That was a tag being born somewhere in the city. Somewhere...somewhere off Elysian Fields? Gentilly, maybe. Probably. *Certainly.* And if he could narrow it down this far...

A breeze swept by the tag, sent it bobbing down Frenchmen Street. Silently, Casey wished it well on its travels and took off walking.

Perry lay enveloped by a darkness so profound that it seemed tangible. He imagined that if he could move his fingers, he could rub the darkness between them and feel its oily slickness. It seemed proper, somehow, this dark. It seemed safe—neither warm nor cold. For an instant, he was back in Da Cut, watching Stagger Lee's bullet sail toward him. He turned his head away, trembling.

But Peaches wouldn't turn away. Peaches was strong, unafraid. Peaches would—

Perry sat bolt upright and took a whooping pull of city air. "Who touchin' me!"

Perry scrabbled to turn himself around. A dark-skinned grown-up with a broad pulpy nose and hair clipped close to his scalp knelt on the asphalt beside him. His right hand was still outstretched, and in his left, he held something small and shiny. Something that blurred Perry's vision when he tried to focus on it.

"You Perilous?" the man asked.

"Who wants to know?" Perry asked.

"I'm Casey," said the man. "I'm here to help. Where's Fess?"

"Where's—?" Perry stopped short. "I don't know." Where *was* Doctor Professor?

"Ain't seen him since last night," Casey said. "I need you to come with me. The Wise Women can tell us what to do next. You got others with you. A sister? Where she at?"

Instead of asking another question, Perry kicked to his feet and scanned his surroundings. The crowd of onlookers were all gone, and Brendy was picking herself up from the sidewalk outside the Pancake House. "Awwwwwwww," she groaned. "What happened? Was it fireworks?"

"A bomb?" Casey asked. "A bomb went off?"

"It wasn't a bomb," Perry said distractedly. He was relieved to see that Brendy was unhurt, but the last thing he remembered was seeing Stagger Lee and Peaches fighting, moving so fast that Perry couldn't quite track their movements. The noise and the force of their blows had buckled the street beneath them, and then—and then they'd disappeared...

"Listen, Mr. Casey," Perry said hastily. "Thanks for your concern, but we gotta go. Our friend—"

"What happened? What are y'all doing?"

Perry didn't stop to consider. He explained in broad strokes.

"Is First Chief still alive?"

"He's safe," Perry said. "He's in my sack. I grabbed him as soon as the fight started. Problem is, my friend and Stagger Lee, they're fighting, and she needs our help."

"What sack?" Casey asked. "What are you—?"

"We gotta get Doctor Professor," Brendy said. "He'll know what to do."

"Fess took off like a scared pigeon," Perry said. "Now, either you call up your haint and have him take us wherever they've gone or I'll trade you for my sack and I'll do it myself, ya heard?"

"I'm scared," Brendy said simply.

"I know," Perry said. "But I'll tell you a secret: There's no such thing as grown-ups, Brendy. They're just old kids, pretending."

A shocked expression appeared on Brendy's face. Perry considered darkly that this must be the same face he'd made when Peaches first told him. "What that means?"

"I'm not a kid," Casey said before Perry could answer. "I'm not pretending."

Instead of looking directly at his sister, Perry watched Casey's face. The two regarded each other as Perry spoke. "It means we're enough. It means we can *do* this."

Something in Mr. Casey's expression changed. A new light seemed to dawn in his eyes. "Okay," he said.

"Okay what?" Brendy asked. "Who you is anyway, Mistuh Man?"

"I have something that will take us to your friend—"

"Well, bust it out," Perry said.

After a beat, Mr. Casey withdrew a brassy locket from the

pocket of his jeans. He took a breath, then, "Compass, can you take us to Peaches?"

Yes, said a disembodied voice. Perry realized after a beat that it was the locket who had spoken. The compass. *Gather.*

"All right," Mr. Casey said. "Get close."

Perry kept watching Mr. Casey's face, and he thought he understood the look the man was giving him. It was one of respect.

A hissing, fizzing noise filled the air. Perry, Brendy, and their new friend disappeared.

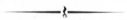

"Where we is now?" Brendy asked.

She, Casey, and Perry had winked back into the world, and Perry found himself up to his calves in mud. He pulled at his legs, trying to turn around and get a look at their surroundings.

"Look," Mr. Casey said. "In the sky."

Perry stopped his struggling to look up into the sunlight. Shadows flitted there, backlit, and Perry recognized a paper condor pursued by a paper dragon with a long, segmented tail. "Kites," he said. "This must be City Park."

"City Park ain't got no mudhole," Brendy said.

"This isn't a mudhole," Perry said, thinking aloud. "This is Big Lake."

A bloodcurdling whoop split the air, and as Perry watched, the middle of the dragon's tail caught fire. It took Perry a few seconds to realize what he was seeing. Someone had loosed a series of flaming arrows at the dragon, and they sliced through him, blackening his body and saving the paper condor from its vinyl claws.

"You got it, Tammara?" called a woman's voice. It was almost musical.

"Wow," Casey said softly.

"Wait," Brendy said. "If this Big Lake, what happened to the water?"

"That must be it right there," Mr. Casey said.

Perry saw what he meant. At first it looked like a flying saucer made of clear and spinning glass, gleaming in the sunlight. But it wasn't. Something had spun all the lake water into the air as a single mass, and here it came, hurtling right back at them at amazing speed. It cast a shimmering shadow on the lakebed around them.

As soon as he recognized it for what it was, Perry understood how stuck they were. If all that lake water came down on them, it wouldn't hit them like rain—it would crush them like concrete, and they'd die before they had a chance to drown.

Perry pulled his sack from his jeans pocket. The more he used it, the more natural it felt to do so. Was he getting stronger, or was it? "Brendy Graves! Mr. Casey!" he shouted. "Click—!"

There! said the Trouble Compass.

The fizzing sound began again, and by now the lake water was so close that Perry could see nothing else. Toy fish, seaweed, Mardi Gras ducks, and even a couple moldering bodies were still submerged inside it. Had some killer dumped corpses into—? No. One of the bodies turned its head, and its wide, staring eyes locked with Perry's.

Of course. What better place for a zombie to get a little rest than the bottom of Big Lake? Perry hoped the undead survived the fall. Then again, would Perry and his companions?

Perry shut his eyes tight as he and the others fizzed away again.

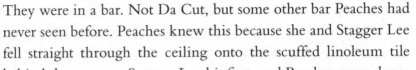

They were in a bar. Not Da Cut, but some other bar Peaches had never seen before. Peaches knew this because she and Stagger Lee fell straight through the ceiling onto the scuffed linoleum tile behind the counter. Stagger Lee hit first, and Peaches came down on top of him.

Someone had left the jukebox on, and a rocking saxophone solo filled the room.

You learned all them dances, the shimmy and the shake
Ain't no use unless you got you a honey to take!

The scents of stale tobacco smoke, beer, and oil soap hung musty in the air. Before her enemy could register what was happening, Peaches grabbed the back of his suit jacket and the seat of his pants and lifted him from the floor like a bag of sand. She heaved him onto the bar top and launched him toward the stacked glasses at the bar's far end. Stagger Lee crashed through them, and his head went right through the wall. He groaned as if in pain.

Peaches looked down at her dirty feet and saw Stagger Lee's purple hat lying between them, daisy-fresh. It hadn't been rumpled in the fight. Peaches grabbed it and stepped around the bar.

She tried not to wonder where they were. Christmas lights, signs, and promotional lamps for beer and booze Peaches had never heard of festooned the barroom walls. What was a Yuengling?

Everything except the bar looked fashioned from plywood, and most of the furniture had been stacked, secured by chains. What few windows there were were closed tight, maybe even nailed shut from outside. Photographs of happy drunks stood out on the walls. In most all of them, white folks and Black folks held their drinks aloft, as if in offering to some soggy spirit.

She remembered Perry showing her one of his schoolbooks—Peaches didn't much like anything had to with school, but her daddy had made it clear before they got separated that reading and books were important. Perry had shown her an explanation of the world that said their planet was always turning and turning through space, that they and everything on it were traveling all the time forever. Peaches wondered now if the titanic force of her fighting with Stagger Lee had unstuck them from the world, made them stay still as the planet turned beneath them. If that was the case, they could be anywhere.

Get ready ready ready
Get ready ready ready
Get ready ready ready
For the Downtown Blue Jeans Ball!

Peaches breathed hard, not because she was winded or afraid, but because Perry had once told her she sounded like a *T. rex* when she did. She could be a *T. rex*. She could be anything he or the city of Nola needed. Her bare hands were dinosaur jaws, and they would crush her enemy with reptilian might.

Stagger Lee pulled his head from the ruined wall and turned to face her. One of his eyes had swollen shut—Peaches wasn't sure she remembered punching him in the eye. Thin worms of blood crawled from his left nostril and from a cut at the corner of his mouth.

I did that, Peaches thought. *Me.* The baddest gangsterest gangster who'd ever lived had been smacked up good by Peaches Lavelle.

As soon as he saw her with his hat, Stag's expression turned mean again, and hatred darkened his good eye.

"What you think you doing with that?" he said softly.

Peaches sipped a startled breath. He sounded like a man.

"You didn't care when I took yo gun away," she said. "But now you getting upset about a silly ole pimp hat?"

"That right there is a genuwine Stetson, and you best hand it back to me fore thangs get complicated." He took an unhurried step forward with his right leg and showed her his left palm. One second it was empty, and the next he held his big old nasty gun. He didn't point it at Peaches, though. Instead, he slid it into his suit.

"What you gone do?" Peaches asked, and for the first time, she felt out of her depth. "You gone breathe fire on me? You gone hurt people just because don't nobody respect you?"

"Don't pretend to know what goes on in my head," Stagger Lee said lightly. "Up till now, we been playing. I ain't never met nobody could stand up to me hand to hand, and my guess is you ain't, neither. But playtime *over*, baby."

"I ain't stupid," Peaches said. "You hurt bad. You can't last much longer."

"Neither can you."

"Why you doing this? Where you gone live if you destroy the city?"

For a long time, he didn't answer, and when he did, it was as if he had drawn his Stagger Lee–ness back around him like a cape. THASS WHAT YOU DON'T UNDERSTAND: I AIN'T VIOLENT; I'M VIOLENCE. I AM VIOLENCE AND I AM HATE.

"You the Devil" was all Peaches could think to say. She had begun to sweat.

BABY, THE DEVIL GOT NOTHIN' ON ME. HE WAS STANDIN' RIGHT HERE, I KILL HIM JUST AS DEAD AS I'MA KILL YOU, YOU DON'T GIMME THAT STETSON. NOW, YOU MIGHT THINK I'M ON MY LAST LEGS, BUT YOU DON'T WANNA BET YO LIFE ON IT.

"I just wanna know why," Peaches said. "I wanna know why you so awful."

"I ain't awful, little bit," Stagger Lee said. "Awful is me."

Peaches considered, then tossed Stagger Lee his prized hat. As it sailed through the air, she planted her feet, squared her shoulders, and brought her hands together as hard as she could, thunder-clapping, just as Stag had done in Big Lake.

The force of the concussion took them out of the world again.

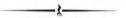

This time, when she and Stagger Lee reappeared, Peaches knew exactly where they were. Congo Circus. It was night, but that meant nothing—it was always night in Congo Square. The darkness made the lights look better. They fell from thirty or so feet above, landing on the tiles maybe twenty paces apart. Peaches dropped lightly into a crouch, but Stagger Lee hit the stones hard enough to crack them.

Even so, when he stood up, his Pimpin' Suit had been restored. His injuries had disappeared as well. Both his eyes were clear, brown, and full of hate.

Peaches knew she should do something. She knew she should rush Stagger Lee, snatch his hat again to distract him, and resume the fight to its finish, but her body wouldn't obey her commands. The stones of the square were cold against her feet, and she just couldn't lift them. All of a sudden she was tired all through her, and she hurt deep inside.

Stagger Lee didn't speak. Instead, he locked eyes with Peaches, pointed at her. He flashed her a pained smile and then shaped his hand into a gun. He mimed a shot at her.

Peaches sank to her knees as if she'd been hit by a real bullet. When she looked up again, Stagger Lee was limping away, and piano chords had begun to sound out of nowhere at all.

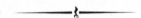

It was Daddy Deke who had first brought Perry and Brendy to Congo Circus. The old man had driven them across town, laughing and joking like usual, but when they turned down North Rampart Street, his mood grew serious.

He found a parking space easily enough, guiding the car into place outside a laundromat shop front. "Now, listen here," he'd said. "The place I'm bout to show you is the holiest place in all of Nola. Holier than all the churches and the boneyards put together."

"How come?" Brendy chirped.

"Congo Square, where the circus at, is where jazz began, way back in Slave Times. The French used to let their slaves congregate at the open-air market and sell their wares, have their church services, and do their drumming. So the slaves, they used to drum and dance all the dances they remembered from Africa. That was how the Rhythm started. That was how the Jazz Spirit first entered the world."

But now? Now the circus had stopped, and the Square had been desecrated.

As soon as they appeared, Perry could tell that he had arrived too late. His heart lurched with cheer as he smelled the roasting peanuts, frying funnel cakes, and spun cotton candy of the circus, but it sank as he noticed the crater. Somehow, the center of the square had been dented in, and a web of wicked cracks radiated from it.

A couple of the tents had fallen down. Figures of people and furniture lay swaddled, covered like cats under bedsheets. The big tent at the center of the square had lost some of its poles in the accident, and now listed badly on its facing side. Doctor Professor sat just beyond the radius of the damage, playing hard as ever, and the fortune-tellers and circus audience had left their seats to dance.

Lord don't let it snow in New Orleans!
Lord don't let it snow in New Orleeeeeeeeans!
I said what I said and you know what I mean!
Don't want that nasty traffic or that ice beneath my feet
Lord don't let it snow in New Orleans!

Instead of the fever to dance, Perry felt a pulsing in his temples. The sight of Fess playing his piano like nothing had happened— like he hadn't abandoned Perry and the others just moments ago— made his head buzz like a hornet's nest.

"Hey!" Perry shouted.

"Oh noooooo!" Brendy wailed and broke to Perry's left.

Perry turned to see Peaches sitting on the flagstones, her legs splayed out in front of her, hugging herself and crying hard. Brendy stretched, enfolding her friend in her arms as best she could. "You okay now. We here. We got you."

Doctor Professor had stopped playing, but Perry paid him no mind as he approached his friend. He squatted in front of her and rested a hand on her thigh, waiting for her to look up at him.

Peaches shook her head and sobbed, inconsolable.

"Are you hurt?" Perry asked.

Peaches seemed to consider, then shook her head again.

"He's gone now, and we're here," Perry said. "You're safe."

She shook her head again, and a heat passed across Perry's face. It reminded him of how sometimes, when he was home sick from school, he could feel his own fever baking up from his skin. He backed away, balled his fists, and turned.

Doctor Professor stood nearby, having left his piano on the far side of the Square. Circus patrons milled around, aimless, as fortune-tellers picked up their overturned card tables and folding chairs, looking to get back to work. Even as he opened his mouth to speak, Perry wondered what he would say. Could he think of anything besides cusses?

"Perry," Peaches said.

He turned back to her. "Yeah?"

"I need to go home," she said. "I ain't quitting, but I just—I need to go home, just for tonight. You take me?"

"Yeah," Perry said. "Yeah, I take you." He turned back to Doctor Professor. "You heard her," he said. "We going home."

"Time growing short, baby," said the ghost.

"We don't care."

"Listen, baby. I'm truly sorry for the way things—"

"That don't mean *nothing*," Perry said. "You left us. There's things you care about more than you care about us, and that's fine. But I care more about Peaches and Brendy and Daddy Deke than I do about your songs. Now, you take us to Peaches's house right now, and we'll take your quest back up in the morning *if we choose*!"

"What about me?" Mr. Casey asked. "Should I go?"

Perry considered. "You can come if you want, but you don't know the danger we're in. You could—You could *die*."

Mr. Casey swallowed. The pain in his expression comforted Perry a little. The man didn't know what he was getting into, but he seemed to understand that the stakes were higher than high. "I know."

"I'll take you home," Doctor Professor said. "But you go to your mama house first, understand? Let her know you alive and kickin'."

"What if we ain't?" Peaches asked just loudly enough for Perry to hear.

THE GOODNIGHT SHOW

N
one of the children spoke as their stretch of Jackson Avenue sprang into being around them. The fog had returned, near solid, like spiderwebs, but after everything that had gone on since they'd left Perry's house, even the clammy, unseasonable cloud wasn't enough to bother Perry. What bothered him was the way Peaches shuddered against him, the way none of them reacted to Doctor Professor's magic keyboard. Had the city's turmoil sapped its potency, or were Perry, Brendy, and Peaches now fortified against it?

As Perry considered the question, he saw his front door open, and three grown-ups exit to stand on the porch. Two, he recognized—his parents, but the shortest, darkest of the three was unknown to him.

"Mama Lisa?" Brendy said.

Perry scowled, wondering how his sister could be silly at a time like this.

"That's right," the woman said. "Hello, Brendolyn."

"Call me Brendy, please!" Brendy chirped. She ran in place for a moment, then zipped to her grandmother and jumped into her arms.

The woman let out a squawk, then kissed Brendy's forehead right on her hairline. Her smile faded as she looked up. "Thank you, Henry. Well done." She gestured with her chin at Mr. Casey. "And here *you* are, as well. What's your name again?"

"Cuh-Casey," Casey said. "My compass Roux gave me took me to the kids. That's no regular storm in the Gulf. It's not just one hurricane, it's like all of them, ever, stacked up together. And it's alive."

Mama Lisa closed her eyes and nodded. Her expression was one of worry and relief. "That is so," she said. "That is why the Ancestors have brought me here."

Perry swallowed, and for a moment, everyone stood silent. Mama Lisa had a glow about her. Like a shadow, it clung close to her, but as Perry watched the woman, he began to suspect that he perceived it not through sight, but by some other sense that had been boosted and refined by the Clackin' Sack. This was his chance to explain to his grandmother that she'd made a mistake, that the sack should not be his.

But he didn't move. He didn't speak. Maybe Mama Lisa and the Ancestors *had* made a mistake, but it didn't matter now. There was no time to give the sack to anyone else, to train them in its use. *We're enough*, he'd told his sister. *We can do this.* He hadn't doubted when he said it, so why should he now?

"Ms. Lisa—?" Doctor Professor began.

"No," said the woman. "You are dismissed."

"What about my songs?" he asked. "I ain't asking for my own self. I got a job to do, and these kids was helpin' me do it."

"I'll summon you when you're needed," she said. "Away."

Doctor Professor wavered, and his expression of shamefaced uncertainty gave Perry a mean little thrill. He shrugged glumly and started playing again:

Gone leave tomorrow on a northbound train!
And ya won't see me no more!
Shut all the windows and turn out the lights
Cuz I won't be back agaaaaaaaaaaaaain . . . !

And he was gone.

Immediately, Mama Lisa's mood softened. The hardness, the formality dropped out of her voice. Perry had often seen his mother shift moods this way, but with Mama Lisa, the change was more pronounced.

"Well, look at you all!" she said, grinning. "Y'all have grown so big!" She bent her knees, bobbing confidently under Brendy's weight.

"Mama helped us get the stuff you left!" Brendy said. "I was so mad! I thought I got a dusty ole rock, but it's got a div inside named Billy Pete!"

"You sure this y'all's gramma?" Peaches spoke into the crook of Perry's neck.

"I dunno," Perry said. "Maybe it's a trick."

"It's no trick," Mama Lisa said. "I'm sorry I've had to wait till now to meet you all."

"Perry—" Peaches's voice cracked, and Perry fought to keep his expression neutral. Crying and wailing wouldn't help now.

"Mama Lisa, Mama, Dad," Perry said. "We're real happy to see y'all, but, uh—but Peaches has been through a lot. Can I take her home and come back, and she'll come see us all in the morning?"

"She can sleep here," Perry's father said. "Shouldn't she sleep here?"

"I need my house. My bed," Peaches said, so low only Perry could hear.

"I be right back," Perry called. "I promise."

"Yvie?" Perry's dad sounded genuinely perplexed.

Perry grinned a grin he didn't feel. "You know how it is," he said. "Peaches does what Peaches does. No use arguing."

He glanced in Mr. Casey's direction. The grown-up searched Perry's face for a bit, then offered him the slightest of nods. "Do what you gotta."

Perry buried his face in Peaches's hair. "Okay," he whispered. "It's okay."

He could tell the words meant nothing to her.

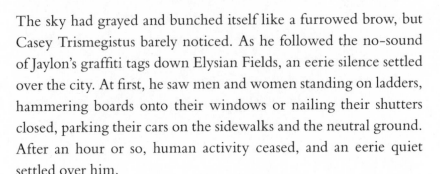

The sky had grayed and bunched itself like a furrowed brow, but Casey Trismegistus barely noticed. As he followed the no-sound of Jaylon's graffiti tags down Elysian Fields, an eerie silence settled over the city. At first, he saw men and women standing on ladders, hammering boards onto their windows or nailing their shutters closed, parking their cars on the sidewalks and the neutral ground. After an hour or so, human activity ceased, and an eerie quiet settled over him.

Casey was intimately familiar with his own version of Elysian Fields. He'd walked and driven down it many many times on his way to UNO. He wondered whether the college existed in this world, and if so, how similar it was to the school he'd attended. It wasn't until he'd been walking at least two hours that he noticed the lack of storm damage. That was one of the reasons this place unsettled him so—he'd seen no storm damage of any kind any-where since he'd come to the Hidden City.

Many of the houses and businesses he passed had been boarded up, or had sandbags heaped against their front doors, but none of the windows were blank and broken. No faded crosses appeared on the sides or fronts of houses. Reverend Keith seemed to hate the Storm, seemed aware of what it could do, but did the people here know about Katrina or the levee failure? If the city had been hidden to protect against the Storm, maybe they had no idea.

Casey spat a string of cusses as the heavens opened above him, but after a beat he realized that the rain didn't touch him.

It wasn't as if he wore a forcefield or had sheltered himself against it, the rain just seemed uninterested in him and contented itself to fall everywhere else. Casey walked through it for several yards, marveling. Then, unable to resist, he began to experiment. He jumped from one spot to another, trying to catch the wet, and failed.

The Hidden City in trouble, baby, and I gotta do my part...

Casey's mother had said that his great-grandpa had come here after his death to deliver something. Had he succeeded? Did it matter?

A ghostly boy rode past him on a white ghost bike. Casey wondered if he'd been killed somewhere along Elysian Fields. He knew the intersection where Saint Claude gave way to Rampart was particularly dangerous for cyclists.

That thought forced Casey to consider the nature of death here in this haunted magic city. If it was possible for dead folks from Casey's own world to come here, what happened when they did? Was the ghost boy one of these? Had Daddy Deke arrived here as a translucent specter or as a living man? Hell, what if he'd become a zombie or some species of talking animal?

Casey *had* to stop thinking about Daddy Deke. About the Storm.

The not-sound he'd followed was stronger now, but it was also harder to interpret. It seemed to ring from everywhere and nowhere at once.

Casey walked another block, listening carefully, and the sound seemed to weaken by just a shade. He retraced his steps to stand in front of a house he'd passed before. It was a camelback positioned a little ways back from the avenue.

A few more experimental steps convinced Casey that he needed to head around back of the place, but he'd seen a couple NPD squad cars pass during his hike, which meant police existed here. He had no way of knowing whether they were as dangerous and unpredictable as the NOPD, and while he had the feeling that his sorcery would stack up just fine against some armed-and-jumpy cops, he knew they might be magic, too.

Cautiously, Casey made his way up the long set of stairs to the house's front door and peered in the front picture window. The place was full of dust-covered furniture, stacks of books, children's toys strewn across the floor. Nothing he could see suggested Jayl's presence. Maybe he'd misread the sound and was standing at the wrong house.

But he felt it again. A brief interruption in the flow of energy.

He turned to look behind him just in time to see a tag wink into sight on the avenue. At first it was hard to see through the rain, but this one said YARBOH!!@. This was the place, all right.

Casey tried the front door. It gave a little, but seemed stuck. He put his shoulder into it, and when the door burst open Casey smelled the must and rot of molded insulation. As high up as it was, this place was water-damaged—likely from leaks in the roof.

He searched the kitchen, a bathroom, and one of the bedrooms before he headed to the converted studio upstairs.

In here, the energy was enough to overwhelm. The air crackled with it, and Casey smelled the same clean-laundry aroma the sky trolley had exhaled. The scent was *much* more powerful, though, and it carried with it a warm golden shine that enfolded both Casey and Jaylon in its aura.

"Oh shit," Casey whispered. His legs failed him. He dropped to his knees. He thought he had driven all doubt from his mind. He'd crossed worlds on this mission because he knew Jaylon was still alive in the Hidden City, but some doubt must have lingered, because the sight of his cousin heated his skull, made it pulse.

All his life, he'd read and heard about people being thrilled. He realized, now, what they meant. An exquisite electricity raced through him, and he didn't think it had anything to do with magic.

"*Jayl,*" he said. Was he shouting? "*Jayl. Jayl. Jaylon!*"

As he walked Peaches home, Perry thought about what Mr. Casey had said. The storm in the Gulf wasn't *a* storm, it was *the* Storm. All storms stacked together. How could a thing be itself—tangible, factual, of-the-world, but at the same time *more*? Well. Wasn't Perry himself an example of this? He was a living boy. He lived with his family, played with his friends, went to school, but did the Clackin' Sack make him *not* himself, or *more* himself? What if it was somehow both?

The Storm. The Storm. The Hanging Judge. Mr. Larry.

When he was very little, before he met Peaches, even, Perry had wanted superpowers. He'd read about Spider-Man and the Phantom in the Sunday paper and ached to pull on tights and fight crime. He would even mix potions from food ingredients and seasonings and choke them down in the hope that they'd give him super-speed, or lightning eyes, or the power to read minds. Of course, none of it had worked.

He checked comics collections and science fiction books out of the Nola Library, searching them for clues, but real life had offered him no magic words, no lab accidents. In real life, there was no such thing as comic book superpowers. The closest he could come to that would be to learn an instrument. But then Peaches entered his life. When Perry had asked her about her strength, her ability to do the impossible, she hadn't understood: *What you mean, how I do that? If something need pickin' up, I just pick it up.*

He'd asked his mother about it.

The world is a big place, she'd said. *With all sortsa folks in it. Everybody got something. Everybody got something makes them special. Even you.*

How I'm special, Mama?

Well, you part of my heart, but you run around on two legs getting into things all the time. If that ain't a miracle, I don't know what is.

But his mother believed he was destined for greatness. She told him all the time. Perry had believed it, too, until the Hanging Judge. His encounter with the Judge had shown Perry that he wasn't special—or that even if he was, it didn't matter. He wasn't strong enough to do magic. He wasn't bright enough. If he struggled so to learn piano, how could he ever—ever—be strong enough to protect himself and his loved ones from monsters like that?

The Hanging Judge wasn't the Storm. But if the Storm was all storms, then couldn't it include such a specter? Or one like Koizumi Yakumo, the living congealed darkness that slept beneath the boneyard? No. The Storm had nothing to do with the Judge, and it had nothing to do with the haint who'd stolen Peaches's letter from her daddy. If Perry was to get through this, he had to keep his eye on the ball. Maybe the Clackin' Sack gave him the power to fight the Judge, imprison him permanently, but he'd have to figure that out later.

As he walked through the fog, one arm around Peaches's waist, Perry imagined that the haze would not close behind them after they passed. In his mind, it made way to let their bodies pass and held its new shape thereafter. If, on his way back, Perry came this exact way, he would see the channel their walking had created in the mist, and he could trace it again if he chose. Thinking this way helped Perry turn his mind away from the Judge, away from musings that did no good. It also kept him from wondering just how he would find the words to ask Peaches what Stagger Lee had done to her. Physically she seemed fine, but it was clear to Perry that she'd been hurt both inside and out.

"Are you okay inside?" he asked as they reached Peaches's back porch. They had to enter the house this way, because she had never had a key to the front door. Several chickens had congregated at the edge of the porch, clucking like church ladies as they pecked after bugs and other food.

"Naw," Peaches said. "But I heal up fast."

Inside, the house smelled damp and dusty, but not rotten. Stacks of newspapers stood in the gloom. To Perry, they looked like gravestones.

"Are your ears ringing?" he asked as they crossed the kitchen and entered the hallway beside the grand staircase. "Do you feel fuzzy? You're not supposed to sleep with a concussion. We could maybe go to Charity."

"Hospital no good for me," Peaches said. "The machines there can't see through me, and even if they could, the knives and razors can't cut me."

"I'm sorry we got separated," Perry said as they climbed the stairs together. He realized now that he'd never seen Peaches climb stairs without running.

"Wait," Peaches said. "I wanna see Fonzy."

She turned and started back down. Perry watched for a beat, then followed. In the parlor on the first floor, part of the wall had given way, creating a gaping hole that led into the walled yard. This was how Alphonse, Peaches's horse, came and went. The house had been raised to keep it from flooding, and Perry knew at the very least that Alphonse couldn't navigate stairs—this was why the entire first floor belonged to him. If that was the case, though, how did the horse get in and out of the hole? Every time he visited, Perry hoped to catch the horse leaving or returning, but he had begun to suspect that he would never know Fonzy's secrets.

"Fonzy!" Peaches called. "Hey, hey! Alfonso?"

She passed out of sight into the junky living room, still calling. A sickness gathered in the pit of Perry's belly as he realized what had happened. Mr. Casey said the horses and mules had all disappeared, taken by Stagger Lee and the Storm. Should he tell her?

Peaches emerged through the kitchen doorway wiping at her face. "He not home right now," she said. "It's fine. He's fine. He go out all the time." She gestured with her chin, and Perry stepped aside to let her pass, then followed her back upstairs to check on the other animals.

Did they have time for this? Perry wondered, but the question angered him. If he couldn't care for Peaches, help her get back into fighting shape, they were all as good as lost, anyway.

After saying their goodnights, Peaches and Perry headed for the bedroom. It was a large chamber full of antique furniture—most of it draped in sheets to keep the dust off. The ceiling in here was even higher than the ceilings in Daddy Deke's house. Exposed beams stretched overhead, and sometimes Peaches climbed up to walk across them, her arms stretched out to either side. Perry had only done so once, and the feeling of nothing beneath him or around him, no floor to hold him up and no handholds to keep him from falling, had been almost too exquisite to bear. He knew that one day he would walk those rafters again, and he would enjoy himself at least as much as he had before, but he kept putting off trying, savoring the anticipation.

Peaches's bed was enormous. It consisted of six twin-sized box springs and two king-sized mattresses stacked together in the western corner of the room. At its foot sat one of those old-fashioned TVs that was less an electronic appliance than a piece of furniture like a sofa or a credenza. The hole where its screen should be was wider than Perry's arm span, and from time to time, the box, which lacked any plug or cord that Perry could see, would turn itself on. Ghostly blue light would flicker across the set's interior, and its neglected innards would be replaced by what looked like a theater stage. It was only ever one program that the children had seen inside it—and that was the only one they cared to see. (Peaches had no interest in *Morgus*, or *News with a Twist*, or even *Tha Jon Reaux Yung Money Sheaux*. No. When they were here, they only had eyes for the *Goodnight Show*.)

As Perry watched, Peaches climbed onto the bed and knelt with her arms crossed, like a king surveying his realm. She made her decision and started grabbing the pillows that lay piled in the bed's left corner and built herself a mound of them. She always arranged things this way to watch the show. When the time came to sleep, she would dole out pillows to whoever was with her and modify her nest to cradle her through the night. Perry wasn't sure she actually did this on nights when neither he nor Brendy were with her—she didn't seem to need food with the same regularity they did, and her need for sleep was likewise either nonexistent or much less than Perry's own.

"Do what now?" Perry asked. Peaches had said something or asked him a question.

"I said I made room for you, too."

"In your pocket?"

"Yeah. In my pocket. You gotta watch the show right next to me this time, heard?"

"You don't like people touching on you while you're sleeping or watching the TV."

"I don't," Peaches said. "But you ain't people."

Perry opened his mouth, but words failed him.

"I know you gotta get home. I know Miss Yvette be worryin', but you got time for this... Please."

"No, it's not that," Perry said. "It's not— She knows where I am. It's just that—something's different. Something's wrong."

"I'm different? I'm wrong?"

"That's not what I mean."

"You think I can't handle a nasty ole gangsta with jewely teeth and a gun?"

"I know you can."

"Because I'm strong as anything," Peaches said. "Can't nobody or nothing get the best of me."

"I know. I know it. It's just— There's something you're not saying, and I don't know if it's because you just don't feel like it, or because you can't."

"Perry," Peaches said with a frown. "I'm not like y'all. I could eat a million million bombs, and I still wouldn't explode. I'm hard inside and out."

Perry knew that this was true, but he also knew that it was somehow *not*. He suspected that Peaches knew this as well but had chosen to make an argument she knew Perry could not refute.

"And you would tell me if something was really wrong? You wouldn't lie to me or try to keep it secret like a grown-up would?"

"I already told you bout grown-ups."

"I know," Perry said.

"So will you come in my pocket with me? Because our show bout to start."

Right now, Peaches seemed both closer and farther away than she'd ever been. Perry's blood still sang at the sight of her, at the smell of her, and he wished he could just let the joy of the invitation pierce the dread enfolding him like a sodden cloak.

As light began to flicker in the depths of the TV set, Perry kicked off his shoes and climbed into the pocket. They half sat, half lay, hip to hip. Peaches reached for Perry's hand and held it lightly as the figures on the stage resolved.

Perry wondered whose bedroom this had been before the Storm. He imagined an elderly couple who had dressed in their best formal clothes and lain down together just as the rain began in earnest. He imagined them holding each other as the sound of the weather swelled like the noise of a passing train, happy alone together after decades. As the house began to shake and shudder around them, they had closed their eyes and dissolved into For-ever. In Perry's mind, this was not death. It was the same sort of thing that had happened to Mama Lisa. It was not a cessation, not even a becoming; it was a going-on to somewhere better, even more full of magic than the city in which they had lived their entire lives, and inside Perry's imagining, there was no room for fear.

The rain started slowly, but it fell with purpose. For now, it seemed to coexist with the fog, tamping it down to lie close against the ground. Mama Lisa stood before the window, staring out at the deserted expanse of Jackson Avenue.

This rain. Should she try to command it?

Mama Lisa could feel the Storm testing its limits, curious to learn just how far it could swell. What would she do if she tried to rebuke the weather, to remind it of its place, and it defied her? Yvette and the babies needed their faith in Mama Lisa's authority. So long as they didn't mistakenly believe her to be all-powerful, their faith would be a comfort to them.

"Your hair is different," Yvette said softly. "You used to wear it long, but now it's short. It suits you."

"Hm," Mama Lisa grunted. "Thank you, baby."

Her body felt like a suit of borrowed clothes. She had been elsewhere—she wasn't sure where exactly, or for how long—and during that time, she must have been formless. The thought didn't entirely make sense to her, but now was not the time to muse on such things. What mattered were this place and this time.

"You looking out for Perry and Peaches?"

"No, hon. Perry's fine. He and Peaches just need some time. He'll be back directly." Mama Lisa chose not to mention that when Perry returned, it would be alone. "I was just thinking about that chocolate cake."

Yvette bowed her head, stifled a grin. "I'm not sure what cake that would be."

"Mmm-hmm," Mama Lisa hummed. "My cakes used to come out wrong every time I baked them. They'd fall, or they'd be dry, and I never quite knew what I did wrong. Your grandmother tried to show me, but it just didn't take. I had to find my own way."

"But you figured it out."

"I figured it out. That cake when you were three years old was the first one that came out just—" She sighed. "—perfect."

"It was so pretty."

"It was. I made my own icing from scratch. Iced it myself."

"And I stuck my little hands right down in it." Even now, the memory thrilled Yvette. "I scooped out giant chunks and just shoveled them right into my face."

"And you wore the chocolate on your face like a fake hobo beard on Halloween."

"I never!"

" 'Mama Lisa, I don't know nothing bout no cake, I promise! You baked a cake? What a cake is, anyhow? Who took it? Where?' "

"If it wasn't for your hands and face, you mighta convinced me," Mama Lisa said.

"Except I stepped in a chunk and tracked chocolate from the kitchen to the bathroom and into my bed."

They laughed together.

"Does—?" Yvette began. She bit the question in half. She looked down, nodded. "Okay, then. Guess we better get cooking."

TURN BACK

The dead taxi glided to a halt in front of Peaches's house. This one was a battered old truck with no wheels. Its body hovered above the asphalt, making not a sound. Peaches took a breath and levered herself into the truck's grimy bed.

The truck offered wooden benches for sitting and a dirty little window through which Peaches could see what looked like a half-rotten zombie nutria, its big ole buckteeth crusted with blue-green mold. The nutria aimed its vacant eye sockets in her direction for several seconds before Peaches remembered what was expected of her.

"Department of Streets," she said softly. The nutria jerked its head like a pigeon, and the truck glided into motion.

Peaches didn't care to see which route they took—and it wasn't as if the drive to the Dead Side ever made sense, anyhow. She knew what she needed to do now, but she wasn't sure her imagination was up to the task. Just the fact that she thought of it as imagination was a bad sign. At the best of times, she could convince herself that the entire exercise was real as real could be.

Sometimes, when she felt desperate and alone, Peaches spoke to her daddy. It wasn't like her memories of his instructions or his telling her about the world as they sailed the Seven Seas. When she summoned him to her in this way, it was as if he alllllmost appeared. Peaches imagined him sitting beside her now, his corn-cob pipe clenched between his teeth, his clothes still damp from ocean spray. Instead of his usual red knit skullcap, he wore a tri-corne hat cocked at a jaunty angle, and a patch instead of his glass eye.

As soon as she could almost see him, Peaches started talking, as if in the middle of a conversation. "Lotta folks still live here," she said, speaking low in her throat so that the taxi driver couldn't hear. "All them people and all the buildings. They precious to me."

They ain't strong like you strong, babygirl.

"I know."

They cain't take what you can take.

"I know it."

What I done tole you?

"You told me protect the weak. Fight for them can't protect themself."

Yeahyouright.

Peaches fell silent for a while and just listened to the no-sound of the dead taxi making its way to its destination. She didn't like thinking about the Department of Streets. In her mind's eye, its windows and doors yawned like graves.

"Daddy, there's a man," she said. "A bad man. 'Cept he ain't even a man. Not really. He something else. He says he ain't awful. Awful is him. And he *strong*."

Stronger'n you?

Peaches felt something at the edge of her awareness. A dim understanding fluttered just outside her grasp. "Ioknow," she said. "Seem like he is."

What about your friend, though?

"Who? Brendy?"

Naw. The other one. Dat boy you like.

Peaches's cheeks heated at the question. "His name Perry."

What about Perry? Perry strong?

"Aw, baby, what you think?" Peaches surprised herself by grinning. "Perry the *strongest*, ya heard me?"

He can pick up a tree, roots and all, right out the ground? Break a boulder in half with one punch?

"Naw," Peaches said. "Naw, I guess not."

Mebbe being strong don't mean being able to hit the hardest. Mebbe being strong means standin' up even when there ain't no hope of winning through strength of arms, you dig?

"Maybe so. I think so."

That bad man, he hurt ya like you ain't thought nobody could. He didn't just do it by punchin', though, did he? He tole you some thangs got you shook up—and that was the point. Just because he can take a punch, that don't mean he stronger than you is, do it? That don't mean you cain't beat him, do it?

"Nuh-no," Peaches said. "I guess it don't."

What else I done tole you?

" 'Ain't nobody invincible. Ain't nobody can't be brought down by somebody stronger than they is.' "

That's it right there. That's it, verbatim.

"Verbatim," she repeated. "That's a Perry word."

Her daddy didn't answer, and Peaches's impression of him thinned a little. Like he wasn't allllllmost with her anymore, like he was almost-*almost*.

"Daddy?"

What?

"Daddy, are you really here with me, or am I just talkin' to myself?" As soon as she asked the question, Peaches wished she hadn't. Not at a time like this.

You tell me. Am I?

"I don't know," she said. Her voice had risen, and now the nutria in the front seat cocked his head. Did zombies hear? Did they hear the way people heard?

"I don't know where you at. The Yardbird Haint stole your

letter to me. He stole your letter, and now I don't know where to find the next one."

Baby, letters is just writing on paper. Ain't I more than that to you?

Overhead, thunder cracked, and fat raindrops fell on the truck-bed's canvas cover, just a few at first, but the flat, moist ring of them promised that more would be along directly. Soon, they would fall by the thousands of millions.

The interior of the dead taxi felt warm and dry and safe—but not for long. Soon enough, Peaches would have to brave the storm. She would have to step into a night after which might come no day.

"I don't know," she said sadly. "I don't know what you are to me."

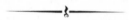

An enormous crack of thunder startled Perry awake. The rain sounded like an army on the march. A gust of wind shook the house, rattled the windows. The Storm was here. It wanted inside. But then, suddenly, the noise ceased, replaced by a sound that was not a sound. It was as if a room full of people standing shoulder to shoulder—no, an entire Superdome's worth of people—all stood silent, holding their breath, fighting to keep from screaming and cheering. Perry lay on his belly, hugging one of the pillows Peaches had given him, and waited.

He strained in the darkness, trying to hear anything at all. No noise filtered in from the street outside, no wind, not even the creaking of the branches on the trees. No chicken clucked; no dog barked. The bed was so full of Peaches's scent that Perry did not realize right away that she was gone. When he did, the bottom dropped out of his heart. He didn't even take the time to tell himself she'd gone to the bathroom or to check on the animals. He'd never been in the house without her, but in her absence, it felt the way he would have imagined if he'd taken the time to think about it: the house seemed to wait breathlessly for her return so that it could live again. The worst thing about it was that this was how Perry felt whenever he was away from Peaches for too long.

Perry sat up and swung his feet to the hardwood floor, and something in the action told him where Peaches had gone. She'd gone to Mr. Larry for help.

Mr. Larry. Lafcadio Hearn. That storehouse of information. Mr. Larry could tell Peaches which song would be next in Stagger Lee's sights because he knew all sorts of things. He knew more about the city than anyone Peaches had ever met. But if he could tell Peaches, that meant he could tell Stagger Lee. If he and the Storm needed direction, who else could provide it?

Sickness gathered in the pit of Perry's belly. The thought had occurred to him before, but he'd brushed it aside, knowing that he couldn't share it with Peaches unless he could prove he was right. But just because he couldn't prove it didn't mean he was wrong.

Why would he do it, though? What did Mr. Larry have to gain from steering Peaches wrong? If the city was destroyed, haint or no haint, he'd be destroyed along with it, wouldn't he? Perry pictured the old ghost in his mind's eye: His stained clothes. The way his good eye drooped. His rounded shoulders. He was already dead, but he was terribly tired. Maybe killing Nola would destroy him—but maybe that was what he wanted more than anything.

He was still missing something. Perry held his head, thought hard. When nothing came, he took a different tack. Instead of thinking as hard as he could, he relaxed, shut his eyes, let thought empty from his mind.

Brendy's voice: *Nuh-Ohleans? What that is?*

New Orleans is a different city, Mr. Larry had said. *Much like this one, but sadly lost to time.*

That was it. That was the moment Perry began to suspect that something about the old ghost was...off. His weary, disheveled bearing. His birdlike stare. The letter. Peaches seemed terribly hurt since her fight with Stagger Lee, but she'd been having trouble for a while now. She'd been showing strain ever since they'd ventured into Mount Olivet after the letter that living dark thing had stolen from her. Why would some haint steal her daddy's letter? How would Koizumi Yakumo even know about the letters to steal one in the first place?

He'd know if Mr. Larry told him.

Unless Mr. Larry didn't *need* to tell him.

Because Koizumi Yakumo and Lafcadio Hearn were the same.

How could the old haint have disguised himself so thoroughly that he fooled even Perry's vision? Perry had no idea, but he was no less convinced. He bit his lip, cursed his stupidity. He was bone weary, but he had no time to waste.

He wished he could hop on Fonzy's back, ride him to the rescue—but Fonzy was gone. Because of Yakumo. Perry remembered the oily black tentacles that had followed Peaches out of the grave back at the boneyard. What if Yakumo disobeyed his command to enter the Clackin' Sack the same way Stagger Lee had? To face Yakumo—let alone the Storm—Perry needed stronger weaponry. Something that could not just contain but *destroy*.

He thought of the story his mother had told him about his fourth-great-grandmother and Grand Lahou. Each of the Last Nine had been armed. Surely, one of them had gotten something Perry could use.

As the thunder cracked and the wind gathered strength, Perry hurried from the bedroom and pounded down the stairs.

The rain had just begun to fall. Dark purple clouds roiled above the Missus Hipp, lit intermittently by lightning that, for now, stayed in the sky where it belonged. The parking lot was mostly quiet. The only sounds to be heard came from the odd car swishing up Decatur Street, and from the pulse of Tha Bangin' Gardens over by Canal Place. From here, its actual magic could not be heard. Instead, one could feel the stuttering beat of its bounce music throbbing through the heels of one's shoes.

One of the empty cars—a powder-blue hatchback—flashed its lights, and its radio played just enough of a tune for Stagger Lee to ride.

He materialized in the driver's seat and sat still, drawing his Stagger Lee–ness about him like a cape. He had scared the little girl pretty good, but he knew she'd snap out of it sooner rather than later. Nobody who could hit that hard could be conquered by fear—not for long. Stag knew he was still hurt deep-deep. Every breath caused him pain.

He'd told her he'd kill her next time. Could he?

The very question made his chest smolder. He had never had to wonder—never in memory—whether he could kill anyone or anything. He was Stagger Lee, damb it, and at one time or another, he'd killed everything that walked or crawled upon the earth.

He gritted his teeth, and instead of opening the driver's-side door, Stagger Lee folded his right leg, turned in his seat, and kicked that door straight off its hinges. It crashed into the car next to it and set its alarm to wailing.

Unhurried, Stagger Lee stepped into the lot and scented the air. Gardenia, the rushing river, and wild, wild magic gathering in the sky. It wouldn't be long now before ambient magic unmade Nola and set Stag free at last.

I know this week done you downbad
I know you feelin' some kinda way
I know they don't treat you right at that job of yours, honey,
And this mornin', it felt like somebody turned the gravity way up!
But it's the weekend now, baby. It's Friday mutha. Fuckin'. Night.
So lemme tell ya what we finna do . . . !

The voice blared from the Garden's speakers, surrounded by an eerie-calm silence. Stag had never encountered this magic before, but something about it felt young, new. It would be no match for him.

Smiling jewels from one side of his mouth, Stagger Lee started toward the high-rise club. He limped slightly. Damn if that little thing couldn't *hit*.

Eyes on the prize, Negro, Stag thought. *Eyes on the prize.* Time to find Tipsy Tina and introduce her to his .45.

———————⚬———————

Perry turned his face to the angry sky. The rain helped him focus, to ignore the hissing voice in the back of his mind.

Too late. You're too late. Mr. Larry's got your Peaches, and it's all all over already.

"No."

Perry couldn't tell whether he'd spoken or thought the word. He thrust his hand into the front left pocket of the jeans he didn't remember drawing back on, and it closed around the Clackin' Sack. He pulled it free, shook it open, and thrust his right arm inside it.

Don't fall in, he thought.

He swept his arm back and forth, his fingers questing for some magic object empowered to set everything right. The not-quite-day was electric around him with lightning and fear. The thunder had begun to roll, and it sounded as if it was gathering strength. Perry ignored it. What would Milo do? he wondered, and now he realized that it had been a long, long time since he'd asked himself that question.

It didn't matter what Milo would do. He wasn't Milo; he was Perry. Milo had never had to save his favorite person. Milo had never faced down Stagger Lee. Milo had never held Moses's enchanted staff—not even for an instant.

Perry's fingers brushed against something metal, and a thrill of power raced up his arm. The energy rang like a bell as it reached the vault of his skull and caromed around it. This was the deepest, most potent magic Perry had ever encountered—except for that of the sack itself.

Perry stood on the dirt floor of what, at first glance, he took for a barn. But barns didn't have high, narrow, stained-glass windows like the ones he saw over the heads of the crowd. And what a crowd! Dark faces of men and women in varicolored shades of tan, beige, and brown who stood before him, wearing old-timey clothes. Some of the colors were peacock bright, but they still gave Perry a sense of murk, a sense of Street. The lines on their faces and the glaze in their eyes told Perry that each one of these people had seen more than he had, and that they were impatient. They seemed to wait for some play or speech to resume, and it was up to Perry to satisfy them.

The room stank. It smelled like the insides of Perry's daddy's running shoes—but the reek was more than that. It smelled of booze, of tobacco smoke—pipe, cigar, and cigarette—a little bit like earwax, a little bit like belly button lint.

Unable to think what else to do, Perry took a big breath and raised his horn to his lips. As he did, it slid from his grasp, and he snapped back to himself again. Was that what had happened before? How many times had he reached into the Clackin' Sack in search of a weapon and been disoriented by a vision that left him empty-handed? He'd never even thought to ask what all was in the sack to begin with! Why hadn't he?

Because he knew his mother couldn't tell him. She was no Wise Woman, after all.

But Mama Lisa was. Mama Lisa would know.

But what if she won't say? Perry thought.

"If she won't say," Perry said aloud, "I'll *make* her tell me."

In some other life, Tha Bangin' Gardens had been a parking garage with a helix of steep spiral ramps coiled together like DNA. That was so long ago that only the garage's skeleton remained, overgrown with tree roots and bioluminescent plants whose glow stuttered in time with the chopped-up beats. One fat, barrel-chested doorman stood at the mouth of the entrance ramp. A tight fade clung close to his scalp, as if imitating his tight black T-shirt with the SECURITY legend in white block caps across the front.

"All right!" said the guard, and something about his tone rubbed Stag the wrong way. "Welcome to Bangin' Gardens. No outside food or drinks, *please*! No weapons, *please*! You strapped, sir?"

Stagger Lee glared at the man until beads of sweat gathered on his brow.

THAT YO WAY OF AXIN' DO I GOT ME ONEA THESE? he said, and the .45 appeared, big as life, in his left hand.

The doorman averted his eyes. "I'm not supposed to let you in with that," he said quietly.

THASS RIGHT. WHAT YOU SAID? NO OUTSIDE FOOD OR DRANK. NO WEAPONS?

"It's not my rule," the guard said. "I got kids to feed."

SIN AND A SHAME, PODNAH. ORDINARYWISE I'D TELL YOU TO FIND ANOTHER JOB, 'CAUSE WON'T BE NOTHING LEFT OF THIS PLACE WHEN I'M DONE UP IN HERE. ONLY THANG IS, THASS TRUE FOR THE WHOLE DAMB CITY, HEARD ME? BEST GO HOME, HUG THEM CHIRREN.

The doorman looked down at his shoes. His expression suggested that he wished he could be anywhere else.

WHAT YO NAME IS, DOORMAN?

"Irwin."

WELL, IRWIN, YOU BEST TAKE MY ADVICE, YOU KNOW WHAT'S GOOD FOR YOU. Stag waited until the man glanced up at him, then gave him a slow, exaggerated wink.

The doorman shook like he would fly apart.

Stagger Lee's grin widened. He took a step toward the man and leaned in close. The man's cowardice smelled a lot like fear, and in Stag's estimation, there were precious few aromas tastier than fear.

SEE YOU NEVER, NEGRO, he said. IF YOU LUCKY...

As he stepped into the club, Stagger Lee heard the fat doorman's running footsteps behind him.

This was shaping up to be a beautiful night.

Inside, the club was like Mardi Gras stood on end. Stagger Lee wasn't sure he'd ever seen a Mardi Gras for himself, but to exist in the city was to be aware of Carnival and its character. Costumed revelers danced up and down the entry and exit ramps or stood in clumps, shouting at each other over the music. The air in the club smelled of wet concrete, motor oil, fried dough, and cooking food.

As Stagger Lee passed, club guests would cease dancing to stare, motionless, or fall silent, their faces clouded with shame. All of them seemed to understand that whatever fun they'd been having was over. When Stag cast a glance over his shoulder, he saw costumed clubbers marching, dejected, down to the exit. Not one person came the other way.

Taking his time, teeth gritted against the throbbing beat and siren noise of the music, Stag made his way to the first dance floor.

The place was enormous. Scanning its expanse, Stag could see that at one time the walls had been open to the elements, but now glowing moss and vines had choked those open spaces until the club was bathed in perpetual twilight. As Stag left the ramp, people gyrated and bounced in twos and threes, doing dances Stagger Lee couldn't have named if he'd cared to. He supposed he'd heard of twerking, but for all he knew, it meant mowing a grassy lawn.

Put your, put your, put your back in it now!
Put your, put your, put your back in it now!
Put your, put your, put your back in it now!
Put your, put your, put your back in it now!
Put your, put your, put your back in it now!

The stuttering clap of the beat and the rough, rubbed-raw bass rhythm gave way to a spiral of notes that sounded almost like horns, and for a moment, Stagger Lee felt light-headed. This Bounce Magic was more powerful than he'd given it credit for, and its potency was boosted by so many of its disciples enacting ritual in the same place. He was a soldier behind enemy lines, and at any moment, the opposing force would notice his presence and demand he state his business.

And then what?

And then nothing.

That little redbone girl must have rung Stag's bell harder than he thought. He'd been thinking like a mere man. Finite, bound to inhabit one moment, once place, at a time. If the Bounce Magicians recognized his purpose, if they turned on him, they would thwart him at worst, delaying the inevitable by hours. Besides: their power could be blunted.

Stagger Lee raised his gun and fired once at the ceiling.

The warm flutter in Stagger Lee's chest told him that even that warning shot had been fatal for someone up above.

At least twenty dancers covered their ears, turned to look, as if they didn't know a gunshot when they heard one. Scores of others scattered like insects revealed by an overturned rock. No one screamed or cried out, and the music didn't stop.

Stagger Lee grinned his jeweled grin and advanced, firing into the crowd.

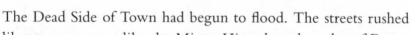

The Dead Side of Town had begun to flood. The streets rushed like streams, more like the Missus Hipp than the calm of Bayou Saint John.

As Peaches climbed down from the bed of the dead taxi, a school of paper boats bobbed by, their bases filling with water as the raindrops and wind gusts buffeted them this way and that. As Peaches watched, the biggest boat was overwhelmed. Its triangle mast dipped into the water and didn't come back up again. Now it was trash. Just a piece of litter floating away and away.

After only a second or two, she was soaked to the skin. Her raggedy dress clung to her like she was all it had.

Won't need no swim this week, Peaches thought as she fished in her sodden pocket for a hell note.

Something made her stop short and look around. She stood on the curb outside what looked like six or seven different houses trying to resolve themselves into one dwelling. Bare wood shaded into candy-colored siding, into wind-scoured paint that was no real color at all, into bricks, into glass and steel, even. Peaches turned back to the taxi, then skirted around it to rap on the driver's door.

"Hey!" she said. "You was sposedta take me to the Department of Streets!"

Slowly, the zombie nutria turned its head to train its eye sockets on her. The emptiness where its eyes should be looked somehow sad.

"No closer," it rasped. "Bad things."

Peaches's skin crawled, but she couldn't tell whether the sensation came from anger or fear. "You shoulda told me that in the first place!" she said. "I don't even know where I'm at."

"Not far, but storm is here," rasped the nutria. "Take shelter. Turn back."

Now Peaches's anger boiled over. It heated her face and make her limbs weak and shaky. "Don't you think I would if I could, dummy?" she yelled. She pulled her sodden Afro puffs away from her face to look the nutria square in his lack-of-eyes. "I ain't like y'all, though! I'm still alive! Somebody gotta do something, and ain't nobody but me! Y'all *kill* me, always needing somebody to fight your fights, and can't never help out or say 'thank you, Peaches!'"

"Thank you, Peaches," said the nutria. "Thank you. No more fight. Turn back. Shelter."

Somehow, the thanks made Peaches even angrier. *"Nutria, is you deaf?"* she shouted. "This is it! This as much as I can do! Stagger Lee gone cuh-*kill* me, this time! Mr. Larry can't help me! Can't nobody help me! I'ma be dead as you—*deader*—*'cause I won't be able to drive no ratchet-ass taxi!"*

Peaches's breath rushed in and out of her chest, and she stood with clenched fists, grateful for the rain that hid the hot tears streaming down her face. She wanted to keep shouting. She wanted to scream. She could feel a scream scrunched down inside her toes, and as soon as she noticed it, it crept up into her calves. It wanted to move all up through her, but if she let it into her throat, there was no telling what would happen. One time, she'd seen her daddy shout a pirate ship to pieces. One blast of his voice had reduced it to matchsticks, and all the cutthroats and swabbies flew this way and that, winding up straight in the drink.

Peaches pressed her fists against her belly and tried to focus on her breathing. She tried to crumple that scream into a little wad of noise and shove it back down inside her. She sobbed as she did, and her back ached. This is what it must feel like for normal people to carry heavy, heavy things.

"Peaches," said the nutria.

Peaches didn't look up right away. When she did, the driver looked sadder than ever.

"Whoever you looking for in that building," he said very clearly—the rasp was almost entirely gone from his voice. "He wa'ant never there, ya heard me?"

"You don't know what you talking bout," Peaches said. "And you can get the hell on. *You* turn back. *You* shelter. I don't need you. I don't need nobody."

The zombie nutria dipped its head, reluctant. "So sorry," it rasped. "Not there. Never was." It wavered a beat, then turned away to gaze out the taxi's windshield again. It didn't touch the steering wheel, but the truck sloshed into motion, then lumbered slowly away.

Peaches glowered after it, feeling as if she'd said a thing, said *many* things, that couldn't be taken back.

WATERS RISE

S tag didn't fire fast—he was looking to kill a few folks and dispel the crowd, not clog the place with bodies. Still, in their panic, some of the dancers couldn't decide which way to run. Almost no one who saw Stagger Lee was willing to chance breaking past him, but neither did it seem a good idea to run farther into the club, what with Stagger Lee stalking that way.

On the fifth floor, a trio of revelers barred Stag's way. Operating as one, they began to perform. The light-skinned man with the dreadlocks began to beatbox while his shorter, dark-skinned, bespectacled friend began to freestyle:

Lemme find out you encroaching on my territory
Cutting up rough, tellin' my boys that you be gunnin' for me
Ya made a mistake and ya done fucked up good
Cuz Kamari the Damaja is the king of the hood!

The beat hit Stag hard, and the lyrics raised welts on his skin. He gritted his teeth against the pain. The dark-skinned rapper glanced at the third member of their crew.

My mans tell the truth and he does not lie
You come at Shaina the Maimer, boy you finna—!

Stagger Lee shot her in the face, and the trio's magic evaporated. With one punch he caved in the other rapper's chest while the beatboxer turned and ran.

Someone pulled a fire alarm, and the club's music stopped. As Stagger Lee turned a corner, he saw that someone had forced open a pair of stairwell doors, and one man in neon bike shorts, a spangled feather boa, and a rainbow Afro wig was directing people through it, trying, as he did, to mitigate their panic. Stag shot him just for grins. He laughed out loud when the man fell over backwards and the doors banged shut. The three costumed women jostling to get out wailed in unison, and Stagger Lee considered capping them, too. He had work to do, though, so he moved on. He sensed his quarry nearby.

He started up the ramp to the next level, and by now, the stampede had begun in earnest. The braver souls streamed down the ramp as Stagger Lee walked up. They had sense enough to give him a wide berth, so instead of shooting at any of them, Stag made a game of it. He would count to five in his head and then lash out, backhand, with one hand or the other, breaking bones or killing on impact.

After the third such swipe, Stagger Lee looked up the ramp and saw the figure he'd been looking for this whole time.

Tipsy Tina had lost a button or two off her top, but she was still decent. Her multicolored hair was awry. It looked like she'd been out partying hard, and when she realized she wouldn't make it home to pass out, she just lay where she was and snoozed. She wore too much foundation, and her makeup was smudged—especially round her mouth on account of all the gin she'd been drinking. Her belly poked out, full of the stuff, but her eyes—mismatched, one gray, one blue—were as clear as they were sad.

As she met Stag's gaze, he grinned like a shark and pointed at her. BE THERE DIRECTLY, he mouthed.

What she did next surprised Stagger Lee all to hell.

Tipsy Tina slung her legs over the railing where she sat and dropped onto the ramp. The clubbers still rushed this way and that, but they didn't matter anymore. Right now, the whole world was Tina and Stag. All he needed to do was summon his .45 and blow her head clean off...

...But he didn't.

Staring into each other's eyes, the two wayward songs closed the distance to stand face-to-face. Tipsy Tina looked up at Stagger Lee, who was a good two feet taller.

"Well, you got what you wanted," she slurred. "You done ruint the party. Shit."

THAT AIN'T WHAT I WANTED, MS. THING. I WANT *YOU*.

"If I'da known you was this bad, I'da turnt myself over long time ago," Tina said. She showed him her palms. "Here I'm is. Go 'head and put it on me. Just don't hurt nobody else because of me, ya heard?"

I DON'T DEAL, BABY. NOTHIN' TO STOP ME KILLIN' YOU STONE DEAD AND THEN KILLIN' EVERYBODY ELSE I CAN FIND EVEN *LOOK* LIKE THEY WAS UP IN HERE WITH YOU.

The statement seemed to shock her sober. "Why, though?" she asked without a trace of her slur. "What these people ever done to you? All they was trying to do is have a good time and dance."

WHY? 'CAUSE I'M STAGGER LEE, DAMB IT. THIS *ME*, BABY.

"You don't have to do this."

Stagger Lee sneered.

"Negro, *listen to me*," Tina said. "I'm not tryna save my life. This life ain't never meant much to me. I stayed in the box till the ole man played me, and then I'd come out to dance, and then I'd go back to sleep. If you do what you finna do, either I'll either be nothing or I'll be free. Being the biggest and baddest, yeah, I imagine that's something else, but you know what? If you don't know why you do what you do, then what difference do it make?"

YOU LYIN'. YOU AFRAID TO DIE.

Stagger Lee willed the gun into his palm and slowly raised its barrel.

Tipsy Tina reached down with both hands and grabbed Stagger Lee's left hand, gun and all. With surprising strength, she wrenched it up and pressed her forehead to the barrel. *"BANG!"* she shouted, and laughed uproariously.

Startled by the noise, Stagger Lee squeezed the .45's trigger.

Everything that had been inside Tipsy Tina's head fled out the back of her skull. Piano music and a bluesy braying voice. The choruses, the verses, all at once, and along with them an inhalation, a sort of negative-sound, as of a sneeze, but backwards.

Even as she fell, her body and clothes dissolved to nothing, and Tipsy Tina was gone. Stagger Lee stared at the spot where she'd stood. He sensed vaguely that the clubbers seemed to fear him less now. They bumped past him in their haste to leave Tha Bangin' Gardens, as if unaware that Stagger Lee was the one they were fleeing in the first place.

Darkness descended like a velvet curtain as the power went out all over town.

There are thoughts so powerful, so freighted with meaning, that the moment one thinks them, one is forever changed. Sometimes a man or a woman—even a boy or a girl—can sense themselves on the verge of one of these changing thoughts, and on rare occasions, can try not to think them. (Which never, ever works.) Sometimes that effort is instinctive, and you try to unthink a thought even as it occurs, like a waiter momentarily losing control of a pile of dishes and regaining that balance before everything can leave his grasp and crash down. That's what Stagger Lee tried to do now.

The thought was simple: *This shit ain't right.*

Just four words, but their implication was terrible.

This was *much* worse than when Stagger Lee had had Jailbird and then the boy with the clackin' bag right in his sights. That time, the mighty little redbone girl had knocked the gun aside, and Stag's shot had gone wild, and then the boy with the bag had defied him, fearless, and confused Stag with his words—the magic ones *and* the mundane—before he disappeared.

But this... Stagger Lee found himself powerless but to admit that he hadn't meant to shoot Tipsy Tina. He hadn't truly made the decision. He wasn't a fool—he knew he *would have* shot her before long, but he would have at least tried to understand where the other song was coming from. How she managed to seem so *unafraid*.

Because, let's face it, that song was terrified... wasn't she? Stagger Lee knew what courage was—the ability to act against the paralyzing influence of fear—but the true absence of fear made no sense to him.

Another, even worse thought: *What if you don't understand a body being unafraid because you scared out your natural mind? What if you scared right now? So scared you don't even know it?*

"Naw," Stagger Lee murmured to himself. "Nuh-uh. No way. I ain't awful, baby. Awful is me."

Maybe, Stagger Lee thought, *but if awful is me, then what Yakumo is?*

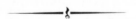

Brendy stood on the roof of One Canal Place, gazing way off into Metry. Rain fell all around her, and wind gusted hard, but Brendy felt the weather as if from far away. She knew with a fuzzy certainty that she was divided, that the Brendy of Dreams stood here in her patent-leather shoes as Real Life Brendy lay sleeping soundly on her parents' living room sofa. If this was a dream, though, it was also *not*. The wet, the wind, the salt smell gusting at her off the Gulf were all as real as real could be. So was the angry purple sky and its cloud-to-cloud lightning that clattered back and forth.

"Okay!" Brendy called into the storm. "Here I'm is! You got sumpthin to say to me, come on wit it!"

Just then, lightning split the air, bathing Brendy's surroundings in stark, false daylight. By the illumination, Brendy saw a white wicker basket like the one Mr. Ghiazi kept by his desk in Brendy's homeroom class. From it rose a flower with a bright yellow face and puffy pink petals. Each of its eyes was a thick black X, and its mouth was a round black circle with two buckteeth right at the top.

At the sight of her old friend, a thrill of recognition lit Brendy from the inside. *"Froggo!"*

Daddy Deke had given Brendy the plush flower for one birthday or another. It hadn't even been her big gift from him—Just a lagniappe meant to sit on the mantel in Brendy's bedroom and make her smile whenever she glanced at it—but in the way of such things, it had captured Brendy's interest immediately, and she had fallen desperately in love with the toy. She'd named it Froggo—or had it named itself? Brendy couldn't remember whether the flower had been capable of speech or if she had simply imagined it so. Some wise, removed part of herself understood that the distinction didn't matter.

Not Froggo, said the flower. *Bilipit.*

"Aw! Billy! Why you look like Froggo? I ain't never seent you before. Can't you look like you?

Must not, said the flower. *Div aspect dire and frighten. Here to protect. Trap.* Trap!

"Protect...? Wait. What's a trap? Me being here?!"

The squeal of metal door hinges sounded several yards to Brendy's left. She turned to see the roof access door swing open, and Gun Man hisself, Stagger Lee, stepped onto the roof, wide-eyed and grinning.

"Wake up," Brendy said, unaware that she spoke aloud. "Wake up *now!*" But nothing happened.

WHAT IT DO, LITTLE BIT? Stagger Lee thundered. MUSTA FORGOT YO BODY AT HOME.

Panic sank like a stone into the pit of Brendy's belly. Brendy knew she should run—but run where? She didn't know how she'd got here in the first place! What could she do? Jump off the roof? She looked this way and that, hoping to catch sight of Billy-as-Froggo, but he was nowhere—Billy shifted, and Brendy realized he was closer than she'd thought. He twined around her left arm like a friendly snake.

I smite, Billy said. His "voice" was low and dangerous.

No, Brendy thought. *Wait*. Then, aloud, "Whatchoo want, Gun Man? If you wanna fight, you finna get one, ya heard?"

AIN'T HERE TO HARM YA, BABYGIRL. JUST THOUGHT YOU MIGHT WANT A VISIT WITH YO GRANDADDY.

"For *real*, for real?" Brendy said. "You take me to Daddy Deke, I won't even hurt you none."

Trap, Billy said. *Smite!*

Oh, I know it is, Brendy thought. *And we gone smite. Just not yet!*

"I know you don't believe me, Gun Man," she said aloud, "but I'm deadass. If you don't mess with me, I won't hurt you, okay? But that's *my* promise, not Perry's. Perry still gone kill you for snatching Daddy Deke and hurting Peaches, all right?"

IS HE, NOW?

"Did I stutter, or did yo mind skip, Mistuh Man?"

COME ON SEE THE OLE MAN, THEN WE SEE WHO DO WHAT TO WHO.

You ready? Brendy thought.

Ready, Billy said.

Then let's do this.

"Awright, then," Brendy said. "Lead the way, Mr. Gangsta-est Gangsta!"

Stagger Lee came forward and held out his big, thick right hand. Brendy gazed at it for a beat, then took it. She glanced up at Stagger Lee's face, and her gaze lingered there. "Oh, wow."

WHAT?

"I didn't know you could look sad."

———❧———

The walk home seemed interminable. By now it was raining so hard that Perry could barely see through it. His visibility was so bad that it was not until he stepped into water up to his waist that he realized how badly the neighborhood had flooded. He trudged, careful not to bring his feet down on anything sharp and to avoid tripping. He wondered whether he was crying and how he would know even if he was. His nose and sinuses were clear, so he supposed it must be rainwater only running down his face. Besides, he felt bad, but he didn't feel weepy. Something had hardened inside him since he awakened to find Peaches gone. It was like a lump of coal or a great diamond. He could have pitched it through a pane of glass and made a satisfying crash.

Mama Lisa was waiting on the front porch when Perry reached the house. She wore one of Perry's mama's sweaters. More than one size too big, it hung on her like an orange sloth on a tree branch, enfolding her neck and chest like furry arms.

They watched each other as Perry's feet found the front walk and carried him out of the grimy waters.

Perry took a deep breath and reached into his pocket for the sack. He didn't pull it out yet—in a quick flash, he remembered the man from the car yard and the look on his face when he had reached for the gun he didn't have and Brendy and Perry had steeled themselves to use their own weapons.

Because that's what Brendy's rock and Perry's Clackin' Sack were: weapons.

He felt the fabric with his fingertips. It comforted him, reminded him that he was not entirely powerless in all this.

"They've got her," he said. "They've got Peaches."

"Yes," Mama Lisa said. "And now we must plan to get her back."

"Tell Brendy it's time to go."

"I will *not*," Mama Lisa said. "I don't lie, and it is not yet time for you to go."

"I can't waste time arguing," Perry said. "I don't have time for you to tell me grown-up stuff that don't make sense. It's up to us. Us kids."

"Come inside. You need to eat, and while you do, I'll do my best to tell you what you need to know."

"Who will decide what that is?" Perry asked. "You?"

"Perry."

"You complicate things on purpose. You know you do. The question is simple, but you'll say something that doesn't make sense, and it's not because you know so much, it's because you *don't*. Peaches was right about you. All of you. You tell lies even when you don't mean to, and there's no such thing as you. No such thing as grown-ups."

Mama Lisa sighed. "Perilous, what Peaches told you about grown-ups is true. But part of being grown up is understanding that a thing can be true and not-true, all at once."

"See?!" Perry said. "Right there! *That doesn't make any sense!* You know what I'm going to ask you, and you're being confusing so you can make up an answer that isn't a lie and isn't the truth, either! I was gonna—! I was going to ask you to tell me what I need to know, but I can't because that's how you do it. That's how Mr. Larry did it. He really *is* Mr. Larry, but he's also Yakumo at the same time. He lies without lying, and he's out to get us."

"Do you think I'm out to get you?"

"No," Perry said. "No, but—but you're not on my side, either, because you don't know about me or what I—what I—! You don't understand what's happening to us."

"I understand what's happening to you, child," Mama Lisa said. "Your power, your…*might* is blooming like a flower. It's stretching up and up like a mighty oak, and the height of its towering dizzies you."

Perry stopped short and ran his grandmother's words back through his mind. Blooming, stretching…She was exactly right, and there was nothing slippery about her description.

"How much will it change me?" Perry asked. "Will I still be me? Am I now? Will there be two of me like Mr. Larry?"

"You're nothing at all like Mr. Hearn," Mama Lisa said. "For starters, you're alive and you're sane."

Perry withdrew his hand from his pocket and crossed to the porch steps. These last few steps seemed longest of all. His throat felt raw, as if he'd screamed himself hoarse. His back ached between his shoulder blades. He felt as if he was still trudging through the floodwaters. As if he always would be. Should he ask his grandmother about the horn? Should he tell her about his... "vision" didn't seem like the right word.

"I'm all wet," he said. "It's bad out here."

"And you need dry clothes, at least, don't you?"

"I touched something. I reached in, and I felt something, and I was someone else. I played music and everyone was sweaty, and the floor was dirt, and they danced."

Mama Lisa's eyes widened. She opened her mouth but said nothing. She closed it again.

"Will you tell me? Tell me what's in the sack that I can use on Yakumo and Stagger Lee."

The shock in her expression softened, but her eyes still looked hollow. The worry in her was plain to see, but Perry wasn't sure what was bothering her so badly. Was it the storm? The threat to the city? The prospect that they were all about to die? Or was it what Perry had just told her? Maybe it was all those things, but Perry wasn't sure what that meant for his present circumstance. She was family, after all. Did that mean she could be trusted?

"Come in and get out of those clothes. Take a shower, and I'll tell you what I can."

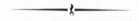

The little girl talked too much. Just talked and talked without waiting for answers, but as long as he ignored half of what she said, Brendy—for that seemed to be her name—didn't even work Stag's nerves.

Leaving Tha Bangin' Gardens took time. Stag had guided the

girl into a stairwell that reached all the way down to the street. He
hoped to spare her the sight of dead bodies, and the fact that to do
so had occurred to him at all bothered him badly.

Stagger Lee tried not to think about what he was doing. He
tried not to think through the implications of his actions. He—

When they reached the seventh floor, Brendy stopped walking.
Stag continued on a few paces before looking back to see what
kept her.

She crossed her arms over her little chest, glowering at him,
obstinate. "I know this a trap," she said. "You think you slick,
Gun Man, but you can't fool me."

I GOT NO USE FOR TRICKERY, Stagger Lee said. His voice sounded
brittle in his own ears. Her accusation had stung him. Was he
going crazy? IF I MEANT YOU HARM, I'D JUST HARM YOU.

"You swear on a stack of Bibles you taking me to by Daddy Deke?"

WE BEEN OVER THIS.

"Yeah," Brendy said. "But I figured you was just lying. I mean
you a criminal and errythang, right?"

Stag creased his neck. AIN'T NO CRIMINAL.

"So you think fightin in the street and breathing fire on folks
something a good, churchgoin' Mistuh Man would do?"

I THINK I WAS A CRIMINAL ONCE. A GANGSTA. BUT NOWDAYS I'M
MORE OF A ELEMENTAL EVIL.

"Hate to break it to ya, baby, but that mouthful o' jewels says
you still gangsta as gangsta get."

With great effort, Stagger Lee spoke like a man. "Listen to me,"
he said. "Listen. Do you know the name Lee Shelton?"

The girl seemed taken aback by...something. The emotion in
his voice? She looked at him sidelong for a beat. "I don't know,"
she said. "Should I?"

"I'm not sure," Stagger Lee said. He hated the sound of his
own voice. He sounded weak and childish, capable of nothing.
He sounded like the kind of sniveling little nobody who could be
done wrong by anyone at all. "I think I had a family. A home," he

said. "We took your granddaddy from y'all, but we was supposed to have turned him loose by now. Keepin' him in the basement going stir-crazy, it ain't...I know what it's like to be imprisoned. I remember, I think."

Brendy's eyes widened. "You remember being inside the Mess Around?"

His nod was slight, not because he felt meek or frightened, but because he was uncertain. He remembered a darkness and a silence, and he remembered being drawn from it from time to time to live again in the throats and instruments—especially the pianos—of sorcerers. But he also remembered something before that. Striped coveralls. Eating gruel in a mess hall. He remembered Billy Lyons begging for his life, and at the time, he'd clenched his teeth and squeezed the trigger.

Brendy crossed the landing to grasp Stag's left pinky in her right hand. The touch caused a spark of static electricity. "Listen," she said. "I know you havin' emotions alla the sudden, and I'm with that, you know? But if you serious about giving Daddy Deke back to me, you best hurry up so I can take him home before the weather get worse."

"You just a little girl," Stagger Lee said. "You tryna disrespect me?"

"That's the thing," Brendy said. "Ain't nobody owe you no respect. And just cuz people afraid of you don't mean they respect you, neither. If we going, let's *go*."

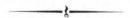

"Where's everybody else?" Perry asked as his mother set plates before him and Mama Lisa.

He sat at the dining room table. Usually he took the middle seat on the kitchen side, but this time Mama Lisa sat at the table's head and Perry sat to her right, in the corner by the horse-collar mirror.

He hadn't realized it till halfway through his shower, but Perry was desperately hungry. Coming down the stairs, he was nearly bowled over by the smell of food. He couldn't remember the last time he'd eaten.

"I thought we were all eating together."

Mama Lisa shook her head. "Just you and me for now. You wanted to talk, and that is what we'll do."

Thunder clattered like bowling balls rolling off a truck. Mama Lisa flinched, blinked her eyes rapidly. With visible effort, she composed herself. "First, we say grace."

"Right," Perry watched Mama Lisa, waiting for her to begin. She just stared back at him until he realized that, for the first time, grace was his job.

"Dear God who divided the darkness and parted the waters of nothing…" Perry began, not sure where he was headed, "we thank—we thank you for this food. Please bless us to use the strength it gives us to…to protect our home from any and all who mean us harm." He paused to consider all the prayers he'd heard before. Thinking of the pressure to open his eyes, look up, fidget, having let his attention lapse. He felt none of that this time. In its place was a stillness, a *listening*, that he'd never felt before. He spoke directly to it. "Great God, we quake with terror as the earth shifts beneath us. We feel the vast, hydrogenous sweep of the cosmos reordering around us, and it is Your joyful and deathless power that we sense and fear. Please, *please*, gift us some of that force so we can accomplish the task you've set before us. Amen."

"Amen," Mama Lisa croaked.

When Perry looked at her, her eyes were wet. She tore a chicken wing in half and took a bite from the drummette. "So," she said.

"How do I fight Mr. Larry?" Perry said. "How do I save Peaches and save the city?"

"I don't know."

Perry's heart sank. "What do you mean you don't know? You said you'd tell me the truth."

"I did, and I am. I don't know how you will save the city and the one you love."

Perry squeezed his eyes shut. He felt as if he'd fly apart, but he found that stillness he'd felt before and grasped it tight. He buttered his waffle, cut into it, took a bite with real maple syrup, and marveled at its malted goodness.

"Okay," he said. "Okay. Then that was the wrong question. How can I make saving Peaches and saving the city the same thing?"

"I don't know that, either."

At first, Perry had hoped the Wise Woman was being slippery, waiting for him to ask the right question, but now he sensed otherwise. "That's the truth?" he asked. "You don't know anything?"

"I know a great deal." Mama Lisa paused to work on her chicken. "I know more than I remember. Your task is almost immeasurably great. The questions you've asked so far are enormous—you've asked more than I'm able to tell. Great questions, however, are usually combinations of many, many smaller questions, and in order to solve them, you must ask a trail of questions that might lead to your answer. This is not a game or a lesson, so start. Smaller."

Perry frowned. He looked at his plate and remembered being small. He remembered his father carefully cutting his smothered chicken thigh from the bone and into small, chewable pieces.

"Okay," Perry said. "Smaller, then. First: Where have you been?"

EXTENDS TO EVERYTHING

Peaches left the rain behind as she stepped into the building. She could still hear the weather marching through the streets like a conquering army. The dead cabbie had said she had no friends here, but he was wrong. Mr. Larry was in here, and he could tell Peaches what she had to do to come out on top against Stagger Lee.

She had walked for blocks and blocks before her surroundings began to seem familiar, and when she reached the Department of Streets, it was shut up tight. At first she despaired, but after a few minutes, she began to walk around the building, looking for a door she could pull open without doing too much damage.

The first couple of times she'd passed this way, Peaches had seen only wooden doors with old-fashioned locks, but this one was metal and heavy—well, what other folks thought of as heavy.

She yanked gently at its handle, and the door stood firm at first. Then, with the sound of popping springs, it came open. She didn't even need to pull it off its hinges.

"Thass right, baby," she said quietly. "I got this. Ain't nobody need to worry none. Peaches on the case."

Inside, she encountered something she'd rarely seen before:

darkness. Peaches's eyes needed *very* little light to see, but the dark in here reminded her of the darkness beneath the boneyard vault.

The thought made her shudder. That dark had been absolute. It had weight and substance. Peaches had rubbed it between her fingers like oil and listened to it squeak...And then? And then nothing. She didn't remember.

But she did. Part of her did.

Peaches had made her way down the steps, walking by feel. She wanted to call out, but the silence cowed her. There was no music beneath the tomb, not even that buzz that only Peaches could hear. That buzz she suspected might be electricity, or magic, or maybe even Life itself.

She wanted to ask her daddy if he was with her, but she didn't dare. It would be wrong to summon him to a place like this. He didn't belong with dead things, because he was alive and well somewhere. He had to be.

Some—

Outside the Department of Streets, lightning crashed.

Peaches shook from the noise. The wind, the storm sound, reminded her of That Night. The smell of smoke as the schooner burned. Of wood Peaches had trusted creaking and splitting.

Peaches had awakened in her little twin bed. It was as if the noise in the heavens had reached down and shaken her with loud hands. Her cabin turned on its side, spilling Peaches from her bed onto the yellow papered wall.

The cabin door fell open, and her daddy ran into the room. He had his do-rag tied around his ginger cornrows, and he hadn't even taken the time to cover his empty eye socket.

"Daddy! What's happening?"

He didn't seem to notice that the cabin had turned on end. The floor had become a wall, but he ran across it anyway and gathered Peaches into his arms. He smelled of sleep-sweat, but also piney and sweet. He smelled like home. As he carried Peaches out of the cabin and up to the foredeck, she knew everything would be all right.

"This ain't no regular storm, swee'pea," he said. "That damb lightning already struck us twice, and we had a deal, me and that lightning."

"Daddy, there's fire!"

"I know it," he said. "These damb elements won't do right." He set Peaches carefully on the listing deck, then tilted her a little to change her balance. "Baby, you got ta go. I'll catch ya up later."

"What? Go where?"

"I'ma— Whoever sent this storm, I know you can hear me right now! Best believe there gone be *consequences and repercussions*! For every onea my crew get kilt, I'ma kill ya twice, ya heard me?"

Peaches glowered and stuck out her chest. "We'll get 'em together, Daddy!" she crowed. "We gone hit 'em fa real!"

"Chin! Highball!" he bellowed. "Furl them damb sails, damb it! We cain't have this damb wind just a-blowin' us all around—!"

He stopped short and turned to put his hands on Peaches's shoulders. "Listen here, swee'pea. *Listen.* You got a mouth on ya, and you got the strength to back it up. Daddy need you ta find somewhere safe, or find somewhere dicey and *make* it safe, and I be along directly, ya heard?"

"What?"

"Thangs getting rough out here on these Seven Seas—the kinda rough I don't want you messin' with till you a little older. This ship goin' down, and I be gott-dambed if you goin' down with it!"

Panic lit up her little body from the inside, like a jack-o'-lantern. "But Daddy—!"

He took Peaches in his arms and held her close. Her heart fluttered in her chest while his beat steady and slow. Peaches found his rhythm, and their hearts beat together once, twice, three times.

Then he pitched her into the air.

Peaches shrieked as she watched her daddy and his ship fall away below her. She wailed, then sputtered as she passed through a cloud bank. The moisture plastered her dress against her body, but it didn't slow her progress. She kept going and going. Before she hit the top of her arc, she had time to see the sleeping face of the silent yellow moon and hear the sound of church bells tolling, tolling as the world she knew gave way to some other.

Peaches's daddy had thrown her so hard and so high that if she wished, Peaches could have kept right on going. She closed her eyes and considered letting herself drift past the sky into space, into whatever came after space.

When she opened her eyes again and looked down, the storm and its clouds had gone, or she had gone so far from them that they were nowhere in sight. She shut her eyes again and willed the weightless flying feeling away, and began to drop toward the moonlit ocean.

It took a long time, but eventually she hit the water with an almighty *slap*, then sank down and down, past fish, past mermaids, into the darkest dark, so dark that it was not dark at all, because dark was something and this was nothing.

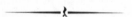

She awakened much later, floating on her back. No human sound came near her, just the roar of the sea, the cries of seabirds, and the workings of her own body.

She was numb. An emptiness had settled in her belly, but she wasn't hungry. All she was was alone.

After a long time—days, maybe—Peaches turned onto her belly and began to swim.

Mama Lisa took her glasses off and set them on the table. She rubbed the bridge of her nose for a beat, then took a sip of her orange juice. This was the moment she had dreaded since her return. Since before her return. To put the quality of her absence into words was not easy, but that wasn't what bothered her. The most troubling aspect of all this was that she knew what her grandson wanted to ask, and she feared the answer would place him beyond her help.

Certainly, she could explain to him what she remembered of her disappearance, and her fragmented understanding of what had become of her afterwards, but the explanation would be worse than useless.

Her own grandmother, Mother Maudell, had appeared to her during her morning run. Lisa stopped short, stunned, as the woman's body broke the summer air. No longer wasted by cancer, the woman stood inches above the sidewalk on Paris Avenue, wrapped in a swirl of chanting female voices. Without a word, she had taken Lisa by the wrist and stepped away with her into a fast-flowing river of time and imagery.

Mama Lisa shook her head, banishing the confusion of memories. Visions of Stagger Lee shooting Lheresday in the belly, of a jazz orchestra playing to beat the noise of a cataclysmic storm, of a thickset, dark-skinned trumpeter angrily turning his back to her—to the city itself?—as he played louder and louder until the music was more than music, and the notes blurred together the way wavelengths of light combine to create a pure-white glare...

"I'm not sure where I was," she said. "Everywhere. Nowhere. But that's not what you want to know, either, Perry. Do you know what I am?"

"A teacher?"

"Yes. A teacher. I consider it my highest duty to impart knowledge to those in need. The young, the old, whoever. But I am also a mother, a grandmother, and I love my family dearly. The answer to your real question is a hard one, but to refuse you an answer would go against— It would be against everything I believe."

"So tell me."

"You want to know whether there is a weapon or an artifact inside the Clackin' Sack that will allow you to defeat your enemies and save Peaches."

"Is there?"

Mama Lisa shut her eyes. A lump had formed in her throat. It didn't budge when she paused to clear it, so she resolved to speak past it. "There is such a weapon, but it's not for you or me to use."

Numerous expressions danced across Perry's nut-brown face. "...What?"

"It's too powerful. It would annihilate you, Peaches, the city, everything. If you had *decades* of training, the danger would still be too great! If I ..." Mama Lisa trailed off. She realized now that she had begun to cry and that her tears colluded with the lump in her throat to distort her words. She fought to make herself understood. "I know you won't understand. I know you think we adults lie or obscure the truth to suit our ends—and—and sometimes we do. But, Perry, if I told you what that instrument was and how to obtain it, it would be as if I killed you myself."

Perry was silent for a long time, but he didn't resume eating. He frowned and looked at his hands, and Mama Lisa knew he was ordering his words. How like his grandfather and his great-grandfather he looked then.

"Mama Lisa," he said, and his voice didn't waver at all. "I've been through so much. We have all been through so much. If there's even the smallest chance I can succeed, I have to try."

"Peaches is strong," Mama Lisa said. "She's a hero."

Perry's voice rose now, but it was still measured. "She *is* strong," he said. "She *is* a hero, but sometimes even heroes need saving. I'm her best friend. She needs me. She's earned our help over and over. Mine. Yours. Brendy's. Everyone."

"Perilous."

"Don't you understand, Mama Lisa? You are the answer to my prayer. God has sent you to help me help Peaches."

"Perry—!"

"*Listen* to me," Perry hissed. "Listen. If you refuse, it's not just me you're telling no. I know you're afraid. So am I. *That's because we've been paying attention.* Do you remember the story of Jonah and the Whale?"

"Of course I remember!" Mama Lisa snapped. "That has—!"

"Look inside yourself," Perry said. "*Look*. Are you resisting because you know it's right? Do you fear for me because you know I can't handle the responsibility? Or are you just...scared?"

Mama Lisa looked her grandson in the eye and realized he had asked her yet another question to which she did not know the answer.

Casey Bridgewater awakened with a start. Even before he fell asleep, a fierce wind had begun to blow through the city. It made him imagine giant children on roller skates gliding through the streets, reaching out to rattle walls and windows. Every once in a while, the wind howled as well, like an idiot swamp-haint declaring its territory. The sound that awakened him was different. It was a voice.

It's time, the compass said again. *We must retrieve it.*

The little girl, Brendy, lay sleeping on the loveseat across from the sofa where Casey slouched. She lay with her head thrown back and her mouth wide open as if to loose a howl of her own. Casey couldn't help but smile to look at her. Better not to make too much noise.

Instead, Casey reached into his pocket and closed his hand around the compass. "All right," he said. "Take me, then."

Suddenly, he stood in water up to his waist. He took a step and slipped on what felt like a slick of underwater mud. He fell backwards, sputtering, trying to keep the floodwaters from invading his mouth.

In the car, said the compass. *Glove box.*

The dirty orange street light was just enough illumination for Casey to make out the shape of a car sitting in what must be the flooded driveway. He swam for it.

He felt blindly for the door handle until his hand closed around it. He pressed the plunger and pulled. He slipped off his feet again, went down. He sputtered and coughed as he took an accidental breath of water. This wasn't working.

Casey shook his head and grasped the door handle with his right hand. Now he paused. A stray quote from the *Hagakure* surfaced indistinctly in his mind. Something about how when sudden showers blow up, people run, take cover, trying to avoid getting wet, got wet anyhow. But if one were to resolve from the beginning to just be soaked, perplexity would evaporate...And the rest of the quote—the important part—resolved clearly in Casey's memory: *And this understanding extends to everything.*

Sputtering and struggling in floodwaters, trying to keep from losing his footing or swallowing water, Casey was filling his mind with noise. If he could resolve to just be in the storm, to accept the weight of his sodden clothes, the rainwater running into his eyes, the mud and slick, the darkness of the night, lit intermittently by bomb-flashes in the heavens, then...He took a settling breath. He braced his left foot against the car's frame and just pulled, thinking of nothing else.

The water had risen. It pressed heavily against the car's door, trying to keep it closed. Still, in his single-minded focus, Casey felt the metal budge. He pulled, straining, and the door began to open. He groaned low in his throat, and the round sound roughened into a scream of triumph as he dragged the car door open. He snatched the glove box open, felt inside.

His hands fell on a velvet drawstring bag much like the one Roux had given him. Casey had no idea what was inside, but it must be important.

"All right," he told the compass. "I've got it."

He fizzed away again.

"Good Lord."

For a split second, Casey thought he'd been dreaming. Then he realized that he was soaked to the skin, sprawled on the couch. Across from him, the little girl lay snoring having moved not at all. The girl's mother stood in the living room doorway. She still wore her apron, and the smell of frying chicken followed her into the room. Casey's mouth watered.

"No wonder you threw in with us," the woman said. "You disappear and reappear like my kids do."

"Oh, Lord," he said. "I'm sorry. I didn't mean to wet up your— Is that chicken and waffles I smell?"

"Sure is," said the woman. She smiled as if to let Casey know that wetting up the couch was the least of her concerns.

She sat down next to her daughter, stroked her hair lightly. "Brendy's a *real* heavy sleeper," she said. "Always has been. The only way to get her up is for me to call her, then turn on the overhead light and call her again, louder."

Casey glanced at the contents of his right hand. Gingerly, he pulled the bag open enough to see inside. It looked like the mouthpiece to a horn.

"Only mama," he said absently. How could this thing help?

"Brendolyn," the woman said, her voice hard with command.

The Trouble Compass buzzed again in Casey's pocket. He ignored it for the moment.

The girl's mother frowned. The overhead light was already on. The girl just as sweet as before, but something was missing.

"Everything all right?" Casey asked.

"No," the woman said. "No, I don't think it is."

Someone had knocked down a wall between two of the bedrooms to create a large, high-ceilinged chamber cluttered with nonsense items—car tires, fast food wrappers from chains Casey didn't recognize, broken ink pens, and a lot of coins and what must be insulation or bright orange cotton batting. Jaylon levitated above the room's center wearing tattered jeans and no shoes. His hair and beard had grown out, making him look like an escaped slave hiding out in the bush. At first, the way his limbs moved made Casey think his cousin was dancing. He wasn't wrong, he guessed, but that wasn't all Jayl was doing.

He gestured as if sawing or shaping the air, working it and

folding it. As he did, Casey began to see the changes he was making. He made brushing motions with his left hand and pulling
motions with the fingers of his right, massaging and massaging
as a tag began to take shape in the air. In his mind's eye—or in
the vision given him—Casey saw Jayl in his Saint Claude studio.
He saw Jaylon drop a can of paint as he stared at the blank canvas
before him and begin making motions like these.

It was as if he uncovered and created the tag at the same time,
but to do so, he manipulated sound, light, and air, stretching and
coaxing them into a desired shape. Casey knew he should do
something, should say something, but he couldn't interrupt. Eventually, he saw that this was a longer tag reading YIK PRAMMA IKLSS.

While Jaylon worked on it, it began to fizz at the edges, sub-
liming like dry ice. Jayl leaned back at the waist, curling his palms
toward his chest as the letters trembled under his enchantment,
then drew his wrists together and formed his hands into a hinged
pair of claws. He thrust them out before him in a "Hadouken"
motion. A tangled bouquet of notes sounded in the room, and
somehow Casey knew that this was *also* the tag. The sound receded
abruptly to the edge of Casey's hearing as the tag winked out of
sight.

"Jayl!" Casey called. "Jaylon!"

Jayl didn't respond. Instead, he began dancing a new tag, summoning it from the fabric of the Hidden City.

"Jaylon, it's me!"

Very carefully, Casey stepped closer. His vision of the room
distorted and bowed, rippling out of shape. Much more disori-
enting was what the energy did to Casey's thoughts. When he'd
dropped acid back at Smith, the most surprising part of it, for him,
had been the conceptual hallucinations—perceiving spacetime as a
viscous substance lying everywhere in puddles and drifts—seeing
alien script threaded into the bark of trees, the bent blades of grass,
unreadable and secret. At the time, Casey feared that if he managed to read any of the messages, he could never return to Earth.

Earth.

The word echoed in Casey's mind. He felt himself moving down a strange corridor, forward and back, at the same time. He began to hear a chorus of distant voices. "Jayl—!" he barked—or thought he did. He felt hands on his shoulders. He felt his own hands on Jaylon's bare shoulders. He felt a sweetness, a hidden union, and felt all of it tremble and flicker, as if ready to wash away.

Casey's vision skipped, and he was half crouching, half kneeling on the cluttered floor. He and Jaylon were both inside a halo almost too bright to bear. A Door stood open behind Casey and to his left. He must have drawn it to take them back to New Orleans. He had thrust his pencil into the floor to anchor him against the pull of an unseen force that held Jaylon, fought to keep him here.

Jaylon's face was expressionless. His eyes were open, but he seemed blind. Whatever they saw was not Casey or the house around them, or the city of Nola, but the alien landscape that Casey had only barely pulled himself away from moments ago.

"Please!" Casey screamed. "*Please!* Come back with me! I need you! I can't do this by myself! Everything's wrong! Everything's wrong without you!"

Jaylon didn't respond. He gave no sign that he'd heard at all.

A burning roughness rested in Casey's throat. He felt as if he'd been crying and puking for hours. So many of his favorite memories included Jaylon. He felt as if it was with Jaylon that he'd become himself.

He realized dimly that he was shouting—"switched beds in Mamaw's third-floor room because H. T. wouldn't move, and yours was under the vent! You kept getting too cold, and even under all them blankets, your teeth would chatter!"

He remembered Jaylon's face, his glow as he recounted meeting President Obama at Willie Mae's.

"You used to copy *Garfield* strips, and you had all the *Calvin and Hobbes* books!"

He remembered Jaylon's red eyes and wet face the night they'd come back from visiting family in Baton Rouge to find Jaylon's pet rabbit, Scrimshaw, dead in his cage.

"You always knew all the names of all the African presidents. *Please!* Please come!"

He remembered Jaylon and H. T. teaching him how to throw a punch. Jaylon lightly grasping his wrist, pulling it gently toward his own chest. *Don't punch at a nigga. Punch through his ass.*

Jaylon made no response.

"I'm sorry! I know you thought I'd go back with you when the city opened up again! I stayed in Baltimore because I knew! I knew something about me was...The—the—the— My *body* didn't fit me! I'm sorry I left you, I swear if you come with me I'll never leave you again, just— Please! *Damn it, Jaylon!*"

Casey saw himself sitting aboard a jet at Dulles Airport, waiting in line to take off on his first-ever international flight. H. T. sat beside him, poking blunt fingers into his side and telling idiot jokes to distract him.

He saw the arcade at the Esplanade in Kenner, himself, Jaylon, and H. T. sitting in the massage chairs at Spencer's Gifts, pretending they were under attack aboard a spaceship. A long, thin scream drifted to him from far away.

The noise snapped him back to the present. His hand was still outstretched, but now so was Jaylon's. A tag hung half-finished in the air, and now Jaylon's eyes were trained on Casey as if he could see again. "Whaaaaaaat's haaaaaaapppening to meeeeee!" he called.

"I don't know!" Casey shouted back. "It's magic! You're doing magic!"

"IIIIIIII'm glooooooowiiiiiing!"

"Yes!" Casey called. "But this world is ending! You gotta come with me!"

"IIIIIIIIIIIII got wooooooooorrrrk!"

"You can work there! *Please!*"

Jaylon's eyes rolled back in his head, and his chin drifted up toward the ceiling. *He is my champion. His power will protect me.*

Casey's voice died midshout. "Is that—? Who's there?"

He is my champion.

The voice he was hearing was not a voice at all. It was Casey's mind translating a wave of communication to him. This was the city making herself understood as best she could. He remembered explaining to Ximena that he felt like New Orleans had cast him out.

It didn't cast you out, Ximena had said. *It's a city. It's not alive. It doesn't love anyone or hate. It doesn't* want.

This was true, but it was also . . . not. Casey felt as if by going to Smith instead of resuming his studies at UNO, he had abandoned New Orleans, abandoned Jaylon. It wasn't that leaving had been wrong, it was that he'd made the decision out of fear. Fear of what was happening to their art. Fear that the city would never again be what it was. That the storm had taken its spirit, leaving behind an aching septic wound.

Nola was not New Orleans, but the same spirit animated it, allowed it to communicate.

"Let Jaylon go," Casey said. "I'll fight in his place. I'll fight with everything I've got."

The Hidden City examined him, considered his offer.

The city didn't respond.

Instead, Jaylon shook his head, as if waking the rest of the way up. He blinked. "Casey?" he said calmly. "You came for me?"

"Of course. Of course I did."

Jaylon glanced over his shoulder as if he'd heard someone else speak. "I will!" he said.

"What?"

"Trismegistus," Jaylon said. "Thrice great."

"It's the name the city gave me," Casey said. His face was numb now. He barely felt his own tears. A sense of deep loss, of futility, cut a deep gash in his spirit, and he wasn't sure why.

"That's dope as fuck!" Jaylon said. He'd never sounded more like himself. "I'ma link up with you later. Don't die."

"No. No. Jay—"

"Nigga, we magic! We everything! Make anything! And—" His voice threatened to break now. "Don't get killed," he said. "If I have to cross the Gulf to find you, I will."

"Jaylon."

"I seen so much. It's the bells, Case. It's hard to— There's a Higher Planet," Jaylon said. "Bells herald you across and you come bursting like a quasar beam. Jewels everywhere. Singing sand. You'll see. It's everywhere."

"I don't understand."

"I'll see you. I'll see you from There."

Now Casey could hear the Storm. Howling, rushing, clattering over the city. Faintly, from far off, he felt wind and wet. "Nuh—"

"Later on, bruh," Jaylon said. "I can't wait to show you."

Jaylon ducked through the open doorway just as the Storm peeled off the roof. Casey let the portal wink shut and lifted his face to the flashing heavens. The rain still wasn't touching him. Not because it didn't want to—because it *couldn't*. Casey laughed.

He shut his eyes and felt inside himself for the part of him that was Bee Sharp. His gut trembled as gravity dropped away from him. He fell headfirst into the sky.

XXIX

GOTCHA WHERE I WANTCHA

Mama Lisa shook her head, then shook it again, but Perry could tell these were not gestures of refusal. His words had moved her—well, of course they had, they'd moved Perry, too. His question had come from a place so deep inside him that he was amazed he'd found the words to clothe it.

The woman opened her mouth to speak, but before she could say anything, a wail split the air of the house, sounding even above the wind and rain battering from without. The sound froze Perry in his seat.

"Mama Lisa, come quick!" This time, it was Mr. Casey raising the alarm.

A deadly calm had settled over Perry. His scalp tingled from it.

Mama Lisa rose so quickly from the table that the motion bowled her chair onto the carpet.

Perry didn't remember getting up. He didn't remember rushing into the living room, but he was there in time to see Mama Lisa arrive. He heard his father charging heavily down the stairs.

Perry's mother held Brendy like a baby, shaking her gently at first, then rougher. "You hear me, baby?" she said. "Mama calling. Wake up, now. *Wake up!*"

Perry's father let out a wordless shout as the power went out.

"What has happened?" Mama Lisa asked.

"She won't wake up," Mr. Casey said. His voice cut through the gloom from somewhere to Perry's left. "She just— I don't know. She's not dead, but Trouble Compass says she's not here."

"*E-nough!*" Mama Lisa bellowed, and light bloomed back into the room.

At first Perry thought the power had cut back on, but it hadn't. The light issued from a halo surrounding his grandmother.

"What effrontery!" she barked. "What *gall*! You dare enter this blessed place to bedevil my family?"

"Who you talking to?" Perry's father asked. He looked at Perry. "Who she talking to?"

Perry shook his head. "Grandma. Mama Lisa. No one came in. Brendy left. She left without me."

The adults all turned to stare at him.

"It's true," he said. "Check her hands and pockets. I bet you her rock is gone."

Perry's mother reached down to feel Brendy's right hand, then shifted her grip on the girl to check the other, then went into Brendy's dress pockets. "Empty," she croaked. "Nothing."

"She'd never leave it behind," Perry said. "She's gone after Peaches or Daddy Deke, or both."

"Why would she do that?" Mama Lisa's voice was close to breaking. "Why would she be so foolish?"

"She's not foolish," Perry said calmly. "She's a soldier and this is war."

"Soldier or not, we gotta get her back," Mr. Casey said. "Trouble Compass will take us to her."

"We can't follow with our bodies." Perry locked eyes with Mama Lisa. "This is a spirit war. Bodies will only slow us down. I need the weapon."

"The fact that you think of it that way..." Mama Lisa began.

Perry just watched her.

"It's...it's called the Elysian Trumpet. Buddy Bolden built it when he first began to suspect he was going mad. No madman should ever wield power like his, so he placed most of his magic in the trumpet and hid it at the Colored Waifs Home in City Park where Louis found it. He gave part of it to your grandfather instead of turning it over to the Powers."

A wave of weightless relief almost made Perry's knees give way. "Thank you," he said.

"Its power is immense, and it could only have grown by now. To blow one note on it, let alone a scale...to make music on it would be impossible."

"It contacted me," Perry said.

"What?"

"On the way from Peaches's house. It touched me when I reached into the sack. I think it wants to help."

"Help who?" Perry's father asked.

"What do you mean?" Perry asked.

"Does it want to help us or the Storm?"

"We fight for the city," Perry said. "It knows who I am."

"It might do, little man," Mr. Casey said, "but this fight has gotten outta hand. Sometimes when two sides fighting over something, there's only one thing to do..." He trailed off.

"Take it from both," Perry's mother said. " 'If y'all can't act right, *nobody* gets it.' You think that's what the horn thinks?"

Perry didn't like the sound of that, but he had to admit the possibility to himself. Still, there was no way he could let his baby sister charge into battle without him.

"It has another name," Mama Lisa said, and her voice was full of menace. "The Horn of Unmaking."

Perry swallowed. Now was the time for action, not thought. With great effort, he stilled his mind. Quietly, he slid the Clackin' Sack from his jeans pocket. *"Perilous Antoine Graves..."* he whispered.

"How can we know?" Perry's father asked.

"...*Clickety-clack*..." Perry hoped speaking at full volume wouldn't interrupt the incantation, but somehow he felt it would work just fine. "Only one way to find out," he said. "I'm gone ask it... *Get into my sack!*"

The living room disappeared, and the adults with it.

"Who car this is, anyway?" Brendy asked.

Don't know, Stagger Lee said. Don't matter nohow.

"It matter if we stealing it," she said. "Stealing is stealing."

The car was a beat-up gold Chevy. Its tires were slightly flat, and its paint job had rubbed raw in places, like patches of mange on a dog. A faded American flag decal was stuck to the left rear window. It too was peeling, its colors leached by time and sunlight until it seemed more sarcastic than patriotic. The backseat was littered with odds and ends of a forgotten life—trinkets from fast food meals, sheaves of paper, and a tattered graduation robe from NOLA U.

Stag and Brendy had left the black stairwell and found the old car parked neatly in front of the building, beaten by rain, floodwater up to its undercarriage.

Ain't stealing nothing, Stag said. All I need a radio or some music.

The Chevy's interior smelled like a gym shoe. The khaki-colored upholstery must have gotten wet and molded over long ago. Stag wondered whether the car would run if he needed it to.

But they didn't need it to.

Git on in, he said. We gone be where we be directly.

"By Daddy Deke?"

Thass right.

"But don't you be double-crossin' me now, Gun Man," Brendy said. "I know I'm little, but I can fight. I won't be locked up."

Ya ain't gotta woof at me, Stag said. Git on in.

The little girl sniffed, nose in the air, but did as he directed.

Watching her, the gangster had to suppress a smile, and the feeling of it was as strange and painful as a snootful of bees.

Stagger Lee went around and got in the driver's seat. He glared at the radio with its broken knobs and WWOZ flared to life.

"Y'all," the DJ said. "*Y'all*. It's bad out there. Wind and rain, and weird-ass lights in the sky? People, Animals, sky trolleys up and disappeared, and now the power out all over town? Turmoil and trouble, baby. But here's some good old barrelhouse piano if ya can hear me a tall. Champion Jack Dupree. Stay inside. Stay safe. One way or another, all this be over soon…"

The music began with an eddy of keystrokes, and that was all Stagger Lee needed.

He took the little girl's ghostly hand, and straightaway, they'd left the Chevy behind to materialize inside a Packard not far from the Department of Streets.

Now that they were close, Stagger Lee wasn't sure of his next move. He could have taken them straight to the ballroom, but there was no telling where Yakumo was, and Stag didn't want to force a confrontation before he could reunite the girl with her granddaddy.

If he was done murdering songs—and that did seem to be the case—and he had defied Yakumo's direct order to kill this little girl and her friends, what was he after? What did he want? Well, he didn't want to go back inside that damb piano. It was worse than prison.

Stagger Lee remembered lying on a cot, then maybe a hospital bed, his strength stolen, his vision dimming.

None of that would matter if Yakumo enacted his plan to destroy Nola and set them both free. Freedom appealed to Stag, he supposed, but the prospect didn't thrill him like the pursuit of prey, or the snuffing of life. Yes, this would be an opportunity to snuff many, many lives, all at once, but perhaps it was the fact that the deaths would be incidental—a side effect of the city's destruction—that made killing on such a scale disinterest him.

No, what drove Stagger Lee was the sense that somewhere, in some other, forgotten time, he had been monstrously wronged, and that everyone and everything must pay for that injustice. If everyone were to die, who would answer for that crime? Besides, these memories that kept bubbling into his mind made Stagger Lee suspect there was something, some piece of information, that Yakumo had withheld from him.

Yakumo had hinted that the old man, Daddy Deke, possessed some special knowledge, some key to their freedom...So, what if giving the old man something he wanted could convince him to tell Stagger Lee and not Yakumo?

Stag was no expert in bargaining or interrogation, but without recognizing the feeling, he had begun to feel desperate. He might as well give this idea a shot. Besides: if his gambit failed, there was always the option of murdering everyone he could find until his mood improved.

Stag got out the car to retrieve Brendy—the Little Girl, he corrected himself. He might not be looking to kill her just now, but thinking of her by her right name seemed dangerously soft. Her identity mattered only relative to Stag's own, and that was as it should be.

He lifted her onto the driest part of the sidewalk and watched for a beat as muddy water ran through her ghostly patent-leather shoes.

Come on, he said. He thisaway.

"Hey, Mistuh Man," the girl said. "You wanna hear a funny joke?"

Naw.

"Well, I'ma tell you anyways cuz I don't like this wind and rain. I was only axin' you to be polite. *So.*" She took a breath. "One time, there was this girl named Brendy, but she wasn't me, and she lived in a house like my house, but she *still* wasn't me, and her friend Moriah said to her one day, 'You know what? There's a hainted house on our block with a haint in it, and you know how I know?'"

How you know?

"Not me. *Moriah*."

HOW MORIAH KNOW?

"Moriah said, 'I was walkin by at midnight last night, and I heard a terrible voice say, I GOTCHA WHERE I WANTS YA, AND NOW I'M GONNA EATS YA! And I ran all the way home!' And *I* said—"

I THOUGHT BRENDY WA'ANT YOU.

"She ain't. Don't interrupt. So *Brendy* said, 'Girl, you don't know nothin' bout haints. I bet that wa'ant no haint anyhow,' and Moriah said, 'Yuh-HUHH!' So I waited till midnight, and I went out to see, and right when I got to the house, something said, I GOTCHA WHERE I WANTCHYA, AND NOW I'M GONNA EATCHA!' And I was like, 'Whaaaaaaaat?!'

"So I went in the house. (The porch was all nasty and rotten.)

"And I went up the stairs. (The stairs was all dusty, and I was coughing.)

"And right at the top of the stairs, there was a creaky ole door fulla spiders, and riiiiiiiight before I touched it, I heard it again! (I GOT YA WHERE I WANT YA, AND NOW I'M GONNA EATCHYAAAAAAAAAH!)"

Brendy's voice dropped to a whisper. "...And I opened the door reeeeeeeeeal slow. And you know what I seen?"

"What?" Stagger Lee asked. "What you seen?"

Brendy stood on her tiptoes for the punchline. "It was a monkey talkin' to a bananaaaaaaaaaah!"

Stagger Lee's laugh was as loud, as flat, as profane as a gunshot.

"Girl, you too much," he said aloud. He paused for a beat as Brendy beamed up at him, then lifted his prized purple Stetson from his head and put it on hers.

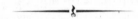

This time, there was no darkness or falling. Instead, Perry found himself standing on a city street in broad daylight. It was hotter than hot out and humid besides—the kind of day that made thermometers scream. He wished he'd worn shorts instead of jeans, but he'd had no idea he'd wind up leaving home this way.

A quick glance around told Perry that he stood outside the McDonald's on Saint Bernard Avenue.

A mechanical hiss caught Perry's attention. He looked up in search of a sky trolley, but there was none. Instead, a big purple-and-white bus with tinted windows squatted at the corner by the traffic signal to disgorge a stream of passengers. Perry had read about city buses, but he'd never seen one. So *big*.

He didn't have time to tease out the riddle of this bizarre not-Nola. He was here on pressing business. He squared his shoulders, then pushed his way into the restaurant.

A roar of conversation greeted him. Old folks, men and women, Black, Hispanic, Asian, white—but mostly Black—filled every table. They sipped coffee or cold drinks, read the newspaper, played dominoes, bid whist, and spades, all of them wrapped in that McDonald's not-quite-food smell of hot grease and almost-meat.

The fact that everyone seemed in good spirits, that nobody was arguing or cussing anyone out, made Perry want to stand right where he was and just let the scene wash over him.

He scanned the room, wondering as he did whether anyone would push inside behind him, grumble at him to make way. Then he saw it. One empty chair opposite a booth where Jailbird Stomp played checkers with a white-haired old man Perry didn't recognize.

Perry made his way across the restaurant's linoleum floor and sat down opposite the song.

"Look who it is," Jailbird said with a grin. His gold teeth glinted in the light, and his suit still looked slept-in. His squashed-up hat had slid back on his head, revealing his wooly, salt-and-pepper 'fro. "Savin' Man hisself. Answer to mah prayers. Y'all don't even know. I said, 'Save me, Jesus, hide me, Lawd, O God,' and Youngin here stepped right up and spirited me away!"

It took Perry a second to realize Jailbird wasn't mocking or complaining. Still, Perry didn't think it wise for anyone to know who he was or what he could do. He squinted a little, shook his head slightly, and Jailbird clammed right up.

"I'm just here to talk to somebody," Perry said.

"Somebody who?" Jailbird's friend asked.

"I think he's an instrument," Perry said. "A horn."

"Baby, we *all* instruments," Jailbird's friend said with an exaggerated wink.

"Well, not *all* all," Jailbird said under his breath.

"Hey, now!" someone shouted elsewhere in the dining room. "Sing!"

Perry turned in his seat to see a sixtyish man in blue velour track pants and a white tank top standing in the center of the room. He was bald, and he wore a constellation of jewelry on his hands and around his neck.

"Whatchall wanna hear today?" asked the man. "Y'all wanna hear some rock'n'roll? Some Johnnie Taylor?"

"NO!" the crowd answered in unison.

"Y'all wanna hear some blues? Some Muddy Waters?"

"NO!"

"Y'all wanna hear some Juvenile? Some 'Back That Thang Up?'"

"NO!"

"Well, thass all right then, baby. Cuz you know, I can't sang just anything, ya heard me? You know, I can't do the thangs I used to done, ya feel me?"

"Yeah!" someone shouted.

"*Praise* Him!"

"*Hallelujah!*"

"I just can't sang like I usedta done since Go-o-o-o-o-od done brought me through, now!" He was already half singing. "Because you *know* I been changed!"

The crowd erupted. A tingle stole through Perry's body. He almost knew what was coming next. Almost, but not quite.

The old man crossed his wrists behind his back and pushed out his chest as he began the song.

Oh, I know I been changed
I-III know I been changed
I-III know I been changed
'Cause the angels in heaven done signed my name
Well, the angels in heaven done signed my name!

The old man's voice was rough, but its power wasn't entirely raw. It sounded weary but bright, full of longing and compassion. Perry remembered the feel of his hand in Daddy Deke's as they walked in City Park. He remembered kissing Brendy's skinned knee, telling her she'd got the run, and in kickball, that was all that mattered. He fought back tears for as long as he could—three seconds, maybe four. He remembered his father telling him, *It's not true that men don't cry. To cry isn't weak. Gangsters and hoods don't cry because they're not strong enough to remember how.*

Perry remembered the last day of school. When he looked back, he barely recognized himself, arguing with Mickey Ledoux, watching *The Phantom Tollbooth* for the umpteenth time . . . He thought of the *Family Circus* cartoons in the *Times-Picayune*. How they'd chart Jeffy's progress through his neighborhood with tracks of black footprints. Perry had left his former self so far behind that he imagined maps of his earlier days marked up the same way. Every photo of him ever taken was of someone who had ceased to be.

And I'm gone now, he thought. *I'm not even in the world. And it's fine. This is what I do.*

Two horses standing side by side
When death rides down and cracks the sky
I been changed I been changed I know I been changed!

Perry slid from his seat to stand on the tile floor, legs planted like a gunslinger, as the old man wailed the last note. He'd been terrified of the sack when he first received it, and on some level, he was terrified still. The fear in him was no longer a hindrance, it was an

408 • ALEX JENNINGS

understanding of power. A respect for the responsibility it entailed. Was it the sack that had changed him, or had Perry changed in order to use it? He had ventured inside it willingly this time. His quest was desperate, but it was *his* quest. He'd formed the plan himself and acted.

The crowd whooped and hollered, filling the restaurant with their approval. Perry couldn't remember whether he'd already wiped the tears from his face. He didn't care. He waited for the crowd to settle down.

"Mr. Horn!" he called.

"Who askin'?" the old man said.

"My name is Perilous Antoine Graves. Do you know who I am and what I'm about?"

The old man looked Perry up and down. He smiled a little, nodded. "I believe I do. You think you got what it takes?"

"I have no idea," Perry said. The steel had gone out of his voice, but bluffing didn't seem the thing to do. "If it can be done, I'll do it."

"There anything you want to ask me before we go?"

"Uh, I don't know," Perry said. "I don't even know what I don't know. How...? How do I make music?"

"That's the easy part," Mr. Horn said. "You don't *make* music, you ax it to come on through. And don't try to out-blow your bandmates, ya dig? You give them a little something, they give you a little something, and together, y'all make something new."

"I think...I think I know what you mean."

Perry looked around the room. Everyone seemed to hang on his words, waiting for what he'd say next. They seemed just as rapt now as they'd been for Mr. Horn's song. Perry thought he should say something to them.

"This place is wonderful," he said. "You're wonderful. I love you, but we got work."

The crowd cheered.

"Perilous Graves, Elysian Trumpet... *Clickety-clack, get outta my sack!*"

Peaches sipped short breaths as she moved through the darkness. At the bottom of the stairwell, she made it out—or did the darkness withdraw, leaving her alone? Without realizing it, she took a deeper, settling breath and took in her surroundings. This didn't look like the Department of Streets at all, but buildings worked differently on the Dead Side of Town, so maybe wherever she was now was connected to her destination.

The concrete floor was water-spotted from floods, and the bare cinder block walls made her think of some sort of Haint School. She was fine with haints, for the most part, but Peaches *hated* school. She wrinkled her nose, not just at the idea of sitting still while some grown-up tried to tell her and a bunch of other kids what to do and what to think, but from the *smell*. It smelled wet and swampy, but also like mothballs and the skeletons of small, dead animals.

Peaches cocked her head to the left as if listening for something, but she was smelling instead. Was that...? It was. Daddy Deke's cologne. Just the barest hint of it, as if it had fallen off his body somehow. Head still cocked, Peaches stole carefully down the hall. She didn't smell anybody else, but haints and criminals didn't always smell the way she expected them to, so it was better safe than sorry.

At the next corner of the corridor, Peaches stopped and balled her fists, not even breathing. Something about this didn't seem right. Would whoever had taken Daddy Deke let Peaches just waltz in and collect him back, like picking him off a shelf at Family Dollar? Why wasn't he hidden? Why wasn't he under guard?

The old man's scent was stronger now, and there was a little more of Daddy Deke in it. There were some other, uglier smells, but those abounded, so she thought little of it. She took another step, and a familiar voice rang out.

Damb it! What you done?! The hell was you thinking?!

Peaches broke into a run.

DEAD AS DAVY JONES

Sometime after several hundred, Koizumi Yakumo had stopped counting the years. He had awakened in darkness in those first, saner days and lain still on his stone slab, certain that at any moment, a seam of light would crack the black that surrounded him, and that soon after, he'd hear Setsu's cooing voice, feel her soft hands on his haggard cheeks, feel her soft lips kissing him awake. Expectant, he had drifted between nothingness and waking, memories of his former life drawing him to this moment or that.

He saw the boats docked on the Mississippi, their varicolored sails furled against the wind like birds sleeping with their heads under their wings. He saw his editor at the *Daily Enquirer* glaring across his desk: *Really, Larry, marrying a Negress? You've given them the rope yourself, and it's no wonder that now you're thoroughly hanged . . .* He saw Mattie, his first wife, her face in her hands, turned slightly away from him as she sobbed. *I can't. I can't be the reason for all this. I love you, but I can't.* He saw his leather-shod feet as he stepped from his steamer's gangplank onto the boardwalk on Martinique.

The air was alive with heat and perfume. An aching void rested in his heart, having taken the shape of New Orleans, but he felt drawn forward as if by an invisible cord, pulled east, and east, and east. Could it have been this way? Could he have felt himself nearing Setsu and their children? The Sea of Japan? The demon- and spirit-haunted islands, the richly folded gowns, the house with its stacked roofs, each curled at the corners? The clop of his children's sandaled feet?

Confusion, memory, and loss fell on him like his father's fists. He couldn't remember his children's names. There were four of them. Two boys and—three boys and—? Being here, there, now, then, was exhausting. The jumble of moments and locales... Unable to bear it any longer, he sat up on his slab and touched his cold hands with cold fingers. He felt them well enough, but where were his legs? They seemed to stop at his knees. Was that what had killed him? Had he lost his legs?

Sleeplessness settled on him like a dirty film. It thinned his skin, roughened his voice. Brought all his worst emotions and impulses to the fore. And this darkness. This black upon black upon black: Why couldn't he *see*? Were his eyes shut?

The years enshrouded him. He felt swaddled in the passage of time. Minute woven to minute, hour to hour, decade to decade, tattered and ephemeral as cobwebs, but strong as the work of spiders, strong as fact. A vile taste rested in his mouth. He smelled grave dust.

If I am dead and dreaming, he wondered, *how is it that I know what I know?*

Startled by the light of language, his thoughts ran like palmetto bugs, this way and that...Something terrible coiled in his belly, growing in a mockery of pregnancy. But he was helpless to stop it. He could feel it stretching filaments into and around his organs. Eventually, it would take him completely.

And would he die? Again? Or would it just pilot him?

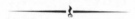

Stagger Lee paused outside a heavy metal door. Up till now, Brendy had been jabbering at him, trying to entertain him and keep him calm. Billy Pete's presence let her know she could fight him if she had to, but if there was a chance he was really taking her to Daddy Deke, she'd rather not lock horns until she had to.

He had changed some since their meeting on the roof of Canal Place. He seemed less angry, more introspective, even worried and a bit sad. Brendy figured it was because he was an old-fashioned kind of man, and that the idea of lying to her about Daddy Deke and leading her into a trap didn't sit well with him. She wasn't sure what to do with that understanding, but she knew it represented an advantage for her team, a chink in Stagger Lee's gangsta armor.

Stagger Lee pressed his palm against the door but didn't push. "You hear that?" he said.

Billy Pete made a mournful, wordless noise that chilled Brendy to the core. "Hear what?" she said as brightly as she could. "I don't hear nothing. Not even the weather no more."

"Every time I come down here, he doing something," Stagger Lee said. "He ain't got nothing in there to entertain him, so he gotta entertain hisself, you know?"

"Maybe he ain't there," Brendy said. Maybe the time had come to stop playing along. "Maybe you just tryna trap me, Gun Man."

HUSH WIT THAT, Stagger Lee said. WAIT HERE.

"Why I gotta wait outside? You said you was bringing me to Daddy Deke."

I AIN'T SURE WHAT WE GONE FIND. HE AIN'T HERE, WE GOTTA FIG-URE OUT WHERE HE AT AND WHAT TO DO BOUT IT. SO WAIT. HERE.

"You on thin ice with me, Gun Man," Brendy said. She hadn't meant to say it, but it was true.

"Girl, I been knowing that. You don't make it easy switching sides."

Rain fell like nails as Perry emerged back into the city. When he had spoken his incantation, Mr. Horn had stood at Perry's left side, but now he was nowhere around. Perry craned his neck this way and that, squinting against the rain and wind, then realized that both his hands were full. In his right hand he clutched the

Clackin' Sack, and in his left he held a gleaming trumpet—except without the mouthpiece.

Perry dimly remembered his friend Troy at his old school arguing that you could too play a horn without one, if you used the proper technique. But that was where Perry's memory ended. Not only did he remember no explanation, he couldn't even recall whether there'd been one to forget.

The weather didn't seem to touch the trumpet. No raindrops ran over its shining skin. Instead, it glowed softly, breathing its shine into the air. Raindrops hit the glow and did not pop, hiss, or steam as they disappeared. The instrument felt alive in Perry's hands. He felt the same way looking at it as he did when he looked at his father asleep. He marveled at its quiet power.

The horn wasn't silent, either. It emitted a faint but steady hum right at the edge of Perry's hearing. It was like the sound you hear after striking a bell, juuuuust before silence.

How magic am I now? Perry wondered, his mouth slightly open. *Could a normal person hear this? Could a normal person feel what I'm feeling?*

He knew that one couldn't hold, couldn't use things like the Elysian Trumpet, like the Clackin' Sack, for long without absorbing some of their magical properties.

As Perry stared at the horn, he felt his left elbow begin to bend. The horn rose slowly up, toward Perry's lips.

Panic tightened Perry's scalp. *"No!"* he said aloud. With great effort, he lowered the instrument, held it at his side. He felt a slight resistance in his elbow; it wanted to bend again. The fingers of his right hand twitched as he held the Clackin' Sack, and he longed to feel his finger pads pressing down on the horn's valves. The longing gave way to cold, quiet fear. He had almost played the trumpet without meaning to. He had almost ruined everything.

Perry knew something else about magical things: they *wanted* to be used, to fulfill their purpose. Unless he acted quickly to learn what he needed to know, to form a plan and enact it, either the

Elysian Trumpet would force Perry to play it or it would play itself. Perry wasn't sure which would be worse. He broke into a run.

Later—much later—after waking and wandering from the tomb in Mount Olivet Cemetery and making his way through some barely perceived veil that made his chest and shoulders ache, Yakumo had stood atop a ghostly dance hall on the Dead Side of Town, watching silvered figures flit up and down the muddy street below, the women's skirts gathered daintily in their ghostly hands. Shining wigs stood piled upon their heads, ringlets falling about their ears.

Where was the port? Where was the cotton gin? He'd come here to collect ghost stories, and—no—to translate articles and write about cotton, the statues, the Negro women (Mattie?) selling rice balls in the dusty streets. The crumbling walls and fountained courtyards, the Italians gesturing with both hands as they exhorted their children, the regrets of ghostly pelicans...

Away to the west, he heard a deep, throaty blast of some awful horn. The stutter of unfamiliar music. Voices raised in chat, in song, the confusion of brass instruments. Something ugly twisted within him, curdled like milk with lemon juice mixed in.

seven hundred seventeen i counted i know seven hundred seventeen years and its been twice that at least since i stopped better to live in new orleans in sackcloth and ashes but this is not new orleans where is my setsu where is she where is she where why is she kept from me   or am i kept from her youll pay for this youll pay youll all of you will pay o yes

But the girl. He had seen a little redbone girl darting through the streets. He'd watched her knock a Garden District mansion off its foundation with a single punch. The mayor, the king and queen sought her out from time to time, solicited her help with crises. She fought the Axe Man to a standstill, trapped his spirit in a jar. The girl would be a problem. He must find a way to weaken her.

Stagger Lee opened the door into the dark and closed it behind him, leaving the ghostly little girl on the other side. His heart had sunk as soon as he touched the door and sensed nothing beyond it. The Ole Man usually had a charge to him. Stag wasn't sure what it was—maybe a touch of music, or even just old-man sass, but whatever it was could always be felt at the door, and it had been strong enough for Stag to elevate the man in his mind from simply an old man to the Ole Man.

Had he stepped in water? Of course there was flooding all over town, but it hadn't gotten so bad that water would have seeped in here just yet—or had Stagger Lee badly miscalculated the completion of Yakumo's plan? What if Yakumo didn't need him anymore? What if it was too late, and he had switched sides just in time to lose?

Maybe the Ole Man was just sleeping. He did a lot of that, but usually his slow, heavy breathing could be heard before Stagger Lee entered the room. Stag took a breath, reached up to the light, and flipped it on.

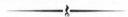

Peaches thought she heard someone call her name as she grabbed the heavy metal door and yanked it open. The latch popped straight off, the door swung wide, and Peaches's mouth fell open as she saw Stagger Lee standing there, holding something limp and familiar in his rough brown hands.

At first, Peaches didn't understand what she saw. The dirty lightbulb swung right to left, right to left, dragging its weak illumination to light one side of the room, then the other. Was that Daddy Deke's purple zoot suit pants and yellow shirt?

Naw, she thought. *Naw, Peaches. That ain't no suit. That's Daddy Deke!*

Panic flared in Peaches's mind. Time slowed as her breathing sped. Something was wrong with Daddy Deke. Something was wrong with his body. He had no eyes, no teeth, and his mouth gaped like a wound. Now she understood why she had confused his body for his suit. His skin was empty, drooping fleshless and boneless in Stagger Lee's hands like a scarecrow without his straw.

As she watched, a wave of roaches, wriggling rats, and other vermin poured from Daddy Deke's empty skin, bursting from the eyeholes, the mouth hole, from the sleeves of his shirt and the cuffs of his pants, splashing together in the black, nasty water standing on the floor.

Her panic left her. There was nothing to fear now because the worst had already happened. She'd failed. She hadn't saved Daddy Deke. An icy calm radiated from the center of her chest.

"Where the rest of him at?" she asked. In her own ears, her voice sounded conversational—as if she'd asked whether someone had stashed the cold drinks in the refrigerator.

"What?" Stag said.

"If that's his skin and clothes, where the rest of him at?" Daddy Deke must be okay after all. He must have shrugged his skin off like that of a snake, gone somewhere else to await rescue.

"This all of him," Stagger Lee said. "This all that's left."

Peaches! The shout was formless, barely louder than a thought.

Peaches ignored it, her gaze fixed steadily on her enemy. Her calm deepened, marbled with relief. She knew exactly what to do next.

She balled her fists and put up her guard, relaxing into the cat stance her daddy had shown her when she was little. "You put him down, and you put up your dukes," she said, her voice slow with command. "'Cause it's you and me, baby, and this time...? This time, I'ma kill you dead as Davy Jones."

Still later, Yakumo discovered the Department of Streets. Its libraries. Its offices yawning empty like graves on Judgment Day. It was connected, somehow, to every place in this mad, thrice-damned mockery of New Orleans.

Every so often, unable to bear consciousness any longer, Yakumo would retreat to his tomb, to the darkness he could draw about him like a blanket, and lie on his slab to sleep, to dream sometimes of Mattie, but mostly of Setsu and his children with her, whose names were still lost in the river of time.

Gradually, Yakumo had realized that the darkness did not stay behind when he emerged back into waking and into Nola. It didn't follow him, either, or reek from his pores; it *was* him, and he was it.

He felt no spores, no fruiting bodies inside him now. Maybe he'd imagined them to begin with. But he knew he hadn't. He knew his mind was likely only an echo of itself. He'd been eaten— well, not *alive*—from within.

am i mad

yes of course the darkness answered utterly madness is the only sane response to the horror we endure

that we endure who are we

we are lafcadio hearn

we are koizumi yakumo

we are this citys secret knowledge that it should not exist

we are its salvation and its end

Yakumo laughed or screamed—he wasn't sure which.

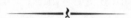

Brendy clapped her ghostly hands against her disembodied cheeks as a wave of dread washed over her. The building rocked on its foundations, and the sound of another heavy slamming impact spread through the air.

Everything had gone wrong. Brendy had come here alone, thinking that when Gun Man inevitably turned on her, she would command Billy Pete to knock him flat and keep him subdued until Perry and Peaches arrived on the scene—but Stagger Lee hadn't turned on her. He'd even seemed like he wanted to *help*, and now—!

Lordy Jesus, Brendy prayed. *What I'm gonna do?*

Billy Pete answered, clear as day: *I stop the fight. I separate.*

Yes! Brendy said. *Billy Pete—!*

Just then, Daddy Deke stepped around the corner. His eyes went wide and his mouth fell open as soon as he set eyes on his granddaughter.

Naw, not you too! he said. *Lord,* please *tell me that stupid-ass haint ain't killed my grandbaby!*

Perry ran down Terpsichore Street at top speed. He couldn't tell whether the street was clear of floodwaters because it was built on higher ground or because Perry was headed in the right direction. Did any of these houses belong to Doctor Professor? He remembered Manda Bird standing at the front of his class, summarizing a report about the sorcerer. She'd mentioned that in life he'd stayed on Terpsichore Street, but damn if Perry could remember the address.

Panic spurred him faster. He held the trumpet steady against his chest as he swung his right arm and worked his legs. He ran so fast that if he were to stop suddenly, he'd fall.

He felt the same panic a mouse feels beneath the shadow of a hawk. He felt a quake deep in the pit of his belly, and he reached for it with an internal grasp and stuffed it into his shoes. Now was not the time to come apart.

He tripped on a tree root and tumbled to the cracked sidewalk. He cradled the horn against his body, making sure no harm came to it. He rolled to sitting as the rain beat down on him.

"What do I do?" he asked aloud.

He looked down at the horn in his right hand. "What do I do?"

No answer came.

"Tell me," Perry said. His words were ragged from exertion, but he spoke without waiting to catch his breath. "You were a man inside—inside the sack, so I know—you have personality and will. I can't blow you—unless somebody shows me how. So if you want to get used, luh-*lead* me."

With some effort, Perry calmed his breathing. He stood and relaxed, holding the horn at his side. He ignored the rain, the thunder, the blasting wind. He barely held the trumpet now. He shut his eyes and waited, willing himself still.

At first, there was nothing. Perry breathed and fought to keep his mind clear. He imagined himself as a dream catcher hanging in someone's bedroom. He imagined himself as a colander, letting pasta water drain through it. He imagined himself as wind chimes, as an instrument himself, an instrument of—

His arm twitched. In his surprise, Perry nearly dropped the horn. He kept his eyes closed and let his legs carry him through the rain.

He tried not to think of Peaches. He tried not to think of her rich summery smell. He tried not to think of Daddy Deke and his beak of a nose. He tried not to think of Brendy, of his father, of Mama Lisa, of Fonzo, of all Peaches's animals.

It occurred to him that if he and Milo ever met, it would be as equals, as two not-quite-boys who had seen and done the impossible.

He's got that car, though, Perry thought. *I could really use a car like that.*

Thunder clattered overhead, but Perry didn't flinch. He opened his eyes but didn't stop walking. His legs carried him up a set of stairs and stood still.

Perry wasn't sure where he was now. He stood at a door on a columned, wraparound porch with crazed white tile that reminded him of the tea eggs he'd eaten when Daddy Deke took him and Brendy to Hong Kong Restaurant.

What am I supposed to do now?

He shrugged, took a breath, and knocked.

When Mr. Horn—Perry still thought of the elderly man as Mr. Horn—opened the door for him, he realized that both his hands were empty.

"Hey!" Perry said. "You can—?"

Mr. Horn put a wrinkled finger to his lips and shushed him. "You hear to learn, ain'tcha, little pitcher?"

Perry couldn't tell whether Mr. Horn had said "here" or "hear," but it seemed imperative to keep quiet. If little pitchers had big ears, Perry had better keep his open.

———— ⚬ ————

"Heavenly God," Mama Lisa prayed aloud into the inky black of the house, "God of my mother and her mothers before her, we approach your throne to entreat you now because you sit high and look low. Dear God, we don't know what to do. Lord, my grandson has disappeared in search of a fearsome weapon, and my granddaughter is shrouded in a sleep from which she cannot or will not wake. Our family is fragmented. Our city is in peril. Help us. Help."

She fell silent then but didn't stop praying. Blindly, she reached for her daughter's hand, and her son-in-law's, and held them tight. She trembled with effort, searching for some sign, some sense of where her grandbabies and their friend had gone.

I thought you returned me to my family to help them fight this fight, she prayed. *I thought you returned me to lead us to victory. Instead, all I have is uncertainty and fear. Please. Show me what to do!*

Outside, the wind howled and rushed. Wave after wave of rain battered the roof and walls, trying to pry its way inside.

Please, Lord. Please!

A piano chord sounded in the living room.

When Mama Lisa opened her eyes the lights were back on, but they shone weakly, dimly. The piano chords walked up and down, and Mama Lisa drew Yvette along behind her as she headed for the living room, knowing exactly what she would find.

The Mess Around took up most of the room. Doctor Professor sat at the keyboard, hanging his head in shame or exhaustion. The stillness of his body cut a bizarre contrast with the constant motion of his hands.

"Henry Roeland Byrd," Mama Lisa said. "Why have you come here?"

He didn't answer right away. He seemed to be listening to his own playing, even though what he played was not exactly a song.

"I come because it's time," he said. "Time I put a end to all this."

SUGAR, HONEY, ICED TEA

The house—was this a house?—was full of laughter and the aroma of simmering beans. Perry's mouth watered at the scent, even though he'd eaten the breakfast of his life just a little while ago.

"Damb it, I told y'all I can do it. Just gimme space, now. Come on, now. I remember!"

Perry had been here, or somewhere much like this, before. The area he was in now seemed like a finely appointed residence with marble floors, dark wooden accents, and art hanging on the walls. To Perry's right lay a combination library and office, and before him, stairs raced up and around to a second floor. To Perry's left stood a living room full of people and antique furniture.

A white man with wavy dark hair sat on a low, broad chair, his legs crossed, a trumpet balanced impossibly on his knee. "Aw, just play the other one!" he called. His voice was raspy and tuneful, as if he had to force himself to speak instead of singing.

"Ain't your turn," said the man sitting at the drums. He was relatively short, light-skinned, and he wore a red baseball cap and a black T-shirt. He was a series of *V*s. His eyebrows, his nose, his mouth, his shoulders and waist. His eyes were clear and watchful. "Let somebody start it off, and the rest of us come in."

"It don't start with no piano." The man sitting at the keyboard sounded mortally offended. "Listen here, mother—"

"Hey, now," the man at the drums cautioned, gesturing with his chin in Perry's direction. "Little pitchers."

Perry had ventured into the room without realizing it. He knew now that all the grown-ups in here could see him, and he wondered why that surprised him. He glanced over at a skinny blind boy leaning in the corner—he knew the boy was blind because of his great dark glasses and the way he craned his neck. The boy seemed to sense Perry and gestured to him, as if to say, *Listen close.*

"I tole you: somebody gonna play this got-damn keyboard, it's gonna be—!"

"Negro, get on up!" a tall, chocolate-skinned woman commanded as she entered the room. "They say age before beauty, but you old as hell, and I ain't that cute."

The woman's hair was wrapped in purple fabric and piled on her head. Her dress was tight, especially in the booty, but she wore it with taste. She strode like a queen toward the bench and sat without looking. The other piano player got up just in time.

"I'ma sing it, then," he said, but without much conviction.

"You don't know it," said the woman. "You would have started already if you did." She started playing high with her right hand and pursed her lips, squinting as if in pain. "*There* it is."

"Have you got the embouchure?"

Perry shook his head and looked to his right. He couldn't see Mr. Horn, but a white woman stood beside him, holding a trombone in her left hand. She wore a black-and-white dress and a maroon shrug, and her blond hair had been swept into a neat ponytail. Her face was round and kind, but something that wasn't kindness lit her gray eyes. It was…excitement? She barely looked at Perry as the piano chords somersaulted across the room.

"The what?" Perry asked.

"The embouchure. It's how you hold your lips. You purse your lips and *buzz*." She demonstrated.

Perry looked back at the woman playing piano. Her expression had softened now, become a little vacant. She was somewhere far-off, concentrating.

"It's about breath control."

"Playing the—?" Perry stopped himself. Little pitchers.

"You have to imagine that the air is alive—because it is. It really is. And you breathe all the way down, into your diaphragm, and let the air come up a little at a time, the way you want it, and when it leaves you, it keeps going. It goes to the wall, past the wall, out and out, into the world, and even space."

Perry nodded gravely, although he wasn't sure he understood. Any moment now, the woman at the piano would begin to sing, and Perry didn't think he'd be able to listen to anything else.

"You want *music*, not noise. You have to have a good tone. If it's not shaped right, it'll go wild and do harm. Music is magic. Noise is just . . . noise."

Up in Harlem on a Saturday night
When the highbrows get together it's just too tight
We all gather at the Harlem Strut
And what we do is tut tut tut . . .

Perry shut his eyes without meaning to. The woman's voice had taken hold of him with more force than he expected . . . If she was a woman. Her voice was low, and it wasn't rough, but there was roughness in it.

"That's it," said the woman with the trombone. "See how it's all the way in you already? It was always there. You have to find it and let it out."

Old Hanna Brown from way cross to-o-wn
Keeps drinking her liquor and she brings them down
Just at the break of dayyyyy, you could hear old Hannah say . . .
. . . I want a pigfoot and a bottle of beer!

Send me, daddy, 'cause I don't care!
I feel just like I wanna clown
Get the piano player a drink 'cause he brought me down!
Got rhythm when he stomps his feeeet—!
He just send meeee right off to sleep!
Take all your razors and your guns
We gonna be 'rrested when the wagon comes!

Behind Perry, a trumpet leaped into the song, following the chorus. It was the white man with the wavy hair. Another white man, this one old and balding, stood up from a low couch and joined him. Their horns dueled, tumbling over each other like alley cats sparring.

Other instruments joined. A bass, at least two other saxophones, and trombone girl had lifted her own horn. When she played, Perry understood many things he never had before. The image of her hand on the slide seemed to stick in the air, her movements lingering as she went from one note to the next. Her music sounded like giant rose petals unfurling in the air, smooth and fragrant…

The horns, the banjo, the piano wandered away from the main tune, following each other happily down one path, then another, like revelers from Away looking for a bathroom during Carnival, and Perry wasn't sure how they all knew when, but they returned together.

Gimme a pigfoot and a bottle of beer!
Slay me, daddy, 'cause I don't care
Slay me, daddy, 'cause I don't care, no, no
Get that piano player a drink because she bringing me down!
Check all your razors and your guns
Send me, 'cause I don't care!
Send me, 'cause I don't ca-a-a-a-are!

The music swelled but didn't stop. It became a current bobbing Perry along, spun this way and that by eddies and whorls. Eventually the horns quieted and ceased, leaving just the bass, the piano, and the drum. Perry wanted to stay here, like this, listening, forever. He realized, in a flash, that he could.

But he had come here with a specific goal...Hadn't he? Perry had the sense that the goal had been fulfilled, but he couldn't be sure. The music was intoxicating. Perry knew that if he had a horn of his own right now, he would join in. He would—

"Hey!" Perry said aloud. "Hey, where's Doctor Professor?"

The music didn't stop, but it seemed to recede. The man at the drums raised his eyebrows. "You looking for Fess?"

"Yes," Perry said. "I have to find him. Right away. I'm...I'm on a mission."

The piano player who'd gotten up for the woman grimaced, clacked his teeth together. "He ain't here," he said. "That is, he *present*, but he ain't here..."

"Do you know where he went?"

Now the music stopped.

"To do his sacred duty," the woman at the keyboard said.

"What do you mean?"

"Sacrifice," she said. She nodded, matter-of-fact, and repeated, "Sacrifice."

"But he's already a haint," Perry said. "How can he sacrifice himself if he's already dead?"

The drummer shrugged. "Dead is as dead does," he said. He counted off *one, two, one, two, three, four!* And the music began again.

Perry was out of time.

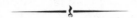

Blood seeped from a cut above Stagger Lee's right eye, running around the orbit and dripping into his upper eyelashes. His top lip had split, and his cravat had come loose at the neck. He knelt in the brackish water on the floor of what had been Daddy Deke's cell, his shovel-hands hanging at his sides. The tips of his middle fingers almost touched the wet.

"You ain't look so good, baby," Peaches said, breathing hard.

"You better put up them dukes. This ass-whuppin' won't be no fun if you won't do your part."

Stagger Lee's lips moved, but Peaches couldn't hear his voice over her own breathing and the blood roaring in her ears. Hardly thinking about it, she lashed out with a hard right that landed on his left breast and rocked his entire body into the wall where a cot lay flush against the corner. The flimsy thing stove in when Stagger Lee hit it, crumpling around his body with a squeal of twisting metal. The wall cracked from the force of the collision, but it didn't crumble. Not yet.

"What was that?" Peaches asked, feeling a mean sort of glee. "What you said to me, you dirty, granddaddy-stealing sumbitch?"

With trembling limbs, Stagger Lee righted himself, levering his palms against the damaged concrete wall. He looked Peaches in the eye and swallowed. Peaches realized now that he was swallowing blood. She could almost taste it herself, warm and metal-red against her tongue.

"I said, ain't no ass-whuppin'," Stagger Lee rasped. "This what I got coming to me, I know that, but make no mistake, babygirl. This ain't no fight. I ain't raised a hand against you. This *murder*, what this is. Kill me if you gone kill me but be straight with yaself about it."

Peaches drew in a big, shocked breath. The air in her lungs felt hot with electricity. "How many people you done shot or beat till they was *nothing*?" she hissed. "How many lives you done stole just because you could? You calling *this* murder? You calling *me* a killer?"

"Countless." Stagger Lee coughed, swallowed again. "My victims are without number. If there one thing I'm a expert on, it's killing folk. I know you ain't heard me, but I'm tryna tell you, I didn't kill the Ole Man."

"You lyin' to live."

Stagger Lee grinned a mouthful of broken teeth. "You think... I want to *live*—?"

Just then, Daddy Deke walked through the wall, holding Brendy's hand.

Peaches's mouth fell open when she saw the old man. For a beat, she let herself believe that the empty skin had been a nasty trick, a prank played by the same haint who'd stolen her daddy's letter, but in the next second she realized she could see right through him and Brendy both. Their figures shone in the dim of the room.

Peaches bit her right fist to stifle a wail.

"Don't worry!" Brendy chirped. "I'm still alive, I think! I think I'm at home, sleep!"

"Stagolee tellin' the truth," Daddy Deke said. "He ain't laid a hand on me. Your friend Mr. Larry ain't the friend you think he is."

"Mr. Larry...? What...?"

"His real name Koizumi Yakumo," Stagger Lee rasped. "And he ain't nothing nice."

"Where Perry at?" Daddy Deke asked. "Where you seent him last?"

"I left him on the Live Side," Peaches said. "He was sleeping at my house."

"We best get back there posthaste," Daddy Deke said. "Yakumo could come back anytime, and we ain't got a hope of beating him without a lil something I got squirreled away."

The cell's heavy metal door squeaked on its hinges as Mr. Larry let himself into the room. "Too late," he said sadly. "Too, too, too late. Did you think I'd leave you all to collude against me if you had any hope of stopping me?"

Peaches stared, dumbfounded, at the haint she'd thought was her friend. She said something then, but she hadn't meant to, and the words left her so quickly that she wasn't sure what they were.

Mr. Larry sucked his teeth. "Profanity, my darling? *Utterly unbecoming.*"

The darkness was itself a substance. Peaches felt it clammy on her skin, like damp newspaper. It filled her nose, flooded her lungs, pressed sick against the pit of her belly as if she'd eaten too much.

I gotta do this, Peaches thought, but the thought sounded faint and tinny inside her skull, as if the darkness had sapped its resonance.

its much worse than that im afraid

Peaches gritted her teeth, clenched her eyes shut, and tried to ignore the evidence that until now, her eyes had been open.

you need not respond im confident you hear me

Don't listen. Don't listen to him, Peaches thought. *Everything he says is lies.*

havent you wondered at the circumstance that brought you to nola doesnt it seem strange that your father has left you alone to live in this cursed city scrambling to find the letters he sends you on a schedule without rhyme or reason

Don't you talk about my daddy, Peaches snarled. *You keep his name out your mouth.*

yes his name what was it again

Peaches clenched her teeth harder and harder until her jaw began to ache. She tried to radiate disdain the way a gas oven radiates heat.

i couldnt say his name if i wanted to your father never had a name because he never was

How could you do us like this? Peaches thought. *How could you do me like this?*

you dont have a daddy peaches youre not a girl at all youre barely a song you are a tuneless little ditty the heathen indians used to hum before the white man ventured into louisiana bits of your melody were repeated over and over until just about every tune born in new orleans exhibited a piece of you that is how you came by your titanic strength you are the intersection of forgetting and remembrance

I remember my daddy, Peaches thought. *I know he loves me.* But did she? Did he? She was sweating now. She could feel the slickness on her skin. She felt a fizzing sensation in her skull, and her chest constricted. Panic strobed within her, a bright, scouring thing that made every thought sharp enough to cut.

does he Yakumo asked, and now Peaches knew he'd been listening to her thoughts all the while. if he loves you peaches where is he your memories of him your silly little letters these are just manifestations of the song that is you

Impossible, Peaches thought. *I know who I am.*

you deserve to know the other songs died ignorant of their true nature but you the greatest of them deserve the truth

You crazy. You out your mind.

Yakumo's voice grew deafening, ringing in Peaches's mind. OF COURSE IM MAD OF COURSE IVE BEEN TRAPPED IN THIS PARODY OF MY BELOVED NEW ORLEANS FOR AN ETERNITY He seemed to struggle for composure and continued in his rasping whisper. thousands of years thousands of thousands i have watched you all go about your idiot business gossiping with talking animals and automatons never never realizing you lived in what amounts to a dirty fishbowl

aeons ago i realized that in order to escape id have to kill the music that holds this sick dreamland together i couldnt bear to sacrifice innocent lives o no o no o o but ever so slowly i came to realize that the alternative is far worse an eternity spent here as the only one who knows the truth id sooner be damned better to roast in hell than to continue decade after decade year after year day after day unliving bound to a locale that by its very nature cannot grow or change

I don't care how long you was trapped here, Peaches thought. *This city better than you deserve.*

DON T YOU DARE I DON T DESERVE THIS TORMENT NOBODY DOES

When the first chords sounded, Peaches's heart leaped. She recognized the tune right away. She'd know "Tipsy Tina" anywhere. But this wasn't "Tipsy Tina." The lyrics were just as hoarse and bluesy, but this song was about someone else.

Baby I'm so damn tired
Because I ain't slept a wink
If you and me baby sailed the seven seas
I'd pitch you in the drink!

Peaches still couldn't see, but hearing Doctor Professor banging out his chords, singing the guitar, the bass, the horns, cheered her anyway. Of course, if what Yakumo said was true—if she had no daddy, if she wasn't a girl at all—then she didn't know how she'd live, but the music made her think she just might find a way anyhow.

You evil when you sleepin'
You cruel when you awake!
Ain't no good at nothin'
But a-kissin' and a-huggin'
Girl you more than I can take!

This was it. This was crunch time. This was Nola's way of thanking Peaches for all she'd done. She'd fought to protect the city, and now the city was reaching out to save her. Peaches went very still, summoning all her strength. Girl or song, damn if she wouldn't go out fighting.

The singing roused Stagger Lee back to waking. He lay in the brackish water, his eyes swollen shut, bruises and abrasions tightening his skin. He savored the pain. He didn't remember feeling physically broken before. That girl Peaches had made him remember a time before he was a monster.

Stag had never heard Professor Longhair sing with such fervor. He seemed to mean every heartsick word.

Stagger Lee opened his left eye just enough to see Yakumo standing legless in the air above him. His head had split open, but not at the neck or the throat. He had split to his waist, and his red-orange tentacles wrapped around Peaches, Brendy, and the Ole Man. No. The Ole Man's ghost. It was the discovery of his remains that had sent Peaches over the edge. That had spurred her to use her whole strength against Stagger Lee.

The shaggy-haired haint wheeled in the air, his tendrils sizzling against Peaches's pale skin.

henry byrd Yakumo sneered. far too late you ve summoned the courage to face me

"I come to stop you killing that girl," Fess said.

what girl the song you mean the song you hid in plain sight when you and your band created this mockery of new orleans

Stagger Lee didn't know what Yakumo meant, but then it dawned on him. Peaches was like him? A song?

"You don't need to sacrifice her," Doctor Professor said. "It won't work, nohow. You wrong about her. You wrong about a lotta thangs. That Storm done got down in ya, ruined yo brains."

Stagger Lee's body seemed to move on its own. One moment he was lying in the muck, the smell of mold and turned earth clogging his nostrils, and the next he was on his feet, gun in hand, aiming at his former master.

Before he could squeeze the trigger, Yakumo's blood-red eye flared to life. It hung from the tattered ribbons of Yakumo's pale flesh, but it worked. Stagger Lee swung his pistol and fired.

Time ground to a halt.

Stagger Lee roared his protest. Yakumo had taken control of his very body and forced him to revise his aim. The bullet entered Doctor Professor's left temple and passed through his skull, dragging most of the musician's brain with it. Instead of a spray of gore, a pregnant sizzling sound unfolded into the thick air of the room. Was Doctor Professor's magic so powerful that even Stagger Lee's gun couldn't end him?

Light thick as egg yolk spilled into the room, and a little chocolate-brown woman emerged from the middle of the air. The little girl—Brendy—her body lay slung across the woman's shoulder, and the way her hand lay against the small of Brendy's back told Stagger Lee that this was her mama or her granny. Only blood could touch a child with such tenderness.

The woman's other hand extended, fingers spread, in Professor Longhair's direction. This must be why the old haint's head was still intact. If she eased her grip on him, even a little, his head would be gone, and the city would die with him.

Yakumo seemed just as surprised to see the woman as Stagger Lee was. Quickly, his head formed again, the tendrils extended from his open mouth. He wheeled in the air to glare at the little woman, but as he did, his control over Stagger Lee's body eased just enough.

Barely aiming, Stagger Lee swung his pistol again and fired once, twice, three, four times, and each report was loud as the Last Trump signaling the End of the World. Stagger Lee had just enough time to worry that the noise would damage the woman's control, force her to let go of Fess, and that all of them, the songs, the little girl, both ghostly old men, would be done for.

That didn't happen. Not quite.

Yakumo fell into the dirty water. Peaches and the spirits fell with him, free of his tentacles. As soon as Brendy hit the muck, she pressed her palms together like a diving swimmer and jumped into her body.

The old man, Daddy Deke, said something unrepeatable, then, *Lisa . . . ? Izzat you?*

"What's happening here?" Stagger Lee asked. "What in hell is going on?"

"What's going on is I bought us minutes if we're lucky and seconds if we're not," the woman snapped. "Brendolyn. *Wake.*"

Brendy stirred on her shoulder, shook her head sleepily, then, *"Haniran sayala alagbara!"* she thundered.

A flock of black shadows exploded into the air from her fist and hung there, chattering.

"Help Mama Lisa!" Brendy shouted. "Make her stronger and help her hold on. *This I command!*"

Mama Lisa exhaled slowly, her teeth clenched tight.

"Now what?" Stagger Lee asked. "I done kilt Yakumo. What else can I do for y'all?"

"You haven't killed me," Yakumo rasped bitterly from where he lay. "You've injured me badly, but still I cling to a mockery of life. My imprisonment persists."

How you still alive? Daddy Deke asked. *Is it because Lisa keeping Fess together?*

"What difference does it make?" Yakumo said. "I'm...I'm still *here*! Still *bound*!"

"Fool," Mama Lisa said. "You were never trapped. The Storm brought you here to act as its agent. You let it twist your thoughts, your love, until you became...*this*. Ask yourself: Have you ever *tried* to leave? You've always been free. Everyone is."

Stagger Lee felt hot and cold all over. "Every...? Even me?"

"...What?" Yakumo asked.

"You searched in vain for a way to free yourself. You schemed and lied. You did everything but *try*. Nothing and no one can make you free."

Yakumo's face twisted. His mouth became a square of hate. But then something seemed to stop him short. The tension drained from his face. He looked less like a pale-faced ghost and more like a little boy. A blood-red tear spilled from his good eye. "I could have left...?" he said. "I could have gone to Setsu and the children?"

Still can, dummy, Daddy Deke said. *You ain't got no reason to stick around unless you wanna. That's the way haints work. Why you think I'm still here after you hollowed me out with your weird-ass tentacles? It's because I ain't ready to let go my peoples. What you holding on to?*

The water around him began to bubble and boil. The disturbance seemed to lend Yakumo a bit of vitality. He surged upward toward the ceiling, rearing like a cobra. This time, he split completely, seemed to turn inside-out. The tentacles emerged from his raw red inside, whipping angrily back and forth.

too late he said. if i am to journey on by god and by damn you re all coming with me

That was when the boy appeared. He hung just above the water, his feet bent toward the floor. He wore a classically cut tuxedo and patent-leather shoes. His bow tie was tied as crisply as any Stagger Lee had seen. A horn hung in his right hand, gleaming so brightly that Stagger Lee could barely stand to look at it. He glared at Stag and raised the horn to his lips.

"Not him!" Lisa shouted. She pointed up at Yakumo. *"There!"*

Perry whirled away from Stagger Lee, and Yakumo expanded across the ceiling. The tentacles spread down, striking in what seemed like every direction.

Perry lifted the horn to his lips and blew.

In that sound was every note of music Stagger Lee had ever heard. Instinctively, he reached out to touch it, and as he stared his hand began to dissolve. He blinked, shocked, and found himself standing on tamped-down dirt. The crisp air smelled of woodsmoke.

Stag looked right, looked left. The sky was untroubled and blue, and a rickety train depot stood forlorn before him.

Stagger Lee touched the knot of his cravat and brushed off his lapel.

He climbed the steps to the train platform and glanced to his left, where an elderly Black man stood with a push broom and a long-handled dustpan.

WHERE WE AT JUST NOW?

"Cain'tcha read, son?" asked the old man. He gestured with his chin to a sign above the ticket booth: BELUTHAHATCHIE.

WHEN THIS TRAIN COME, WHERE IT GONE TAKE ME?

"What you doing out here if you don't know nothing, boy?" the old man asked. He shook his head, disgusted. "This here line is the train to Hell."

THEY GOT MUSIC IN HELL?

"Naw," said the old man. "Can't say as they do."

THEY BOUT TO, Stagger Lee said. He took a breath and felt his chest expand. Hell. That sounded right up his alley. THEY BOUT TO.

He thought of them kids. Of the flooded cell and the mad city teeming with musical life. But those memories were already fading.

XXXII

To Miss New Orleans

Peaches's heart leaped as Perry appeared. She watched him aim his magic horn at Stagger Lee, then watched him turn away from the demon song as Mama Lisa pointed at Yakumo. "Perry!" She called. "Perry, you gone be—?"

Her voice was lost in the blare of the horn. Music and light filled the air, burning so brightly that Peaches couldn't tell them apart. Maybe she didn't need to. Maybe they were the same. She squinted, visored her eyes, and looked toward the ceiling. Yakumo's blanket of darkness tore and evaporated against the musical onslaught.

"That's it!" she called. "Put it on 'im!"

Perry didn't seem to hear. He kept blowing, and a sustained note of magical force poured from his horn. The light brightened further, pulsed, and Peaches felt the sound abrade her skin. She realized then that she had to get everyone out. Their bodies couldn't handle this.

Peaches locked eyes with Mama Lisa. "Come on!" she shouted. "Everybody! Everybody *OUT*!"

She had just enough time to wonder where Stagger Lee had gone as the rest of the family fled the room. Only Mama Lisa stayed behind, using her power to hold Fess's body in suspension. Her glow was brighter than ever, but the strain stood out on her dark face. Her eyes were beginning to redden.

The Mess Around trembled and made a noise Peaches didn't recognize. Peaches rushed to the keyboard, thinking to play just anything, anything at all, to keep the city from coming apart. She couldn't tell whether Perry had played another note or whether the Mess Around itself was giving up the ghost. It exploded in a riot of color and force, and Peaches shielded her eyes. She felt wooden splinters pierce her left forearm and opened her mouth to scream.

The other man, the one she didn't know, shouted at her as he pressed something hard and metallic into her hand.

Hurry! You got to go!

A fizzing noise carried Peaches elsewhere.

Peaches smelled old stone and something like electricity. Magic? Somewhere outside, a storm roared and raged, but the timbre of its voice was different from the storm Peaches had left behind. It was dark in here, but Peaches could still see. The rocky floor was rough, uneven. This place seemed to be at once a cell and a cave.

"Hey!"

The familiar voice turned Peaches's head, and when she saw her daddy, her heart lurched in her chest.

"*Daddy!*" she shouted. "He told me you wasn't real! He told me *I* wasn't real!"

Peaches's father, Renard Two-Times Jackson Lavelle hung against the rough stone wall, his arms and legs spread, suspended as if by manacles. A darkness coiled around him, darker than the dark of their surroundings. It was similar to the shadows of which Yakumo was made, but older and oilier, seething and vibrating at a lower frequency.

Peaches's daddy craned his neck, staring into the dark. "Baby-girl?" he asked. "Zat you?"

"Daddy! Daddy, yes!" Peaches called. She started toward him, but the distance between them lengthened with every step, the way it might have in a nightmare. Peaches didn't care.

Nightmare, fire, flood, drama—none of it could stop her. "It's me! I'ma bust you out of here!"

"*No!* Don't you come near this place! Don't you come after me, now, ya heard?"

"Too late," Peaches called back. "I'm already here."

"No, you ain't, and don't ya come nowhere in the vicinity! Promise me, now!"

"No, Daddy, I—!"

"Promise," he shouted. *"Promise!"*

Peaches stopped trying to trudge toward her father. She squared her shoulders and glared at him. "You can't tell me what to do," she said. "You may be my daddy, but I'm Peaches damn Lavelle. I go where I wanna, and I do what I do! If I decide to come save you, then damn it, that's what's getting done!"

Her daddy sagged in his bonds. His barrel chest deflated, and his knotted arms lost some of their definition. Peaches watched, horrified, as tears spilled from his good eye.

"Please," he sobbed. "Please don't. I cain't let them get you, too."

"Who, Daddy?" Peaches demanded. "Who they is? The bird-ladies?"

But he was already gone.

Peaches stood in a pool of light shed by a fixture overhead. A cold checkered marble floor spread beneath her bare feet, and plush sofas squatted against walls on either side of the room—if it was a room. It might have been simply a widening of a hallway.

Perry stood at the far edge of the pool of light. Everything behind him was lost in shadow. He was dressed up, like for a church wedding—he wore a fine tuxedo with a royal purple bow tie and cummerbund, and purple patent-leather shoes with spats. He held a softly glowing horn pressed against his wrinkled forehead. He hissed at someone Peaches couldn't see:

"...or I won't do it, you heard me?" he said through clenched teeth. "You bring her to me now. *Right now.* Bring her here and let me know she's safe. She don't get saved, *nobody*—!"

"...Perry...?"

Perry straightened, surprised. "Peaches? Is that really you?"

"Did you bring me here? Just now?"

"The horn brought you," Perry said. "But I made him do it."

"How?"

"I...I told him I wouldn't play him unless I knew you were safe."

"Me? Because you love me?" Peaches heard herself speak the words and couldn't read her own tone.

"Yes, but..." Perry crossed the puddle of light to take Peaches's left hand in his right. "There's no time. I have to play to get the city back. It's already half gone. Wild magic is tearing Nola apart."

"It was—!"

"Mr. Larry," Perry said. "I know." He paused for a beat. "Peaches. *This is it.*"

"What?" she said. "This is what? I got so much to tell you. Like, I thought I was a song, but I'm not but maybe I am, but I'm real, too, and my daddy is real, and you saved us, but I think maybe that hasn't happened yet."

"What do you mean?"

Peaches frowned. "I don't know. In the boneyard, I saw what happened to my daddy. The storm that broke our schooner, it wasn't just a storm. It was these giant bird-ladies with lightning in they mouths, and after Daddy threw me away, they ate him."

"They ate him?" Perry said. "But the letters—!"

"I know," Peaches said. "That's why I believed Yakumo when he said the letters weren't real, but I think they were. They are. I think my daddy writing them so I won't come looking for him. And—and I think your horn missing this."

She held up the mouthpiece given to her by the man she didn't know.

Perry swallowed hard. "Damn," he said sadly. "That's ... *damn*."
He began to cry.

"Perry," Peaches said. "Perry." She gathered him into her arms.

"How can they ask me?" he sobbed. "How can they ask me for this?"

"For what?"

"I don't want to die."

Peaches stiffened. *"No,"* she said. "Oh, no. Oh, baby." She cradled Perry gingerly, so as not to break him. "I'm so sorry. I shoulda known."

"It's true, isn't it," Perry said. "Even with the mouthpiece. If I do this, it'll kill me."

"It's—yes," Peaches said. That sensation of ice lodged in her chest returned to her again. To lose Perry—for him to die, even in triumph—might destroy her. If she could only—

A thought occurred to her.

"That horn so magic, I don't know how you can mess with it and survive ... When you show up to fight Yakumo, I dunno if you *you* anymore. But, Perry ... if there's one thing we know from living in Nola, it's that death ain't the end. And you, me, Brendy ... we ain't like other folks—or we are, and it's true for everybody: We *have* to do what we can do. We *have* to. Think about all the people who can't. The people who get in their own way or who don't get the chances we get."

"I just want to be with you."

Peaches pulled back to hold Perry at arm's length and look him in the eye. "We will be together," she said. "I don't know how, and I don't know when, but we will. I *promise*."

Perry half smiled, tears still rolling down his cheeks. "I used to be so sorry I wasn't super like you," he said. "I didn't know it was this hard."

"It's hard," Peaches said. "Sometimes it's real scary, too ... but ain't it cool as hell ... ?"

He smiled, for real now. "Yeah," he said. "Yeah, it's cool as hell. I'm finna play a magic trumpet and save everybody. Not even Milo did that."

"He didn't," Peaches said. "Just please remember…" She searched her heart for the words. For a way to put them together as beautifully as Perry himself would. "I love you, and I have always loved you, and you are the joy of my heart."

She drew Perry close again and kissed him now, a grown-up kiss. Their breath mingled, and the world went away. When it was over, Peaches was crying again.

Perry brushed the tears from her cheeks. "Okay," he said, and there was steel in his voice. "Okay. Yes. I'm ready."

Perry didn't know what he had expected, but he was stunned when he stepped onto the hardwood stage. Nobody announced him. The band didn't even stop playing. The drums ticked rhythmically along—there were two sets, both at the back of the stage, one on either side.

At first, Perry didn't recognize the place, but then he recalled coming here before with Brendy and Doctor Professor. It had seemed much smaller then, more enclosed. In here—if Perry was, in any way that mattered, indoors—were stadium seats reaching up and up. He did not see, but sensed that there might be, walls somewhere in the distance. The ceiling was open to the sky—or no. The ceiling *was* the sky. It existed, but not the same way the ceiling of the Superdome existed, back in the world Perry knew and understood. Almost every seat was occupied.

The drums slowed to an expectant crawl as Perry took in his surroundings. Every so often, the horn section would sort of sigh quietly, waiting to assert itself. High above, the Storm swirled, blotting out the stars and constellations. It was a raging ring of wind and cloud and water, lit now and again by colored lightning flashes. Its noise was loud, but removed from the music, as if Perry sensed it by something other than hearing.

The auditorium seemed to go on forever. Beyond the footlights was a sea of faces—some Perry knew, most he didn't—but he had encountered each of them before, and even the strangest, the most forgotten of them, tugged at the edges of his memory, saying, *Hey! It's me!*

Papa Nguyen from Da Cut, the policeman from the car yard in Nola East, the Pie Lady, Perry's mother and father, Mama Lisa—even the Moon Lady from Perry's long-ago dream. Even the goddess Denkine, from his adventure in the Canaries. Perry's eyes slid over each of them, and the people in between, looking for one face in particular.

All at once, Perry remembered he was holding the Elysian Trumpet, that he was expected to play. A wave of invisible force rolled toward him from the crowd, broke over him, making his skin tingle and sweat. Perry wiped his brow and tried to tell himself he wasn't afraid.

Oh, you ain't afraid...that rasping voice whispered from the back of Perry's mind. *You* petrified.

Just then, the banjo began to play. Perry cut his eyes stage left and saw a white man with big old sunglasses sitting cross-legged with the instrument over his knee. He strummed confidently and flashed Perry a toothy grin.

Now the trombones groaned into action. Their noise sounded like citrus peel curling behind a zester, or flower petals, beaded with dew, opening to the sun. The elongated notes made Perry's sweating all the worse. *I can't do this*, he thought. *I can't!*

He sighted Peaches in the crowd. He didn't know why it had taken him so long. There she was in the second row, center, sitting between Daddy Deke and what must once have been a P-body. The woman wasn't a woman anymore. She wasn't crusted in dried paint; she was an animated graffito, a living cartoon.

Perry implored Peaches with his eyes. *Help*, he looked. *I'm so afraid!*

Peaches returned his gaze, steadily and level, and for a moment,

Perry feared he had failed to make himself understood. Then he felt a sensation like a door opening in the back of his skull, and Peaches climbed inside him.

Warm up in here, she thought. Then, *Damn. That horn hot as hell. No wonder you spooked.*

Perry could tell the trombones were stretching, waiting for him to come in. What should he do? Play a solo?

Naw, Peaches thought. *That ain't how this one go. You know the song—sing!*

Lord, I'm gwine down to Saint James Infirmary
See my ba-a-a-a-a-aby there!
She stretched out on a long white table
So cold, so sweet, red hair!

Aw! Peaches thought. *Is that me? Lemme do one!* This time, Peaches opened Perry's mouth and sang in his voice:

Let her go, let her go, God bless her
Wherevah she-e-e-e-e may be
In this whole world or any other
She ain't never find a sweet baby boy like me!

Peaches threw the controls back to Perry, and he sang again.

When I die, put on my straight-leg britches
a box-back coat and my Stetson hat
Put a gold piece on my watch chain
So you can let all them boys know I died standing fast.

Perry lifted the horn to his lips and felt the breath swell inside him. He blew without thinking, but he felt it in his toes. At first, the notes he played followed the melody of the verses he had sung; then, as the breath swelled in him, took on strength, it raged forth like a herd of horses, running in rhythm together, but each one with its own particular gait.

Perry lost track of himself. He felt taller than tall. If he could see himself, he would see starlight shining through him—had the Storm gone? Had it ceased to trouble the air?

No. His feet left the stage as he lifted up and up, into the living Storm. The winds whipped and gusted at Perry, spinning him this way and then that. He kept playing, but any moment now, he knew he'd lose the thread of the song. He shut his eyes, but doing so dizzied him. It—

Perry felt an arm wrap around his shoulders, steady him.

He opened his eyes to see Mr. Casey—or no. Not Mr. Casey. Not quite. This man had a full beard. His hair was more carefully faded at the temples, and his eyes were compounded like those of a fly—or a bee. *Just play*, he urged. *I'll do the rest.*

As Perry played, this new version of Mr. Casey turned from him to face the wall of whirling clouds. They hung in a tunnel. The black clouds, the lightning, the wind pressed against it, fighting to consume them.

A chain of lightning broke through the barrier, flashing at Perry. Mr. Casey stretched out his arms toward it and little black flecks leaped from them to form a living shield. The lightning turned back on itself, and Perry heard the winds howl over his own playing.

Perry watched Mr. Casey and let the music calm him. The man hung in the air, surrounded by a cloud of— They were bees, weren't they?

Mr. Casey bowed his head, and fireworks bloomed in the tunnel. No. Not fireworks. The lights were colorful, but they didn't burst and fade. They were graffiti tags. And not just words. Colorful figures appeared—A cow in a pink ten-gallon hat bearing a machine gun who fired into the storm. A neon robot with laser eyes whose fists exploded from his arms to tear holes in the dark clouds.

Lightning struck again and again, but every time it hit a drawing, made it disappear, two more appeared to take its place. How long could Mr. Casey keep this up?

Perry finished a note and glanced below him as he took a breath. What he saw almost made him forget to pick up playing again. A squadron of P-bodies, of living cartoons, rose toward them, each one's face a glare of concentration.

Perry started blowing again as the first wave of P-bodies poured into the storm. The holes they made in the clouds seemed to open channels that Perry filled with music. He felt rather than heard a growl, a howl of pain. It was working. They were tearing the Storm to shreds.

Perry let the music carry him up past the Storm. Now it lay below him, lit with multicolored flashes. It was both there and not-there. Perry could see through it.

From here, he thought he'd be able to see the whole world, but it wasn't there. He saw the city and the surrounding area, but it was as if the rest of the world had been masked, divided from it. Perry realized that his memories of leaving the city—of traveling to Houston, to Pensacola, to the East Coast—weren't from his life in Nola, but from the world before. Before what, though?

Before the split, Mr. Casey's voice sounded again in his mind. *Before the Powers divided New Orleans from itself and hid it from the Enemy.*

The explanation created a seam in Perry's consciousness; it glowed like the light from underneath a door, illuminating Perry's life, illuminating knowledge Beyond. This was how he learned that the Storm was not the same as the Hanging Judge, the spirit Casey had unwittingly given life with his inherited magic before it fled into Nola to keep from fading away, but also that it *was.*

He knew now that Casey was kin to him, through the brotherhood of sorcery, yes, but through blood as well. Before Daddy Deke had come to Nola with the horn, he had lived and died in New Orleans, fathered Casey's grandmother, Charlotte.

The world spun slowly beneath Perry, but while it was greater than him, he was also greater than it. He felt its foundations at his feet, the pressure of its hopes and fears against his heart. Somewhere in time, somewhere impossibly, long ago, but also *now*, Nola had split off from the world, become hidden on its own plane. Amazed, Perry used his breath to investigate the city he knew and how it had come to be.

He reached down with his musical grasp and found a shining band extending from its other side, off, off, back into the branching of time and the fracturing of place. Casey let go of Perry, grinning wide.

I did it, he said. *I did my part. Just like Daddy Deke.* And now Perry could see through his cousin, knew he'd willed himself home again.

Perry heard himself playing the opening bars of a song he didn't know, and at the same time, he was singing:

I'm singing my praise to Miss New Orleans
So beautiful that she gleams.
To eyes from Away, her Carnival is gay
And music runs in her streets.
The gold in her teeth, the flowers in her hair
The pigeons strutting her square
Gardenias bloom and spread their perfume
Crepe myrtles and moss hang shaggily down in the breeze
When I'm away, I yearn everyday
And feel such exquisite loss.
I'm singing my praise to Miss New Orleans
So beautiful that she gleams.
To eyes from Away, her Carnival is gay
And music runs in her streets.

Here, Perry felt the wound. A wound that predated the killing of songs and skycars crashing down. This was the wound that had worried them all for thousands of years. Perry stood astride the river of time and watched the Storm bear down. It swelled the river and Lake Pontchartrain, it bowed the Seventeenth Street Canal and threatened to rip the roof from the Superdome.

Perry played right into the center of the Storm, into its eye. He played Daddy Deke, and his parents, and Jelly Roll Morton Academy. He played the summer days so hot and wet that walking through the city air was like crossing the bed of a boiling sea. He played crepe myrtles, he played crawfish curling in the boil. He played the Ninth Ward, the Seventh Ward, he played Creole Jesus, Lafayette Square, the Jazz Market, and Congo Square.

He shook with the effort of his breath. With the unbroken note of it, pouring through the bell of the horn as he pressed the valves and buzzed his embouchure. He played Mardi Gras and the Indians meeting in ritual combat. He played every pebble in each gravel lot. Every pothole and cobblestone on Felicity Street, the drunks, the church ladies, the aroma of meat pies sizzling in deep fat fryers. He played the palm trees shimmying hello, the sno-ball stands, the scrubby grass, the Mardi Gras ducks, and the kites and blimps of City Park.

A burning halo had settled upon his scalp. It sizzled there without pain. The music left his ears but was still inside his body. He knew he was playing one single high note that reached up and away to infinity. He divided from himself then, possibly because Peaches was still with him, but he couldn't be sure.

He couldn't leave the song this way. He had to bring it back. He had to reconcile the two songs together, make them one, and whole.

Gimme six crap-shooting pallbearers
Have a chorus girl sing me a song
A red-hot marching jazz funeral
Now you done heard my story
So if anybody aski-i-i-ing . . . !
Tell 'em I got them Saint James Infirmary blues!

Perry sat between Peaches and Brendy in the audience, holding both their hands. Together, they were a circuit of force—something magic but *more* than magic. Perry played as the Storm fled the sky.

Stars wheeled untroubled overhead. As the last solo began, Perry tapped his foot, anticipating each note. He watched himself age and grow, his body elongating, filling in, and beginning to wizen. A beard sprang up on his face, turned gray, then white. His hair whitened and thinned, all while holding that same note, and then, when he released it, his body had thinned again and shrunk. His reduced frame swam in his natty dress clothes.

In the second row, Peaches's hand sought Perry's. She held it tight, but not tight enough to hurt.

We together, she said, or thought. Perry wasn't sure which.

Like rum and Coca-Cola, Perry said, or thought.

The band ceased.

The audience held its breath.

Where before they had been individuals, now they were one body, transubstantiated by the performance into a single organism with one thought, one mood, one faith.

Silence descended.

Onstage, Perry lowered the Elysian Trumpet, wavered on his feet, and collapsed.

The music resumed as Perry-in-the-audience and the rest of the crowd followed the band from the concert hall into the street outside. Another Perry raised his trumpet to his lips to play again as a new song began. There were so many of him. The crowd that had been in him, all playing in harmony. Perry—one of him—felt his family, his friends, lay hands on him in turn.

On they walked, buoyed by the sound, rejoicing for Perry's life. This was everything. This was all he had ever needed.

XXXIII

...WHO KNOWS THE WAY

So to review, these are our priorities," Dr. Pullen said, his brow furrowed. Casey, Dr. Pullen, and the rest of the Leadership Team sat at a curved table in the International School's first-floor conference room. The meeting was running long—again. It was no wonder with the chaos of the school year's second half.

"We have fifty-seven students we didn't have before," Pullen continued. "Or we did. We *did* have them, or we had memories of..." He heaved a sigh, shook his head. "New students. New-old students. Some of whom are...what's the word?"

"I think they prefer *Animals*," Casey said. "With a capital A. And capitals for their specific species."

"Yes, ah—" Pullen said. "But then, there are also..."

"The doubled students," Ms. Rolonda said.

Casey shook his head. What a mess this cosmic storm had left behind. Sky trolleys, talking Animals, zombies, and god knew how many doubles who remembered snatches of *long*, strange lives lived in the Hidden City.

"I vote we test them," Mrs. D'Antoni, the History Chair, said. She was an owlish, auburn-haired woman with a light Mississippi accent and a sweet, round figure. "We can put them through practice LEAP tests and use those to decide how to register them next fall."

"If they're still here," Mrs. Thornton added.

"They'll still be here," Casey said. "I won't get into how I know, but this is our city now. This is our circumstance. We need to adjust."

Mrs. D'Antoni said something else as Casey's phone buzzed in his pocket. He tried to still the beating of his heart as he slid his hands into his jeans. He withdrew the phone and glanced down at its screen:

WHERE U AT???

"I'm sorry," Casey snapped. Everyone turned to look at him. "I have to go. Something's— I think I'm done here."

"What?" Dr. Pullen asked. Casey didn't know whether he was asking what had come up or expressing a mood of general consternation.

"I think I'm done here for good," Casey said. "My cousin— Jaylon's back. He finally made it."

"Negro, you got to *go*!" Dr. Pullen said.

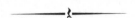

Casey tried not to think about the last time he'd come here the night Jaylon—died? He still wasn't sure that's what had happened. The explosions. The screams tearing their way out of his throat. He'd been here several times since Nola and New Orleans became one again.

The joining of the cities had restored the building. Numerous houses and businesses had returned from oblivion. Just like the students at work, some of them had been transformed or doubled. Three Muses, in fact, now stood next door to Tree Muses, across the street from two Favela Chics.

And what about Casey? After aiding his young cousin in what must be the greatest working of musical sorcery in history, he had awakened on his living room sofa and ventured into the master bathroom for a look in the mirror. Everything about him seemed to be in its right place, but he was a couple inches taller and his beard was gone. He still hadn't decided whether to grow it back.

Casey pulled his battered car into a vacant spot on Saint Claude and jogged around the corner to the studio's entrance. The door was unlocked, no chain, no padlock. Casey went inside.

The studio was full of tags. They stood jostling each other like a school of eager fish. Jaylon stood among them, stroking this one and then that one like pets. This time, he looked like himself. His dreadlocks were tight and neat, hanging down to the middle of his back. He wore a Saints jersey—Number 1 Kamara—and a pair of patchwork jeans. A cloud of sewing moths hovered around him, and when he saw their quilted wings working, Casey wondered how he knew what they were if he'd never seen them before.

Jayl wore his beard and mustache cropped short, and now it was shot through with gray. That detail reminded him that more time had passed for Jaylon than it had for him. Or had it? He still didn't understand it.

"Jayl," he said, and Jaylon looked round at him.

Casey meant to walk over for a hug, but instead he broke into a run. The tags parted to let him pass. It was only when he reached his cousin, took him in his arms, that Casey remembered what it felt like to touch one of these artworks.

Casey held Jaylon tight, sobbing, and Jaylon returned his embrace. "I wanted to wait for you after the Merge, but I got called away."

"Called away where?"

"I don't know if I can explain," Jaylon said. He disengaged to hold Casey at arm's length. "Oh," he said. "Oh wow. Did you *grow?*"

Casey sucked his teeth. "Sheeeeeeeit," he said. "Don't even get me started."

They laughed.

When their laughter subsided, Casey looked Jaylon up and down. "Last time I saw you, you was *glowing*, my nigga."

"I still am," Jaylon said. "So are you."

"So we playing Madden now, or do we got some more cosmic shit to handle?"

Jaylon shook his head. "I wish we could," he said. "We don't have to leave Earth yet, but the Doctor wants to see us."

"In his garden?"

"City Park," Jay said. "At Delgado. You drive."

"Mane, I think I stopped driving when I parked the car," Casey said. "They don't call me Trismegistus for nothing. Take my hand."

Together, they disappeared, and the graffiti sang a mourning song for their absence.

The night air was hot and thick. The scents of jasmine and cut grass crept in through the darkness, insinuating themselves among the smells of fried dough and brewing coffee. Perry tapped his right foot on the red tile of the patio as he stared out into the park. On impulse, he pulled the letter from his pocket and unfolded it on the table:

Dear Perilous Graves,

As Chancellor and Archmage of Delgado Community College for Spellcraft and Sorcery, it is my pleasure to announce your acceptance into our upcoming fall class. If you are currently deceased, it is imperative that you resume living at once and begin preparing for your first semester. Gifts as profound as yours must be nurtured and developed as well as shielded from harm or exploitation. To that end, we have waived all tuition and fees and welcome you on full scholarship. I look forward to meeting you.

Sincerely,
Dr. James Carroll Booker III, MSoD
DCCSS

"Hey, there, champ."

Perry turned to look as a brown-haired white man took the seat opposite him. He wore horn-rimmed glasses, a Cuban shirt, and khaki pants flared at the cuffs.

"Who are you?"

"I'm a friend, friend," the man said. "I know a thing or two about what you've been through. I'm here to tell you that just because you got a fancy letter in the mail doesn't mean you have to do what it says."

"You sound like a preacher."

"I've been called many things, and that's far from the worst of them."

"I miss my family, though. My sister. Peaches."

"I get that," said the man. "That's natural. But have you asked yourself how you'll go back and be just you after everything you've seen and done?"

"I don't know," Perry said. "How did Milo?"

"You're still comparing yourself to him?"

"He's still with me," Perry said. "His story still means something to me."

"What would you say if I told you Milo got invited to a fancy school after his adventure, just like you?"

Perry squinted, doubtful. "It's not fancy, though. It's right here in City Park. It's *Delgado*."

"Plenty fancy," said the man. "That James Booker, he plays a mean piano. But you play the horn."

"You're the one trying to talk me into something."

"Am I?" asked the man. "Well...and what about your hero, Milo? Will you take him with you next time?"

"Next time?" Perry said. "There's nowhere to go. It ended." But even as he said it, he knew it wasn't true. "The world was enough for Milo after he saved the princesses. The book says he wouldn't have had time to go back even if he'd had another booth."

"Books say a lot of things."

"Why do you care so much if I go to Delgado or stay dead?" Perry said. "Who are you, and what's your stake in all this?"

The preacher—if that's what he was—just watched him evenly until the waitress interrupted to set Perry's frozen café au lait before him. Perry put the decision out of his mind and gazed at the sweating drink. He'd never seen anything so beautiful. He picked it up and sucked some through his straw.

"If you ever meet Milo, ask him," said the man. "Ask what happened next."

"I don't know you," Perry said. "Go bother somebody else."

The man shrugged. "If you say so," he said. "But I know one thing, Perry: You didn't defeat the Storm. The Storm is eternal and undying. Eventually, you and everyone else will be dead, and it will just go on." With that, he rose from the table and walked away toward the natatorium.

Perry watched him go for a moment, then shrugged. The drink was frightfully cold. It locked up Perry's jaw and sent pain shooting across his forehead. Perry clenched his eyes shut and shook his head, trying to get rid of the brain freeze. All his senses ran together and then—

And then—

And then he opened his eyes.

ACKNOWLEDGMENTS

This book was made possible by so many that I barely know where to begin. Many hands made this work light, either by assisting me directly or by helping me live a life worth commenting on. It is my mother, Sharon Hardiman Jennings, who taught me that life is not about how I feel. My father, Hartford Jennings, without meaning to, tasked me to write the Blackest fantasy I could concoct. My brother, Brandon MacDonald. Erin, Aunt Donna—who saved my dear mother's life—and William "Soopaman" MacDonald.

H. T. and Rebecca Jennings and their children Max, Vanessa, Veronica, Xavier, and Tre. Lisa Jennings Léandre—who taught me to read and write in the first place—and her children Trenton Pierre, Vérida, Alexandra, and Yvette. Cousin Judy, Tracy, Cookie—Tanisha, Allen, and Stephen. Eugene Marion "Mike" Jennings, whose courage, intellect, and open heart inspire me every day. Thanks to Casey Grayson for this service and example. Thanks to Billy Martin, who helped me begin reshaping my heart.

Cousin Andrew, Uncle Larry, Cousin Laurel Ann, Cousin Houston, Shelly, Brian, and Kevin.

Mike Nan and his wife, Felicia. Aunt Naomi, Uncle Raymond, Aunt Harriet, Uncle James, Aunt Louisa, and Elizabeth Jennings, who taught me Story.

To Mimi Mondal for hours upon hours of shop talk and companionable conversation.

To Preston Spradling, the first person outside my family to truly love my fiction.

456 • A<small>CKNOWLEDGMENTS</small>

To each of the brilliant teachers who sped me along, including Frankie Ayeh, Tom Fox, Liz Thornton, Nancy Gregory, Dorsaf Kouki, Nellie Bridge, and Sandra Yannone. China Miéville, Samuel R. Delany, Elizabeth Hand, Nisi Shawl, Octavia Butler, and K. Tempest Bradford. Eliani Torres, of course, of course. Neile Graham, Leslie Howell. Sheree Renee Thomas, who paved the way for so many.

April Blevins Pejic, Rade Pejic, Creighton Durrant, Jennifer Kuchta, Connie Zeanah Atkinson, Elizabeth Blankenship, Dan Doll, Shaina Monet and Aaron Maus, Maurice Carlos Ruffin, and Wendy Bolm.

My fellow Dogfish producers: Jessica Kinnison, Taylor Murrow, and, of course, Cate Root. Sara D'Antoni, Erica Aargraves, Winfield Yaw, Lola Oyohochitto, Amanda Emily Smith.

Thanks to Benjy Ferree, whose music and friendship saw me through some dark-ass times. Vince Gulino with his companionship and bedroom eyes (*ew*, girl). Jennifer Gutierrez, Jason Stratton, Domenica Clark, Aelva Duckhugger, Aubrie Brown. Renata Brito-Cherrin, Brittany Whittenberg, Tanks Transfeld! Meg Elison! Njeri Campbell! Alex Smith! Kytara Epps, Keely Lewis, and Karate Valentino, who helped hold me together during the Pantene Pro V.

Special thanks also to Shawna McCarthy, my agent, without whom none of this would be possible. Thanks also to Bill Campbell and, of course, to my editor, Nivia Evans.

Finally, a thousand thousand thanks to the city, culture, music, people, and spirit of New Orleans.

MAP OF NOLA

lakeside
uptown · downtown
riverside

N · W · E · S

CITY PARK

NATATORIUM

DELGADO COMMUNITY COLLEGE
FOR SPELLCRAFT & SORCERY

GAS STATION

S. CLAIBORNE AVENUE

R.I.P.

FERRET STREET

PROFESSOR LONGHAIR'S

INTERNATIONAL SCHOOL

FERRET STREET CAR YARD

PERRY'S

DRYADES ACADEMY

AUDUBON PARK

ST. CHARLES AVENUE

DADDY DEKE'S

PEACHES'S

missus hipp

tchoupitoulas street